UNENDING LOVE

A Medieval Romance

By Kathryn Le Veque

Printed by Dragonblade Publishing in the United States of America

Other Novels by Kathryn Le Veque

Medieval Romance:

The White Lord of Wellesbourne
The Dark One: Dark Knight

While Angels Slept
Rise of the Defender
Spectre of the Sword
Unending Love
Archangel
Lord of the Shadows

Great Protector
To the Lady Born

The Falls of Erith
Lord of War: Black Angel

The Darkland
Black Sword

Unrelated characters or family groups:
    The Whispering Night
    The Dark Lord
    The Gorgon
    The Warrior Poet
    Guardian of Darkness (related to The Fallen One)
    Tender is the Knight
    The Legend
    Lespada
    The Wolfe
    Lord of Light

The Dragonblade Trilogy:
Dragonblade
Island of Glass
The Savage Curtain
The Fallen One
Fragments of Grace

Novella, Time Travel Romance:
    Echoes of Ancient Dreams

Time-Travel Romance:
The Crusader
Kingdom Come

Contemporary Romance:

Kathlyn Trent/Marcus Burton Series:
    Valley of the Shadow
    The Eden Factor
    Canyon of the Sphinx

The American Heroes Series:
Resurrection
Fires of Autumn
Evenshade
Sea of Dreams
Purgatory

Other Contemporary Romance:
    Lady of Heaven
    Darkling, I listen

Note: All Kathryn's novels are designed to be read as stand-alones, although many have cross-over characters or cross-over family groups.

Novels that are grouped together have related characters or family groups.

Series are clearly marked. All series contain the same characters or family groups except the American Heroes Series, which is an anthology with unrelated characters.

There is NO particular chronological order for any of the novels because they can all be read as stand-alones, even the series.

For Lord MR, Linda, Kris, & Rozz –
Thank you for your encouragement and patience! Now, here it is – read
it!
And to Jennifer –
Thank you for keen eyes and swift work!

As I stare on and on into the past, in the end you emerge,
Clad in the light of a pole-star piercing the darkness of time:
You become an image of what is remembered forever.
    ~ excerpt from 'Unending Love' by Rabindranath Tagore

CHAPTER ONE

Canterbury Castle, England
The Month of May, 1234 A.D.

He could hear the battle before he ever entered the bailey.

Swords clashing, one against the other, echoed off the great stone walls of Canterbury Castle, ancient barriers with some Roman origin that had seen much war and strife throughout the centuries. The knight's trip had been a relatively leisurely journey up until that point as he returned from France. It was a spring day that had shown remarkable weather for the eight and a half miles it took when he disembarked his ship at Herne Bay to Canterbury Castle.

But the sounds of distant warfare had him snapping into battle mode. The road was rocky and uneven as he thundered towards the castle astride his new gray Belgian charger, a gift from his father. The horse had been cooped up on a boat for over a day and was feeling energetic, which meant he was having a devil of a time controlling the beast as it raced towards the enormous castle compound. The wrestling was distracting him from his battle-readiness.

The knight bellowed at the sentries on the wall as he approached and the men, recognizing both his voice and his armor, began to lift the steel-fanged portcullis from its already half-open position. By the time he pounded through the Roman arch of the gatehouse that lead to the keep, he was bloody well angry at his new horse, as well as deeply concerned over the sounds of a battle. It made for a snappish situation.

As the knight entered the ward, he didn't have far to look to find the source of the swordplay; two well-armed knights were slugging it out just inside the gate, trying to kill each other in the area between the gatehouse and the massive keep. The knight on horseback unsheathed his enormous broadsword as he charged towards them, yanking his enthusiastic charger to a halt and trying not to lose his balance as he dismounted. The horse didn't seem to want to come to a complete halt, which meant the knight nearly lost his footing with the momentum. But he was off his horse; broadsword gleaming wickedly in the early afternoon sun. He was ready for battle.

Although the knight was focused on the combatants, he could see people in his periphery, standing and watching. As he swung his broadsword in a swift, controlled motion, preparing to enter the fight, he could hear hissing off to his right.

"Maddoc," someone was calling his name. "Maddoc, *hold*."

Sir Maddoc du Bois came to an unsteady halt, and the only reason he stopped at all was because he recognized the voice. He could see his liege, David de Lohr, Earl of Canterbury, standing on the great retractable stairs that led up into Canterbury's red-stoned keep. David was waving him over. Broadsword still flexed defensively in front of him, Maddoc edged his way over to his liege.

His expression, once stone-hard and focused, was now rippling with some confusion. "My lord?" he asked as he drew near. "What goes on here?"

David, a handsome man with graying blond hair who had been a very great knight in his youth, was actually grinning. More than that, he looked very calm for a man with two knights battling it out in front of him. He crooked his finger at Maddoc, beckoning him closer. Maddoc obeyed.

"Those two idiots have been dueling for about an hour," he told him. "Leave them alone. One of them is about to break the other soon."

That explanation didn't help Maddoc's confusion. Still, he had his sword up as he watched the two men try to kill each other. But he was beginning to see exhaustion in their movements now that David had brought it to his attention.

"What goes on, my lord?" he asked the obvious question. "Who are they?"

David chuckled. "Adalind is home."

Maddoc had no idea what the man was speaking of. "What do you mean?"

David accepted a dented chalice of ale from a servant who emerged from the keep and extended it to him. His eyes were on the fighters as he spoke to Maddoc.

"Adalind," he repeated. "My granddaughter – Christina's daughter, the one who has been at court these five years past. You remember Adalind, do you not?"

Maddoc did. He nodded his head. "Of course, my lord," he replied. "The little girl with the…." He caught himself before he could say it. *The little girl with the bucked teeth who used to follow me around like a lost puppy.* Instead, he cleared his throat and tried to cover his stumble. "The little girl with the hair down to her knees. I remember her well."

David laughed softly. "You are too tactful for your own good, Maddoc," he replied. "She was the girl with teeth like a rabbit and a penchant for making a nuisance out of herself. For some reason, she liked you in particular although I have no idea why."

He spoke the last few words drolly. Maddoc gave him a half-grin, finally lowering his sword as the two knights continued to hack away at each other. It was no great secret that Maddoc du Bois was a man of great honor and skill, and he had a particular reputation for being an object of many ladies' affections.

With black hair, bright blue eyes and an enormously muscular build, Maddoc had more female admirers than he could handle. He was a great knight from a long line of great knights and something of a legend. De Lohr liked to say there was a star in the sky for every heart Maddoc had unknowingly broken, and he said it quite a bit. Not wanting to hear that over-used adage again, Maddoc diverted the subject by gesturing at the battling knights.

"That still does not explain why I could hear a sword battle a half mile away," he said. "Who are these two and why have you not driven them away?"

David took a long drink of his ale, watching the spectacle like a good sporting event. "They followed Adalind from Winchester," he said, a twinkle in his blue eyes. "Meet Rolfe ap Athoe and Deinwald ap Athoe; brothers who are attempting to woo my granddaughter. At least, they were *attempting* to woo her; one from the other, until the nooning meal whereupon Deinwald insulted his brother. This has been going on ever since. I am anxious to see which fool falls first because neither one of them are worthy of her."

That explained a great deal. So there was no crisis; only morons battling to the death over a woman. Maddoc unlatched his helm and pulled it off, wearily, raking a hand through his black hair as he watched the two ap Athoe brothers succumb to bone-grinding exhaustion. Now they were simply swiping at each other more than they were actually doing battle. Maddoc watched a moment longer before shaking his head.

"Are you sure you do not want me to break this up?" he asked. "They are making an embarrassing spectacle of the knighthood and I find that I am personally offended by the display."

David drained his ale cup, laughing in between swallows. "You are the upholder of knightly honor, Maddoc. Are you sure you would not rather see them beat each other to a pulp?"

Maddoc just looked at him. Then, with a shrug, he handed David his broadsword and marched purposefully over to the two combatants, who were by now showing serious signs of collapse. In full armor and with great mail and leather gloves, Maddoc walked up to the pair and reached out fearlessly to disarm the first knight. The second knight was disarmed shortly thereafter and both broadswords were tossed to the ground several feet away.

Without missing a beat, Maddoc balled a fist and cocked the first knight on the jaw so hard that the man went flying back on his arse, skidding to an unconscious heap. With one knight down, Maddoc turned to the second warrior and the taller one, and did the same thing to him. The tall knight fell like a rock to Maddoc's massive blow.

Several men-at-arms were standing around, watching, clapping and laughing when du Bois finished off the battling pair. But Maddoc didn't spare a reaction to the applause.

"Pick up those broadswords and hide them," he commanded. "If those two want their weapons returned, tell them to see me personally and we shall have a discussion about the idiocy of a swordfight over a woman."

As the soldiers moved to do their commander's bidding, David came down from the stairs and clapped Maddoc on a big shoulder.

"You are much like your father," he said, grinning. "Rhys would not tolerate foolishness, either."

"He still doesn't."

"And how is your father? Did your visit go well?"

Maddoc nodded. "Very well," he replied. "My father is enjoying excellent health and is showing no signs of slowing down even though he has my three brothers to help him rule and administer the fiefdom of Bellay. My uncle, the Duke of Navarre, gifted the lands to my father a few years ago. They are very rich lands."

"I remember," David nodded. "And how is your mother?"

"Elizabeau is very well also. She sends her good wishes and affections."

Now up to date on the health and welfare of Maddoc's parents, David put a hand on Maddoc's shoulder and directed the knight towards the keep. "I am glad your visit went well," he said. "But I am also glad you have returned. When my Captain of the Guard leaves, even for a week or two, we all feel rather lost around here. As you can see, much has happened in your absence."

Maddoc lifted his dark eyebrows, arched over those brilliant blue eyes. "So I see," he said. "But I do not recall that Lady Adalind was returning from Winchester. I thought she was a permanent fixture there, hoping to be a lady-in-waiting for the queen."

Some of David's humor faded. "That was her hope," he said. "She has great aspirations, you know. With all of my brother's connections, we were able to place her very well within the court hierarchy. But it seems that my granddaughter has some enemies at court."

David's older brother was the mighty Christopher de Lohr, the Earl of Hereford and Worcester, and one-time champion of Richard the Lion heart. His political contacts were deep and endless. Maddoc frowned at the last sentence.

"Enemies?" he repeated. "Why?"

David shrugged. "Evidently, some of the senior ladies-in-waiting have taken to gossiping against her," he said, lowering his voice as they mounted the steps for the keep. "It took both Christina and my wife some time to drag it out of her, but from what they can make of it, there was much attention on Adalind of the male persuasion and the other women were jealous. So Adalind has come home but the men seemed to have followed her."

Maddoc paused at the top of the steps, with the big Norman herring-bone pattern arched doorway hovering overhead.

"Was she sent home in disgrace?" he asked.

David shook his head. "Nay," he said quietly. "It seemed to be her choice. Some of the women were quite mean to her from what I gather and she'd had enough."

"Shall I ride to Winchester to avenge her?"

David grinned. "You would, wouldn't you?" He slapped Maddoc on the shoulder and stepped inside the entry. "I do not see a need for that, although I appreciate your offer. Come greet Adalind and see what the years have done for her. How long has it been since you last saw her?"

Maddoc followed the man into the cool, dark entry with the great hall just beyond. Canterbury actually had two halls; a giant separate building in a corner of the bailey for more formal feasts and a smaller one inside the keep that the family used. However, it was still an enormous room with big stone columns. It was warmly lit and he could see movement inside. He felt comforted to be in the big, old keep, as it had been his home for a number of years, and the smell of smoke and fresh rushes settled him.

"She was nine years old when she went to foster at Warwick Castle," he replied. "Then she returned to Canterbury when she was around twelve or thirteen years, I believe, before she was off again to Winchester Court. It's been at least five years since that time."

"Five years, six months, and twenty-two days to be exact."

Another voice entered their conversation, causing both Maddoc and David to turn in the direction of the golden-lit hall. A woman of unearthly beauty was standing in the archway, smiling at Maddoc, and it took the man a moment to realize that it was Adalind. His bright blue eyes widened.

"Lady Adalind?" he couldn't help the awe in his tone.

The Lady Adalind Alianor de Lohr de Aston smiled hugely. "So you recognize me?" she asked. "I wondered if you would. It has been a very long time since I last followed you around the grounds, annoying you to tears. 'Tis good to see you, Maddoc."

Maddoc had to make a conscious effort to keep his mouth from hanging open. The skinny, irritating child he'd watched grow up was no longer the awkward little girl he remembered. Somehow, someway, Adalind had grown up and filled out, creating something of a heavenly vision.

Like most of the de Lohr family, she was blond, but her hair was a darker shade with streaks of copper through it, and her eyes were a vibrant shade of green. With her delicately arched brows, pert little nose with a dusting of freckles, and rosebud lips, Maddoc could instantly see why she apparently had hordes of men following her around in Winchester. Something this exquisite would not go unnoticed.

"'Tis good to see you as well," he responded, trying not to appear too stunned. "How long have you been back at Canterbury?"

Adalind moved out of the archway, heading towards him, and it was all Maddoc could do not to stare like an idiot at her. She was average in height but there was nothing average about the womanly figure she had developed over the past few years, deliciously embraced by the yellow surcoat. She reached out her hand to him as she approached and he instinctively took it.

"About a week," she replied, tugging on his hand. "I have been waiting impatiently for you to return from France. Come inside and tell me all about your trip."

Maddoc let her hold his hand, following her into the great hall with its enormous table that could easily seat forty people. Servants moved about, kicking the dogs out of the way as they set food and drink upon the scrubbed surface. Maddoc steadied Adalind as she sat on the bench, lowering his big body next to her.

David wasn't far behind them. He collected another chalice of ale and took a seat. "Do you not want to know what happened to those two fools who were dueling to the death outside? You haven't even asked me about them."

Adalind turned her nose up. "That is because I do not care," she said. "They are both idiots. I hope they will give up their pursuit and return home."

David snorted as he settled back in his chair, the only chair at the entire table. Every other seat was a bench.

"They are still here," he said, "but Maddoc put an end to their battle. By now they are probably picking themselves up off the ground, wondering what hit them."

Adalind turned her smiling face in Maddoc's direction. "Did you champion me, then?"

Maddoc still wasn't over the shock of Adalind having become such a beautiful creature; made worse when she smiled. Her smile was no longer bucked-tooth, but white and radiant. He returned her smile, modestly.

"That is my job," he said. "I am sworn to champion everyone in the Earl of Canterbury's household and you happen to fall under that directive."

Adalind stared at him, her smile fading after a moment. "Of course," she said, taking her eyes off of Maddoc to claim a cup of wine. "Ever the loyal servant, Maddoc."

Maddoc could sense her happy mood fading. All of that radiance seemed to dim suddenly and he found himself repeating their conversation, wondering what he had said that might have upset her. Was it the fact that he had said it was his job to champion her? All seemed to sober after that statement. He wondered why.

"I would like to hear of your stay in Winchester," he tried to keep the conversation going, feeling oddly confused at the moment. "Did you enjoy your time spent?"

She shrugged, toying with her wine. "There were times when I enjoyed it," she said. "I enjoyed the parties and the festivals. Oh, and Grandfather, I ran into an old friend of yours at the Street of Merchants a few months back. He sends his greetings."

David was sipping at his ale. "Who?"

"Lord Forbes," she said. "A very big, bald man. He lives at Dunster Castle. He had some grandchildren with him; all girls. He says to tell you that you have not cornered the market on female children."

David started laughing. "Gart Forbes," he shook his head at the memories. "Other than Maddoc and his father, Gart was the best knight I have ever seen. A truly powerful and frightening man. Before your Uncle Daniel was born, Gart and I used to joke about all of the female children I had. I once told Gart that I was going to trade him two of my girls for one of his boys."

Adalind grinned because he was. "Would you still do such a thing?"

David shook his head. "Of course not... although there were times when I would have gladly traded away your mother's sisters. Emilie had two younger sisters, and then Emilie and I had three girls in a row before Daniel was born. Then...."

Adalind cut him off. "Then my mother had two girls, Aunt Caroline had two girls, and Aunt Catherine finally had a son." She shook her head, teasing. "How do you put up with so many women?"

"It is not easy."

He was snorting into his cup as he said it, taking a long drink. Smiling at her grandfather, Adalind glanced at Maddoc to see that he was grinning also. She pointed a finger at him.

"And you," she said. "How old are you now, Maddoc?"

Maddoc met her intense green gaze. "If you recall, your mother and I were born on the same day three years apart," he replied. "I have seen thirty-one years."

Adalind cocked her head thoughtfully. "And you have not yet found a wife? I find that astonishing."

Maddoc's humor faded somewhat as he reached for his own cup of wine. Before he could reply, David answered.

"Addie," he admonished softly, sternly. "'Tis an inappropriate question. You...."

Maddoc lifted a hand, cutting him off. "She does not know," he defended her. "She has been away for many years. She could not have known."

"Know what?" Adalind's focus shifted between Maddoc and her grandfather.

Maddoc looked at her. "I did have a wife," he said, his tone somewhat quiet. "In fact, we were married about six months after you left for Winchester Court. But she died in childbirth before we had even been married a year."

Adalind's jaw dropped, her eyes round with horror. "Oh, Maddoc," she gushed softly. "I had not heard. No one ever told me."

He shrugged, returning his attention to his drink. "There was no reason to, I suppose," he said. "As I said, it was a long time ago."

Adalind was still mortified. "If it was shortly after I left for Winchester Court, it was no more than four or five years ago." She shook her head, putting a soft hand on his mailed arm. "I am so sorry, Maddoc. I did not mean to sound callous. I did not know."

The twinkle was back in his eyes as he looked at her. "I know you did not. No harm done."

Adalind was still feeling very bad. "Who was she? Anyone I know?"

Maddoc shook his head. "She was from Navarre," he said. "My father selected her for me. In truth, I only met her a few days before our marriage. She was a tiny brown-eyed French girl who, I found out later, had always been in ill health. The pregnancy simply took its toll."

Adalind squeezed his arm before letting him go. "Still, I apologize for being insensitive," she said, trying to think of a way to salvage her blunder. "Before I make a complete fool out of myself and embarrass my grandfather further, you asked about my time spent in Winchester. Let us speak of the great and terrible times I had there."

Maddoc was back to smiling; Adalind had grown more animated over the years and her bright personality was something of an anomaly in a world where demure women were the preference. He rather liked her vivaciousness and he could easily see why it would threaten other women. There was something very magnetic about her.

"Speak of the great times," he said. "I do not think I want to hear of the terrible."

Adalind wriggled her eyebrows. "Nor do I wish to speak of them," she said, sobering somewhat. "Although there were more terrible times than great times. It was unfortunate that...."

She was cut off by a big bang followed by something that sounded like a growl. Adalind, David and Maddoc turned towards the source of the sound; seeing the two beaten brothers standing in the entry to the great hall. They were dirty, and somewhat pale, but the fury in their eyes was unmistakable.

"You!" the taller brother jabbed a finger at Maddoc. "You will pay for your actions, knight."

Adalind was on her feet. "Deinwald ap Athoe," she snapped, putting herself in between Maddoc and the hall entry. "I have told you and your hard-headed brother repeatedly that I do not want you here. I have no interest in either of you, as you have known from the beginning, and nothing you can say is going to change my mind. I have asked you to leave twice now, yet still you remain. I want you to leave Canterbury immediately, do you hear?"

Deinwald was weaving unsteadily somewhat, still fighting off the after-effects from Maddoc's devastating punch. His mouth was swollen, his pimpled skin red and flushed. He ignored Adalind's orders.

"You will change your mind," he said firmly. "I am to inherit a great deal, my lady, and you must give me a chance to show you what a fine husband I will make."

Beside him, his brother started to move into the hall, heading for Maddoc. "You shall feel our wrath, fool. You had no right to interfere."

David was on his feet now, moving towards the aggressive young men. "Get out of here," he pointed a finger at the door. "Adalind has asked you thrice to leave yet still you remain. Now I am ordering you from

Canterbury. If you are not out within the hour, I will turn du Bois loose on you and I promise you will both regret such a thing."

Up until this point, Maddoc had remained seated and silent, watching the situation unfold. He was waiting to see how David reacted and prepared to take his direction from the man. When David ordered the brothers from the hall, however, they were disinclined to obey right away. They stopped their advance for a moment, lingering by the door, before looking at one another in both confusion and defiance. At least they had some sense, knowing they would not get much further with the lady if they defied her grandfather; a very powerful earl. But when they refused to leave as ordered, Maddoc stood up.

"The earl has commanded you to vacate," he rumbled threateningly. "Since you seem incapable of following his directive, allow me to assist."

It was said in the most dangerous tone possible. The brothers remained by the entry, but they took a healthy step or two in the direction of the keep entry as Maddoc began to stalk them. The shorter and more foolish of the brothers threw a finger in Maddoc's direction.

"You shall not lay a hand on us," he commanded, but his voice cracked in fear as he spoke and completely ruined what he had hoped would be construed as a threat. "What right do you have to assault us? You are the hired sword and unworthy of engaging us in combat."

It was the wrong thing to say. Ever stone-faced, Maddoc simply lifted a threatening eyebrow as he advanced and mentally planned on all of the terrible things he would do to the pair once he reached them. But his building steam was interrupted when Adalind put herself in between Maddoc and the foolish brothers.

"*He* is my betrothed," she said, pointing to Maddoc. "He will beat you within an inch of your life if you do not leave this moment. Get out, I say!"

Every man in the room looked at Adalind with some shock, including Maddoc. But David quickly caught on to her game.

"She is already pledged," he reiterated. "Go home. I will not see you again."

The brothers lost all of their steam. Jaws hung open in surprise. Maddoc returned his gaze to the pair and, without so much as a crack in his façade, resumed stalking.

"I am certain you will not like the pain I shall put you through if I get my hands on either of you," he said. "You have been told to leave. Do it now or suffer the consequences."

The shorter brother took off at a dead run, hurling himself from the entry and down the stairs to the bailey. The taller brother, however, stood his ground even though he was incrementally backing away as Maddoc advanced. He eyed the enormous knight who had so effortlessly subdued him and his brother.

"If you are the lady's betrothed, then... then I challenge you." He pointed an imperious finger at Maddoc. "To the winner go the spoils."

Maddoc was within arm's length of the man and reached out, snatching his hand and squeezing so hard that bones could be heard snapping. As the brother screamed in pain and tried to jerk his hand away, Maddoc grabbed him by the neck and literally tossed him out of the hall. The brother ended up in a heap near the door, scrambling to get away from Maddoc, who was by now bearing down on him. As Maddoc reached down to pick the man up, his brother came back through the entry with a broadsword in his hand.

Maddoc caught the glint of steel in his peripheral vision. He heard Adalind shriek. In that split second, he lifted the grounded brother and used him as a shield just as the shorter brother thrust the blade forward. The sword caught the taller brother in the shoulder and the man howled in pain, but it was enough of a distraction for Maddoc to release him and go after the brother with the weapon.

A massive fist dropped the shorter brother, the blade, and with the taller brother still attached to it. They all went down in a pile on the entry floor as David rushed forward to pull the broadsword out of the maelstrom. He wanted it out of the way, unable to wreak any further damage, as Maddoc grabbed both brothers and heaved them from the entry. By this time, several soldiers and at least two knights, who had heard the noise coming from the keep, were just mounting the stairs. They were not surprised to see du Bois standing whole and sound on the entry landing as two hapless victims rolled down the stairs.

"Remove them," Maddoc commanded his men. "Escort them to the river crossing and make sure they are well across it before you return their weapons to them. If I see them here again, I will kill them both. Make it known."

With that, he turned back for the keep, gesturing for the startled Adalind to go back inside. She had been standing behind him with wide eyes, obeying when she saw his directive. David, however, stood at the top of the stairs, watching his men untangle the wounded brothers before hauling them away. His blue eyes were wrought with knowing as he watched them go.

He knew that wouldn't be the last time such a thing would occur with the fair Adalind returned. It was just a feeling he had.

I seem to have loved you in numberless forms, numberless times...
In life after life, in age after age, forever.

CHAPTER TWO

"Did he even say anything to you, Addie? Anything at all?"

Seated by the fish pond back near the buttery where the castle was supplied with fresh fish, Adalind sat with her sister, the Lady Willow, in the early morning sun. A new day was dawning, the sky streaked with the muted colors of sunrise. The ladies glanced up when a flock of geese noisily flapped across the sky, soaring off into the deep blue sky. As the kitchen yard around them bustled with servants preparing for the morning meal, the question hung in the air between them.

"Nay," Adalind replied, trying to sound casual. "I did not expect him to. Why would he?"

The Lady Willow Lillibet de Lohr de Aston shrugged her slender shoulders. She was a beauty, like her sister, a tall and lanky young woman of sixteen years who had only recently returned from fostering herself. Adalind and Willow had not seen each other in five years, a long separation for sisters who had once been inordinately close. For the past three days, they had been inseparable as they became reacquainted.

"Because you have grown up," she said simply. "You have matured a great deal and you are no longer that silly, gangly child that used to follow him about. Has he not even noticed you have grown up?"

"It does not matter. I am still the grand-daughter of his liege. He sees me as a member of the de Lohr family and nothing more."

Willow shook her head in disbelief, her pale hair licking at her cheeks. "I cannot believe the man to be so blind," she said, eyeing her sister after a moment. "When you saw him for the first time yesterday... did you feel the same as you have all of these years?"

Adalind was staring into the pond, watching the fish mingle amongst the vegetation. "Of course I did," she murmured. "I have loved him since I was nine years old. That has not changed. I thought I could forget him as I went away to foster, but I did not. He was always lingering in my mind, like a shadow over my heart that would allow no other man to have it. It is both a wondrous blessing and a horrible curse. Why should I love a man so much who will never return my feelings?"

Willow gazed at her sister, so lovely and sweet. Adalind was the oldest of the grandchildren, the leader of the troops, and when she spoke, they all had listened. She was intelligent and compassionate, but somewhere in the years she had spent in Winchester, she had developed something of a shell. Willow could see it. Adalind used to be so open, a bright spirit that happily embraced the world. That didn't seem to be the case any longer. She was guarded.

"He is a fool," Willow took her sister's hand reassuringly. "Maddoc du Bois is a stupid fool if he cannot see what a wonderful wife you would be to him."

Adalind smiled weakly. "I cannot imagine such a thing," she said. "I have dreamt of it for so long that it does not seem attainable to me. I think that it if were to ever happen, I would faint dead away from surprise."

Willow giggled, squeezing her sister's hand. "Then let us speak of men who are more attainable," she said, eyeing her sister's lowered head. "Surely there was someone at Court who caught your eye?"

Adalind cocked an eyebrow as she looked at her sister. "You have been speaking with Mother."

"I have not. But I *did* hear her speaking with Grandmother."

"What did you hear?"

"That you had more suitors than you knew what to do with and the women at Court were jealous."

Adalind returned her focus to the fish pond and the schools of silver-scaled fish. "There was no one special," she replied. "A few tried to catch my attention; perhaps a few that even tried too hard."

"Like the ap Athoe brothers?"

Adalind rolled her eyes. "Idiots, both of them," she said, standing up and brushing the dirt off her bum. "Who knew that men could be so foolish?"

Willow stood up as well, brushing off her surcoat and then picking a few dead leaves off of Adalind's hip. "I did not," she said. "But I was not so fortunate that men were fighting over me."

Adalind cast her an expression of displeasure as she turned for the keep. "I wish they would not. I have no use for them."

Willow followed. "You will someday. You will need a husband."

Adalind gathered up the hem of her surcoat so it would not drag through the moist ground. Being that they were in the kitchen yard, the ground was covered with the leavings of chicken, geese, goats and other animals, and she didn't want to soil her coat.

"Perhaps," she replied vaguely. "But I do not wish to speak of it. Let us speak of something else."

"Why?" Willow pressed. "Addie, what *happened* at Court? I heard Mother tell Grandmother awful things. What did those jealous women do to you?"

Adalind simply shook her head. They crossed the yard and she reached out to unlatch the postern gate that lead into the main ward, but Willow reached out and stopped her.

"Please tell me," she begged softly.

Adalind's green eyes were soft was sadness. "Why?" she asked. "Willow, I do not wish to speak of it."

"You are my sister. I can see how you've changed, Addie. You seem so... protected. You are not the girl I remember."

"I am most definitely not the girl you remember."

"Will you not let me come to know the girl you have become, then? Please tell me what has changed you so I may understand."

Adalind gazed at her sister as the soft morning breeze blew strands of blond hair across her eyes. It was a cool breeze, chilling her, and she pushed the hair from her face and looked away.

"People are cruel," she finally said, softly. "Suffice it to say that people can be vicious and cruel and hateful. They took my trust and faith and threw it beneath their shoe, crushing it. If I have changed, it is because I have learned something of the true world. It is not a kind place."

With that, she moved through the postern gate and out into the ward, coming alive in the early morning. It was clear that Adalind was in no frame of mind to speak of her experiences at Court, so Willow followed Adalind through the gap and took her hand as they passed by the stables. There would be time later to discover what had sent Adalind home and Willow knew enough to stop pestering the woman until she was ready. The time would come at some point.

Around them, dogs barked, horses nickered, and men were bustling about. Guards upon the walls were changing and young soldiers gave the women a wide berth as they headed for the keep entry. Somewhere in the midst of it, a chorus of shouting began to take up upon the parapets. From man to man, the cry traveled and eventually, the heavy iron portcullis of Canterbury began to lift.

Adalind and Willow weren't paying attention to the creaking of the portcullis as it laboriously climbed its chains. The subject had shifted between them and now they were speaking of going into the town to the *Shipshop* import merchant because the man usually had all manner of textiles and other items for purchase. He was a particular favorite with the de Lohr women and the girls knew it wouldn't be a difficult thing to convince their mother, and her purse, to come along. As they neared the great retractable steps that led into the keep, Adalind heard someone call her name.

It was a shout, really, like a desperate plea. Midway up the steps she came to a halt, turning to see who was calling her name. Her jaw dropped.

"Oh... Dear Lord," she muttered. "Please, not him. Not today."

Willow was anxiously looking to the portcullis, the bailey, and trying to find what had her sister so distressed in all of the bustle. There was a crowd of people in the ward, so much so that she truly had no idea what her sister was referring to.

"What is it?" she asked. "What is your trouble?"

Adalind's gaze lingered on the bailey and a certain point of reference before gathering her skirts and dashing inside. Confused, perhaps even bewildered, Willow followed.

***

"What did you say his name was?" David asked.

Adalind's expression suggested that she had a sour stomach. "Eynsford du Lesseps," she said. "He is the son of Baron Wallingford of Preston Castle in Oxfordshire. Papa, I want nothing to do with him. Please send him away."

David eyed his granddaughter, who looked rather distressed. She had come charging in to the great hall of Canterbury not a minute before, upset about something. Now David was coming to understand what had her so worked up. *Another suitor.* He snapped his fingers at the nearest servant and ordered the entry door bolted until he could get to the bottom of things. The servant went on the run.

"What about this man, Addie?" he asked. "What do you know about him?"

She shook her head, frustrated. "He is not unkind," she said, "but he is a bore. Papa, he is a horrid bore and he plays a *citole* worse than anyone I have ever heard. All he wants to do is sing sonnets to me. And his voice; terrible! I will go mad if you allow him to remain here, I surely will."

"The man is an entertainer?"

She shook her head again. "Nay," she replied, increasingly agitated. "He is a knight, but he is a very unaccomplished one. All he wants to do is sing songs and give recitations to anyone who will listen. I have seen him get up in front of a room full of people and declare his interest in me. It was the most humiliating moment of my life."

David fought off the urge to grin. He could see that Adalind was sincerely distressed. Moving from his position near the hearth where he was trying to warm his hands in the cold early morning hour, he came over to the feasting table where his granddaughters were sitting on a well-worn bench. He sat between her and Willow.

"I will not allow anyone to remain if you do not wish it," he said quietly. "But I know Baron Wallingford. He is an ally to both me and your Uncle Christopher. Before I chase his son away with nary an explanation, I should at least be hospitable to the man. I do not want it getting back to the father that I was rude. Can you understand that?"

Adalind was looking at her hands. Miserably, she nodded and David put his arm around her shoulders, kissing her on the head.

"At least allow me to sup with him tonight and then I will send the man on his way tomorrow," he said. "You do not even have to come to the meal if you do not want to. You can stay to your rooms until he is gone."

Adalind's head shot up, her green eyes full of gratitude. "Oh, *thank* you, Papa," she said, hugging him tightly. "Thank you so much."

David smiled at her, patting her cheek as he stood up from the bench. "You and your sister can sup in your chamber tonight," he said. "But I should probably go outside and greet the son of an ally. If I am going to run the man off tomorrow, then I should at least be cordial to him today."

Adalind breathed a sigh of relief. She was about to reply when there was a loud knocking at the entry to the keep. In fact, it was a heavy banging that threatened to knock the door down. Thinking it was Eynsford in all of his minstrel glory, Adalind made a face but David was obliged to answer it, especially now that he knew the situation. He had the hovering servant lift the heavy iron bolt and shove it out of the way. The big door creaked open.

Maddoc was standing in the doorway. Dressed in mail, a heavy tunic, heavy gloves, and enormous leather boots, he appeared every inch the intimidating and warring knight. Maddoc simply had that look about him, as if a single glance from his bright blue eyes could melt steel. But today, those eyes were puzzled as he looked to David.

"My lord," he said, pointing into the bailey. "There is a man with an instrument in the bailey who swears he will not leave this place until he speaks with Lady Adalind."

David cleared his throat softly, straining to look around Maddoc's bulk to see the man he was speaking of. He could see an expensive horse, tacked in expensive gear, at the base of the stairs but not much else. He put an arm out, pushing Maddoc out of the way to see a very round and tall man standing at the base of the stairs.

David had to make a conscious effort to keep from reacting. The man was not young by any means, dressed in some kind of red silk tunic that was so frilly and fine that it looked like a woman's surcoat. He had matching red hose and black boots with a peculiar pointy toe that was about a foot long. It was extremely odd. On his head he wore an elaborate hat with silk streamers and big peacock feathers sticking out of it, and in his hand he held what looked to be a heavy and expensive *citole*. David could only catch a glimpse of it before the man swung it up against his chest and began to strum.

"My lord," he called, rather dramatically, punctuating his statement with a few chords. "I have come seeking the Lady Adalind de Aston. Would you be her father, good sir?"

David tried not to let his jaw drop at all of the ridiculous fanfare. "I am her grandfather," he replied. "Her father is dead. What is it that you want?"

Eynsford smiled brightly, as if he had just landed upon extremely good fortune, and began to strum away at the guitar-like instrument that had been imported all the way from Italy. It was elaborately carved and painted in shades of red and yellow. His stubby fingers licked the thick gut strings with flourish.

"Lady, lady, my fair and beautiful maid,
Lady Adalind of virtue, most beautiful flower.
My heart beats for you, my soul to sing,
Be mine, fairest lady, and fulfill my every desire."

When he was finished, he looked rather proud of himself, as if he had just accomplished something rare and great, but David was having a difficult time controlling himself. It was the worst thing he'd ever heard, sung off-key in the most terrible voice possible. David was coming to quickly see what had Adalind so upset, for the man was truly a pathetic example of an ostensibly normal male. In fact, he was rather a joke.

David didn't dare look at Maddoc, who was standing beside him. If the man even gave a hint of a grin, David would lose his composure for sure. Struggling with all he possessed not to break out in laughter, he cleared his throat softly and descended the steps towards the wayward suitor.

"What is your name?" David asked.

"Eynsford du Lesseps," the man replied grandly. "My father is Baron Wallingford. He has spoken most highly of you and your brother, my lord. It is a distinct honor to meet you and my father sends word that it would please him greatly if our two families were united by marriage. I have come to ask you for Adalind's hand in marriage, my lord."

David was having trouble looking at the big buffoon with the crooked, toothy grin. *Over my dead body*, he thought. He could see that the man needed to be handled gently, especially since he was invoking his father's name this early in the conversation. It was a strategic move. Again, he cleared his throat softly for lack of a better action, thinking quickly on how to discourage the eager man. There was truthfully only one thing to do to end this pursuit before it gained any momentum. He would make his own strategic move.

"It would indeed be agreeable to be linked to your family by marriage," he began, "but I am afraid that Adalind is already spoken for."

The big, toothy grin immediately fell. "*Spoken* for?" Eynsford repeated, shocked. "But... but that cannot be. She is intended for me. I have followed her all the way from London and she is intended for *me*."

David hoped God would forgive his convenient lie. "She is pledged to another," he said firmly. "I am sorry you had to come all this way to discover the news. Please stay as my guest tonight before returning home. I should like to hear of your father's health and welfare."

Eynsford was crushed beyond crushed, hurt beyond hurt. He looked at David as if the man had just quashed every dream he'd ever had, now left with nothing. The naked emotion on his face was without question. Rather than respond to David's invitation, he simply turned away.

"Woe," he moaned, then threw up his hands and wailed louder. "Woe, I say! My goddess has slipped through my fingers like... like sand as it drains through... through... through a shattered chalice with holes all about it. My beautiful Adalind belongs to another and I am woeful! It cannot be!"

"It is."

"Then I am *ended*!"

It was a comical and dramatic emotion at its best. David dared to turn around and look at Maddoc, who was still standing at the top of the steps next to the keep entry, watching Eynsford stomp about with an impassive expression on his features. David wished he was so adept at keeping a straight face.

"Eynsford," David tried not to giggle as he spoke to the man. "There is no need to despair. There will be other fine ladies, I am sure."

Eynsford suddenly fell to his knees in the muddy floor of the bailey. "Nay," he threw up his arms. "No more ladies. There will be no more ladies for me. *Argh!* When I think of another man touching Adalind as only I should, I... I...!"

With that, he fell over onto his back, sprawled out on the ground as he gazed up at the sky. Then he clumsily clutched his *citole* to his chest and began to strum despondently.

"'Painful! Grossly painful and wretched heart, you pain me stubbornly!
If only I could rip you free, free of the bondage of a love unreturned!
Hateful bastard!'"

He was singing at the top of his lungs and David wiped a hand over his face because he couldn't help the smile now. It was horrible and dramatic and funny as hell. The man was making a spectacle of himself, drawing attention from those in the bailey.

"Eynsford, get up," David commanded softly. "There is no need to wallow in the dirt. Get up before you make a fool of yourself, boy."

Eynsford shook his head, grinding his elaborate hat into the mud as he moved. "I will stay here forever," he moaned. "If I cannot have my beloved Adalind, I will waste away in the dirt of her home so I will forever be a part of her."

"Get out of the dirt."

"At least she will walk over me at times. If I cannot have all of her, at least I can have her feet."

David turned away, biting his lip because he wanted to burst into laughter. He truly did. He made his way back to the steps leading into the keep, taking them quickly until he came to Maddoc. The knight was still standing at the top of the stairs, watching de Lesseps make an ass out of himself.

"See if you can get him out of the dirt and into the great hall," David muttered. "Let us get this meal over with in a hurry so I can get the man out of my keep."

Maddoc's expression was neutral but the bright blue eyes were flickering dangerously. "I can get him out now."

David put a hand on Maddoc's arm. "No, lad," he said. "We must be polite to this jackass because his father is a valuable ally. Just... make sure he does not hurt himself in his grief. God's Blood, now I see what Addie was talking about. The man is boorish to say the least."

"May I at least attempt to get rid of him, my lord? His behavior is shameful."

David eyed him. "Not now," he replied. "Let us see if he comes to his senses first. If he is still laying here come nightfall, I will permit you to do as you must to remove him."

Maddoc wasn't pleased with the directive but he understood somewhat. The situation was delicate. With a lingering glance to the odd fellow lying on his back and strumming his *citole*, David disappeared into the keep. Maddoc remained at the top of the stairs, however, watching the fool as men walked around him and dogs sniffed his feet. He eventually shook his head with disgust.

So this is what men in love do? Although he'd never been in love before, he hoped he was wrong. He couldn't imagine allowing himself to succumb to such deplorable behavior. He'd seen ample displays of it in the past two days.

As Maddoc continued to stand there and observe, he caught sight of someone beside him. Turning his head, he saw Adalind standing behind him, using him for a shield as she peered down into the bailey at Eyndsford. She was very close, bumped up against him as she tried to hide and Maddoc found himself studying the shape of her eyes. She had very beautiful eyes. But Adalind wasn't looking at him; she was focused on the fool down in the bailey.

"God's Beard," she hissed. "Has he not gone away? What is he doing?"

Maddoc's gaze lingered on her sweet face, appreciating it through new eyes, before returning his focus to the ward.

"He is lamenting your loss, I believe," he said.

She looked at him. "What did Papa tell him?"

"That you are spoken for."

"With you again?"

"He was not specific, but it was enough to send your suitor into fits."

Adalind's gaze returned to the idiot with the *citole*. After a moment, she shook her head with displeasure.

"I wish he would go away," she said. "He is humiliating me just like he did before. All that man does is humiliate me."

Maddoc looked at her. "How has he humiliated you?"

Adalind didn't want to speak of it, just as she didn't wish to speak of the series of events that eventually had her fleeing Court for home. Those were painful memories she didn't wish to discuss even though her mother and grandmother had already forced it out of her. But Maddoc had asked a reasonable question based on her statement so she did him the courtesy of answering. She sighed heavily.

"I first met Eynsford back in January when the king had a Masque for the advent of the New Year," she said quietly. "I was attending the Lady Margaret, Hubert de Burgh's wife, and somehow Eynsford saw me. He was a guest of the Duke of Norfolk, evidently. He tried to catch my attention at first but I ignored him, which turned out to be my mistake. When the meal commenced, he came to my table and announced he was deeply in love with me and would proceed to woo me. It was simply awful."

Maddoc crossed his big arms thoughtfully. "Have you spent all of this time running from him?" he asked. "Perhaps it would be better if you simply told him you were not interested."

She gave him a look of disgust. "I *have* told him," she said. "I was polite at first but he would not listen. He kept following me, playing that... that stupid *citole*, singing stupid sonnets until I was nearly mad with it. Finally, I was quite nasty with him and told him I had absolutely no interest in him at all and I'd sooner wed a goat. It did not seem to matter to him. He continued to try."

Maddoc returned is attention to the man on the ground. "How did he find you here? Did he know of your family?"

Adalind seemed to dim. "Someone must have told him, for I never did," she said softly. "Those terrible women who... well, it does not matter. Someone must have told him."

Maddoc was focused on her statement; *those terrible women who....* It seemed to reinforce what David had told him about the women at Court chasing her away. He could only imagine what those sly and worldly women were capable of and he began to feel strangely protective of Adalind, something beyond his normal sense of duty. The sensation was surprisingly strong and while it should have rattled him, unfamiliar as it was, he found it rather overwhelming. He wasn't rattled at all. It seemed completely natural.

"So he did not listen to you when you told him you had no interest?" he asked.

She shook her head. "No," she replied, her gaze on the red-silked figure. "He was much like the ap Athoe brothers; he did not listen to me at all. Maddoc, why on earth do men not listen to a woman when she has something to say?"

He looked at her. "Because they think they know a woman's mind better than she does," he said, his gaze lingering on her a moment. "Your grandfather told me to give him time to come to his senses before I take action, but if you wish for me to run him off now, I will do it."

It was a chivalrous declaration. Adalind looked up at him, into those bright blue eyes that were so intense and beautiful, and her cheeks began to grow warm. She realized how close she was standing to him, up against his big and powerful body and feeling the heat radiate off the man.

When she had been a young girl, her emotions for him were untried and uncontrolled, silly thoughts from a silly girl. He could make her heart race and make her feel giggly, but there had never been any heat to it, not like now. Now, the warmth she felt from the man was nearly searing and she had to make a conscious effort to take a step away or she was fearful she would go up in flame. The sentiment she felt for him were no longer those of a foolish young girl. They were the emotions of a woman, with all the depth and heart those feelings entailed. It made her heart ache with longing simply to be near him.

"You had better not," she said quietly, taking another step away and hoping he didn't notice the dull flush in her cheeks. "If Papa told you to wait, then you had better do as he says. I do not want you to get in trouble on my behalf."

Maddoc smiled faintly, something he rarely did. But something in that beautiful face made him feel like smiling. "It would be an honor," he said. "May I?"

She looked doubtfully between Eynsford and Maddoc. "Well," she said slowly, "if it does not involve beating him to a pulp or throwing him over the wall, I suppose you could try."

His smile vanished, though there was humor to the gesture. "I do not beat anyone to a pulp. Well, not without good reason, anyway."

Her eyes narrowed playfully. "I *saw* you," she said. "You beat the ap Athoe brothers within an inch of their lives."

"I had good reason."

"Then you admit it."

He shrugged. "If anyone comes calling for you, or any of the de Lohr women, they will have to answer to me first. What I did was purely in your interest. Those two fools were unworthy of you."

She eyed him. "Who *is* worthy of me, Maddoc?"

He shook his head. "God has not yet created such a man, I think. You are not meant for mere mortals."

She threw up her hands. "Sweet Lucifer!" she exclaimed softly. "Am I to become an old maid, then?"

His smile was back. "I have a feeling you will marry well and be very happy, my lady. I would stake my life on it."

She tried not to smile in return, unable to help the comment that came from her lips. "The only man I have interest in has no interest in marrying me, so perhaps you were not far wrong the first time. Perhaps I will indeed be an old maid because if I cannot marry him, I do not want anyone."

Maddoc was caught up in the gentle flirt. He was untried and unused to such games because he usually walked away when some young woman would make the attempt, but Adalind was very practiced. She batted her eyes and flashed the dimple in her right cheek appropriately, and he was swept away. For a man who kept himself very tightly locked away from any emotion, Adalind seemed to have the ability to turn the key and he wasn't even aware of it.

"Is that so?" he countered. "Who is this saint of all men, then? And who on earth would be foolish enough not to want you?"

She looked at him, giggling. "He is a *very* big fool," she scolded lightly. "He is such a fool I cannot tell you how truly foolish he is. It defies explanation."

"Do I know him?"

"Of course you do because the fool is *you*," she said, then sighed dramatically. "Alas, I suppose you will always view me as that silly girl with the bucked teeth, so I suppose I have no other choice than to accept another's proposal. Perhaps you should go down to the bailey and see if Eynsford has not changed his mind about me. It might be my last chance at marriage. Perhaps I will have to listen to him wail like a tomcat for the rest of my life, but I suppose it is better than being alone or confined in a convent."

By this time, Maddoc's smile had faded. The impact of her words hit him and although they had been said in a flirtatious and jesting manner, he realized for the first time in his life that he was actually touched by them. Adalind had made no secret about wanting to marry him when she had been young, but now, as a grown woman, he no longer saw a joke in her words. He saw something that greatly intrigued him, and the mere thought that he might actually be interested scared him to death.

"Perhaps we should return inside," he said, taking her elbow to direct her back into the keep because he didn't know what else to do, startled by his alien thoughts. "I shall give du Lesseps until sundown to come to his senses, and if he has not, I shall be forced to find his senses for him."

Adalind wasn't unaware of his swift change in demeanor. He suddenly seemed stiff and distant. Realizing that her reference to marriage must have turned him, inwardly, she was furious with herself for daring to bring up the subject. She knew the man didn't want her. He had always made that very clear. All of the love and adoration she felt for him, the admiration and respect, would never come to fruition. Disappointment and sorrow consumed her.

Without another word she allowed the man to escort her back into the keep. Then she went up to her chamber and wept.

My spellbound heart has made and remade the necklace of songs,
That you take as a gift, wear round your neck in your many forms,
In life after life, in age after age, forever.

CHAPTER THREE

"He has been singing like that for hours," Christina de Aston, David's eldest daughter and Adalind's mother, was standing at the window of her daughters' chamber, her attention drawn to the torch-lit bailey below. "One would have thought he would have grown weary of it."

Adalind was lying on the bed with Willow. The room was warm, well furnished, with a giant feather and straw-stuffed mattress made of linen and heavy coverlets of fur. The heaviest top coverlet was canvas stuffed with dried straw that held in the heat, covered with a silk duvet. Nights were very cold and even though the small chamber had an enormous fireplace, Adalind was always cold and required a good deal of blankets for comfort. Tonight was no different as she lay swathed in a heavy brocade robe over her wool surcoat.

Willow was brushing the elder sister's hair as all three women listened to the baying down below. It had been going on all day. Sunset was upon them and the night was growing cold and dark, and a fog was rolling in from the east. The torches upon the battlements were giving off a ghostly glow through the coming mist.

"Is Maddoc still down there?" Adalind asked.

Christina's lips twitched with a smile as she strained to see down below. "He is nearly standing next to him," she said. "I have no idea how Eynsford can concentrate with Maddoc standing over his shoulder. The man is positively terrifying."

"I think he is trying to scare him to death."

"It is not working. I must give the man credit for his bravery."

Adalind lay there, listening to all manner of terrible and hoarse singing, before rising from the bed and going to the window where her mother was standing. Christina put her arm around her eldest fondly.

"Life is never dull with you around, Addie," she teased softly. "When you were young, it was one crisis after the next – wayward animals, injured birds, scraped knees, and missing teeth. Now it would seem we are destined to revisit those lively years with more adult predicaments."

Adalind smiled weakly at her mother, a woman she favored a great deal with her blond hair and green eyes. "I hope not," she said quietly. "I have had quite enough excitement over the past few years. I simply wish to be left in peace."

"I am not entirely sure that will be the case tonight. Do you realize that young man has been singing all day?"

Adalind did. As she listened to the howling, she began to grow more and more frustrated. She tried to forget about it, returning to Willow and braiding her sister's hair, but the noise continued. It reminded her of moments in her life of great humiliation that she would rather forget about, memories of people laughing at her, whispering behind her back. Things she never wanted to remember, ever. It reminded her of the horrors that had driven her home and back into the safety of her family's bosom. This was *her* place for safety and comfort, and he was destroying that illusion. Finally, she couldn't stand it any longer.

Gathering her skirts, she fled the chamber, ignoring the calls of her sister and mother. Descending the stairs far too quickly, she hit the entry with full fury and even ignored the calls from her grandfather who was seated in the warm and stuffy great hall off to her left. At the moment, she was singularly focused with ridding Canterbury of du Lesseps. She'd reached her limit. Every pain, every shame, that she had felt over the past five years was about to come out all over that pitiful fool with the *citole*. He was in for a thrashing.

The early evening was moist and cold as Adalind charged out of the keep and took the steps down to the bailey. All fit and fire, she charged up on Eynsford, who was now sitting up in the mud as he brayed forth his lament. When he saw Adalind approaching through the dark, his fat face lit up and his singing immediately stopped.

"My lady!" he exclaimed gratefully. "I have...!"

Adalind interrupted him with an angry snap. "Enough!" she roared. "Eynsford du Lesseps, I have listened to you screech and howl all day and I am sick to death of it, do you hear? I have told you repeatedly, since the day we met, that I am not interested in marrying you, and no amount of horrible singing or nauseating poetry is going to force me to change my mind. Do you understand me? You are the stupidest, foulest, and most disgusting man I have ever met and I want absolutely nothing to do with you. I want you to get out of Canterbury and never come back. Is this in any way unclear?"

She was sincerely raging. By the time she was finished, Eynsford was looking at her with a great deal of shock and amazement. The smile was gone from his face.

"But...," he was genuinely puzzled, "my lady, I am desperate for want of you. Do you not understand that my feelings are...?"

She cut him off again. "Go away," she nearly shouted. "I have tried to be patient and I have tried to be kind, but you are so foolish that you cannot understand what I am telling you. Pleasantries have evidently masked the meaning of my words, so I am no longer pleasant. I don't like you. I don't want you. I will not marry you. I want you to go away and never come back."

Eynsford rose to his knees, stiffly struggling to his feet. "But if you will only give me a chance, I am sure...."

"No!" she roared. "No chances. No nothing. Stop humiliating me with your idiotic singing and go *away*!"

Eynsford was on his feet now, looking genuinely hurt. It was clear that the concept of rejection was foreign to him. A wealthy lord's spoiled son, he had always gotten what he wanted. *Always.* He began to look around the bailey.

"Your grandfather," he said. "I will speak with him. He will understand my proposal and consent."

With a shriek, Adalind flew at him, pounding him on his silk-covered chest before slapping him, hard, across the face. She was so livid that she had lost her self-control. There happened to be a rather large stick on the ground, debris from the storm they'd suffered two days before, and she picked it up and swung it at him, catching him on the hip.

"Go!" she bellowed, smacking him with the stick again. "Go away and never come back. I do not want to see you ever again, do you hear me? Stop ignoring what I am saying. You will not speak with my grandfather. You will *get out!*"

She punctuated the last two words by smacking him again with the stick. Eynsford flinched from the blows, startled by the loud cracking sound more than he was actually hurt. The stick's noise echoed against the battlement walls. Adalind's fury was working the desired effect; he was backing away and heading towards the gatehouse.

"My lady, please," he began to plead, trying to dodge her flying stick. "You do not understand. I mean only the best and...."

She screamed with frustration as she swung the stick, catching him on the shoulder. "Go!" she yelled. "I hate you, I hate you! You have made my life miserable and horrid, and I hate you!"

She was chasing him now, violently swinging the stick as he finally ran for his life. Maddoc, who had stood by silently and observant during the exchange, broke from his stance and went after her before she could beat the man to death. Coming up behind her as she swung, he grabbed her around the torso with one big hand and grasped the wrist holding the stick with the other.

"Enough, Addie," he murmured, his lips by her ear. "I will handle it from here."

Adalind's response was to burst into gut-busting sobs. Concerned, Maddoc wasn't sure what to do at that moment, so he did what his instincts dictated – he hugged her tightly, briefly, and gently let her go, pulling the stick out of her hand as he went. By this time, Eynsford had already collected his horse, which had never been formally stabled but merely tied up, and was making a break for the gatehouse. Maddoc really didn't have to do anything more than simply make sure the man left and the portcullis closed behind him. After that, his attention returned to Adalind.

Her mother and sister had come down from the keep and had tried to comfort her as she stood sobbing in the middle of the bailey, but she wanted no part of it. She ran away from them and as they watched her go; indecisive as to whether or not to follow her, Maddoc silently indicated he would follow her to make sure she came to no harm. Willow wasn't so sure but Christina agreed, thinking that perhaps Adalind would find more comfort in the attention of the man she had always been in love with rather than her mother and sister. Something was coming to a head in her quiet and sad daughter, something that perhaps family couldn't help her with. Maybe Maddoc could.

It was just a hunch she had.

***

Maddoc found Adalind in the stables. It hadn't been difficult; he had simply followed the sounds of her weeping. It was dark in the stables with occasional sounds of a snorting horse or the meow of a cat. The animals shifted listlessly when they sensed humans. Patiently, he made his way back into the depths of the structure to find Adalind sitting in a storage area where they kept piles of dried grass. The smell of wood and hay was heavy in the air.

She was sitting against the wall, her back turned to him, weeping softly. Maddoc watched her for a moment, finding himself thinking on that skinny little girl who used to drive him daft. He'd run from her and hid from her, when he'd never run or hid from anything in his life. It had been rather embarrassing behavior from the serious young knight. But somehow, she would always find him. She had popped up more than once when he had been using the privy, something that had infuriated him at the time but now brought a smile to his lips. Adalind was, if nothing else, fearless and persistent. But he didn't see those qualities in her now and that concerned him.

"My lady," he said softly. "It is cold out here. Would you permit me to escort you inside?"

Her back was still to him. She wiped at her face, sniffling. "No," she said after a moment. "I do not want to go inside now. I simply wish to be left alone and if I go inside, my sister and mother will hound me mercilessly. They mean well but I do not want their company right now."

"Will you accept mine?"

The question hung in the air between them. Adalind's tears faded as she thought on it. She'd known the man her entire life and he'd asked her dozens of questions during that time. So why was this question so different? She swore she heard something in the tone. It was soft and hopeful. But perhaps she was simply imagining there was anything more than polite concern to the question. She remembered earlier in the day when his manner had abruptly changed as they had discussed suitors and marriage.

Still, she felt such painful longing for the man, more and more as the hours went by. Since his return yesterday, she could feel her emotions for him magnifying. He was such a handsome, sweet, compassionate and powerful man. She'd known him her whole life; she knew his character. She was so far gone in love with him that it would surely ruin her life.

"Maddoc?"

"Aye?"

"I have come to a decision."

"What is that?"

She sniffled, wiped at her nose, and shifted so she was facing him. She gazed up into that handsome face, feeling the tears at her throat again, feeling more pain and sorrow than she'd ever known.

"I... I have decided to commit myself to the cloister," she said. "It is the only alternative, you see, for I shall never marry. My grandfather and grandmother are great patrons of Canterbury Cathedral, so it would be a simple thing to join the Augustine order there. I have been familiar with it all of my life. Besides, if I join the order at the cathedral, I will still be close to home."

Maddoc gazed down into her sad face. "This is the first time I have heard you express any interest in joining the cloister."

She shrugged. "Perhaps it is the first time I have spoken of it," she said. "But I have been thinking of it for a while, I truly have. It is not a new idea to me."

He looked at her thoughtfully. Then, he took a few steps and lowered his bulk down next to her. Sitting side by side, leaning up against the wall, they gazed at each other. It was the first time Maddoc could remember that he openly inspected her, as purely a man to a woman, noting the slight tilt of her lovely eyes and the dusting of freckles across her nose. She had such beautiful skin, so creamy and smooth. She was the most spectacular woman he had ever seen.

"When you were about eight or nine years of age, you first declared that you were deeply in love with me," he said softly. "I was very young and a newly knighted. I ignored you for the most part, so you hid under my bed in the knight's quarters. I thought you were waiting there to murder me in my sleep. Do you recall?"

Adalind fought off a grin, averting her gaze. "I do."

"Do you recall that it was a safe haven until I lay upon the bed and the mattress sank?"

She was struggling not to giggle. "You nearly squashed me between the floor and the mattress."

His grin broke through. "Thank God you had the presence of mind to yell before I smothered you."

She started to laugh. "I nearly passed out."

He was starting to laugh now, too. "It would have served you right, you pint-sized assassin."

Her laughter deepened. "I thought I *was* going to kill you, after all, but as I thought on it, I would miss you too much. Perhaps I was just going to make your life miserable for a while. I believe I succeeded, too."

He shook his head. "You never made me miserable. Frustrated at times, but never miserable. You were too sweet to make me truly miserable."

Her smile faded, hearing tender words from his mouth that she could have easily believed to have been romantic rather than simply kind. Maddoc had always had a soft spot for the girls in the family, showing more compassion and understanding than most. But he only let a select few see that side of him. Adalind had always been one of them in spite of her annoying presence at times.

As she gazed back at him, her heart swelled so that she thought it might burst from her chest and words of longing and adoration came to her lips, but she bit them off and looked away. She couldn't stomach to look upon the man and not tell him what was in her heart. He didn't want to hear it, anyway.

"You were patient to tolerate a young girl who gazed upon you with stars in her eyes," she said softly. "I always appreciated your kindness and your discretion for not telling my mother half of the things that I did in my quest to conquer you."

He was looking at her lowered head, her dark blond hair, resisting the urge to reach out and stroke the silken strands.

"I hardly recall any of it," he said quietly. "It seems that fostering had taken the edge off of your rebellious spirit. You have returned to Canterbury refined and proper. Why put all of that time and effort to waste at a convent?"

Adalind shook her head faintly, her gaze on the straw-covered floor. "It would not be a waste," she murmured. "Maddoc, where did you foster?"

"Northwood Castle in Northumberland. It is one of the great border castles in the north."

"Did you like it? Did you make any friends there?"

"I made many friends. They are like my brothers."

She sighed. "That is what I had hoped for as well," she muttered. "But I found little companionship when I fostered, only jealousy and evil. I simply wanted to belong. I hope that the nuns would not be so judgmental or wicked. Perhaps... perhaps I would finally found where I belonged with them."

"Is that what you truly want? Simply to belong somewhere?"

She grew frustrated. "You make it sound as if I wish for something foolish or trite," she said, snappish, and attempted to stand. "It is easy for you to ask that question because you belong here, or with your friends at Northwood. Maddoc, I have not been home in five years. It is not even my home anymore; it is simply a place where my family lives. I suppose Winchester Palace was my home, but I did not belong there, either. The people there, people who were supposed to be my friends, were cruel as you can imagine. I feel as if I live nowhere or have no one. Ever since I returned to Canterbury, I have this feeling of drifting and awkwardness."

He reached up and grasped her wrist before she could get away. "I am sorry," he said gently, soothingly. "I did not mean to sound judgmental. I would never presume to do that. Please do not leave."

She tried to yank away but she didn't give it a very good effort. Eventually, she plopped back down onto her buttocks but she wouldn't look at him. He continued to hold on to her wrist, fearful she was going to try to get away again. He studied her profile, wondering where all of these strangely warm feelings for her were coming from. Since they had gotten reacquainted yesterday, that spark of surprise he had experienced when he had first seen her was morphing into something different. He'd never experienced anything like it. All he knew was that he didn't want her to leave.

"Addie," he said in a low, soft voice. "This is your home. You will always belong here with people that love you. In that respect, I am very envious of that because the only family I have is in Wales or in France. I was raised by my grandmother and my uncle, and went to foster when I was ten years of age. When I was seventeen, I found out that my father, who I believed had been killed when I was a child, was in fact alive and living in France. Although I am now close with my father and step-mother, the truth is that I only came to know them as an adult. I do not have fond or happy memories of my childhood with them. Even if you feel as if you do not belong at Canterbury, the truth is that you have a family that loves you a great deal and you do indeed belong with them. You are very much loved and cherished."

Adalind was still staring at the ground. When she was finished, she reached down and picked at a piece of straw off the hem of her surcoat. Her manner was sad, fidgety.

"I know they love me," she said, almost guiltily, "but I... oh, I do not know what more to say. I feel as if I want to run away from the world and hide."

"So that is why you want to join the cloister? Because you want to hide?"

She simply nodded. After a moment, he saw a tear roll down her face and drip off her chin. His manner softened.

"Hide from *what*, Addie?" he whispered. "What are you hiding from?"

She burst into soft tears and shook her head. He thought perhaps she wouldn't answer him but after a few moments, she began to speak.

"I am hiding from fools like the ap Athoe brothers and Eynsford du Lesseps," she wept. "I am hiding from the lords who would see me in the halls of Winchester and send me secret messages that were intercepted by servants who then spread vicious rumors. I am hiding from the wives of those lords who would slap me in public or tear my surcoat in church and call it an accident. I am hiding from maidens that were supposed to be my friends but when attractive suitors would call upon me. These same maidens would steal from me or break my hair combs, or refuse to talk to me and cause me to eat my meals alone. Someone even cut my hair one night when I was sleeping. They cut off the bottom of one of my braids and I had to cut my hair to even it out. I am hiding from all of these horrible people, Maddoc, and I will not allow you to judge me for what I feel nor stop me from what I feel I must do. If I want to join the cloister to remove myself from these terrible things, then I will do so."

She was wiping her face furiously by the time she was finished, angry and heartbroken tears coursing down her cheeks. Maddoc sat still and silent against the wall, letting her vent, feeling overwhelming sadness for her. It was probably more than she told her mother and grandmother, embarrassing and painful things to tell. He sighed heavily.

"I am so sorry," he murmured. "It sounds as if you bore the brunt of some very mean and petty actions. Is that why you came home?"

She nodded, wiping at her wet chin. "I withstood it for three years," she said, finally looking up at him. "Three long years of abuse until I could stand it no longer. I had hoped to secure a high position at court, perhaps even a lady-in-waiting to the queen, but that dream will never know fruition. Everything I wished and worked for is in ruins."

Maddoc watched her face, feeling so very sorry for her. God, how he wished he could have protected her or helped her. Poor Adalind didn't deserve any of what had evidently been dealt her.

"You know why they did it, do you not?" he asked quietly.

Sniffling, she eyed him with confusion. "Because they hated me."

"That is only a small part of it, I am sure. But there is a greater reason."

"What is that?"

He smiled faintly. "Because they are jealous," he said. "Look at you; I have never seen a more beautiful woman and I am quite certain I am not the only one to have noticed your beauty. All of these women you speak of are simply jealous. You have something they will never have and they will punish you for it. It is envy, pure and simple."

The words from his lips warmed her, eased her sorrow. Still, she knew he was saying it out of kindness. Perhaps he really didn't mean any of it. He was simply trying to make her feel better. Averting her gaze, she wiped the last of the tears from her face.

"You are very sweet to try and ease me," she said, "but you do not have to say such things. It does not matter why those things happened, only that they did. But I would appreciate it if you did not tell anyone. It is my shame to bear."

"I will take the information to my grave," he assured her. "But I did not tell you those things simply to ease you. I told you because they were the truth."

She shrugged. Then she cast him a side-long glance, a weak grin on her face. "You have never said such things to me before," she said. "Have you grown so foolish in your old age?"

He snorted. "I have grown wise beyond measure," he told her, smiling. "What a fool I was to resist you those years ago."

"That is your misfortune."

"More than you know," he agreed, eyeing her. "Is it too late to consider that marriage proposal you presented to me when you were eleven years of age?"

She laughed softly, displaying her pretty white teeth. "You must be getting desperate," she said, rising to her knees and brushing off the straw. "As I recall, you never had any shortage of female admirers. Grandfather used to say that there was a star in the sky...."

He cut her off, finishing for her. "For every heart I have broken," he pretended to be annoyed as she giggled. "Perhaps I resisted you all of those years just to throw you off of my true intentions towards you. I did not want to make such an easy conquest."

She laughed out loud as she began to make her way out of the stable. "You have no true intentions towards me, Maddoc du Bois," she said, glancing behind her as he followed. "Stop teasing me. You will only break my heart again and I do not think I can stand it."

The night outside the stables was cool and misty as they emerged from the stable. Adalind immediately wrapped her arms around her torso, chilled, as they headed off towards the keep. Maddoc took her elbow politely, escorting her, but at some point he realized he had hold of her because he wanted to. He probably should have let her go at that point but he didn't want to; he knew he would miss the feel of her in his hand.

"It was never my intention to break your heart, you know," he said softly, his gaze moving about the posts up on the parapets that were being set for the night. "You must remember that I was rather young at the time as well."

She cast him a side-long glance, a smile playing on her lips. "And you were therefore completely ignorant of women?"

"Absolutely."

"But now you are not. You are wisened and experienced."

He shrugged with some hesitance. "Wisened, yes. But I am not entirely sure about experienced."

"Why not?"

"Because I am a busy man. A woman takes time and I've none to spare these days."

"Surely you must have spared time for your wife."

He nodded. "I did, but I had no choice. She was my wife and by virtue of that station deserved my attention."

Adalind fell silent as they crossed the darkened bailey, drawing closer to the keep. She was interested in his wife, this mysterious woman who had held the one thing in life Adalind had ever wanted - she'd had Maddoc. She tried to be careful in her approach.

"What was she like?" she asked after a moment.

He was thoughtful. "She was very well-bred," he replied. "She was well-educated and spoke appropriately. She had been well-schooled in how to behave for a husband."

"But what was she *like*? Was she humorous? A shrew?"

He grinned. "I am not entirely sure I know," he said softly. "It seemed to me... well, it seemed to me at times that she was simply doing what she was told to do, as I was. I cannot say there was any affection in our marriage. Simply duty."

She gave him a disapproving expression. "Did you even *try* to get to know her? Perhaps she was a very nice woman."

He could see she was mostly teasing him. "Of course I tried," he insisted weakly. "But I am afraid to tell you the rest."

"Why?"

"Because you might become angry with me. This I could not abide."

She fought off a grin. "I will not become angry with you."

"Swear it?"

"Tell me, you coward, before I become angry."

He tried not to laugh. "Very well," he said. "She was a very plain woman with a plain personality. She cried for three hours after we first met. She saw me as a fear, as a duty, and nothing more. When she became pregnant, she wept nearly the entire time, every day, so I mostly tried to stay away from her. Any sight of me greatly upset her. In hindsight, I do not think I was a very good husband to her, although I did try. She simply wanted nothing to do with me."

Adalind paused as they reached the wooden stairs that led up into the keep. Her eyes glittered warmly at him.

"She was a fool, then," she said softy, a smile on her lips. "I am glad I was not here to see it."

"See what?"

"Her indifference. You deserve a woman who will worship everything about you. I am afraid I might have had to slap some sense into her."

A smile spread across his lips as he looked at her. "You are my champion, then?"

She nodded firmly and turned for the keep. "If I cannot have you, then I will make sure whoever has you is well aware of your worth."

The smile faded from his face as he watched her take the steps. *If I cannot have you.* Those words had never bothered him until this moment. Now, they bothered him a great deal. In fact, the past two days had seen to destroy every notion he'd ever had about Adalind de Aston. He was coming to feel like the annoying little girl from the past and this glorious creature in front of him were two different women. Had he only just met Adalind, as the magnificent beauty in front of him, he would have pursued her in an instant. He'd never pursued a woman in his life, although he'd had ample opportunity. Therefore, this was all uncharted territory for him and he was vastly uncertain.

"My lady," he called to her.

Adalind turned to look at him. He was standing at the bottom of the steps, partially shrouded by the darkness of the night.

"Aye?"

He paused before answering and his insecurity was evident. The usually confident knight seemed uneasy.

"I would ask that you reconsider committing yourself to the cloister," he said quietly. "You never know what opportunities will be presented to you. You would not want to do anything in haste."

Adalind visibly sobered. "Perhaps," she said, not particularly noticing how uneasy he seemed. She was thinking of her own future, or lack thereof. "I appreciate your concern, Maddoc. Thank you for lending your ear."

"Always, my lady," he said softly as he turned away. "For you, always."

Adalind wished the soft tone he used equated to interest in her, but she knew better. With a sad sigh, she entered the keep.

Whenever I hear old chronicles of love, it's age-old pain,
It's ancient tale of being apart or together.

CHAPTER FOUR

Adalind didn't sleep very well that night. Whenever she closed her eyes she had visions of Maddoc. Although the two of them had many conversations over the course of the years, they had never had a conversation like the one they'd had in the stables. The kind and polite knight she had known all these years had somehow turned warm and deep. It only made her love him more, now with a love borne from an adult woman's heart and not a child's. She fell in love with qualities she didn't know he had. Her heart ached for him more than she could bear.

Consequently, she woke up exhausted and grumpy. Her sister tried to talk to her, as did her mother and grandmother, Emilie, but she didn't want to speak of such things. She didn't want to speak of Eynsford, or Maddoc, or anything else. She simply wanted to be left alone, which is what she told her mother and sister in a fit of angry tears, so they left her alone for the most part. They understood Adalind was dealing with a great many things and it was necessary to be patient with her. If, and when, she needed an ear to listen, they would be there for her.

After the nooning meal, the hall in the keep was silent for the most part as the occupants of the castle went about their business. The main level of the keep housed the hall, her grandmother and grandfather's private chamber, along with a small receiving room for her grandmother and a solar for her grandfather. As far as keeps went, it was a very large one, and it was a fairly simple thing to gain some privacy.

Adalind sat in her grandmother's receiving room working on an embroidery loom. She had started the piece yesterday, sketching out a scene of hummingbird and flowers with charcoal on the fine piece of linen. She was quite an accomplished artist, drawing and painting beautifully, and she was also very accomplished in her sewing. Her years of fostering had seen to that and, fortunately, she had a talent for it. It was an escape as well as a hobby, and she had been quietly doing her work since the early morning hours. Everyone had stayed clear of her as if she carried the plague.

David wasn't unaware of the situation with his granddaughter. He had seen what had happened yesterday when she had exploded at du Lesseps, but he had wisely stayed away as her mother and sister and grandmother attempted to comfort her, only to be pushed away. Du Bois was the only one who seemed to be able to communicate with her and, not surprisingly, ease her, which was causing David to closely watch the interaction between the two. Adalind was fragile and he didn't want Maddoc's well-meaning attempts to give the girl false hope.

David had been in his solar since early morning as well, having received word from his brother, the powerful Earl of Hereford and Worcester, that one of their allies along the Welsh Marches was being harried by a Welsh prince who was gaining some momentum. Christopher de Lohr had stopped short of asking his brother for immediate assistance, but he had put him on notice. Canterbury carried almost a thousand men and David was sure his brother would request three-quarters of that number.

He was therefore studying a map of the area in question, a beautiful piece of cartography etched upon an enormous piece of yellowed vellum. He had the entire country on various pieces of vellum in his solar, for he and his brother had done their fair share of troop movement and maps of this sort were necessary. The maps were old and well-used, pieces of art as much as they were maps. This particular map had been passed down from David's father, Myles. But as time went by and thoughts of Adalind caused him to lose his concentration, he set aside his quill and casually wandered over to his wife's receiving room.

Sunlight was streaming in through the big arched window on the north side of the room. Dressed in a soft yellow surcoat and looking radiant and lovely, Adalind sat before her loom, patiently piercing the material as she wove her tapestry. When she caught movement out of the corner of her eye, she glanced up without lifting her head to see her grandfather standing in the doorway. She smiled faintly.

"Greetings, Papa," she said softly. "I thought you were busy with the fate of England today."

He smiled weakly as he entered the room. "I was," he said. "But I thought I would come and visit you for a few moments. I've not seen you all day."

"That is because I have been busy," she said, refocusing on the loom. "If I plan to give this piece to Uncle Christopher and Aunt Dustin by Christmas, then I must be diligent."

"Christmas is several months away."

"I know, but this is an ambitious piece. It will take time."

David moved into the room, looking over her shoulder at what she was working on before moving to the window and gazing outside. The sky was clear and blue with a hint of cool breeze. He inhaled deeply.

"Your Uncle Daniel should be here in the next few days," he said, glancing over at her. "It has been a long time since you last saw him, hasn't it?"

Adalind stabbed the material with colored thread. "I saw him almost a year ago when he came to visit me at Court," she said. "He stayed for a few days and we had a wonderful time. Papa, why has he not married yet? He would make some woman a wonderful husband."

David lifted an eyebrow as he turned from the window. "Your Uncle Daniel is in no hurry to marry," he said. "Although I wish he was. I would see at least one son from him to carry on the de Lohr name before I die."

"Perhaps you should find him a wife."

"Perhaps," he said, eyeing her. "Did you have anyone in mind? Perhaps a lady you knew at Court?"

She shook her head. "I would not burden him with any of *those* women," she said, but then she looked thoughtful and stopped sewing. "I did have one friend, however, that could very well be a suitable match. She was from the de Royans family, far to the north in Yorkshire. She had a brother I met a few times, a very powerful knight who, I believe, served Norfolk. In any case, she was one of my few friends in Winchester. She is a pretty and obedient girl. Perhaps she would be a good match for Uncle Daniel."

David put his hands on her shoulders. "Did you at least introduce them when Daniel came to visit?"

She shook her head. "I did not," she replied. "I did not think to."

"What is her name?"

"Glennie de Royans," she replied. "Her father is the Constable of Yorkshire."

David rather liked the sound of that. "Perhaps I shall consider her," he said, kissing the top of her head before removing his hands from her shoulders. "As for you, my fine lady, what are your plans now that you have come home? We have not discussed the subject, you know. Are you planning on leaving us again? Perhaps you would like to travel?"

Her good mood was fading rapidly. "I do not wish to travel," she said as her movements came to a complete halt. She was gazing at her loom. "Papa, I was thinking... thinking that perhaps I should consider joining the cloister. I know that you would suppose that to be a foolish decision, but I do not. I do not believe I shall ever marry so rather than become a burden, I would like to dedicate my life to something productive and meaningful."

David gazed at her lowered head. "The cloister?" he repeated, somewhat surprised. "This is the first time I have heard you express interest in such a thing."

Adalind hung her head. "I realize that, but I do believe it is something to consider."

"Why?"

"I told you – because I shall not marry."

David scratched his head as he thought on his reply. "I do not believe that to be the case," he said quietly. "You are still young, Addie, and you are very beautiful. You have an entire world of suitors at your feet. Of course you shall marry."

She shook her head. "There is only one man I would consider and he has made it clear that he has no interest in me," she murmured. "I know you think I am foolish, Papa, but believe me when I tell you that I know my own heart. I always have. The richest and most eligible man in all of England could come to my door and still, I would refuse him. The heart wants what the heart wants, and I could never be married to another man if I loved someone else."

David pondered that for a moment. The he sighed. "Addie, I know you have always been infatuated with Maddoc, but now that you are grown, surely you see that it is not meant to be."

"Why not?"

He looked at her, rather painfully. "Do you truly want me to speak of it?"

"I do."

"He has watched you grow up. You are like family to him."

"But I am *not* family," she said passionately. "Papa, I have spent my entire life loving one man and now that I am a grown woman, those feelings have only gotten stronger. For the rest of my life there will only be Maddoc in my heart and soul and if I cannot have him, then I do not want anyone else. It would only make me miserable forever. Do you not understand that?"

David gazed into her lovely face, his heart hurting for her. He knew how she felt and he was sure the reintroduction to Maddoc yesterday had only exacerbated those feelings. After a moment, he reached out and stroked her cheek.

"I understand," he said quietly, "but let us not make any hasty decisions today. You only just returned home; be patient until year's end and if you still feel the same way at that time, then we will make some decisions. I only want you to be happy, Addie. You know that."

"I know, Papa."

"There could still be someone to win your heart, you know."

"They could not win what does not belong to me."

He cocked an eyebrow. "You are going to make it difficult on your sister and your cousins, then," he said. "You are the oldest. You must be spoken for before they can entertain invitations. Willow is already eyeing the men around her."

"When I enter the cloister, she will be free to entertain all the suitors she wishes."

David shook his head, rather resistant to her reasoning, and opened his mouth to say so. But a voice from the doorway interrupted him.

"My lord," Maddoc said. "We have a visitor."

Both Adalind and David turned to Maddoc. He was dressed as he usually was, in mail and leather, looking as if he was a hair's breadth away from going into battle. David focused on his face as Adalind let her gaze drift over his enormous body, muscular arms, and trencher-sized hands.

Hands that would never touch her in love and muscular arms that would never hold her as a man holds a woman. She began to think on their conversation from yesterday, of her dreams of him the night before, and she was both eased by the sight of him and hardened. She wasn't sure how much more she could take of seeing him daily, knowing there could never be anything between them. It would drive her to the convent sooner than expected. Maybe returning home had been a mistake, bringing her back into Maddoc's orbit where she would be more miserable than she ever was. She was deep into those reflections when David spoke, jolting her from her thoughts.

"Who has come?" he asked.

Maddoc lifted a dark eyebrow. "Walter de Burgh," he said, somewhat quietly. "He is brother to Hubert de Burgh. In fact, I...."

"No!" Adalind suddenly bolted up from her seat, her green eyes blazing. "Not him. He is *not* welcome. Send him away, Maddoc."

"Hold," David put up a quelling hand, looking at his granddaughter with curiosity. "Why would you say that, Addie? Do you know him?"

Adalind's frustration was evident; she was red in the cheeks and as both men watched, she angrily stomped her feet, verging on a tantrum.

"Of course I know him," she said, furious. "He has pursued me relentlessly for almost six months. He is a shriveled old man who thinks that his family name will gain him his wants. Papa, he is older than you are!"

David eyed Maddoc before focusing on his granddaughter. "I know the man," he assured her quietly. "What's more, I do not like him. He is a dim-witted brother of a powerful family. Are you sure he is here for you?"

Adalind threw up her arms in frustration. "Why else would he come?" she wanted to know. "Were you, in fact, expecting him?"

"I was not."

"Then it surely stands to reason he has come to see me."

"Perhaps there is another reason, I would hope. If the man has indeed come to see you, then I will personally toss him out on his arse." He stood there and shook his head as if baffled by the entire circumstance. "Is this how it is going to be from now on, Addie? A new suitor every day that I must throw from the keep?"

Her anger turned to a pout and, genuinely frustrated, she plopped down on her chair, struggling not to cry. When she lost the battle and began to weep softly, David went to her and kissed her on the head.

"I am sorry," he said, giving her a gentle hug. "I did not mean to make you cry. But this is going to become exhausting for us both."

The statement did not ease her tears. She wiped at her eyes. "I did not tell these men to come," she said, frustrated. "It is not as if I extended an open invitation for any fool to bid for my hand. I never gave any of them any encouragement, but from appearances, it would seem that I have. They made my life at Court a nightmare and now they have followed me here. All I want is a measure of peace, Papa, *please*."

"You told the first four suitors that you are already betrothed," Maddoc said from the doorway. His voice was low, quiet. "We will simply tell anyone else who comes to Canterbury with the intention of courting you that you are already spoken for."

"They will want to know to whom and, at some point, a wedding would be expected," David turned to him. "Word tends to travel and I do not want to jeopardize Addie's chances of obtaining a true husband with lies to throw off the rabble."

Maddoc's expression didn't change. "It would not be a lie, my lord, if you consented to a betrothal between Adalind and me. I will marry her if she will have me."

David's jaw dropped. Adalind's tears were instantly forgotten and her head shot up, looking at Maddoc with such astonishment that her jaw, too, fell open. Stunned speechless, Adalind tried to rise from her chair but her knees gave out and she ended up toppling onto her bum. Maddoc rushed forward to help her as David stood there like an idiot.

"You *what*?" he managed to stammer. "Maddoc, are you *serious*?"

Maddoc had hold of Adalind's arms, gently pulling her up from the floor. "I am," he said steadily. "Moreover, she proposed marriage to me some years ago. I have made up my mind to accept her proposal. I apologize for the delay."

Adalind was staring at him as if she could hardly comprehend what he was saying. By the time he set her to her feet, she began to laugh, like a woman losing her mind, but just as quickly she shifted to tears and began to weep. She pulled out of Maddoc's grip and knocked over her loom in her attempt to get away from him. Hysterical, she ended up slumping against the wall near the hearth.

"You... you are horrid," she sobbed. "How can you joke about something like this?"

"I am most certainly not joking."

"You are!"

"Addie, I swear that I am not. I have never been more serious about anything in my life."

That statement only caused her eyes to widen, as if he had just said something terribly offensive. Then she pointed an accusing finger at him.

"You are *not* serious," she wept. "It is only out of pity that you say such things. That is all this is to you, Maddoc - pity. You cannot even suggest such a thing. I hate you for it!"

Maddoc felt rather bad that he had upset her so. His offer hadn't been planned, in fact; it had come out of his mouth before he could think about what he was saying but upon reflection, he wasn't sorry at all. The past two days with Adalind had opened an entirely new world for him, one of a beautiful young woman with intelligence and grace that he was deeply attracted to. He could no longer deny it.

He didn't know if he loved her because he'd never truly loved anyone in his life, at least in the romantic sense. All he knew was that the feelings he was developing for her were consuming him and he couldn't stomach the thought of her with someone else or, worse, sealed up in a convent. He wasn't sure he could explain all of it to her but he was willing to give it a try. He didn't have a choice; he'd opened wide the door and now was the time to step in.

"Addie, I want you to listen to me and listen closely," he said in a deep, quiet tone. "I do not do anything out of pity. It is a weakness and I am not weak. When I saw you for the first time after having not seen you in many years, I felt as if I was introduced to someone I'd never before known. All I could see was a beautiful and brilliant woman with kindness and fire and intelligence. I could also see why four men in two days have come vying for your hand; you are truly an astonishing example of womanhood and you would be a wife a man could be proud of. *I* would be proud, Addie. But if you no longer feel as you did those years ago, I understand. You were a child then with a child's dreams. Perhaps you have outgrown me, but I hope not. I could never forgive myself if I did not ask if you see anything within me that you still find attractive."

Not only was David's mouth still hanging open, but now his eyebrows were lifted and his eyes were bugged. He stared at Maddoc as if the man had grown two heads, but Maddoc only had eyes for Adalind. When David looked at his granddaughter, he could see that nothing else in the world existed, either. Maddoc had all of her attention.

"I... I do not know if I can believe my ears," she said, tears fading as she labored to regain her composure. "This... this cannot be real."

"It is real."

"I am not dreaming?"

"Nay."

She just stared at him, stunned, before wiping away the last of her tears. "Do you swear, Maddoc?"

"I swear."

"You are not jesting?"

He smiled faintly, finding her disbelief understandable and humorous at the same time. "I would not jest with you on a subject as important as this."

Adalind continued to stare at him. Now that the wave of hysteria had rolled over her, she was strangely calm. Pensive, even. But she still leaned back against the wall for support; she didn't trust herself to stand under her own power just yet.

"Maddoc?"

"Aye?"

"Go away and come back later. Say the same thing to me at that time and perhaps I will believe you."

With a twinkle in the bright blue eyes, his gaze lingered on her a moment before he turned away without another word. Before he reached the door, however, he spoke.

"De Burgh is in the bailey, my lord," he said to David. "If I am in competition with him for Lady Adalind's hand, then you will understand I will do what I must in order to rid myself of my competition."

David still wasn't over the scene he had just witnessed but he forced himself to focus on what Maddoc was saying.

"You may not challenge him, Maddoc," he said quietly. "De Burgh must be treated with care. I would not bring the whole family down around us."

"I will not challenge him," Maddoc turned to look at him. "But I will not welcome him, either. I ask that you send another to deal with de Burgh, for I cannot do it. Forgive me."

David gazed at the man with some astonishment. He had always known Maddoc to be the most responsible, stable, and wise knight he'd ever known. Maddoc had been mature beyond his years at a very young age and his wisdom and common sense in all things was second to none. To hear those words come forth from the man was quite extraordinary. He believed him implicitly. He took a few steps in Maddoc's direction.

"Maddoc," he began, grasping for words. "I must ask. Are you… are you truly serious about Adalind?"

"I am, my lord."

"In all the years I have known you, and in all of the years she annoyed you to tears, you have never once expressed any interest in her. Why the change of heart?"

Maddoc's gaze was intense. "The woman who came to Canterbury two days ago is not the Adalind either one of us remembers," he said quietly. "She is cultured, poised, wise, humorous, and undeniably beautiful. She is also vulnerable and sad. I… I cannot explain why my heart has changed only that it has. You will have to take me at my word."

David's gaze was equally intense. "Then if you are serious about courting her, I will have to treat you like any other suitor."

"What do you mean?"

David expression flickered, no longer the liege of a knight but the grandfather of the woman the knight intended to pursue. He wasn't sure how else to behave but he wanted to make his thoughts clear to Maddoc.

"As my captain, you have unrestricted access to the entire family, including Adalind," he lowered his voice. "If you truly intend to court her, then your access will be limited. You will be watched when you are with her. You will no longer be permitted to be alone with her, and any and all requests for her time will have to come through me. Am I making myself clear?"

Maddoc nodded. "You are, my lord."

"Do you still intend to pursue her, then?"

"I do."

David couldn't help it; he still wasn't over his astonishment and slipped. "Do you *really*?"

"Absolutely."

David took him for his word. He was no longer astonished because Maddoc seemed very sincere If he thought on it, he was rather delighted, not only for Adalind's sake but for his own. He had always adored Maddoc and to have the man as a son was something of a dream for him as well. A hint of a smile came to his lips.

"I will say this only once but if you ask me to repeat it, I will deny ever speaking the words," he said softly. "I could ask for no better husband for Adalind. I have raised her, you know, since her father died those years ago. She is not only my granddaughter but my child as well. She deserves every happiness in the world and I know you would be good to her. But I swear upon all that is holy if you hurt her or mislead her in any way, I will kill you myself. Do you understand?"

Maddoc knew the threat was sincere. He was unafraid in his reply. "I do, my lord. Implicitly."

David's gaze lingered on him as if to emphasize his point. He wanted to make sure Maddoc knew he would slit his throat and take great pleasure in it if Maddoc hurt Adalind in any fashion. But Maddoc's gaze held firm, eye to eye, and they understood each other. It was an oddly tense moment but a necessary one. After a moment, David nodded shortly.

"Very well," he rumbled. "Go about your duties but stay away from Adalind. I will greet de Burgh."

They vacated the room without another word, leaving Adalind still standing against the wall, wondering what they had been whispering about. More than that, she was still coming to grips with what had just happened. She still couldn't believe it. Surely she had imagined it.

Pushing herself off the wall, she collected her fallen loom, off balance herself as she tried to right it. It ended up falling again and she left it, too unsteady to pick it up again. Her mind was elsewhere as she staggered out of the receiving room and up the spiral stairs to the third floor where her small chamber was.

Thankfully, Willow wasn't anywhere to be found so Adalind had it to herself as she flopped down on her bed and lay there, staring up at the ceiling, wondering what on earth had just happened. *Maddoc has offered to marry me.* Dear God, surely it was still a dream!

She fell into a deep and exhausted sleep for five straight hours.

***

Adalind woke up to the soft voice of her mother.

"Addie?" Christina was stroking her head gently. "Addie, wake up."

Adalind's eyes popped open to find her mother gazing down at her, her lovely face softly bathed in firelight. The small chamber was dark and warm and Adalind lay there for a moment as she oriented herself. The last she recalled, she had been in Emilie's solar with her grandfather and Maddoc had come in to....

Maddoc! Adalind sat bolt upright and nearly smacked her mother in the process. Christina had to move swiftly to get out of the way as Adalind leapt out of the bed.

"Mama!" she exclaimed. "Maddoc told Papa that he wants to marry me!"

Christina was fighting off a grin. "I know," she said. "Everyone knows. Papa told me but Willow heard us speaking, and she quite happily spread the news until Papa told her to stop. Unfortunately, she did not listen so he spanked her. Now she is in my chamber weeping, Grandmother is with her, and I am here with you. How do you feel?"

It was a concise outline of the past few hours and it took Adalind a moment to absorb it all. She looked at her mother with wide eyes, both confused and elated. Truth be told, she wasn't quite sure what she was feeling. Excitement didn't quite encompass it all.

"I... I am not sure," she said. Then, she ran to her vanity and grabbed the bone comb, running it through her long blond hair swiftly. "I must find Maddoc and make sure he meant what he said. Perhaps he was momentarily mad. Perhaps he was under a spell!"

Christina couldn't help the smile that spread across her lips. "He was not momentarily mad nor was he bewitched," she assured her daughter. "When Papa told me what had happened, I immediately sought him out and we had a very long conversation. He meant what he said, Addie. He has asked permission to court you."

Adalind looked at her mother with shock. "I do not believe it," she hissed, throwing the comb down and snatching the alabaster pot of beeswax to rub over her lips. "I must speak with him."

Christina laughed softly. "Papa has forbidden you from being with Maddoc without a chaperone," she said. "Please come down to sup. You will feel better when you have eaten something."

Adalind grabbed her woolen cloak, brown and lined with rabbit fur. "I do not want to eat," she said. "I cannot. Mama, do you realize what this means? Maddoc is... he is... merciful heavens, I still cannot believe it!"

Christina continued to chuckle as Adalind wrapped up in her cloak and bolted to the door. She reached out a gentle hand to stop her daughter.

"Where are you going?" she asked.

"To find Maddoc," Adalind said. "I told you, Mama – I must speak with him. I must understand what has happened."

"I just told you that Papa does not want you to be alone with him. If Maddoc is truly a suitor, then he will be treated like one."

Adalind lifted an eyebrow. "You may trust me that nothing unsavory will occur between us," she said. "I promise to behave. I will not throw myself at the man. Please, Mama... *please*?"

Christina knew better than to try and stop her. Adalind had been waiting her entire life for this moment, a moment she never truly believed would come. Propriety aside, she couldn't deny her daughter. The glow in Adalind's face had her relenting.

"I left him in the knight's quarters," she said softly. "Papa and everyone are in the smaller hall where the evening meal is commencing. I do not know if Maddoc is still where I left him, but you can slip outside and find him. Oh, and Walter de Burgh will be supping with us tonight."

Adalind's features hardened. "Then I will not eat in the hall. I do not want to see the man."

"I did not think so," Christina murmured, stroking her daughter's soft hair. "I will tell Papa you are not feeling well."

Adalind kissed her mother on the cheek, hurriedly, and slipped from the chamber. Fortunately, the stairs were out of sight of the great hall in the keep but the entry door was not. Christina, who had followed her daughter downstairs, made sure that everyone's attention was elsewhere before directing her daughter to quit the keep.

A fog was rolling in once again from the east as Adalind entered the bailey. The air was cold and moist, and the sentries on the wall with their dogs and torches were eerily shrouded in mist. She pulled her cloak tight as she headed for the knight's house, a small building set against the massive fortress wall that housed the army commanders. There were four good sized rooms and then a bigger common room. She knocked politely on the door, her stomach in knots.

After several additional knocks, it was clear that the quarters were empty. With a slower pace, she headed back across the bailey towards the enormous feasting hall that was built all by itself in the southeast corner of the castle. It was only used for big events; the rest of the time, the soldiers tended to gather in it to eat their meals or sleep. The family almost always used the smaller, more private hall in the keep. Thinking Maddoc might be in the bigger hall, she made her way towards it. She was just into the shadows of the structure, shielded from most of the bailey, when she heard a voice from behind.

"What are you doing wandering out here?"

Adalind recognized Maddoc's tone as she whirled around to face him. He came up behind her, the bright blue eyes glittering as their gazes locked.

"'Tis cold," he said, his voice softer. "Why are you not inside supping with de Burgh?"

Adalind found she was rather breathless at the sight of him. Her heart was beating so loudly against her ribs that she was sure he could hear it.

"Probably for the same reason you are not supping with him," she said. "I do not wish to be near him."

He gave her a half-grin. "That is the truth," he agreed. "But in my case, it is more likely that your grandfather forbade me from going anywhere near the man. I am therefore assigned to the night watch so I can stay away from him. I am supposed to stay away from you, too."

Adalind shrugged, as if she hadn't time for such nonsense. "That does not seem natural to me."

"Nor to me."

It was a warm and perhaps leading answer. Adalind gazed at Maddoc with a rather wide-eyed stare. It was the man she'd always known, the man she'd loved from her earliest memories, but as she gazed at him, she could only think of one thing to say to him.

"Maddoc, *why?*"

He cocked his head. "What do you mean?"

She swallowed hard for her mouth was dry. Nerves were causing her to tremble. "Why...?" she swallowed again. "Why did you say those things earlier?"

His grin broadened. "I believe I was quite clear."

She shook her head. "But it does not make any sense to me," she said, almost pleadingly. "As a child I would follow you around until you would chase me way. Do you remember? You would tell me to go away or you would turn the dogs on me. Then I would run off and hide for a time before writing you notes in the dirt apologizing for making you angry. Do you remember that as well?"

His gaze was warm. "Of course I remember. You only knew a few words so your notes were mostly gibberish, but I will tell you a secret about them."

"What?"

"They always made me smile and then I would feel tremendously guilty for being so harsh with you."

She smiled faintly, but just as quickly sobered. The subject at hand was too serious to get off course with other recollections.

"Maddoc, please do not toy with me," she begged softly. "Tell me why you have changed your mind about me. Surely you must know how this has affected me. All my life... all my life I have dreamed of you and now...."

She trailed off, unable to continue as she averted her gaze. Maddoc could see how confused she was; in truth, he had been confused as well. He'd spent the entire afternoon reflecting on what he'd said, and a good hour discussing the situation Christina. The woman's only concern had naturally been for her daughter and Maddoc had been duly interrogated. By the end of the conversation, his confusion had transformed into certainty. It was as if reasoning his thoughts out with the mother had clarified everything. Now, as he gazed at Adalind, he had never been more certain about anything in his life.

"Now you will make my dreams come true," he murmured, taking a step closer to her. "I explained my reasoning this afternoon. I am not sure I can elaborate on that, Addie."

She wasn't convinced. "You do understand that I have been asking you to marry me since I was about five years of age, and you have been resisting me since that time?"

"Sometimes it takes me quite a while to make up my mind."

"It took you thirteen years?"

He shrugged. Then, he cocked his head pensively. "You never did answer me, you know."

"Answer what?"

"I asked you if you still found anything attractive about me. You did not answer me."

She looked at him as if he was daft. "Are you serious?"

"Of course."

She threw up her hands. "That is the most foolish question I have ever heard," she declared. "Maddoc, I have spent the past several years unsuccessfully attempting to put you out of my heart and out of my mind. When I first saw you two days ago after having not seen you in years, it was as if every thought and dream I ever had about you was confirmed and I knew I could never forget you no matter how hard I tried. When I spoke of committing myself to the convent, it was not an attempt to force you into a proposal. It was because I knew I could never marry another man while my heart belonged to you. I would be doing both him and me a great disservice. Papa thought that perhaps someone would eventually come along that would change my mind, but I assured him that was not the case. The heart wants what the heart wants."

Maddoc's expression was soft. "And it still wants me?"

Adalind could feel her nervousness, her disbelief, fading as she looked into his eyes. She was coming to realize this was the moment she had waited for her entire life; face to face with Maddoc spilling her most personal feelings to him. The best part was that he was actually listening. Maybe this wasn't a dream, after all.

"Aye," she finally murmured. "It still wants you. It always has."

His smile returned, a tender gesture she had never seen from him before, one that sent her heart racing again. When he reached out and took her hand, bringing to his lips for a tender kiss, she thought she might truly faint. She actually felt lightheaded, giddy as she had never felt in her life.

"I do not honestly know what has changed my mind," he whispered. "All I know is that it has in fact changed, which is more of a surprise to me than it is to you. I see such joy and warmth and passion in you, Addie. I see a perfect and beautiful woman, and I do not blame these men who have made fools of themselves as they attempt to gain your attention. Now, I would do it, too. I want to get to know you, as an adult, and understand this magic you seem to have. It intrigues me like nothing ever has."

Adalind was back to trembling again as he continued to hold her hand. She closed her eyes tightly, briefly, as his words sank deep.

"I have waited so long to hear those words from you," she murmured, opening her eyes and fixing him with her teary gaze. "You cannot know how much this means to me."

"Actually, I think I do. The words mean a great deal to me as well. I have never spoken them before, to anyone."

She stared at him for a moment before a hint of a smile came to her lips. Then, the smile grew until it was broad and beautiful. She was positively glowing.

"Truly?" she breathed.

"Truly."

"You will not try to chase me away again or turn the dogs on me?"

He laughed softly. "I will not, I swear it." He brought her hand to his lips again, depositing a warm and sweet kiss on her knuckles as his gaze bore into her. "Will you accept my suit, then?"

Adalind was having difficulty breathing as he tenderly kissed her flesh. All she could do was nod her head, rather recklessly, before throwing her arms around his neck. She'd only meant to hug him, thrilled beyond measure, but she never got that far. Maddoc's face, and mouth, were suddenly in front of her and their lips met with such force that he audibly grunted as he tipped back, thrown off balance by her passionate attack. But just as swiftly, his arms were around her and his warm and soft lips were kissing her as he had never kissed a woman in his life.

She was sweet and hot, incredibly delicious. The sweet scent of her filled his nostrils as he suckled her lips, tasting her, acquainting himself with her. He could have very easily lost himself in an even deeper kiss but he wasn't oblivious to the fact that they were in the bailey, though shielded. It was possible that someone might see them and he knew he would be in a good deal of trouble if news of the encounter got back to David. So he kissed her firmly one last time and set her on her feet.

"I would not make an even greater spectacle of ourselves than we just did," he said, breathless himself. "If your grandfather hears about that, he will beat me soundly."

Adalind was panting, hand to her mouth, tasting and smelling the man's scent against her flesh. "I am sorry," she breathed. "I did not mean to throw myself at you like that. I simply meant to... oh, I do not know what I meant. Please do not think me wicked."

He grinned. "I would never think that," he said, winking at her. "In fact, I very much enjoyed it. I am glad you threw yourself at me."

She was torn between giggling and embarrassment. "Perhaps I should go before I do it again. There is no guarantee that I will not."

With a twinkle in his eye, he gently took her elbow and turned her for the keep. He properly escorted her as far as the stairs in warm silence, both of them reflecting on the turn of events. Around them, the castle was alive with soldiers and servants, moving swiftly through the foggy air, but in their world it was just the two of them. More than once they would glance at each other, grin, and look away. When they finally reached the steps, Adalind stopped and turned to him.

"I am going to go into the hall right now and tell de Burgh to leave," she said firmly. "I do not want him here. He is most certainly not welcome."

Maddoc tried not to agree with her. "Perhaps your grandfather has already done that."

"I cannot be sure."

"I would tread carefully, Addie. You do not want to make a mess of things. Let David handle the situation, please. Go back up to your chamber and stay out of sight for now."

Her gaze lingered on him a moment. "Is that what you wish?"

"It is."

She smiled. "Then I shall do it."

He returned her smile, feeling a bolt of giddy warmth shoot through him. She had such a lovely smile, now reserved only for him. Like her, he was still having trouble believing what had transpired and, like her, it all seemed very perfect and dream-like. It was heavenly.

"Thank you," he said sincerely. "I will...."

He was cut off by a loud voice at the top of the steps. "My lady!" the voice nearly shouted. "Alas, I am fortunate enough to gaze upon you!"

Adalind whirled around so fast that she nearly lost her balance, for standing at the entry to the keep was none other than Walter de Burgh. David was standing right behind him and he did not look pleased.

Maddoc knew the displeasure was directed at him.

As I stare on and on into the past, in the end you emerge,
Clad in the light of a pole-star piercing the darkness of time:

CHAPTER FIVE

"How is it possible you have grown more beautiful since last I saw you?" Walter demanded as he began to descend the stairs in Adalind's direction. "I am very glad to see you. Come and greet my properly, my love."

Adalind backed away from him and ended up practically hiding behind Maddoc. She was frowning deeply.

"I am *not* your love," she snapped. "I told you that I was not interested in your suit, my lord. I am greatly displeased to see that you have come to my home."

Walter de Burgh was a few years older than David, a short man with a bulbous nose, a big belly, and pocked skin. His gray hair was wavy and long, oily, and he often reeked of cheese. It was a horrific combination. Having already buried three wives, he was on the urgent hunt for the fourth because with five daughters, he was desperate for a son.

But the heir would not be from Adalind. At her sharp statement, he came to a halt with genuine astonishment on his face. He was torn between disappointment and surprise.

"Addie, how can you say that?" he asked, his arms open wide as if to embrace her. "You know how fond I am of *you*."

Adalind wedged herself even tighter behind Maddoc, afraid Walter would make a grab for her. "I am not fond of you," she said. "Go away, Walter. I do not want to see you."

Walter wasn't sure how to react. He looked rather speechless before turning to David. "Women do not know what is good for them," he said, his good spirits returning. "It is fortunate that they have no negotiating power in a marriage contract."

David gazed at the man with veiled tolerance. "Perhaps that is true in some cases," he replied, "but not in this case. As I told you when you arrived, my granddaughter is already betrothed and Adalind has made her wishes clear. There is no room for negotiation."

At David's words, Adalind, still standing behind Maddoc, reached out and discreetly grasped his hand. She squeezed, thrilled that David had apparently given Maddoc permission to court her. It was the most wonderful thing she could hope for and wasn't at all peeved that she found out in a rather roundabout manner. All that mattered was that David had given his permission. Maddoc, thinking all of the same things she was, squeezed back.

Walter seemed to be the only one in earshot who wasn't thrilled with the fact that Adalind was evidently spoken for. He simply shook his head.

"No offense to her betrothed or to your taste in a husband for your granddaughter, but no marriage would form a more solid alliance than a marriage to a de Burgh," he said, a hint of sinister arrogance in his tone. "I know you are not that foolish, de Lohr."

David cocked an eyebrow at the insult. Rather than try to humor the man or maintain his cool, he went for the throat.

"I was foolish enough to invite you to sup and listen to your supercilious boasting for the past three hours," he fired back. "You have always been an arrogant buffoon, Walter, and I never liked you. Not even when our brothers were in the king's service together and we were forced by alliances to serve with one another did I like you. Now that you have come to my castle and insulted me, I like you even less. You will leave now and forget about Adalind. She is too good for you and your narcissistic ego. Find a mate elsewhere."

Walter wasn't accustomed to being insulted. He lost all of his humor and his jaw went slack. "You dare...?"

David didn't let him finish. He gave him a shove in the direction of the gatehouse where his horse and several retainers had been waiting patiently since his arrival. The man nearly stumbled to his knees as David pushed.

"Get out," David gave the man another shove. "Get out before I do something I regret. And if you think to tell your all-powerful brother what happened here today, he has his own problems right now and will more than likely disregard you. But if he, in fact, shows interest in your whining, know that I will tell him exactly what I told you. He thinks you are an idiot, anyway, so I would not be surprised if he laughed in your face."

Walter's shabby face went red with anger. He turned on his heel and ran back to his horse as fast as his fat belly and spindly legs would allow. He began yelling at his retainers, pushing them around, slapping one, until he reached into one man's shirtwaist and yanked forth a long, slender dagger. Then he turned and ran back in David's direction, the dirk held before him.

Maddoc swung into action. He released Adalind's hand and placed himself between David and Walter. As big as he was, he made a rather massive barrier, one that not even Walter was immune to. But Walter was as stupid as David had accused him of being; he ran right at Maddoc with the dirk. The intent was apparent and given the fact that he was a de Burgh, he did not expect the knight to resist his charge. He fully expected to stab Maddoc in the midsection without a fight. But when Walter drew near, Maddoc reached out and disarmed him.

Walter screamed as Maddoc twisted his wrist hard enough to crack bones. The dirk went flying and Walter fell to the muddy ground, howling in pain as he cradled his injured arm.

David moved up next to Maddoc, gazing grimly at Walter's writhing form. Then he lifted his gaze and, seeing Walter's men standing rather stunned several feet away, motioned to them.

"Get him out of my sight," he commanded.

Walter's men rushed forward as David backed away, grasping Adalind and quickly escorting her into the keep. Only Maddoc remained behind, like a massive and intimidating sentinel, watching as Walter's men dragged their screaming lord back to their horses and forcibly mounted the man. Walter continued to scream, with the addition of angry cursing, as they forced him and his horse from the bailey of Canterbury. It made for a tense and rather chaotic scene.

Maddoc and a few soldiers followed them to the gatehouse to make sure they left. In fact, by the time they reached the portcullis with the green fields of Kent beyond, there was a solid line of de Lohr men herding them from the ward to ensure de Burgh's compliance.

With nowhere to go but out, they soon left. Maddoc's gaze was intense as he watched the group fading off into the distance. The fog that had been so heavy the past few days was oddly lifting, and a nearly full moon was revealed against the black sky. It would make for easy travel to the village of Harbledown, which was close by.

"Should we follow them, Maddoc?"

Maddoc turned to the young knight standing slightly behind him. Gerid du Reims had been in charge of the fortress while Maddoc had been in France visiting his family. A strong man with uncanny intelligence and piercing black eyes, he was a younger son of the Earl of East Anglia, a local and strong ally to Canterbury. He was Maddoc's second-in-command, and Maddoc shook his head to the quietly uttered question.

"I do not believe that will be necessary," he told him. "I am sure du Burgh will return to his brother's seat of Montgomery Castle, rally his brother's troops, and return to lay siege."

Gerid gave him a lopsided smile as the soldiers forming the unbreachable line at the portcullis began to disburse.

"That will give us time to prepare," he said.

Maddoc nodded, somewhat in resignation of what was potentially to come, before eyeing the knight. His gaze settled on the man rather fondly.

"I have been returned from France for nearly two days," he said. "Why have I not seen you in that time?"

Gerid lifted his eyebrows. "*You* are the one who has been in hiding," he pointed out. "You have been with the earl and his family since your return."

Maddoc cocked an eyebrow. "I have been on the walls most of the afternoon. Someone told me you went into town."

Gerid nodded. "Fordwich," he said. "I escorted the countess. She went to visit the church and dispense alms. She does that every week, you know."

"I know. But next time, tell me directly where you are going."

"I tried to find you but was told you were with Adalind."

Maddoc cleared his throat softly, nervously, because it was a subject he didn't particularly want to elaborate on, even with someone as trusted as Gerid.

"I was," he said. "This steady stream of suitors since her return has her on edge. I have a feeling that de Burgh will not be the last."

It was a subtle shift of subject. Gerid nodded and started to reply, but something over Maddoc's shoulder caught his attention. His eyes narrowed to better see the movement in the dark, causing Maddoc to swing around to see what had his attention.

With the ghostly glow of the landscape, it wasn't difficult to see that something was moving along the road towards the castle. It was short, whatever it was, and seemed to be wailing. Curious, not to mention mildly concerned, both Maddoc and Gerid made their way out of the gatehouse, standing just outside of it so they could see whatever it was as it made an approach. Suddenly, Maddoc hissed a curse.

"God's Blood," he muttered. "That *idiot*."

Gerid had no idea what, or whom, he meant, but when Maddoc broke out into a jog down the road, Gerid followed. They soon came upon the subject of their focus; Eynsford was walking up the road on his knees, playing his *citole* and singing hoarsely at the top of his lungs. As Maddoc and Gerid came upon him, Eynsford came to a weary halt.

"I have come to apologize to my lady," he announced, his voice rough from singing for hours on end. "I spent yesterday thinking on how I could apologize to Lady Adalind and it came to me; God shows mercy to the penitent man. Perhaps Lady Adalind will show mercy to me as well if I am repentant, so I started crawling on my knees and singing her praises. Please do not make me go away until I have apologized to her."

Maddoc stood over the fat young man, shaking his head with a mixture of disbelief and disgust. "How long have you been crawling?" he demanded.

Eynsford pointed over his shoulder, back towards the smoke-shrouded village of Harbledown. "I started at the Snow Dove Inn," he said, looking back up at the knights. He appeared rather fearful. "It has taken me since this morning to make it this far. Please do not make me go away."

Maddoc snorted, looking at Gerid, who seemed genuinely puzzled. "The Snow Dove Inn?" Gerid repeated. "That is almost three miles away, at the far end of town. You have been walking on your knees from that place?"

Eynsford nodded hesitantly, intimidated by the way the man raised his voice. "I have much to atone for."

Gerid looked at Maddoc. "Is this not the entertainer you chased away yesterday?"

"You saw that?"

"I saw part of it. Lord David had me assigned to an errand, but I returned just as Adalind was taking a switch to him."

Maddoc slapped Gerid on the shoulder. "There is much more to it than that," he said. "Right now, I suspect we had better get du Lesseps inside so the physic can take a look at those knees. My guess is that they are in terrible shape."

Eynsford conceded the point. "They *do* hurt."

Maddoc reached down and grabbed a fatty arm as Gerid reached out and grabbed the other. Together, they hauled the young man to his feet. Eynsford could barely walk, but his attention seemed to be on Maddoc.

"You promise you will not turn me away?" he asked.

Maddoc nodded patiently. "I promise I will not turn you away, at least for tonight."

"And if Lady Adalind comes after me with a switch? Will you tell her I can stay?"

"I will tell her you can stay. But you do understand she is spoken for, do you not?"

Eynsford didn't look pleased. "I do."

"You will not try to woo her again?"

"I will not," he sighed dramatically. "Given what happened yesterday, I do not think she would be receptive."

"Probably not."

"Do you know this man she is promised to? Is he worthy of her?"

Maddoc struggled not to grin. "He thinks so."

"Is he a fighting man?"

"Most definitely."

Eynsford looked both thoughtful and intimidated. "Then he would try to kill me if I attempted to steal her from him."

"More than likely. It would be best not to tempt fate."

Eynsford grunted in pain as Maddoc and Gerid helped him walk over a slippery, muddy patch. When he slipped because of his stiff gate, Maddoc easily steadied him. Eynsford acknowledged the assistance gratefully.

"You, good sir, are a saint," he declared. "I will compose a song about you. What is your name?"

"Maddoc."

"I shall call it Maddoc the Magnificent!"

Maddoc and Gerid looked at each other from over Eynsford's head. As Gerid fought off a grin, Maddoc just rolled his eyes.

He wasn't so sure Adalind would think him magnificent as he gave her nemesis safe haven for the night.

You become an image of what is remembered forever.

CHAPTER SIX

"I had to tell her, Maddoc," Christina said. "She would have gone to break her fast in the small hall and found him there. What on earth were you thinking to bring him here?"

Maddoc was properly contrite. It was early morning after the night he'd brought Eynsford back to Canterbury, bloodied knees and all. David had been shocked to see the man but had understood when Maddoc explained the man's presence. In fact, he had struggled not to laugh about it. It was a rather pathetic situation.

Therefore, Eynsford was allowed to sleep in the small hall by the enormous fireplace after the castle physic, a spindly little man with red hair, tended to his cut knees. But the moment he lay down and started to play his *citole*, David emerged from the master's chamber adjoining the hall, snatched the *citole*, and refused to give it back until morning. His good will and good humor only went so far.

"He left early this morning," Maddoc assured the woman. "Gerid escorted him back to Harbledown. As for my bringing him here last night, the man had just spent most of the day crawling on his knees to the castle; I simply could not leave him out of the road. What else was I to do?"

Christina cocked an eyebrow. "You are very kind to a man who wants to court your intended."

Maddoc grinned. "Not usually," he said, "but I suppose I felt sorry for him. The man does not have a chance in the world with Adalind, yet he continues to try. That kind of determination is admirable. Foolish, but admirable."

Christina's lips twitched with a grin. "I am not sure Adalind agrees with you," she said, tilting her head in the direction of the closed chamber door. "She is quite cross. I would suggest you think of some way of soothing her or this courtship might be over before it begins."

He laughed softly. "I would like nothing better than to soothe her, but I have been forbidden to be alone with her and I am not sure I want an audience when I grovel at her feet. Perhaps I should simply let it blow over."

"Or you could take her in to Fordwich to collect her new surcoat she is going to wear to Lady Victoria du Bose's birthday celebration next week."

He cocked his head. "Ridge du Bose's daughter?"

Christina nodded. "She will have seen sixteen years."

Maddoc's dark eyebrows lifted. "God's Blood," he muttered. "I remember when the girl was born. She is *that* old?"

"She is," Christina replied. "Perhaps... perhaps my father will allow you attend the event as Adalind's escort and not simply a family escort."

Maddoc's bright blue eyes glimmered as a smile played on his lips. He realized he was nearly embarrassed by the suggestion, finding himself in a position he never dreamed he'd be in. The man was supremely confident in all areas but now with the transition into an entirely new and different relationship with Adalind, he felt rather uncertain. This was all new territory to the serious and often austere knight who had never held a very high opinion of anything romantic.

"I will ask his permission, of course," he ventured hesitantly. "I have never... well, I have never done this sort of thing before."

Christina laughed softly at the usually-confident knight exhibiting some uncertainty. "You are not without experience with women," she said. "Do not forget that I have known you for many years. I have seen women throw themselves at you and I do believe there were one or more occasions that you entertained a young lady."

He waved her off. "That was a long time ago," he said, somewhat embarrassed. "Since my wife died, I have not had the time or inclination to pursue that aspect of life. It is too much trouble."

Christina's smile faded. "I am sorry if my comment was hurtful. I did not mean to bring up painful memories."

He shrugged. "They are not painful, but I will admit that sometimes I wonder what my son would have looked like had he lived. My mother died in childbirth with me, also. I do not know if you were aware of that."

Christina shook her head with sadness. "I was not," she murmured. "I pray you have much better luck with a future wife, especially if she is my daughter."

He gave her a lop-sided grin. "Which I suspect might not occur if I do not throw myself at Addie's feet and beg forgiveness."

Christina laughed softly and gestured towards the door. "I have already chased Willow out, so Adalind is alone," she said. "Go in and see what you can do. I will be here in the corridor should you need me."

It was a kind way of saying she would have her ear against the door to protect her daughter's virtue. Maddoc grinned, full-on, and silently thanked the woman who was only three years older than he was. The truth was that he more than likely should have been interested in the woman closer to his age, but Christina had no interest in any man since her husband passed away several years earlier, and Maddoc frankly had no interest in her. All of his focus was on the woman's exquisite daughter. He made his way to the chamber door and knocked softly.

"Who comes?" Adalind's voice was muffled.

He didn't hesitate. "Sir Maddoc FitzPeter Crewys du Bois."

There was a very long pause, causing Maddoc to turn and look questioningly at Christina. She balled a fist and shook it at him, a suggestion for what he should do. Biting off a grin, Maddoc rattled the door loudly without actually trying to open it.

"Open this door right now," he barked as he had never barked at her in his life. "You will not treat your intended this way. Open it, you ungrateful wench."

Christina had to cover her mouth to keep from laughing. Maddoc began silently laughing, too, until the chamber door flew open and Adalind was standing in the doorway. She was clad in a deep green surcoat with white rabbit lining around the neck and wrists of the garment. With her long hair braided carefully over one shoulder, she looked exquisite. However, she was furious and Maddoc struggled to wipe the smile from his face, but not fast enough. Adalind had seen the smirk and her eyebrows flew up in outrage.

"So you mock me?" she was livid. "Since when do you call me wench?"

Before Maddoc could reply, Christina stepped in to save the man. "Addie," she scolded softly. "He was jesting with you, so calm yourself. You honestly have no earthly reason to be angry with him, so behave yourself. He will take you to Fordwich to collect your new garments for Victoria's party."

Adalind was frowning as her gaze moved between her mother and Maddoc. As they watched, her pout grew more and more dramatic until she finally turned around, in a huff, and stomped back into her chamber. Both Christina and Maddoc stood in the doorway, watching her collect her fur-lined cloak with sharp gestures, until she stomped back over to the door.

"Help me, please," she nearly commanded as she held out the cloak to Maddoc.

He dutifully took the cloak and shook it out before holding it up for her. Eyeing him, just to emphasize the fact that she wasn't in a forgiving mood, Adalind stepped into the cloak as Maddoc settled it around her slender neck. She stood there, lips pursed in a pout, as he smoothed it around her shoulders and spun her around to tie it at her neck. But she refused to look at him, pretending disinterest, until he finished securing the cloak.

68

When their eyes finally met, he gave her a knowing smile and she stuck her tongue out at him.

Maddoc laughed softly as she turned away and began her angry march down the stairs, waving Christina off when the woman geared up to berate her daughter. He followed Adalind down to the main level, which was now rather vacant once the morning meal had finished, and took her out into the cool and breezy day. Outside, as they descended the steps to the bailey, he grabbed the first soldier he came across and sent the man on the run for first Gerid. Once the organization of the escort party was in motion, he turned to Adalind.

"I am sorry if you are upset with me," he said quietly, "but you truly have no need to be. Eynsford is gone. You will not have to see him again."

She put her hands on her hips. "Why did you bring him back? You know I did not want him here."

He was patient. "Because he had crawled on his knees all the way from Harbledown and I could not let him spend the night outside the gate with bloodied knees," he said as his tone shifted to a nearly scolding one. "In spite of what you and everyone else thinks, I do have some measure of compassion. I did not bring him back to Canterbury to torment you; I did it because it was the right thing to do. The physic tended his wounds and this morning, he was sent along his way. If you wish to remain angry over that, then I will not stop you. Do what you must."

By the time he was finished, her feisty stance had eased. The hands came off the hips and her expression softened. After a moment, she sighed heavily and gave up.

"You know very well that I cannot be angry any longer," she said, trying not to appear too contrite. "And I never said you were without compassion, only I wish it had not been for Eynsford."

He gave her a half-grin. "He is no threat to us, my lady."

She softened further. "Of course he is not," she replied quietly. "Nothing can take my attention away from you. Surely you know that."

"Then you are no longer cross with me?"

"No."

His smiled broadened. "Good," he replied. "Now, what is this I hear that Victoria du Bose is sixteen years of age?"

Adalind nodded eagerly, all fit and fizzle from a few moments before forgotten. "Her father is having a massive celebration for her in two days," she said. "Everyone of note will be there. It will be good to see old friends I have not seen in years."

Maddoc cocked an eyebrow. "And I am sure the young men who only remember the skinny and annoying Adalind de Aston will be greatly surprised to see you. I will be beating them away by the dozens."

She giggled. "Not when Papa tells everyone that you are courting me. They shall all run away in terror at the thought of you."

He broke into a grin. "They will congratulate me on my good fortune," he replied, noting that the horses were being brought forth from the livery. He took her elbow gently and turned her around as they approached. "Which brings me to the subject of our foray into town – I must approve of the dress you wear to the party, of course."

She tried not to laugh at him. "Why is that?"

He pretended to scowl. "Why do you think? I do not want some foolish pup salivating over what belongs to me."

She cocked her head, teasing him. "My, my," she murmured. "Already I belong to you? Our courtship has worked rather quickly."

"I offered to marry you yesterday. Your grandfather has accepted my suit. Our courtship is over and already you belong to me."

She was back to giggling. "As you wish, Maddoc," she relented, watching him wink at her. "But I am not sure I need your approval for my party dress."

His lips twisted wryly. "Not too much flesh," he said. "I know what women wear these days. They show far too much skin. Perhaps I will have to put you in a sack and tie it at the neck, cutting out holes for your arms and legs. That way, I will not have to kill some fool because his gaze lingers on your lovely shoulders or… well, you know, lower… down below your neck."

Adalind burst out laughing. "Do you mean my breasts?"

He averted his gaze, looking up to the cool blue sky. "It is lovely traveling weather, do you not think?" He deliberately changed the subject. "We should make good time into town. If we make short work of your task, perhaps we find something else to interest you. An entertainment, perhaps."

She moved closed to him, putting her hands on his big arm. "You will not get out of this so easily," she said, flirtatious. When his eyes finally met hers, she grinned broadly. "You can refer to my breasts, you know. It is your right, as my intended. You can also look at them if you wish. I will not be offended."

He let out a hissing sigh and weakly tried to pull away. "Lady, you are bold and unrestrained," he said, still trying to step away from her but not doing a very good job. The truth was that he liked her hands on his, feeling the warmth of her body against his. "It is unseemly to discuss such things in public."

"We are not in public. This conversation is between you and I."

"People can hear. "

"Let them. We are betrothed, are we not?"

He stopped pulling and eyed her. "We are."

She bit off a smile at his nearly embarrassed expression. "Then at some point, you may actually want to see my breasts. Does this shock you?"

He held out an even expression for a split second longer before breaking down into snorts of laughter. "You naughty wench," he muttered. "I should spank you here and now."

She was laughing with him. "Are you telling me you do not want to see them? Maddoc, I am devastated. How can you say such cruel things to me?"

He was still laughing as he grabbed her by the arms and pulled her up against his chest, his hot lips against her ear.

"I never said I did not wish to see them," he whispered. "In fact, I am looking forward to that more than you can know. But they are for my eyes only and I do not wish to share with anyone. That is why I must approve of what you wear; I am a selfish man and your beauty is for me alone."

Adalind was crushed up against him, feeling his hot mouth on her ear. His closeness, his maleness, seemed to suck all of the ability to breathe right out of her. Chills ran down her spine as he murmured against her flesh, so much so that she could hardly focus on what he was saying. All she knew was that the man ignited a fire deep within her belly, something scorching and liquid that she could hardly understand. When he let her go, suddenly, she nearly fell. Maddoc had to reach out to steady her.

"Do you understand what I told you?" he asked, holding on to her arm as she regained her balance.

She gazed up at him, all of the giggle and flirt vanished. All she could do was nod. "Aye," she murmured. "I understand completely."

He grinned faintly and winked at her. "Good girl," he said, then looked over her shoulder as her palfrey was brought close. "Come along, now. We have a trip to make."

Adalind didn't say another word. His hot words and heated grip had sucked the flirt and conversation right out of her. She simply did as she was told.

***

The trip to collect Adalind's new garments for Victoria du Bose's celebration had been uneventful. Maddoc and eight men-at-arms had taken her in to Fordwich to the seamstress who made all of the de Lohr women's clothing. The woman had a rather large shop where she, her two daughters, and her sister made beautiful and quality garments. The moment Maddoc saw the gown they had fashioned for Adalind, he heartily approved.

There were several pieces to the garment – a ruby red shift of silk that glimmered and shined, and then a surcoat that went over the top of it of ruby and gold brocade that had a plunging neckline edged with fox, and long bell-shaped sleeves that were also lined with fox. The bodice of the surcoat was stitched with gold thread and glistening pieces of red-colored glass that looked like jewels, and a ruched belt that made Adalind's torso looked slender and shapely. All in all, it was a magnificent garment, and Maddoc had no complaints.

They took their time heading back to Canterbury, stopping at a vendor's stall that was filled with cakes and other delicacies. Adalind had a bit of a sweet tooth, so he purchased cinnamon and currant buns for her, morsels she happily shared with him. They chatted about food, travel, and the weather. They spoke of his trip to France to visit his father and step-mother, and they spoke of his half-siblings who were growing up rather quickly and becoming young adults. They spoke of Maddoc's hopes for the future and of what he would like to accomplish.

It was a level of conversation they'd never had before, adult to adult, and Maddoc was becoming increasingly enamored with Adalind's wit and intelligence. She was very funny, and very bright, and he liked that a great deal. Memories of that annoying young girl were long gone from his memory. The woman before him was something quite different.

Full of sweet buns and bearing Adalind's garment for the party, they headed back to Canterbury at a leisurely pace. Adalind seemed to be doing all of the talking as they traversed the two miles back to the castle. Maddoc listened with a grin on his face as she spoke of attending a feast at Berkhamstead Castle where the dogs ran mad through the feasting hall one evening, ripping up the careful display of food set forth by the baron's wife and leaving a mess in their wake.

It was a rather funny story and she told it very well. Maddoc was enjoying himself so much, in fact, that he didn't notice a small group of men riding parallel to them on a road about a half mile in the distance. It was a smaller road to Canterbury that cut in from the north, partially shrouded by trees and small hills, but a glint of armor finally caught Maddoc's eye and his attention was diverted from Adalind in an instant. For a few tense moments, he watched the movement of the distant party before emitting a low whistle. The escort swung into action and four of them surrounded Adalind while Maddoc and the other four formed a protective barrier between the lady and the approaching party.

It all happened very quickly, in a matter of seconds, and Adalind didn't realize something was amiss until Maddoc placed his helm atop his head and unfastened the sheath that contained his broadsword. He wasn't carrying his shield, but he was fully armed, and she grew very fearful as the distant group of me approached. The unfortunate thing was that from the angle of the roads, the unidentified party was now between them and Canterbury. Tension mounted.

"Maddoc?" she called, apprehension in her tone. "What is happening? Who are those men?"

Maddoc would not be diverted; he kept his eyes on the men in armor who were riding fairly swiftly in his direction. "I do not know," he said evenly. "Stay where you are and do what I tell you."

Tears tightened her throat, tears of anxiety. "The castle is within view," she said. "Perhaps we should ride very hard for it. We can outrun them."

"Stay where you are. Everything will be all right."

Adalind kept her mouth shut after that. He was in command mode, his manner confident and his voice authoritative, and she would have to trust him. She was frightened for him more than herself; she didn't want to see anything terrible befall him, not now when her future was opening up and he was the light at the end of the tunnel. So she sat upon her horse, holding on tightly, fearful of what was to come.

The party riding towards them was odd in that there were only four of them; four heavily armed, and exceptionally large, knights. There were no men-at-arms, no wagons, and no support group; just four knights. As they drew close on their massive, battle-hardened destriers, Maddoc charged forward to block them.

"Come no further," he bellowed. "Tell me your business and do not delay."

It was a booming, authoritative command. The four knights drew to a halt, horses snorting and pawing. When two of the knights helmed heads turned to look at one another, perhaps in confusion, Maddoc unsheathed his broadsword and held it aloft.

"Your business now," he commanded, "else you will not like my response."

Adalind was wrought with terror. She was close to jumping off her palfrey and begging for their lives. The thought of Maddoc speared through the heart in front of her made her feel faint and panicky. As she endeavored to plan a course of action that would save them, she heard a faint noise. It was odd, like a low and steady rumble, and confusion began to mix with her fear. She couldn't tell what it was, or where it was coming from, until one of the four knights suddenly flipped up his visor. It took her a moment to realize that the man was laughing.

"You are right, my friend," he said. "I would not like your reaction. You could take out all four of us and not even raise a sweat."

Maddoc's eyes widened and the broadsword nearly dropped to the ground. "De Wolfe?" he nearly gasped. "My God...*William* de Wolfe?"

Sir William de Wolfe was having a great time at Maddoc's expense. He back-handed the knight next to him in the chest. "It has been so long that he hardly recognizes me," he said to the knight, who flipped up his visor as well. The other two did the same. "He is getting senile in his old age."

It was evident that Maddoc knew these men. He sheathed his broadsword, making a conscious effort not to gape at the group. After a few moments of studying the other faces, he hissed.

"I do not believe my eyes," he said. "De Norville, Hage and de Bocage. What in the hell are all of you doing so far from Northwood Castle?"

William de Wolfe was an excruciatingly handsome man with golden eyes and well-shaped dark brows. It was all that could be seen through the open visor. He was also a very large man, as Adalind had previously noted. She studied him closely, curiously, as he reined his frothing charger near Maddoc and threw out a gauntleted hand. Maddoc took it the extended hand, holding it strongly.

"We were in London on business for the earl," he said. "There is great disharmony on the Scots border and Longley sent us to the king to solicit support."

Maddoc grew serious. "That is nothing new," he said. "Is the threat serious?"

De Wolfe half-shrugged, half-nodded. "Serious enough," he replied. "We suffered through a siege last month that went on for days. Bad weather was the only thing that drove them off in the end."

"What more support do you need? Perhaps de Lohr can spare me."

De Wolfe grinned. "I should only be so fortunate, my friend," he said, "but you may have problems of your own. While were in London, we heard your name mentioned a few times so we thought we'd pay you a visit. Last I had heard, you were at Canterbury so we took a chance that you were still here."

Maddoc still held on to the man's hand, forced to let it go when the horses caught wind of each other and, sensing a battle, began to get excited.

"I am still here," he said. Then his brow furrowed. "To what regard did you hear my name spoken?"

William didn't reply right away; in fact, he deliberately avoided the question as his golden gaze fell on Adalind, surrounded by men-at-arms. He dipped his head in her direction.

"My lady," he greeted.

Maddoc sensed William's hesitation to answer his question, which both intrigued and disturbed him. But he took the man's lead and focused his attention on Adalind.

"This is the Lady Adalind de Lohr de Aston," he introduced her to the collection of knights. "Lady Adalind is the eldest grandchild of David de Lohr, Earl of Canterbury. My lady, these are my very close and dear friends, Sir William de Wolfe, Sir Paris de Norville, Sir Kieran Hage, and Sir Michael de Bocage. A more powerful group of knights you will never meet. They serve the Earl of Teviot, whom I fostered with. The five of us fostered together."

Adalind still wasn't quite over her initial fear of four strange knights but she dipped her head politely as each man was introduced.

"My lords," she said.

Maddoc's bright blue eyes glimmered at her. "Prepare yourselves, gentle knights," he said. "I have great and shocking news for you. Adalind is my betrothed."

That drew a reaction from the knights. "Good Gods!" de Norville exclaimed. "You mean you actually found a woman who would have you? I find that astonishing."

The others were chuckling and Adalind could see that they meant it in humor. She smiled timidly as she spurred her little palfrey forward, heading towards the castle that was in plain view. After this fright, even though it had turned out for the better, she found that she was anxious to return to the safety of Canterbury.

"I do believe it is the other way around," she said as she trotted past. "Ask Maddoc about the annoying little girl who used to follow him around everywhere and you shall see that I am the fortunate one."

The knights watched her go by with various expressions of amusement and perhaps a greater measure of curiosity. Any woman to win du Bois' heart was a woman worth a second look. The men-at-arms began to follow Adalind, as did Maddoc. He waved his big arm at the group.

"Come along, lads," he said. "Let us spend the evening together reliving good memories and drinking to the future."

It was an attractive invitation and one they had hoped for. The collection of armored men turned their horses for the castle as de Norville spoke.

"Perhaps I shall try to convince the woman that I am a better prospect for her than you are," he said.

Maddoc's gaze was on Adalind's blond head. "Do that and I shall kill you."

De Norville glanced at de Wolfe as they followed. "So we have heard," he replied casually.

Maddoc turned to look at him. It was at that moment he began to suspect why they had come.

You and I have floated here on the stream that brings from the fount.
At the heart of time, love of one for another.

CHAPTER SEVEN

"The ap Athoe family is very powerful in Wales," de Wolfe said. "They are related to the Welsh princes and command thousands. Those two foolish whelps you whipped are declaring they are going to bring half of Wales down around Canterbury and take Adalind as a prize."

The group of knights from Northwood, plus Maddoc, Gerid, and David were crowded into David's solar. It was inching towards sunset, the sky turning shades of pinks and golds, casting slender fingers of light through the lancet windows of the solar. A fire crackled softly in the hearth and David's big, gray Irish wolfhound was spread out in front of it. David had to keep rolling the dog out of the way so he could warm his legs.

"The ap Athoe brothers came to Canterbury, uninvited, in an attempt to woo my granddaughter," David said frankly. "They made a nuisance of themselves, were pushy and rude, and when I told them to leave; they essentially ignored me, so Maddoc did his job. He removed them. But it was not without a fight."

De Wolfe was leaning against the wall, helm removed, as was most of his armor. He was rather swarthy looking in a magnetic sort of way, as if those golden eyes held untold mysteries of life and love. He was a deeply introspective man, calm and wise, and had a natural air of command about him.

"According to those two idiots, Maddoc unfairly ambushed them and they barely escaped with their lives," he said. "Of course, no one believed them, but what happened?"

David shook his head with disgust. "They tried to attack him, two against one," he replied. "I saw the entire incident. Maddoc was perfectly justified in what he did. The issue is not that Maddoc defeated them – the issue is that the two of them were too stupid and unskilled to make a good fight. It was over before it began; once Maddoc pushed them both down the stairs. They were humiliated, pure and simple."

De Wolfe grinned, glancing over his shoulder at de Norville, Hage, and de Bocage. As the latter two snorted, De Norville wasn't holding back his audible laugh. The mental image of strong, serious Maddoc shoving those two down the steps was a comedic gem.

"I would have liked to have seen that," de Norville said. A tall, blond man who was a great admirer of the female sex, he was one of the most arrogant men Maddoc had ever met, but a wise and loyal companion. It made for an odd combination. "Maddoc, those two were making a nuisance of themselves in their attempt to get to young Henry. It would seem that the ap Athoes were threatening to create an incident over this if the king did not intervene."

David lifted his eyebrows. "They went to *Henry* with this?" he rolled his eyes. "God's Beard, what a pair of dolts. What in the hell do they want? Adalind? Because I can tell you for a fact that I will defend her until the last stone of this castle. Those morons are not going to get their hands on her."

"Truthfully, I do not know if their demands met Henry's ears," de Wolfe said. "But they were creating quite a ruckus until the Captain of the Guard finally banned them from the Tower. After that, the brothers seemed to think that was an act of war and threatened to return to London with an army. That is when we thought we should take a detour to Canterbury to inform you of what happened. I did not want you to be surprised if half of the Welsh border turned up on your doorstep one day."

David merely shrugged. "Although I appreciate the effort you went through to deliver the message, I am unconcerned," he said. "Those two will more than likely burn themselves out by the time they reach home. It would take a good deal of money and effort to lay siege to Canterbury, as we are quite far from the Welsh border. My brother, however, is not. He is right along the Marches at his fortress of Lioncross Abbey. They could harass him just to make a point."

Maddoc was looking seriously at David. "Should I ride for Lioncross and warn him, my lord?"

David shook his head. "Nay," he said. "I will send a messenger but no more than that. I simply cannot believe that those two pups would create so much drama over their own bad behavior. Had they left when I ordered them to, none of this would have happened."

Maddoc simply nodded, glancing to de Wolfe and de Norville with a rather resigned expression. There wasn't much any of them could do about it but hope the brothers grew weary of the subject and moved on.

By this time, Hage and de Bocage were up from their seated positions, moving to the large pitcher of wine that had been brought in earlier. They had already drunk most of it, being weary, and were looking for more. But David was at the end of his patience with the subject at hand; he was sick of hearing about the ap Athoe brothers and their quest for vengeance. He was anxious to move on to better things.

"Come," he said, standing up rather stiffly as the dog at his feet stirred. "Let us retreat in to the hall and dine together. Let us speak of something other than foolish Welsh pups I wish I had never met."

The group of knights was more than pleased with that idea. It had been a long ride from London and now that they had delivered their message, the time had come to reap the rewards of de Lohr's hospitality. Maddoc began herding them towards the door.

"I suppose we shall get to sup with the Lady Adalind tonight, eh?" de Norville turned to Maddoc. "I am anxious to see what has you so smitten."

Maddoc kept a straight face at the man's braggadocio manner. "She has a sister," he said. "She is not yet spoken for. I could put in a good word for you."

De Norville made a face at him. "Never," he declared. "I intend to live freely and by my own rules until such time as I can no longer walk or feed myself. Then, and only then, will I consider a wife."

Maddoc snorted, looking over at Hage and de Bocage as they wandered in his direction. "And you two?" he wanted to know. "You were both attached at the hip, even as young squires. I see nothing has changed after all of these years. They used to call the pair of you the Bull and the Tree. Remember?"

Kieran Hage came from an old Saxon family whose seat was Southwell Castle in Nottinghamshire. His father, Sean, was the current Earl of Newark, and Kieran had been named for his father's long-dead brother. Kieran had the broad Hage build and blond hair, and his manner was rather subdued and thoughtful. He grinned as he glanced over at his best friend, the extremely tall Michael de Bocage. The knight was at least a head taller than even the tallest man. A tree, indeed.

"They still call me the Bull," Kieran said. "Even my wife."

Maddoc's eyebrows lifted. "So you married? I had not heard."

Kieran pointed at William. "I married his wife's cousin," he replied. "Scots."

Maddoc looked at William with some confusion. "Scots?" he repeated. "Not the kind you are having difficulty with, I hope."

William grinned, a sort of sly gesture. "It is a long and detailed story," he said. "Feed me before I delve into it. I will need all of my strength to get through the story."

With a smirk, Maddoc moved with the group out into the entry hall and then deep into the smaller feasting hall where a veritable mass of culinary delights were laid out for all to sample. Already, there were several people at the table, including de Lohr's family. Much to de Norville's delight, they were all women.

Emilie sat with David in the center of the feasting table, a gracious and lovely hostess for the visiting knights. Adalind sat with her mother and with Willow, who was seriously eyeing the visitors and in particular eyeing de Bocage. Along with his height, he was very handsome with his blue eyes and dark hair. Willow didn't even seem to notice that all he did was respond to Kieran once in a while or laugh at jokes. He never really said much of anything, or take the lead in the conversation, but that didn't preclude her interest. She never even noticed the man had a bit of a stammer, which more than likely explained why he was so quiet. Willow had been eyeing Gerid over the past few days but with the introduction of the handsome stranger, she was shifting loyalties.

After the guests were seated, Maddoc had taken a seat between Adalind and Christina. His gaze was warm on Adalind, who was looking quite luscious in a gold brocade surcoat and he was looking forward to the evening of introducing her to his friends. He hadn't taken two bites of his food when a soldier bolted into the warm and fragrant hall, heading directly for David.

"My lord," the man said, "we have sighted an army approaching."

Maddoc didn't hesitate; he was on his feet. "Lock down the gatehouse," he ordered, already moving to quit the hall. "Send out the scouts. Did we receive a missive or warning?"

The soldier moved to Maddoc's side as David, Gerid, de Wolfe and the other visiting knights jumped up from the table and began to follow as well.

"No missive, my lord," the soldier replied. "Our scouts spotted them a few miles south towards Ashford. They are moving in our direction, a battalion of men and animals."

Maddoc's mind was quickly processing what he was being told. "Ashford," he muttered. "Chilham Castle is in that direction."

"De Digges is loyal to Pembroke," David said. His mind was working furiously as well. "Pembroke and de Burgh are allies."

Maddoc looked over his shoulder and glanced at the man. "Do you suppose Walter ran to de Digges and demanded his army?"

David shrugged. "It is as good a theory as any."

Maddoc didn't like that theory at all, but it unfortunately made sense. He looked at the knights trailing after him, unimaginable firepower at his disposal. De Wolfe himself was called "The Wolf" by the Scots because of his cunning mind and vicious bite. He was perhaps the best commander in the entire north of England and his reputation was legendary. Maddoc's gaze fixed on William.

"Your assistance would be appreciated, William," he said quietly. "De Digges carries nearly two thousand men. This could be bad."

De Wolfe nodded coolly. He was collected and calm, as were the others. This was what they were born and bred for, fighting men whose lives involved death and defense on a daily basis. A siege was nothing out of the ordinary. It was the fabric of their existence.

"I am at your disposal," he said to both Maddoc and David. "Little does de Digges know what he is up against. We shall make short work of him and be back in the hall before dawn."

Maddoc wriggled his eyebrows. "It is not de Digges that concerns me," he said, shoving the entry door aside as the group began to descend the stairs into the dark and cold bailey. "It is de Burgh. If it is truly him, and he truly seeks some kind of twisted vengeance, then I will seek the man out and destroy him. He threatens me, Adalind, and everyone at Canterbury; and this I will not stand for."

David should have been the one to caution him again based on de Burgh and his family connections, but he did not. He agreed with Maddoc completely. He was infuriated that the man would move against his castle and, worse, his family. Canterbury was peaceful for the most part but this night threatened to change that. He was bloody well enraged.

Torches on the battlements were now being quickly put out by orders to douse all lights. As the knights came off the steps and Maddoc began to issue orders, he glanced behind him and caught sight of a figure up at the head of the stairs, the entry. It took him a moment to realize it was Adalind. David caught sight of her, too, and waved Maddoc off as he took charge of the knights. When Maddoc resisted, David pointed at Adalind, made sure Maddoc understood the silent message, and moved off towards the gatehouse. Maddoc attention lingered on the departing group of knights before turning his focus to Adalind.

When she saw he was alone, standing at the base of the stairs, she gathered her skirt and made her way down to him.

"What is happening?" she begged softly. "Will you tell me? I heard you mention de Burgh."

He was in battle mode, struggling to soften his manner as he gazed at her. After a moment, he held out his hand to her and she took it tightly in both of hers. Her hands were warm and soft as she squeezed his big, rough fingers.

"An army approaches," he said. "We do not know for sure if it is de Burgh. In fact, we do not even know if they are truly hostile but it would be foolish not to set our defenses. To that regard, I want you to go back inside and bolt the door. Throw the shutters and lock yourselves in. Do not open the doors for anyone but me or your grandfather. Do you understand?"

She looked at him with big eyes, nodding, and he could see the tears coming. "I do," she whispered. Then she bit off a sob. "Oh, Maddoc, why is this happening? If it is de Burgh, why will he not leave us alone? He is a hateful, hateful man."

He gently tugged on her hands, pulling her against him. His big arms went around her, their first true and solid embrace that was warm, tender, and strong. Maddoc held her tightly, his face in the top of her head, smelling the faint sweet scent of her hair. It was heavenly. His heart, so recently filled with rage and battle, softened with the feel and smell of her. He'd never known anything so wonderful, melting him, causing all of the anger and aggressiveness he was feeling to drain right out of him. It was a struggle for him to maintain focus.

"He is of no consequence," he murmured. "If it is him, then he shall be sorely disappointed, for Canterbury will hold and he shall not have what he came for. He shall not have you."

Adalind was trying to be brave, she truly was. But she was genuinely distressed that they were facing potential danger, with Maddoc in the middle of it. She felt so guilty, as if she was the cause of all of their troubles. Her arms were wrapped tightly around his waist, her eyes closed as she buried her face in his tunic. How long had she dreamed of this moment, to be held by Maddoc in a way that a man holds a woman? It seemed like a lifetime. Now, he was finally hers to hold and she never wanted to let him go, not ever.

"I know," she whispered. Then she pulled her face from his chest and gazed up at him. "I simply want you to be safe. Nothing else matters to me but you. Please take care."

He smiled faintly at her, brushing a bit of stray hair from her eyes. Then he cupped her face in one big hand and kissed her tenderly on the cheek. But that wasn't good enough, like a teaser for his passion, so he kissed her on the lips as well. She tasted like the cherries she had been eating in the hall, tangy and sweet. It was enough to spark his lust and he pulled her tightly against him as his lips devoured her, tasting her, his tongue licking her lips and begging for admittance. When she opened her mouth, timidly, he took full advantage of it. He kissed her until she had to gasp for air and even then he pulled away purely out of necessity. Men were yelling at him from the battlements.

"Rider!"

Maddoc could hear the cries. Leaving a breathless Adalind standing by the stairs, he moved towards the gatehouse where David was ordering the gates opened. There was still the portcullis, squat and tough, lowered against all threats that would wash upon Canterbury and providing some measure of protection, but Maddoc could see something beyond the iron grate as he made his way towards the gatehouse. A rider was indeed approaching in the darkness.

Men were scrambling upon the walls, dogs barking at the excitement. Maddoc reached the gatehouse, standing with David, William and Gerid as the rider came barreling towards them. It seemed as if the rider had no control over his mount because the horse was going in all directions, unsteadily. It ran straight up to the gate and nearly crashed into it, taking a sharp turn to the right at the last moment to avoid a collision.

The action would have dumped a normal rider and the rider did indeed topple, but the entire saddle went with him, rolling to the underbelly of the horse but not coming off. Rider and saddle were still strapped to the horse, who started to panic because it could no longer freely move.

David shouted orders for the portcullis to lift as Maddoc and William slipped underneath the grate to grab the horse. As William took hold of the panicked and frothing steed, Maddoc dropped to his knees beside the upside-down rider. It took him all of two seconds to see what he was dealing with. A beaten and bloodied body, gagged, was tied to the saddle. He was quite dead.

"God help us," he hissed. "What madness is this?"

We have played along side millions of lovers, shared in the same
Shy sweetness of meeting, the same distressful tears of farewell-

CHAPTER EIGHT

"Poor Eynsford," Adalind sobbed. "He was a nuisance but he was not a terrible person. Why would Walter do this to him?"

Christina didn't have any answers. Nor did Emilie or Willow. The four of them sat in the small feasting hall, a warm blaze crackling in the hearth behind them, keeping the hall rather cozy even though the mood of the room was fearful and somber. Christina had her arm around her daughter's shoulder, trying to offer some comfort.

"Papa told you not to worry," she said gently. "He and the knights will do what needs to be done."

Adalind was devastated. Somehow, someway, Walter de Burgh crossed paths with Eynsford du Lesseps and had killed the man, sending him back to Canterbury tied to a horse. No one even knew how Walter had known the man, but Eynsford, being a bit of a dramatic character, must have said something about Adalind somehow and Walter, furious over his expulsion from Canterbury, must have taken his fury out on the young man.

It had been a horrific sight, one that Adalind had unfortunately witnessed. David had tried to spare her when he realized who the dead rider was, but Adalind had caught sight of Eynsford anyway. The man had been wearing his bright red silks and had been hard to miss.

David had taken the hysterical Adalind into the keep and spent a few minutes trying to calm her down before retreating to the bailey. An army was approaching, one that apparently meant serious business, and he could not spare more time to soothe his granddaughter. It was evident that defending her was to be the order of the night.

So Adalind, Willow, Christina, and Emilie had been in the hall since Eynsford's tragic appearance. The keep was buttoned up tightly while Canterbury waited with quivering anticipation for the siege. The women had no way of knowing what was going on outside considering all of the windows were shuttered and they were deep in the keep, far away from doors or openings. They had no way of knowing that the army that had sent them all into lock-down was really no more than one hundred men that had marched upon Canterbury in a rather unorganized group. They had no way of knowing that the collection remained in a black, shadowed tide just outside of the range of Canterbury's archers, waiting and watching. All they knew was that bottled up in the keep made them deaf and blind to all, which only fueled their fears.

"I simply do not understand why Walter would do this," Adalind sniffled, trying not to think of Eynsford's broken body. "I told him I was not interested in him. Does he believe that murder and destruction will make me want to marry him?"

Christina glanced at Emilie before replying; the older women were more astute to the real world, where men's hearts and actions were not motivated by feeling but rather by greed and pride. Adalind was too young to fully comprehend that.

"Nay," she said softly. "He does not believe he can win your love this way. He has come to take what he wants."

Adalind shook her head firmly, wiping delicately at her nose. "He cannot have me," she said, turning beseechingly to her mother. "I am so sorry to have brought this upon Canterbury. All was peaceful until I came home and now...."

"You are not to blame," Emilie spoke up from the other side of the table, cutting her off. "Addie, men like Walter de Burgh are spoiled little bullies. If they do not get their way, in any fashion, they throw a tantrum. That is all this is – a tantrum."

Adalind was no longer sobbing but tears still dripped from her eyes. "It is a deadly tantrum. I am responsible for Eynsford's death."

"Nonsense," Emilie snapped softly. "Worrying about this is not going to change things. In fact, I suggest we all try to get some sleep. If the siege begins, we will hear it, so until that time we may as well try to rest."

Adalind started to shake her head but her mother firmly agreed. "That is an excellent suggestion," she said, standing up and pulling Adalind to her feet. "Let us try and get some rest. "

Adalind realized that her mother and grandmother were joining forces to coerce her into going to bed. She resisted even as her mother bodily pulled her away from the feasting table but eventually relented as Willow took her hand and began leading her up the narrow spiral stairs. She had fallen silent by the time they reached their shared bedchamber, the long stone room with the roaring fireplace and piles of furs and coverlets stacked both on and under the bed.

It was a cozy place, a young lady's place, and it brought instant comfort as Adalind passed through the door. Her things were here, things that had followed her around for the past five years, and she was comforted among her things. She truly was exhausted from her eventful day. She stopped thinking of Eynsford and Walter, at least for the moment. At least until the sound of bellows in the bailey caught her attention. Rushing to the window that faced out over a portion of the bailey, she and Willow strained to see what was going on.

There was some manner of confrontation occurring at the main gates.

***

"Surely you understand the de Burgh war machine," Wallace de Digge was a middle-aged man who fought for his older brother, the Lord of Chilham Castle. He appeared tired and impatient and resistant to being in the position he was in. "Walter de Burgh is demanding satisfaction, my lord. My brother has sent me to seek the truth of the matter. What on earth happened today that has that old man so riled up?"

David knew Wallace. They had co-existed peacefully for years. Although not truly an ally, he wasn't an enemy, either. They simply lived a few miles from each other but not much more than that. Politics had seen them on opposite sides most of the time.

David sighed heavily. He kept the portcullis down, conversing through the big iron bars. "He came to court my granddaughter," he explained, anger in his tone. "My granddaughter is not interested in him, nor am I, and when I asked him to leave, he became rude and threatening. When I physically threw him from my keep, he produced a weapon. My captain defended me."

Wallace listened to the story before scratching his dark, oily head. "Is that du Bois?"

"Aye."

Wallace shook his head, disgusted. "Walter wants him."

"Why?"

"To punish him, I would presume. His arm is badly broken and he said du Bois did it."

"He did it whilst disarming him," David said, his fury growing. "Make no mistake; Walter pulled a dagger and was fully intending to use it on me until Maddoc stepped in. The broken arm is the unfortunate byproduct of a stupid man's stupid actions."

Wallace scratched his head again and looked him in the eye. "So what shall we do?" he asked. "My brother forced me to come here at de Burgh's request. I was asked to bring back du Bois and if I do not, I am to return to my brother and inform him of your refusal to produce the man, whereupon my brother will provide a thousand men to lay siege and either kill du Bois or take him prisoner. My lord, I have no desire to lay siege to Canterbury because of the idiot de Burgh. I do not like him, my brother does not like him, but we all fear his brother. I would not want to offend the de Burgh family."

David's eyebrows listed. "So you would offend the de Lohr family instead?" he shook his head. "My brother commands five thousand at Lioncross Abbey plus another six thousand from his various garrisons. By tomorrow noon, I can have four thousand men here from my garrisons at Denstroude Castle and Kemberland Castle, and I will send word to Fitzwilliam at Dover Castle to reinforce me with another four thousand. If you think you can survive nineteen thousand men, by all means, return and lay siege."

Wallace held up a hand in surrender. "My lord, I do not wish to invite your ire, either," he assured him. "I am simply doing what I was told to do."

David knew the man was a pawn and he struggled to calm himself. But he was sincerely furious at de Burgh.

"I understand," he said. "My anger is not directed at you. But you will return to Walter de Burgh with a message from me. You will tell him that he will cease his harassment of my granddaughter and forget any misplaced sense of vengeance against Maddoc du Bois or I will send word to my brother and we will both march on Montgomery Castle where his beloved brother Hubert resides and burn the place to the ground. If this is any way unclear, he can come personally to discuss it with me, for as of this moment I will consider any further action from him, or Chilham Castle, an open act of war and will react accordingly. Chilham shall fall, as will Montgomery, and any other de Burgh holdings my brother and I decide to raze. Do you comprehend?"

Wallace's expression was a mixture of apprehension and resignation. "I do, my lord."

"Good." David's gaze lingered on the man in the darkness. "Then, when Walter leaves Chilham, tell your brother that I would have you and him as my guests. We will feast and drink and try to determine why we have not been better allies. Perhaps we will remedy that situation."

Wallace nodded faintly. "Perhaps, my lord."

"Good eve, Wallace."

"Good eve, my lord."

With that, Wallace turned and headed back to his collection of mounted men, snapping orders to retreat. As David stood and watched, Maddoc, William and Gerid came to stand beside him, watching the small army organize and move off into the dark of the night. They had heard every word spoken. When the army faded from view, David turned to Maddoc.

"You will watch yourself over the next few days," he said. "I would not put it past de Burgh to lie in wait for you somewhere. Stay to the castle."

Maddoc wasn't afraid of anything much less a shriveled old man. He struggled not to become angry with David's directive.

"I do not believe that is necessary, my lord," he said evenly. "I can watch out for myself."

David lifted an eyebrow at him. "That is *not* a request," he said. "Maddoc, perhaps it is an overabundance of caution, but I know de Burgh. He is conniving and wily. I do not trust the man, so for the next few days I would ask that you remain confined to the castle for your own safety."

Maddoc was fairly close to fuming but hid it well. "What of Victoria du Bose's celebration?" he wanted to know. "That is in two days. I am to escort Adalind."

David turned from the gate with the collection of knights following him. "She will not go, either," he said. "De Burgh could lie in wait for her, also, and I would have a mess on my hands because I would go to war against the entire de Burgh family for so much as touching my granddaughter. Moreover, the Dukes of Navarre would come down on them as well because I know I could not keep you out of the mix. All of England would be in turmoil because of one stupid old man and his inability to accept a refusal."

Maddoc didn't say anymore. He was afraid it would turn into an argument if he did. However, he was embarrassed by the directive in front of his fellow knights, as if he was a weakling who needed to be protected. As David headed back towards the keep, Maddoc let him go. He didn't want to be around the man at the moment, disappointed and humiliated.

As he stood there and stewed, de Wolfe came up behind him and clapped a big hand on his shoulder. "Do you know how many directives I have had from my liege like the one you just received?" he asked, grinning when Maddoc turned to look at him. "Too many to count. All of Scotland is out to get me so I receive orders like that constantly."

Maddoc appreciated the man's sense of comfort; it was evident he understood what Maddoc was feeling. "What do you do?" he asked.

William shook his head. "I do not listen to him if that is what you mean," he said. "I continue to do my job as I see fit because I know I am smarter than the Scots, just as you are smarter than de Burgh. Do not let that old man have such control over you. You are better than he is."

Maddoc wriggled is eyebrows. "It is not de Burgh I am worried about," he said. "It is de Lohr. He is not beyond trying to beat me if I disobey." Then he sobered and averted his gaze. "It will not end, you know. De Burgh will return to his brother and tell him what has happened, and this entire situation will veer out of control. Adalind and I may not know a measure of peace for quite some time, at least as long as de Burgh feels the sting of rejection."

William's mysterious golden eyes seemed to flicker. "I would not worry over that too much," he said quietly. "We will be leaving on the morrow and perhaps find our way to the same road de Burgh will be taking as he leaves Chilham. Perhaps we will run into him. Perhaps he will insult us. Perhaps we will have to defend our honor against him. You just never know what will happen."

Maddoc had been staring at the ground as de Wolfe spoke, but when the knight's words registered, his head came up. The blue eyes glimmered with shock and understanding.

"I cannot ask this of you," he hissed. "Although I appreciate the offer, I cannot ask you to eliminate the man on my behalf, even for the sake of peace."

"Would you allow me to eliminate a threat against Adalind, then?" he asked quietly. "You said yourself that she will never know peace so long as de Burgh believes he has been slandered. There is no telling what he will do. Moreover, you heard David earlier - if de Burgh was to abduct or injure Adalind somehow, the de Lohr and du Bois war machines would come down over him and the entire country would be in turmoil." De Wolfe lowered his voice pointedly. "To protect Adalind, would you do anything in the world?"

Maddoc stared at the man. After a moment, he nodded faintly. "I would."

"Then consider it done."

"I will, but under one condition."

"What is that?"

"That when the moment comes, I do the deed." His expression was deadly. "For Adalind, for the threat dealt against me, and for that poor dolt Eynsford, I will dispense justice."

De Wolfe understood. "As well you should."

When Adalind awoke the next morning, Maddoc had disappeared with his friends from Northwood. David had no idea where they were and he spent the entire day angrily chastising Maddoc for disobeying him. It came to the point where his wife began to ply him with fine wine mid-day simply to calm him down and by sunset, David was so bloody drunk that he was openly weeping over Maddoc and how much he loved the man.

Adalind sat with her grandfather most of the day and evening, trying not to weep herself over Maddoc's disappearance. She knew the man wouldn't abandon her, but she was despondent over his absence. She was very frightened for him.

When she finally went to bed that night, she wept for him all night.

Old love but in shapes that renew and renew forever.

CHAPTER NINE

"Addie!" Willow raced into the small solar where her sister was working steadily on her loom. "He is back! Maddoc is back!"

Adalind nearly stabbed herself with her needle in her surprise. It had been three days since Maddoc's disappearance and three days of hell as far as she was concerned. Turmoil such as she had never known had been her constant companion but at Willow's shouted words, all of the turmoil was replaced by hope and gladness. She was exhilarated. Shoving the needle into the fabric to hold it fast, she jumped up from her seat.

"Where is he?" she demanded as she ran from the room.

Willow followed. "He and grandfather are in the bailey," she said. "I saw them speaking."

Adalind was filled with euphoria. Dressed in an emerald silk surcoat, she had dressed carefully every day, hoping and praying for Maddoc's return, and now the moment was upon her. She wanted to look lovely for him and make him glad he had come back. Or perhaps she wanted him to see what he had missed in his absence. Whatever the case, she smoothed the garment and fussed with her braided hair before purging herself from the keep and rushing down the stairs to the bailey below.

The ward was rather busy at this time in the morning with supply wagons, soldiers, and peasants moving about. The ground was moist, keeping the dust down. Near the squat gatehouse, she could see Maddoc and her grandfather in deep conversation. Maddoc was still clad in full battle armor, holding the reins of his exhausted and frothy charger as the horse swung its head about nervously. Neither man seemed particularly animated, conversing rather seriously, as Adalind rushed up.

"Maddoc!" she exclaimed happily. "You have returned!"

Maddoc and David turned to look at her. Before Maddoc could reply, David spoke. "Go back inside, Adalind," he snapped quietly. "Do it now."

Adalind's happy expression fell. "But... why?" She was crushed. "Why are you angry?"

"Do as I say."

Adalind's mouth popped open, surprised and hurt, but she didn't turn away. She stood her ground.

"Papa, what is the matter?" she pleaded. "What has happened?"

David glared at her. Then, he just turned and walked away. Adalind watched him go, greatly confused and concerned, before returning her attention to Maddoc.

"Is he angry because you left?" she asked.

Maddoc's gaze was still on David, lingering. When Adalind asked the question, he simply looked at her. For a moment, he didn't say anything. He just looked at her. Then, he reached out and collected her hand.

"Walk with me," he said quietly.

Adalind gladly followed him across the bailey as he headed towards the stables. She clung to his hand, wondering why her grandfather was so upset but those concerns being overshadowed by the thrill of Maddoc's return. He was as real as rain, as strong as the heavens, and as handsome as summer sunset. She skipped alongside him, her gaze never leaving his face.

"Maddoc, where did you go?" she asked softly.

Maddoc's mind was elsewhere even as he walked with purpose towards the stables. He could feel Adalind in his hand, hear her soft voice in his ear, and it affirmed to him that he had done the right thing. He had no doubt.

When they had caught Walter de Burgh traveling north from Chilham Castle with his eight soldiers, de Burgh's group had been no match for five very seasoned and powerful knights. Maddoc had made sure de Burgh had seen his face, and he had made sure the man understood why he was there. De Burgh was a threat in every sense of the word and Maddoc didn't hesitate to destroy the man as William, Paris, Kieran and Michael went after the other eight men. There could be no witnesses to what had happened; they all knew that. It was vengeance as much as it was a preventative action. It was justice.

The words 'murder' or 'ambush' never came up, simply because although fundamentally that may have described the circumstances, morality and common sense and reasoning called the action something far different. Maddoc had never thought otherwise, but David wasn't so sure. Even now, the earl was wrestling with what Maddoc had done. Maddoc knew he would eventually see reason but until that time came, the relationship between them would be rather tense. It was an unusual state between men who were so fond of one another.

"I had a task to attend to," he said, holding her steady when she tripped in her haste. "Your grandfather does not particularly agree with the motives behind my task, but it is nothing to worry over."

"What task?"

They came to the stables and he came to a halt, facing her in the noise and stink of the stable yards. Around them, dogs barked, goats bleated, and horses nickered, but Maddoc didn't notice any of it. His focus was solely on Adalind. The more he looked at her, the more he could feel himself soften.

"I will say this only once to you, so please listen carefully," he said, not unkindly. "Honesty and truth are of paramount importance to me, and I will always be truthful and honest with you. Do you believe me?"

Adalind's somewhat confused eyes were wide on him, but she nodded solemnly. "Of course, Maddoc."

"There will also be times that I will choose not to divulge information to you, but that does not mean I am not being truthful. It simply means that I will withhold information because I feel it either does not concern you or it is something you do not need to know. Do you understand?"

Again, she nodded seriously. "I do."

"And if I tell you it is none of your affair, you will do me the courtesy of not asking again. Agreed?"

"Agreed."

"This is one of those times. Where I have been over the past three days and what I did during that time does not concern you."

Adalind felt somewhat rebuked by his answer but she nodded anyway, somewhat demurely, and lowered her gaze. Maddoc could see that he hurt her feelings, however slightly, so he kissed her hand as they resumed their walk to the entry to the stables where he turned his charger over to the one of the grooms. When the big black and white beast clip-clopped away, Maddoc returned his attention to Adalind.

"Now," he said, attempting to change the subject. "If I am not mistaken, today is the day we were set to travel to Victoria du Bose's party. Are you packed?"

She looked up at him, rather surprised. "But Papa said that I could not go because of de Burgh's threat. He said...."

"There is no threat. Are you packed?"

Adalind may have been young, but she wasn't foolish. Simply the way he said the words made her look at him closely. He was stone-faced, meeting her gaze steadily, but there was something in his statement that belied the true meaning. Even though he told her not to ask any more questions, she knew that she must. Something in his words demanded it.

"Why would you say there is no threat?" she lowered her voice. "Papa said he was worried about de Burgh and that is why I could not attend the party. Now you tell me there is no threat. Why would Papa say that if it was not true?"

He sighed faintly. "Again, this is not something you should concern yourself with. Suffice it to say that there is no more threat and we can attend the party as you wish. I am eager to see you in that lovely dress."

Adalind could sense he was holding something back, something terrible. She didn't know why she felt that way, but she did. Maddoc had been missing for days, her grandfather was angry with him, and now there was no longer any worry with de Burgh. She began to feel apprehensive.

"Maddoc," she said, her voice very quiet. "Please tell me why there is no more threat."

"You promised you would not press me if I did not wish to speak of it."

She pulled her hands out of his grip and took a step back, out of his arm range. But her gaze never left his face.

"I would like to make something very clear as well," she said softly, verging on tears, although she did not know why. "I am not an empty-headed chit. I have a mind, and a very good one, and I am a woman of deep thought. I hope you do not expect me to go through life being mindless and satisfied just because you want me that way. There is supposed to be trust when two people are courting, or fond of one another, and at this moment I sense that I do not have your trust."

He shook his head. "Of course I trust you," he said. "But it is as I said; there are some things I simply do not wish to speak of."

"Why?"

"Because it is not necessary."

"Because you wish to keep me mindless and obedient? If it is control you seek over me, this is not the way to go about it."

Maddoc could have easily flared, but he didn't. He thought about what she said and realized she was right. He also realized that Adalind had not only grown up physically over the past several years, but mentally as well. She was sound of reason and mind. In fact, she was very logical and level-headed. He'd seen much of that since her return and he liked it very much. The next few moments would tell just, exactly, how much she had grown and if their budding relationship could weather a serious occurrence. He was aware that he was somewhat reluctant to tell her, afraid she might actually think less of him.

"Walter de Burgh's infatuation with you had grown into something of vengeance and threat against all of us," he said, lowering his voice. "You know what he did to Eynsford. That speaks of madness. It was no longer an issue of rejecting his suit; that became the least of Walter's issues. In his mind, we had all slandered and shamed him, and he was going to seek revenge. Therefore, with the help of de Wolfe and my friends, we stopped the threat. We stopped Walter."

Adalind was listening intently. When he finished speaking, he could see the edginess, the fear, in her eyes, but she held it admirably. "What does that mean?" she asked. "How did you stop him?"

"I killed him."

Her mouth popped open and she inhaled sharply, just as quickly closing her mouth and slapping a hand over her lips. Mouth shut for the moment, her eyes were wide on him.

"You did?" she hissed through her fingers.

He nodded slowly. "I had to, Addie," he murmured. "The man was bent on vengeance. He was out to kill me, hurt you, hurt your family, and anything else he could accomplish. What I did, I did to spare you and your family. If there is a threat against you, it is my duty to do all in my power to end it."

She began to look rather sick and the hand came away from her mouth.

"*Sweet Jesú*," she breathed, hand now on her belly. "I have driven you to murder."

Maddoc took a big step to close the distance between them. His enormous hands closed in on her arms as he held her still.

"You did not," he whispered. "It was my choice and the only choice I could make. But know this; I would kill every man in this entire country if it meant keeping you safe. I will always protect you, Addie. Surely you know that."

She gazed up at him, tears swimming in her big green eyes. "I know that," she murmured. "But what will happen when Walter's brother discovers what has happened? He will come for you."

He pulled her into his powerful embrace, overwhelmed with the feel of her against him. She was soft and warm and supple, and he was quickly succumbing. Each successive embraced between them was more powerful than the last. He was very quickly becoming deeply enamored with her, more than he ever imagined.

"He will not come for me because there were no witnesses," he murmured into her hair. "We eliminated Walter and his entire escort, so there is no trace. Whoever finds him will think bandits set upon him. We made sure of that. There will be nothing linking him to Canterbury or to me."

Adalind clung to him, tears spilling over. "But I am frightened," she wept softy. "Hubert de Burgh is a powerful man. Do you not think he will trace his brother's path back to Chilham and find out from de Digge what transpired between Walter and you? That will bring him right to Canterbury."

Maddoc sighed faintly. "Even if it does, there is no proof," he murmured. "Anyone who knows the truth will not tell a soul and even if they did, what happened was justifiable. Walter had made it plain he was out to kill me, so I defended myself, and for that poor idiot Eynsford, I exacted justice. There is nothing dishonorable in any of it."

Adalind thought on his words, thinking they seemed logical. It hadn't been cold blooded murder; it had been a necessary action of justice and self-protection. She understood completely. But she was still frightened.

"You are the most honorable man I know," she said, releasing her strangle hold on him and gazing up into his face. "I never thought otherwise. But I am still scared that Hubert will discover what happened."

Maddoc looked into her sweet face, feeling warm and giddy feelings wash over him. He could have stared into that face all day.

"He will not," he assured her. "I do not want you to worry."

"I will try not to."

He smiled faintly. "Good," he said, thinking he should probably let her go because the urge to kiss her was growing quite strong and he didn't want to make a spectacle in the stable yard. "Now, let us return to the subject of Lady Victoria's party. It is mid-morning now; I would suggest you return to your chamber and pack for the journey. And tell Willow she may not bring her bedding with her. I seem to remember a young girl who used to like to drag her entire bed along when she traveled."

Adalind grinned. "I do not think she does that any longer," she said. "At least, I hope she has outgrown such things. Speaking of my sister, however, she was quite smitten with one of your friends – the very tall knight with the blue eyes and dark hair. What was his name?"

He gave her a wry expression. "Michael," he replied, releasing her from their tight embrace. "Tell your sister to seek her companionship elsewhere."

"Why?"

"Because de Bocage is not meant for her."

Adalind frowned terribly. "What do you mean by that?" she demanded. "That is an awful thing to say."

He held up his hands in supplication. "I simply meant that he is titled and meant to inherit a fortune," he replied. "He is looking for a wife of connections and standing, which an earl's granddaughter is not. Willow will not have any trouble attracting a lesser knight."

Adalind's frown deepened and she put her hands on her hips. "I am an earl's granddaughter, too," she pointed out. "I seem to be a fine match for you, as the grandson of a duke. My sister is good enough for any man."

He was having a tough time biting off a smile. He didn't want to say what he was thinking. *That may be true, sweet girl, but she's not nearly the beauty you are.* So he simply took her hand and kissed it submissively.

"Michael is a bit of a rake," he said softly. "I would not want your sister to have her heart broken by such a man. Perhaps she will find a husband at Victoria's party."

It was a good way to soothe Adalind and distract her at the same time. Now she wasn't quite so insulted by what he had said about Willow's infatuation with Michael. In fact, it was enough of a distraction to shift her thoughts completely to the party.

"I had better go and find Papa, then" she said. "We will want to leave before the nooning hour, don't you think?"

Maddoc was thankful for the complete change of focus. "Aye," he said, glancing up at the clear blue sky. "Providing the weather stays good, we can make it to Shadoxhurst Castle by sunset. But we must move swiftly."

Adalind was already gathering her skirt, preparing to move quickly to the keep. "Can we take the wagon?"

Maddoc watched her as she skipped away. "Can we not travel more lightly than that?" he asked.

"Nay!"

He grunted, resigned. "One trunk each, then, and one trunk only. I do not escort a baggage train."

She giggled as she came to a halt, grinning at him. "No, my lord, you escort me, and if I need more than one trunk because I want to dress appropriately for the man who has pledged for me, then I shall. And no argument from you."

"Can I argue just a little?"

"If you do, you will lose."

"I am coming to suspect that."

She giggled again and ran off. Maddoc watched her go, a grin playing on his lips. "Be ready to leave by noon, Addie," he called after her.

She waved at him and said something he didn't quite hear; she was too far away. He lost sight of her as she disappeared around the keep. Still, the memory of her lingered in his mind and resulted in a constant smirk as he went about his duties arranging the escort.

Gerid, roped into helping him, noticed that foolish grin on Maddoc's face but said nothing. The man had been acting strangely ever since he had returned from France and, consequently, became reacquainted with Adalind de Aston. Moreover, he suspected Maddoc's disappearance had something to do with the woman as well.

Gerid didn't know all of the facts yet, but he was a bright man. He was coming to think there was something more than acquaintance between his big, brooding liege and the earl's granddaughter.

95

Today it is heaped at your feet, it has found its end in you
The love of all man's days both past and forever:

CHAPTER TEN

The trip to Shadoxhurst Castle had been uneventful. David, though still in the throes of dealing with Maddoc's solution to Walter de Burgh, had been unable to deny his granddaughter the trip she had so been looking forward to. Adalind had known little joy over the past few years and the past few days had been particularly bad, so David was disinclined to deny her something that was already bringing a smile to her face. A thrilling party and the opportunity to see old friends were too much to resist.

He had therefore succumbed to her pleading and by noon, Adalind, Willow, Christina, and Emilie were packed and ready to move out. David reasoned that if what Maddoc said was true, then de Burgh was no longer a lurking threat so there was no reason not to leave the safety of Canterbury. Maddoc, efficient as always, had organized a sixty man escort to Shadoxhurst, including two wagons, so David had very little to do but mount his charger and ride escort along with the rest of the knights.

It had been a strained ride, at least between Maddoc and David. David barely said a word to the man as they had traveled southwesterly during the course of the cool and breezy afternoon. Maddoc had taken point while Gerid and David had ridden back near the wagons; therefore, no one noticed any tension between David and Maddoc because they were apart most of the time. The only person who might have noticed was Adalind, and her gaze was on Maddoc the entire time as he rode strong and proud at the head of the column. She had didn't see or hear much other than him.

Shadoxhurst Castle was a smaller castle with a rather compact, square bailey surrounded by tall gray walls, and a big round keep smack in the middle of it. It was part of the barony of Ashford, one of David's vassals, and manned by a seasoned knight, Ridge du Bose, and his lovely daughter Victoria. In fact, Victoria had just returned from fostering at Lewes Castle in Sussex, so the party was as much an opportunity for the proud father to show off his grown daughter as much as it was for her birthday.

Arriving well after sun set, there were several houses already in attendance for the morrow's activities. The castle was open for the most part as the guests set up their encampments both in the bailey and outside of the walls, and already it was like one giant party as guests mingled at different campfires as the food and drink flowed. As Maddoc, Gerid, and the host of Canterbury soldiers set up their encampment just inside of the gatehouse, Adalind and Willow went in search of Victoria but were told she had retired for the night. Their disappointment faded as they found entertainment and food with several visiting houses, people they had known in their childhood who were now very glad to see them.

David, too, loosened up as the night progressed and he visited with several old friends and allies. Even as he chatted and drank, his mind kept wandering back to Maddoc as the man saw to the organization of their encampment. He was coming to think he'd been too harsh to judge Maddoc for his actions against du Burgh, knowing that the knight only had their best interests at heart.

After they had been at Shadoxhurst a couple of hours, David noticed that Adalind and Willow were sitting before the campfire of allies from Folkestone, and several young men were quite happily enjoying their company. Adalind had imbibed a little too much wine and was being her usually vivacious self, but the young knights were being overly flirtatious with her. It gave David the excuse he needed to find Maddoc and speak with him. He was weary of being angry with a man he looked upon as a son and was glad to find a reason to re-establish communication.

He found Maddoc dealing with a locked wagon wheel on one of the wagons he didn't want to bring in the first place. The smithy was having difficulty with the axel and had summoned Maddoc for assistance, mostly because Maddoc had the strength of a bull and was able to help the man manipulate the wheel. But David pulled Maddoc off the wagon, uttered a few words to him about his betrothed and her current social situation, and Maddoc was off like a flash in search of Adalind. David watched him go with a grin on his face.

Maddoc found Adalind surrounded by the young bucks and, without a word, took her hand and led her away. Adalind had no idea why he was upset with her because in her alcohol-hazed mind, the young men were focused on Willow, but Maddoc knew better. He stopped short of scolding her but made sure she knew that the young men were not, in fact, focused on Willow. Only a blind man would have paid more attention to Willow with Adalind's glorious beauty standing right next to her. And with that, he made his tipsy lady go to bed, but the situation only grew worse the next day.

It all started when the festivities started at noon. Ridge du Bose, a handsome and skilled older knight, had all manner of entertainment arranged for his daughter's celebration, including a tournament of sorts involving his guests. There were eleven houses attending and each house had at least two or more knights, so he solicited entrants from his guests, including Canterbury, and not only did Maddoc and Gerid enter the contest, but David did as well just for the fun of it. His wife was horrified, but David assured her he would be careful.

Adalind and Willow were thrilled at the competition, and Adalind had dressed carefully in her new garment. It was a glorious surcoat that, once secured upon her shapely frame, gave her the appearance of a goddess. She was luscious and curvy, something that did not go unnoticed by nearly every man in attendance. Maddoc felt rather like a dog guarding his bone as he escorted her to the makeshift field to the north side of Shadoxhurst where the guests were gathering for the first event. He was so proud he could burst, a sensation he'd never known in his life. It was alien and somewhat disorienting but wholly wonderful as he walked with Adalind on his arm. It was pride in something other than himself.

In fact, Adalind was so radiant and lovely that the gossip was flying fast and furious, and it flew straight to Victoria du Bose's ears. Young, lovely, silly, giggly and petty, Victoria's reaction was not entirely unexpected. When she was supposed to be the center of attention, it ended up being Adalind de Aston, and when Adalind made an appearance at the field and greeted Victoria for the first time, the claws were out.

"Victoria," Adalind said as she took the woman's hands and kissed her cheek. "It is so good to see you again. How lovely you look."

Victoria was indeed a pretty girl with brown eyes and long blond hair. She smiled thinly at Adalind. "And I see the rumors of your beauty were not exaggerated," she said, her gaze riveted to Adalind and all but ignoring Willow. "I have heard nothing but tales of your beauty since I have returned home. I must say, now that I see you, I understand the rumors."

Adalind could immediately sense an insult. It wasn't so much in the words but the way the woman spoke, the condescending tone in her voice. Her smile faded into a grimace.

"Whatever do you mean?" she asked.

Victoria shrugged, her gaze trailing down Adalind's stunning figure. "You are very beautiful, Adalind," she said. "Surely you know that."

"You are quite beautiful, also," Adalind replied, having difficulty with her temper. "Surely you know *that*."

Victoria laughed rudely. "'Tis not I who has every man's attention today," she said, her tone growing nasty. "They are all looking at you in that rather revealing coat, but I am sure you planned it that way. How dare you turn all attention to you."

Adalind was flabbergasted at the attitude. "I have done no such thing," she said hotly. "Why do you say such terrible things to me? I thought we were friends, Victoria."

Victoria turned her nose up. "We were until you tried to outshine me at my party."

Adalind's outrage cooled. The same thing had had happened at Winchester was happening here and she could hardly believe it. She was stunned.

"It was never my intent to outshine you," she said, lowering her voice. "It was my intent to wish you a blessed celebration but I see that I am wasting my breath. I had no idea that your years at Lewes had taught you that blatant envy is good manners and that offending someone who has done nothing to deserve it makes you a fine hostess. Since it seems that the only conversation you wish to have is one full of insults, I will wish you a good day and be done with it."

With that she strolled away, leaving Willow sputtering at the turn in conversation. But Adalind kept walking, heading towards the edge of the makeshift lists where she could see Maddoc and Gerid as they prepared for the upcoming contest. She marched right up to Maddoc and by the time he looked up from fixing one of the straps on his breastplate, he was faced with a teary-eyed lady.

"I want to go home," Adalind hissed, wiping furiously at her eyes. "I do not want to be here. Will you please take me home?"

He was very concerned. "What has happened?" he asked gently, his hands comfortingly holding her arms. "Why do you weep?"

Adalind was trying to speak without sobbing but it was difficult. "Victoria is upset because she feels that I have dressed provocatively and now all men are looking at me when they should be looking at her," she sniffled. "She was rude and insulting, and I do not want to be here any longer. I want to go home."

Maddoc grunted softly with both disbelief and sympathy, looking over her shoulder to see Willow and Lady Victoria in the distance. It looked to him as if the conversation was growing heated.

"Your dress is lovely and I would be the first person to make you wear something different if I thought it was even remotely provocative," he said softly. "Do not let her jealousy hurt you so."

She frowned deeply and the tears surged. "You cannot say that to me," she hissed. "I spent five years dealing with petty jealousies and this is the last place I expected to find them again. You have no idea what it was like."

She was starting to get agitated so he hastened to soothe her. "You are correct; I do not," he said, collecting her hand and turning to Gerid. "Lady Adalind and I are going for a walk. I will return shortly."

Gerid wasn't oblivious to their conversation, nor to what had been transpiring between them in general. In fact, it was becoming common knowledge at Canterbury now because de Lohr wasn't making any attempt to hide it. Moreover, du Bois had disappeared for several days and dark rumors were about as to the reasons for his absence. He had fled with the four visiting warriors in the middle of the night and had returned days later, exhausted and filthy. Some said that de Lohr had sent him on a mission of vengeance involving Adalind, but no one knew for certain. Whatever the reason, things were different with du Bois now. The man had changed.

Maddoc took Adalind away from the temporary field, holding her elbow as they strolled past people who were heading for the spectacle. A few competing knights passed them by, looking at the heavily armored Maddoc curiously as he headed in the opposite direction. But he ignored the stares, instead, focused on Adalind as they walked through the very green and very wet grass. Her fine slippers were getting wet but he couldn't pick her up because his armor was in the way. When they came to an old, rotted stump near the giant curtain wall, he lifted her up on to it to get her out of the wet.

"Now," he said, looking her in the eye. "I have also heard the gossip this morning, men speaking in hushed tones about you. All I have heard is how you are a treat for the eyes but nothing more. Whatever Victoria brought up to hurt your feelings was fed by petty jealousy and I understand you are weary of such things. However, we cannot simply make it stop. People have a tendency to be cruel when faced with something as bright and shining as you because they feel inadequate. No one can compete with you, sweetheart. You must understand this so you will not be dissolved to tears every time it happens. Take it as a compliment, understand your worth, and do not let it disturb you. Will you at least try?"

He was so wise and rational. Adalind had stopped crying by the time he finished, her red-rimmed eyes now gleaming with something he'd never seen before. There was joy and adoration and appreciation in the green depths.

"You are right," she said softly. "I should not let words bother me so. I suppose I am very sensitive to them because at Winchester, words were usually accompanied by some manner of humiliating action."

He shook his head firmly. "No longer," he said softly, moving towards her and taking her hands in his big mailed gloves. "No one will touch you again, I swear it. Man or woman, I will punish them. Do you believe me?"

"Of course I do."

"Then you will no longer be upset by incidents such as this. Know that none of it matters because you have my complete attention and adoration. Nothing can hurt you ever again."

She sighed dreamily, a smile coming to her lips. "Do you know I have waited my entire life to hear those words from you?"

He grinned in return. Then, he kissed her hands, sweetly, but that wasn't good enough so he kissed her mouth as well. Standing on the stump, she was nearly at eye level with him and it didn't take long before her arms went around his neck and he wrapped his big arms around her body. It was as much a spectacle as either one of them had ever made, but they didn't care; lost in a heated kiss, scents and sensations and tastes consumed them.

"Maddoc!"

The shout disrupted what was a decidedly heated kiss and Maddoc's head snapped around to see David approaching. The man did not look pleased.

"Maddoc, let her go," he snapped quietly, complete with separating hand gestures. "You know better than to take advantage of her in public."

"I am to blame, Papa," Adalind leapt to Maddoc's defense as he lifted her off the stump and put her on her feet. "I made him kiss me. I told him I would never speak to him again if he did not."

David scowled at her, letting her know just what he thought of her foolish explanation. "Next time, I throw a bucket of water on you both," he grumbled, pointing in the direction of the event field. "Go, Maddoc. I will escort Adalind to the field."

Adalind clung to Maddoc's arm. "Nay, Papa," she said. "I want to walk with Maddoc, not my aged though still-handsome grandfather. I am sure you understand how humiliating it would be for me."

David was trying not to grin because she was being rather charming with him, trying to soften him. "You little snippit," he rumbled. "Do as I say or I shall swat your behind. Let him go so he can go compete. They are about to start."

Her eyebrows flew up and she let go of Maddoc, giving him a shove towards the field for good measure. "Hurry, then," she told him. "Do not so much as show your face to me again if you do not beat every one of those fools. I will accept nothing less than complete domination and victory."

Maddoc grinned lazily as she continued to push. "For you, my lady, I will smite my foes and lay their heads at your feet."

She stopped pushing and made a distasteful face. "Seems a little severe to me, but if you must." She winked at him as she took David's arm. "Go, my beautiful boy. I will watch you with great pride."

His grin turned real and he bowed gallantly as he turned for the field. "I shall endeavor not to shame you."

"See that you do not."

He laughed softly as he headed off for the event area at a slow jog. Mail jingled and creaked as Adalind and David watched him go. When he was well out of earshot, Adalind sighed happily, gaze lingering on him, before turning to David.

"Would you really throw water on me?" she asked.

He cocked an eyebrow as she wrapped her hands around his forearm rather manipulatively.

"Well," he said reluctantly, "perhaps not you, but definitely him. He knows better than to make such a spectacle."

"But we are in love. Why can we not shout it to the world?"

"Has he told you he loves you?"

She shook her head. "He said he adored me. I can live on that for the rest of my life."

David couldn't help the chuckle as they headed towards the field and sounds of the coming event. Women in love were odd creatures, indeed.

***

The first event of the day was a mêlée, a competition where two teams of opposing knights would face off against each other until the last man standing. Instead of swords they had clubs, and once a man was down he was not allowed to get up again. Any blow was fair, including those to the face and groin, so after the event marshals explained the rules, they tossed a yellow flag into the air and when it hit the ground, the men went at each other to the roar of the crowd.

Since David was the highest ranking nobleman in attendance, it was his team against Ridge du Bose's team, and David was in command of his team. When the flag fell, Maddoc charged forward with the club poised over his left shoulder, as his left hand was his dominate hand, and began swinging it in several calculated strikes. Men fell at his feet in rapid succession as the spectators cheered.

Standing at the edge of the field since the very small lists were for Victoria and her family, Adalind and Willow were cheering like mad. Every time Maddoc would fell a man, Adalind screamed his name. The pair of them jumped up and down eagerly, causing Christina and Emilie to laugh at their enthusiasm. Watching them was more fun than watching what was happening on the field. But that all changed when David went down only a few minutes into the fight. Then, the mood decidedly dampened.

For an elderly man, David was still very spry and very skilled, but with his reflexes diminished from age, he was no real match for the younger and stronger knights. When he went down, Maddoc beat his way through a couple of men to make it to his side, slinging David over his big shoulder and fighting his way to the edge of the field to get him out of the line of fire.

Emilie and Christina were waiting for him and took David gently as Maddoc carefully unloaded the man. But as he did so, he was hit from behind by a pair of fairly large knights, causing him to lurch forward and plow a big shoulder into Adalind. As she fell to her bum, Maddoc furiously turned to the pair that had attacked him and plowed into them with his fists.

Blood splattered as Maddoc's enormous hands did severe damage. One man fell almost immediately while the other put up more of a fight. Adalind watched with terror and fascination, picking herself up off the ground, as Maddoc's fury was unleashed. It was truly a sight to behold. She didn't even notice that her mother and grandmother, plus a host of Canterbury men, had carried David away. The only thing she was aware of was Maddoc and his unearthly strength and skill as he battered the second man to a bloody pulp. Even after the man finally went down, Maddoc gave him a swift kick in the kidneys for good measure. Then he turned to Adalind, somewhat out of breath. Beating arse the way he did was something of an exertion.

"Are you all right?" he asked.

She nodded, her eyes wide with surprise and perhaps some realization as to Maddoc's true capabilities.

"I am well," she assured him. "You did not hurt me."

Satisfied with her answer, he winked at her as he turned back for the field, collecting his club, which had fallen to the ground, as he went along. As Adalind watched, he jumped back into the fray, pounding man with either fists or club. Blood spurted, men fell, and the crowd went mad with approval. It was a gory bit of fun.

The mêlée actually took a few hours. It wasn't an easy game, nor was it quick. It was quite brutal. There was a good deal of blood and broken bones, split scalps and the like. Since David was out of commission, Maddoc took charge and corralled the earl's team into a circle, and that circle was making its way slowly through the battle and destroying men as they went.

Every knight in Maddoc's circle was back to back with another knight so they covered each other from the rear and formed an unbreakable bond. It was classic warfare tactics, now employed to ensure Canterbury's team emerged the victor. All went well until two hours into the fight when a new and fresh knight was introduced.

That's when things started to change.

Universal joy, universal sorrow, universal life.

CHAPTER ELEVEN

The field marshals had allowed the new knight to enter at Victoria's insistence. The man had arrived late to the festivities and had very much wanted to compete in the battle. Usually, late entrants were not allowed but Victoria begged enough so that her father forced the marshals to make an exception.

The fresh knight was dangerous against the weary ones, and began destroying everything in his path. The crowd, smelling blood, got in behind the newest arrival with their cheering. New life was breathed into the waning event.

The first thing the knight did was go after Maddoc's circle. Adalind and Willow, no longer jumping and screaming but standing wearily on the sidelines, noticed the unfamiliar knight from the onset. He was very big, with expensive armor, and he went straight for Maddoc the moment he entered the field. Maddoc, having survived two hours of battle, was on the defense as the knight swung the club at his head.

It was a nasty fight from the inception and Maddoc's circle began to get pummeled from all sides by other combatants now that Maddoc was distracted. Maddoc's reflexes were cat-like as he countered the fresh knight's attack and, soon enough, he began to retaliate. As his weary circle began to crumble, Maddoc broke ranks because he had no choice. The new knight was attacking him as if he had a personal vendetta against him, so Maddoc's tactics changed. To hell with the group; now he was out for himself.

Maddoc's stamina was strong. He went after the knight with a vengeance, pummeling him so hard with his club that he eventually knocked the knight's weapon out of his grip. As it clamored to the dirt, the knight balled his fist and slugged Maddoc in the neck. Maddoc staggered back and inadvertently dropped his club. The club had no sooner hit the ground when Maddoc threw two punches at the knight, in rapid succession, and knocked the man off balance so decidedly that he ended up on one knee. Seeing his opponent on the ground fed his frenzy and Maddoc pounced, grabbing the knight around the neck and pummeling him with a deadly fist on the side of the head.

Somehow, the knight didn't go down completely. He was big and strong, and managed to sweep Maddoc's legs out from under him before Maddoc could knock him unconscious. Maddoc fell heavily on his left side but rolled out of the way before the knight could leap on top of him. Then Maddoc rolled to his knees and grabbed the man around the neck again, shoving him face-first into the once-green grass that had now become a mud pit.

It was clear that Maddoc intended to hold the man's face in the mud until he passed out. But the knight somehow managed to dislodge Maddoc's grip, bringing up and elbow and smashing Maddoc in the side of the head. Even though he had his helm on, the blow dazed him and Maddoc fell onto his side, his ears ringing and stars before his eyes. But he wasn't senseless and as the knight, who was now showing distinct signs of exhaustion, moved to pounce once more, Maddoc brought up a massive foot and kicked the man right in the groin. He fell like a stone.

It had been a particularly brutal and nasty fight. Since Maddoc was on the ground he could not get up again per the rules of the event, so he lay there as the last of the mêlée dwindled down around him. He watched Gerid take on two men who were determined to send him to the dirt, but Gerid held fast. He was strong and steady, and three hours after the mêlée had started, Gerid finally emerged the winner.

The moment his victory was announced and the crowd cheered wildly, Adalind dashed onto the muddy, bloody field and ran straight to Maddoc. "Maddoc!" she cried, skirts hiked up as she raced through the muck. *"Maddoc!"*

He heard her coming, sitting up as he wearily pulled his helm off. His ears were still ringing and his head was throbbing. He turned to Adalind just as she fell to her knees beside him.

"Are you all right?" she asked anxiously, her hands on his shoulder, his arm. "Are you hurt?"

Maddoc shook his head. "I am not injured," he replied. Then he realized she was kneeling in the muddy mess and he labored to his feet, pulling her up with him. "Get off the ground, sweetheart. You will soil that beautiful garment."

Adalind still wasn't over the abject terror she'd felt since the moment she saw Maddoc and the new knight in mortal combat. When they both fell to the ground, it was all she could do not to run out on the field. She was convinced Maddoc was badly injured, waiting anxiously until the event was declared over so she could rush to his side.

"Are you sure you are well?" she pressed even as he pulled her to her feet. "You are not injured?"

He shook his head, his exhausted eyes glimmering at her. "I am not injured," he assured her. "You need not worry yourself so but I am grateful for the concern."

She frowned. "Of course I will worry," she snapped softly. "I saw you and that knight and... he hit you so hard. It seemed as if he was furious with you. Who *is* he?"

Maddoc turned in the direction of his worthy opponent, who had struggled to his feet and was now exhaustedly unlatching his muddy helm. The blow to the groin had the man hunched over somewhat. Maddoc's eyes narrowed at him.

"I do not know," he admitted. "But I intend to find out."

Both Maddoc and Adalind were looking at the knight when the helm finally came off. His blond hair was close cropped and as he turned in their direction, they could see his square-jawed, rather handsome appearance. His blue eyed gaze lingered on Maddoc a moment, perhaps with some interest as well as respect, before focusing on Adalind.

"Lady Adalind," he greeted rather gallantly. "You are looking as lovely as ever."

Adalind's eyes widened and her jaw dropped. "*Brighton?*" she ventured. "Brighton de Royans?"

Sir Brighton de Royans grinned, displaying straight white teeth and big dimples in his cheeks.

"So you do remember me?" he said. "You had better. My sister is your best friend and I will never forgive you if you do not recollect me."

Adalind was torn between shock, outrage, and some pleasure at his appearance. "Of course I know you," she said. "Where on earth did you come from? Is Glennie with you?"

Brighton shook his head and took a few exhausted steps in her direction. "Alas, no," he replied. "My sister is at home and I have come today because I was invited. Lady Victoria's older brother is a friend of mine."

Adalind realized she was rather pleased to see the man, although she was not pleased at what he had done to Maddoc. In fact, she remembered that she was still holding on to Maddoc with a death grip and she turned to look at him as if to explain her familiarity with someone who had tried to do him some damage.

"Sir Brighton is Glennie de Royan's brother," she explained. "She was my very best and only friend at Winchester. He serves Norfolk."

Brighton heard her, nodding as she divulged the information. "I am now a ranking knight in Norfolk's army," he said rather proudly, his gaze moving to Maddoc as he rubbed his lower abdomen, "and you, my lord, are a formidable foe. I am somewhat regretting my attempt to defeat you."

He had a rather friendly personality, his eyes twinkling with the mirth of the situation. Maddoc, however, wasn't a particularly outgoing or friendly individual so he responded somewhat formally. More than that, he didn't like the way the man looked at Adalind. Pure and rank jealousy was beginning to rise in his chest.

"I thought perhaps I had unknowingly wronged you and you were out for vengeance," Maddoc said. "You are formidable as well."

Brighton shook his head. "I do not know you, my lord," he replied. "I simply looked for the leader of the biggest group and chose my target accordingly. But that arrogance cost me."

Adalind grinned because Brighton was truly comical the way he delivered the last sentence. She could see that he was attempting to ease the situation.

"You could not know that Maddoc du Bois is the one man in all of England that you cannot defeat," she said, gazing up at Maddoc fondly. "He is the greatest knight in the country."

Maddoc, who had been staring at Brighton and mentally sizing the man up, tore his gaze off of him to look at Adalind. Her expression softened his harsh stance.

"She speaks the truth," he said, his lips twitching with a smile. "She is as wise as she is beautiful."

"I would agree," Brighton said, aware of the soft and loving expressions between Adalind and Maddoc. "Since my sister and Lady Adalind have fostered together, I have, in a sense, watched her grow up. She has always been one of the less flighty and silly females I have known."

He was teasing her, winking at her with a grin, and Adalind giggled. "Thank you for your kind words, Brighton. How you must flatter the women with your smooth tongue."

She was jesting with him in return but before Brighton could reply, Maddoc interrupted. "I have known her since she was very young," he said, making sure that Brighton understood he had known her longer, and better. "She has always been an exceptional lady."

Brighton could sense that Maddoc was not pleased with his attempts to communicate with Adalind, perhaps sensing it as competition or, worse, flirtation. He had only just emerged from a battle with the man and was in no condition to enter in to another. As good a knight as he was, he knew from recent experience that Maddoc was a daunting opponent. Wisely, he changed the subject.

"Of that I have no doubt," he said, shifting focus. "Sir Maddoc, whom do you serve?"

"I am Canterbury's captain," Maddoc replied, not completely unaware that the man was trying to change the subject. "I have served de Lohr my entire life, as did my father."

Brighton nodded in understanding. "He is fortunate to have you, then," he said, eyeing the man a moment before finally extending his hand. He felt as if he had to. "I tried to best you today and was turned away. No hard feelings?"

Maddoc hesitated before slowly claiming the man's hand and shaking it, once. "None," he replied. "It made for an exciting battle."

"I nearly got my brains beat in."

"Had I not been so weary, you most certainly would have."

Brighton grinned. "Perhaps you will allow me to join your camp later for food and drink, Sir Maddoc. Perhaps you will allow me to make amends for our rough introduction."

"Did you come alone?" Adalind asked.

Brighton nodded as he looked at her. "I am heading to Gloucester on business from Norfolk," he said. "I knew that Victoria's celebration was happening this week so I took a detour to see her brother and to wish her well. Little did I know I would find you here."

Adalind smiled. "I am eager to hear of Glennie," she said. "It has been two months since last I saw her. The last we spoke, she was heading home with the hope that her father may have arranged a betrothal for her. Has this happened?"

Brighton wasn't oblivious to the fact that Maddoc was quite literally staring him down. More than that, he could feel the protectiveness and animosity radiating off the man every time he focused his attention on Adalind. He got the hint. So he did what any mannered knight would do; he deferred to the man who appeared to have the claim on the lady.

"If Sir Maddoc will be gracious enough to allow me to visit, then I will tell you all I can," he replied, "but you have seen my sister more recently than I. The last I saw of her was several months ago."

"Still, I would like to hear any news you may have heard." She turned to Maddoc hopefully. "Is it acceptable for Brighton to join us?"

Maddoc's gaze lingered on Brighton one last time, attempting to determine if the man had an ulterior motive for wanting to be near Adalind other than to discuss his sister. Given the record of the past several strangers that had been in Adalind's orbit, he was naturally suspicious and protective. But he graciously acquiesced to her request because it seemed to mean so much to her.

"If you wish it," he said, taking her hand. "We will see him tonight at the feast. For now, however, we must see how your grandfather is faring."

Adalind clutched him as he began to walk away. She waved at Brighton when she managed to free a hand from Maddoc's iron grasp.

"We will speak tonight," she said. "Until then!"

Brighton smiled weakly, lifting a hand as he watched them go. Mostly, he was looking at Adalind and her striking hourglass figure in her red surcoat. It was true that he had known her the past several years, watching her grow from a young girl into a young woman alongside his sister, and it was further true that he always thought she was quite lovely but far too young. At twenty years and eight, he had thought he was simply too old and prestigious for her. But now, he didn't think that any longer. He was coming to think he'd been an idiot. In fact, he knew it.

Maddoc du Bois notwithstanding, Brighton couldn't help his thoughts from lingering on beautiful and sweet Adalind de Aston.

The memories of all loves merging with this one love of ours –
And the songs of every poet past and forever.

CHAPTER TWELVE

David had not fared well after the mêlée. A blow to the head, followed by one to his back, had injured him fairly seriously. The attending physic thought he might have blood on his brain because his left ear was discharging some bloody fluid and his back was so painful that he couldn't stand or walk. More than just the usual bruises that came with such events, the Earl of Canterbury seemed to have suffered real damage.

His condition dampened the mood for the entire party from Canterbury. The celebration at Shadoxhurst was no longer fun but serious. Emilie and Christina stayed with David, tending him, while Maddoc conferred with the earl on what the man wanted to do next. It would do no good for him to remain, ill and injured, in a tent. They needed to get him home and Maddoc was trying to convince him of that. But David didn't want to spoil Adalind and Willow's fun, knowing how much they had looked forward to the festivities, so it came to the point where Maddoc brought Adalind to his bedside to speak to her grandfather and convince the old man it was in his best interest to go home.

It was slow going with the stubborn man. After much pleading on Adalind's part, David's best response was that he would think about returning home on the morrow. As dusk fell over the cool and shadowed land, David grew too exhausted to speak any longer and Maddoc pulled Adalind from the tent. She was distraught and worried over her grandfather, and Maddoc sought to provide her with some comfort. He felt rather bad for the way the day had ended.

A large fire was burning in the center of the Canterbury encampment, spitting sparks into the evening sky. Soldiers moved about as the enormous hindquarter of a cow, provided by their host, roast on an open spit. The smell of smoke and cooking beef was heavy in the air as Maddoc procured a cup of wine for Adalind. He set her down by the fire on a small leather and wood chair, collapsible, as she sipped on her drink. The mood was very somber.

"He is going to be all right, isn't he?" she gazed up at Maddoc with her bottomless green eyes. "The physic can heal him, can he not?"

Maddoc folded his enormous arms across his chest. "He shall recover," he assured her. "Your grandfather just needs time to heal, which is why we must take him home."

Adalind nodded in agreement, sipping at her wine as the physic, a small man with bushy white hair and a red beard that trailed to his waist, emerged from David's tent. He fumbled with his bag as he glanced up at Maddoc and Adalind.

"I have left instructions that he not sleep," he told them. "With a head injury, there is always the chance that he will not wake up again. He is to stay awake for the next several hours at least. His wife and daughter said they will see to it so there is nothing more I can do for now. I will be back in the morning but send for me if you need me."

Maddoc nodded his head as he reached into his tunic and pulled forth a few coins for the man. Paying the physic, he watched the little man fade away into the growing darkness. Then he returned his attention to Adalind.

"Since we will be here until at least tomorrow morning," he said, "perhaps you will allow me to escort you to the festivities in the great hall. The party should go on all night."

Adalind had been staring into the fire, her mind in the tent with her grandfather. Her gaze was distant, her expression pensive. When Maddoc spoke, she looked up at him.

"I am not sure," she said hesitantly. "It does not seem appropriate to celebrate while Papa is lying injured."

Maddoc cocked his head. "He would be the first person to demand you attend," he said. "Go and prepare yourself and I will escort you to the hall. Willow, too."

Adalind thought of her sister in their tent, upset with the turn of events and particularly upset over her exchange with Victoria after the woman's attack on Adalind. She sighed reluctantly.

"I am not sure she will want to attend," she said. "She and Victoria had an awful fight."

Maddoc had suspected as much, having seen the two argue earlier. "About you?"

Adalind nodded and hung her head. "Willow slapped her," she said, peering up at him. "Did you hear about that?"

Maddoc struggled not to grin. "I did not. It seems as if I missed a great deal while I was occupied in the mêlée today."

Adalind tried not to look too embarrassed or contrite. "In fairness to Willow, Victoria slapped her first when Willow called her a stupid fat cow. I suppose that provoked her."

Maddoc put a hand over his mouth so she wouldn't see his lips twitching. "I would imagine so."

"Victoria slapped her first and I suppose Willow did not slap her as much as she punched her."

"*Punched* her?"

"In the face. She said Victoria's nose was bleeding."

Maddoc couldn't help the chuckles as he shook his head. "Great Gods," he hissed. "No wonder she is hiding in the tent. I wondered why she was in there and not begging to attend the party."

"Now you know."

Maddoc couldn't help the grin as he thought of Victoria slapping Willow in a huff and Willow, who was a fairly tall and rather solid girl, punching her in return. He would have liked to have seen it. Better entertainment than the mêlée as far as he was concerned. But he pushed past all of that, focusing on the enticement of escorting Adalind to a celebration where he could spend time enjoying her and perhaps even dancing with her. He hadn't danced in years but he was willing to do it, just for the night. The allure of holding her in his arms was almost more than he could bear. He reached down and pulled the half-empty cup of wine out of her hand.

"Go now," he said, gently grasping her arm and pulling her to stand. "Go and prepare for the celebration and tell your ruffian sister to do the same. I will escort you both."

Adalind was still uncertain. "But what if she does not want to go?"

"Then tell her I will carry her into the hall if I have to."

Adalind knew he would, too. As she thought on attending the celebration on Maddoc's arm, a smile played on her lips. It brought back so many memories of events past where she could only watch him from afar. Tonight, she would not have to watch him. She would be *with* him.

"I can remember many celebrations or events in days gone by when you would escort my family," she said. "I can remember specifically a celebration at Rochester Castle. It was for a Christmas feast, I believe, and I must have been nine or ten years of age. Do you remember that trip? It was snowing and very cold, but once we reached Rochester, the feast went on for three days. It was the last time I saw my father healthy, I think."

Maddoc nodded as he recollected the event, thinking on quiet and scholarly Merric de Aston. He'd not thought of the man in years. Tall, blond, rather slender but physically strong, Merric had never enjoyed the best of health. He always had something wrong with him. The trip to Rochester in the snow had caused the man to develop a lung infection from which he had never recovered.

"I recall," he said softly. "He passed away in the summer following that trip."

Adalind thought on her father, a man she had loved a great deal, but the memories didn't bring tears like they used to. Now she remembered him warmly, with bittersweet tidings. She smiled as she recollected the trip to Rochester.

"I remember watching him dance with my mother and thinking that I had never seen him dance before," she said. "I remember watching you dance, too, and I was so terribly jealous of the young women in your arms. I remember them fighting over you."

He chuckled, embarrassed. "I did not want to dance at all but your grandfather forced me to. He said I needed to be social. I hate dancing."

She grinned. "Will you dance with me tonight, then?"

"You will have me all to yourself."

"Promise?" she whispered hopefully.

His mirth faded, his eyes glimmering intensely at her. "I do," he said softly. "You will have me all to yourself forever."

"Are you still sure you want to marry me?"

"More than ever."

"Tell me again."

His smile returned and he went to her, wrapping his arms around her even though David had warned him about such displays. He couldn't help it.

"I wish to marry you," he murmured, kissing her tenderly on the forehead and feeling her tremble. "I was a fool to have resisted you for so long. How much longer must I continue to tell you the same thing over and over?"

"Until I no longer believe I am dreaming."

"Do you still?"

She nodded, looking up at him with adulation in her eyes. She was wrapped up in his arms, her heart beating a mile a minute, thumping against her ribs. She finally let out a ragged sigh, dragging her index finger across his bottom lip.

"I am still having difficulty believing that my hopes and wishes have finally come true," she murmured, watching him kiss her finger. "I swear I will be a good wife to you, Maddoc. I promise I will be gracious and kind and obedient, and I will love you the rest of my life as no woman has ever loved a man. I belong to you now as I have always belonged to you and I will worship you the only way I know how – with unbridled passion and enthusiasm and hope. I hope for so much for us, my handsome lad. So very much."

He was warmed by her words, feeling her sincerity as if she had seared it into his heart. He pulled her tighter.

"I had no idea how fortunate I was until this very moment," he whispered. "To have your love, Addie, fills me like nothing I have ever known. I had no idea what I was missing until you came back into my life and now that you are here, I want to live in this moment with you forever. I am not a man of great words but I can tell you what is in my heart, and my heart tells me that I am truly blessed. Thank you for being patient all of these years and for never giving up hope in a future for us. Your strength of faith is the most powerful thing I have ever witnessed."

Deeply touched, Adalind laid her head against his chest, hearing his heart beating strong and steady in her ear. The feel of him, the warmth of him, was heavenly.

"You know you have my heart, Maddoc," she said softly. "Perhaps someday I shall have yours."

He chuckled softly. "What makes you think that you do not already?" he said, hugging her tightly. "As I said, words do not come easy for me and emotions are even more difficult. But know... know that my heart belongs to you. Can you not feel it?"

She lifted her head, gazing up at him, her eyes full of adoration. "I feel it," she murmured, putting a hand on his chest. "And I hear it. I hear it strongly and steadily."

Maddoc didn't want to talk anymore; he only wanted to kiss her. Dipping his head, his mouth slanted hungrily over hers, feeling her respond ferociously. As the fire blazed a few feet away, Maddoc lost himself in the most powerful kiss he'd ever known, wishing he could simply take her to her tent, kick the sister out into the elements, and have his way with her.

His emotions were running wild and, as he suckled her lower lip, he began to realize there was no private place for them to go. If he didn't remove himself from her this instance, he would be creating a spectacle for the gossips that seemed to be so fond of Adalind as a subject. He didn't want to contribute to that misery for her, even if they were betrothed. But until the formal announcement was made, for all anyone knew, Adalind was simply letting him have his way with her. With a final and lingeringly sweet suckle, he let her go.

"Go now and prepare," he said huskily. "I shall return for you and Willow in a short time."

Breathless, Adalind nodded unsteadily as she licked her lips, tasting Maddoc. She was coming to crave that musky flavor.

"I will try and convince her," she said, struggling to collect her wits as she turned for the tent several yards away. "I cannot promise success, but I will try."

Maddoc watched her go, winking at her when she turned around to look at him again. She simply smiled, that beautiful smile he was coming to cherish. He'd seen the gesture his entire life but it meant more now to him than he could comprehend. When she eventually disappeared into the heavy canvas tent that housed her sister and mother as well, Maddoc went back to check on David before heading to his own shelter.

He was aware that he wanted to clean up and be presentable for Adalind. Perhaps he might even shave. As he dug out his clothing from his traveling satchel, he further realized that his thoughts were rolling quickly and all of them seemed to revolve around Adalind. He was excited for the evening at hand, thrilled to be spending it with Adalind, and thought perhaps he might convince David to announce their betrothal that night. He was thinking many different things. Then he came to halt; *Great Gods*, he thought, *I am giddy. Have I actually become what I have professed to hate? A man who would make a fool out of himself over a woman?*

When Gerid entered the tent several minutes later, it was to Maddoc shaving and whistling a tune. Gerid had never heard Maddoc whistled like that. Given the fact that the man had on a clean tunic and was washing up, Gerid figured out what had the man so happy. He'd heard about men in love but he'd never seen one before. He suspected he was seeing one now.

When he ventured to tease Maddoc on the subject, Maddoc hit him in the chest so hard that Gerid fell backwards, hit the support post, and collapsed the entire tent.

***

It took Maddoc, Adalind, and Gerid to escort Willow to the great hall of Shadoxhurst where a loud and exciting party was taking place. Willow was literally dragging her feet, fearful of showing her face at Victoria's celebration, but Maddoc assured her that their skirmish would be forgotten. Still, Willow wasn't so inclined to charge on in to the party like a conquering hero. She tucked in behind Adalind as they entered the warm, smoky hall.

Adalind had her hand draped through Maddoc's elbow, holding him tightly as they ventured into the room. It was an enormous place with a vaulted ceiling and great beams supporting the thatched roof. It was also an older style hall with the fire pit in the center of the room as smoke escaped upwards and exited through a hole in the ceiling. The giant fire made the room very warm, stinking of burnt meat and fresh rushes, and the room itself was stuffed with guests enjoying a feast.

A page escorted their little group to a table that was already full of guests. Maddoc cleared away space on the over-crowded bench for

Adalind and Willow to sit, but he and Gerid remained standing because there simply wasn't enough room. Along with the large dining table where Victoria and her family and a host of close friends sat, there were at least eight other hastily built tables to accommodate the guests, but there were more guests than tables, so many of the men were left standing.

This included Brighton de Royans. He had been in conversation with another knight near the fire pit but when he saw Maddoc and his party enter, he casually made his way in their direction.

His focus was on Adalind in a deep gold surcoat that displayed her ravishing curves, something he found he couldn't keep his eyes off of. It was fashionable for women, especially courtly women, to be slender and rather flat-chested, as they used odd corsets that concealed their figures, but there was no corset in the world that could conceal Adalind's luscious figure.

The woman looked like a goddess and as he approached the table where she sat with her tall, blond sister, he forced himself to look away lest du Bois take offense. Already, the man was on edge around him. Already, the lines were drawn between them and it was only going to get worse. Brighton had done a lot of thinking that afternoon about Lady Adalind, and he had done a lot of planning. It was time to put that plan into action.

"My lord," he greeted Maddoc and Gerid first before bowing gallantly to the ladies. "My ladies, your beauty puts all other women in this room to shame."

Willow perked up at the sight of Brighton. He was handsome and friendly. She had seen him at the field earlier after he and Maddoc had made peace, but she hadn't thought to ask about him. She had been preoccupied with her conflict with Victoria. But now, she was quite appropriately focused on the handsome knight. As she blushed demurely, Adalind beamed.

"Again with your smooth tongue," she said. "You are going to swell my head, Brighton. Now, I want you to sit down and tell me everything you know about your sister over the past few months."

Brighton was wise to the protocol when dealing with Adalind; he'd learned well at their afternoon encounter. He looked at Maddoc.

"May I sit, my lord?" he asked.

Maddoc was standing directly behind Adalind, a great hulking and protective presence, and his gaze was most decidedly on Brighton. But he nodded graciously and Brighton shoved a male guest down the bench to clear a space, crashing the unfortunate guest into the woman next to him, who in turn plowed into another woman. All down the bench, people were shoved as a result of Brighton until the man at the far end slid right off onto the floor. Adalind and Willow burst into giggles as Brighton claimed his spot.

"Now," Brighton said, claiming an ownerless cup of wine. "Who is this lovely woman beside you, Adalind. You must introduce us."

Adalind grinned at her sister. "This is the Lady Willow de Aston, my sister," she said. "Willow, this is Sir Brighton de Royans. His sister, Glennie, was my very best friend at Winchester Castle."

Willow put on a good act of being properly modest and shy. She batted her eyelashes fittingly. "Sir Brighton," she said sweetly. "It is an honor to meet you."

Brighton flashed his dimples at her. "And you, my lady," he replied. "I see that all of the de Aston women have astounding beauty." As Willow giggled and averted her gaze, Brighton focused on Adalind. "In answer to your inquiries, the last I heard from my sister about a month ago. She sent word to me about a feast to be given in honor of her returning from Winchester and she wanted to know if I would be attending."

"A feast?" Adalind repeated. "Will you be going?"

Brighton shook his head. "Netherghyll Castle is too far to the north and I have no time for such things," he said. "Did Glennie tell you all about Netherghyll? We were both born there, you know, although I was already fostering by the time she was born. I was around ten years of age. In fact, Glennie and I have never spent more than a few weeks together in our lives. She is my baby sister but we did not grow up together, unfortunately."

"That is sad," Adalind said. "It is sad that you had to grow up without your family. I grew up with my sister and also with Sir Maddoc. I was around six years of age when we came to live with my grandfather at Canterbury Castle. My father's home, Oakley Manor, was destroyed by fire and we had nowhere else to go, so we went to live at Canterbury. Maddoc was a young knight of twenty when I first met him. I remember telling my mother that I would marry him someday."

Brighton's grinning gaze moved between Adalind and Maddoc. "And how has your master plan worked out so far?"

Adalind laughed softly. "We are betrothed."

"Formally?"

She shrugged. "Papa has not announced it yet, but he will. He has given Maddoc his consent to court me."

Brighton's gaze lingered on her a moment before shifting his focus to Maddoc. One could nearly feel his curiosity in the air; it bordered on challenge. "Did you always know you would marry her, Sir Maddoc?" he asked, his tone not belying his thoughts. "Surely there were times when it crossed your mind."

Maddoc's intense gaze was riveted to him, watching him. It was scrutiny in its most penetrating form. After a moment, he looked away.

"I did not," he replied, seeming to find interest in the rest of the room. "She would follow me around constantly and it was all I could do to get away from her. Things have changed considerably."

Brighton's focus lingered on Maddoc a moment before returning his attention to Adalind. "You are a fortunate man," he said. "I envy you your good fortune. Perhaps I shall be so blessed one day."

"Do you have anyone in mind?" Adalind wanted to know. "Is there a special lady somewhere that has your interest?"

He shrugged coyly. "I was going to plead for your hand but I see that Sir Maddoc has beaten me to it."

She thought he was teasing her and she laughed. "It would not have done you any good if you had," she said. "There has only been Maddoc in my heart as long as I can recall. However, my sister is not spoken for. Perhaps she would accept your suit."

Willow blushed furiously, thrilled that her sister had suggested her to the handsome knight, but Brighton found himself in an awkward situation that could go very bad very quickly if he didn't handle it tactfully. The truth was that he hadn't been jesting about offering for her hand and was testing the waters, so to speak, but her response had him rethinking his tactics. It was a dangerous game he was embarking on with du Bois around, but before he could reply, Maddoc interrupted.

"Come," he said, pulling Adalind up from the bench. "Let us dance."

Adalind looked up at him, surprised, as he practically hauled her to her feet. "But we have not yet eaten," she said. "Are you not hungry?"

"Nay."

He lifted her over the bench and took her hand, pulling her towards the big area to the west of the fire pit where guests were collecting for the next dance. Gerid, interested in the lovely women looking for dance partners, followed them and lost himself in the crowd. The hall didn't have a second floor gallery so the minstrels, eight of them on different instruments, sat against the western wall with a leader that dressed much like a mummer in brightly colored silks. He played a flute of some kind and happily encouraged people to dance.

A rondelet was preparing, or a certain type of dance where dancers formed a circle and held hands until they broke into couples to complete the reel. Maddoc positioned her in the circle and took her hand as other dancers joined up and held hands as well. Maddoc scrutinized anyone of the male sex who tried to hold Adalind's other hand, so much so that the man who ended up holding it switched places with his female partner so she ended up holding Adalind's hand. All the while, Adalind was watching Maddoc very carefully.

"Why do you wish to dance?" she leaned in his direction.

He wouldn't look at her. "Why not?"

"Because we only just arrived and have not eaten yet. I am hungry."

He sighed heavily but still wouldn't look at her. "Is it not enough that I wanted to dance with you? Must you know every reason why?"

Adalind wasn't foolish. She suspected why. "You do not like Brighton, do you?"

"I could not know what you mean."

"Aye, you do. You do not like him."

He knew he couldn't get around it. She was too sharp. The corners of his mouth twitched. "If you must know, I do not like the way he looks at you."

"He looks at me as the friend of his sister."

"He looks at you as a man looks at a beautiful woman."

"You did not have to give him permission to sit."

He did look at her, then, with a droll expression that suggested he knew better. "You wanted to hear of your friend," he said. "How would you have reacted if I told him he was unwelcome? You would have kicked me in the shins."

Adalind fought off a grin. "Maddoc, I do believe you are jealous."

He looked away. "Call it what you will," he said. "But I do not like the way the man looks at you and wanted to remove you from his company. Perhaps now he is conversing his fill with Willow and will soon leave us and seek his entertainment elsewhere."

The music began, cleaving further conversation between them. As the smoke lingered in the air overhead and the heavy smell of roasting meat and body odor filled their nostrils, the dancers began to skip in a circle in beat to the music. There were two circles, one within the other, and they shifted direction in time. Eventually, the couples paired off and Maddoc had the pleasure of whirling Adalind in a series of intricate steps, his hands grasping hers, always touching as the music played.

It was magical, sweet, something that he never imagined to experience with something as foolish as dancing. Truth was that he had never even been a casual dancer and, as he had told Adalind, only participating in the event when forced. But at this moment, he was coming to think he'd been ridiculous for resisting something as sweet and sensual as dancing, at least where Adalind was concerned. He could touch her, greedily, for all to see and it was perfectly acceptable.

Adalind was feeling much the same way as Maddoc. His bright blue eyes never left her, his warm fingers around her hands, and he would twirl her hard enough to send her off balance and then smile when she would giggle uncontrollably. There were times she would pass close to him and she could feel his face in the top of her head or the brush of his other hand as if holding her with one hand was not enough. He had to touch her with two. It made her tremble, his close proximity and searing presence, and she was coming to think that she wasn't hungry any longer. Food was such an unnecessary thing when she could dance with Maddoc forever.

Towards the end of the reel, the couples passed within close proximity of each other, so close that Adalind ended up pressed against Maddoc's torso, her back to his chest, while one of his big arms was wrapped around her. It was too much, too close, and she began to grow quite breathless. I had nothing to do with exertion and everything to do with attraction. She'd always loved the man, God knows she had, but now there was something more than simply the dreamy ideals of a young girl. Now, there was physical element to it that his heated kisses had ignited. The moment Maddoc gently spun her around to face him, she cupped his big face between her hands and slanted her soft mouth over his.

The middle of the dance floor was no place for so lusty a kiss, but neither one of them could control it. The reel dwindled down around them as Adalind and Maddoc stood in the center of the dancers, tasting of one another deeply. Maddoc regained the last threads of his senses and broke away, pulling her off the dance floor with him and making haste for an alcove that had a narrow, angled passageway that dead-ended in a privy. It would become a private haven for their purposes.

The angle of the passage was enough so they could not be seen easily from the main hall; in fact, they were quite shielded in the dark and private corridor. Once Maddoc realized they were far enough away from prying eyes, he backed Adalind against the dim and shadowed wall and let go his self-control. She fed his senses, in every sense of the word, and he was without a shred of inhibition as he began to ravage her with his mouth. There was no more time for talking or dancing. Now was the time to dig deeper, touch deeper, than ever before.

Adalind gasped as Maddoc's heated kisses came fast and furious. He was sucking the life right of her but she was willingly allowing it, relishing every touch and taste. She was finished thinking all of this was a dream; she knew for certain, as he suckled her tongue as if it was the most delicious morsel, that what existed between them was real and solid and deep.

Adalind wasn't entirely naïve to the intimate relationships between men and women but her education on that particular subject had come from the halls of Winchester where the lines of fact and fiction were often crossed. But she knew that, eventually, the man she married would have rights over her body. When Maddoc's hand drifted to the swell of her bosom and lingered there a moment before pulling away, she thought that was an odd thing for him to do. She belonged to him, utterly and completely, and he knew it. Why did he not take what belonged to him? She therefore took his hand and placed it firmly over her left breast.

"You may touch me however you wish," she murmured between heated kisses. "From the beginning of Time I have belonged to you and until the end of the world, I will be yours. You may touch me in any fashion you wish and taste what belongs to you. I will not stop you."

He stopped kissing her long enough to look her in the eye, great passion and great indecision in his expression.

"My sweet girl," he cupped her face with his left hand because his right hand was still on her breast. "I understand and appreciate what you are saying, but the fact remains that I should not take more liberties than I already am. In fact, I should not be doing anything at all. If your grandfather found out...."

She kissed him, suckling his lips fiercely to quiet him. "He has agreed to a betrothal," she murmured. "In that sense, I belong to you, but in my heart, I have always belonged to you. You *know* this, Maddoc. You are to be my husband and I beg you to show me a taste of the joy I will know for the rest of my life."

He stared at her a moment before his right hand, very slowly and gently, squeezed her right breast. He watched as Adalind closed her eyes, feeling his touch upon her, gasping when he ran his fingers across a puckered nipple that strained against the fabric. When he pinched it, she cried out softly and he covered her mouth with his, absorbing her gasps of awakening desire as he kneaded and caressed her breast.

The bodice of her surcoat was fairly snug on her torso but there was enough give so that he was able to pull the neckline down and expose a bare breast. Wrapping an arm around her very tightly so she was pressed against his hard body, he held her fast as his hot, wet mouth descended on a naked nipple. Suckling strongly, sweetly, he was driven into madness as she writhed and gasped against him.

Maddoc was in a haze as he nursed hungrily on Adalind's flesh. She was soft and warm, so incredibly luscious, that it drove all other thought out of his mind. He was about to take even more liberties, or at least try, when a pair of very drunken guests entered the dark passageway, laughing when they realized they had come across a very compromising scene. The sudden noise in the confined space was loud and startling, driving Maddoc and Adalind apart.

Fortunately, it was dark enough so that they didn't truly get an eyeful as Maddoc quickly helped Adalind rearrange her neckline, but the implication was enough. As Adalind blushed furiously, Maddoc took her by the hand and plowed through the two giggling guests, knocking them both down and not bothering to apologize. As they fell to the floor, he simply stepped on them.

Adalind stumbled after Maddoc as he took her back into the smoky, stale hall. She was still a little dazed, a little breathless, reflecting on wicked sensations she'd never before known. She really didn't know where her mind was, only that it was lingering still in that dark and smelly alcove. It was still back where the magic had occurred. Before she realized it, Maddoc had taken her back to the table where Willow was sitting in conversation with the woman next to her. Willow caught sight of her sister making a return.

"Where did you two disappear to?" she asked.

Adalind was struggling not to grin, blush, or otherwise give their business away as Maddoc politely helped her to sit. It was a struggle to collect her thoughts.

"We were dancing so much that... that we ended up over there somewhere," she said somewhat haltingly, pointing towards the other side of the room. Not wanting to discuss the subject any further, mostly because she wasn't very good at lying to cover their activities, she hastened to change the focus. "Where is Brighton? Did he leave?"

Willow was successful diverted. "He said he had business to attend to," she said. "What do you know about him, Addie? Is he really looking for a wife?"

Adalind shrugged. "I would not know," she replied. "Truthfully, I have only met the man four or five times in my life when he came to visit Glennie at Winchester. Glennie adored him. She would always make such a fuss over his visits. All I know is that he serves Norfolk and that his father is Baron Cononley, Constable of Yorkshire. Brighton will inherit the title from his father."

Willow was very interested. "A titled knight," she said quietly but with excitement. "That would please Papa a great deal. I would be Lady Cononly. How exciting!"

"Perhaps you should speak to Papa so that he may bring it up to Brighton. The Earl of Canterbury would hold much weight behind such a proposal."

Willow was thrilled with the idea. Eager to speak with her grandfather on such a marital prospect, she feigned a sour stomach so that Maddoc and Adalind escorted her back to their encampment. It was fairly quiet and dark but for the white-hot bonfire burning low and snappy in the center of their tents. Willow made the excuse of visiting David because she wanted to bid him a good sleep when, in fact, what she really wanted to do was speak with him about Sir Brighton.

As Maddoc escorted Adalind over to her tent and began the long process of bidding her a good sleep, Willow lingered at the entrance to her grandfather's tent. She could hear voices inside and, curious, she leaned in to hear what was being said. A man whose voice she did not recognize was speaking with her grandfather and as more of the conversation became apparent, Willow realized that she did, in fact, recognize the voice. But the words he was speaking were not the words she hoped to hear. It didn't take long before she barged into the tent.

What happened in the next few days would change their lives forever.

The memories of all loves merging with this one love of ours –
And the songs of every poet past and forever.

CHAPTER THIRTEEN

"My lord, I appreciate that you would see me at such an inopportune time," Brighton said. "I heard you were injured in the mêlée today."

"I was," David eyed the man. "I would be grateful if you would quickly state your business."

Brighton nodded quickly. "Of course, my lord," he said. "But I would preface my intrusion with an apology. I am sorry if this is not an appropriate moment, but I feel compelled to beg a few moments of your time. It is important."

David was propped up with furs and pillows, his aching head resting against a silk pillow that Emilie had embroidered. He wasn't prepared to see visitors, but Sir Brighton de Royans had called upon him and invoked the name of Norfolk so, not wanting to be rude to a Norfolk envoy and more than curious as to the man's business, David agreed to see him.

"You say you come on behalf of Norfolk?" David asked. "I have not seen Hugh D'Aubigny in many years. I am surprised he still remembers me."

Brighton smiled politely. "Of course he remembers you, my lord," he replied smoothly. "All of England remembers and respects the House of de Lohr. Your brother is the mighty Earl of Hereford and Worcester, former champion of Richard the Lion Heart, and you yourself are the influential and powerful Earl of Canterbury. You and your brother's adventures are legendary. I was raised on such tales of valor."

David chuckled faintly. "Those stories have grown over the years, so much so that I have come to believe them myself," he said, sobering. "What would Norfolk have of me, de Royans? A call to arms?"

Brighton shook his head. "Nay, my lord," he said. "In truth, this visit is of a personal nature. "

"Personal? For whom?"

"For me."

David looked at him curiously. "Do I even know you?"

Again, Brighton shook his head. "Nay, my lord, you do not," he said. "My father is the Constable of Yorkshire, Baron Cononley, a title I will inherit upon his passing. My family seat is Netherghyll Castle, a large and prosperous stronghold that has been in my family for four generations. My great-grandfather and Henry the First were close friends, which is how the hereditary title of Constable of Yorkshire came to my family."

David wasn't exactly sure why the man was standing before him but he remained polite. "I see," he said. "I would take it as a favor if you would speak plainly of your purpose, Sir Brighton. Surely it was not to recite your lineage."

Brighton gave him a wry grin. "It was not," he said. It was evident the man was formulating his thoughts. "I am, as you see, an accomplished knight, as a senior warrior in Norfolk's stable and successor to the Barony of Cononley. It is for this reason that I come to you, my lord; I wanted to be clear that I am a man with property and holdings. I am successful, and I receive the full support of Norfolk."

"Please come to the point, de Royans."

Brighton was starting to show signs of nervousness but he fought it. "My lord, I have known Lady Adalind for nearly five years," he said. "She is the best friend of my sister, Glennie."

David was suddenly interested. "Glennie is your sister?"

"She is, my lord."

"Hmmm," David looked thoughtful. "Adalind and I were only just speaking of her. I thought she might make a match for my son, Daniel, who is in need of a wife." He looked hopeful. "Is that why you have come? Because you and Adalind have discussed your sister as a match for my son?"

Brighton shook his head. "We have not," he said. "This is the first I have heard of such a thing."

"Do you think your sister might be interested?" David wanted to know. "Daniel will inherit my earldom. He should make a very fine husband once he settles down. The right woman can do wonders for a man."

Brighton wasn't particularly concerned with his sister or the earl's son, but it did bring about an idea. In fact, it was a very good idea, or so he thought. If Brighton was one thing and one thing only, he was clever. He was very clever. And he never missed an opportunity.

"Perhaps I can arrange for a meeting," he said. "I would be most happy to introduce my sister to your son, but in return, I would appeal for your consideration."

"Consideration for what?"

"Consideration for me as an appropriate match for Lady Adalind."

David didn't react at first. It was as if Brighton's proposition confused him because his thought processes were still lingering on Daniel and Glennie. Then, when he realized what the man was saying, his expression slackened with surprise.

"Adalind?" he repeated.

"Aye, my lord."

"But... but I thought you said you have known her these five years."

"I have, my lord."

"And you think to make an offer for her hand *now*? Why did you not do it two or three or four years ago?"

"Because I was a fool."

David eyed him, somewhat in disbelief. Then, he weakly shook his head. "Your timing is poor," he said. "Although I appreciate your offer, she is already betrothed."

"Formally?"

"Formally enough."

"Has there been an announcement? A contract brokered?"

"Not yet. But I gave my word."

Brighton wasn't going to play dumb. He knew the facts and he knew why. "I understand that du Bois is a fine knight," he said. "I have the greatest admiration for him but I will also tell you that I have spent some time observing du Bois and Lady Adalind and I am convinced that du Bois is only infatuated with her. I do not see it being a viable marriage and I do not see Lady Adalind being happy over time. Men like du Bois... their attention is finite and when it burns out, he will focus on something, or someone, else. Adalind will suffer as a result."

David listened to the rather passionate statement with growing distain. "Who are you to make such a bold declaration about Maddoc?" he asked. "I have known the man for fifteen years and he is the finest knight I have ever seen. Adalind is in love with him, and he with her, and their marriage will be a happy one. I will say again that I appreciate your offer but I will decline. Adalind is spoken for."

Brighton knew he should probably leave it at that. He was, in truth, an honorable knight, but he saw something in Adalind he wanted very much and he was a man unused to denial. He wasn't sure why the past few hours had turned his head so dramatically towards Adalind de Aston, but he knew more and more as the minutes passed that she was something worthy of his attention. Worth fighting for. When Adalind and du Bois had gone to dance, Brighton had politely conversed with Adalind's sister for a few moments before excusing himself and going in search of Adalind's grandfather. He knew who Canterbury was; everyone did. He was quite sure du Bois would try to run him through when he found out what he was up to, but it was a risk he was willing to take.

"May I ask what du Bois brings with him to a marital contract?" he asked. "Prestige? Money? Lands?"

David was coming not to like this brash young knight. "He is the grandson of the Duke of Navarre," he said. "His father is one of the finest men I have ever known. He comes from a very fine family, although I am not sure why that is any concern of yours."

Brighton was playing it cool. "A duke's grandson," he murmured, almost to himself. "Very fine indeed. Will he inherit any titles?"

"Not that I am aware of."

"Does he have property?"

"Again, not that I am aware of."

"Then what does he have to offer Adalind?" Brighton asked, thinking he was driving home a particularly strong point. "I can offer her all of these things. She will be a baron's wife and, more than that, have all of the property and titles that I can offer her. She would be well cared for and never want for anything. No offense to du Bois, but I can offer her so much more than he can, including the support of Norfolk's army. D'Aubigny would be thrilled to be linked to the de Lohrs by marriage, even if it was only through the marriage of one of his knights. Still, the loyalty, and the promise of power and support, would be there. Is that not offering more than du Bois can bring?"

"Adalind?" Came a voice from the entry to the tent. "You… you have come to speak of Adalind?"

Both men turned to the entry to see Willow standing there, her expression full of confusion. Confusion was rapidly turning to disappointment. David propped himself up on an elbow in an attempt to face her.

"Willow," he scolded softly. "You know better than to eavesdrop on a conversation. You were not invited here."

Willow was wide eyed with shock at what she had just heard. "I was not eavesdropping," she insisted, her voice growing angry. "I was simply standing at the doorway because I heard voices and I overhead what Sir Brighton said. He has made an offer of marriage for Adalind?"

David could just see by the look on her face that she was bordering on some kind of tantrum. "Sir Brighton has made the offer but I have informed him that Adalind is pledged to Maddoc," he said steadily. "Willow, I want you to leave and not repeat anything that you have heard, is that clear? This is a private conversation and you will do us the courtesy of respecting our confidentiality."

Willow acted as if she hadn't heard him. Her big green eyes were focused on Brighton as if he was the lowest form of life. Her lips molded into a pout and her eyes filled with tears. Angrily, she stamped her foot.

"You…," she sputtered before breaking in to tears. "You are hateful, Sir Brighton, just *hateful*!"

In sobs, she ran from the tent and David knew he had a mess on his hands. He wasn't sure why, or how, but he knew things were going to go from bad to worse. He shouted for a soldier who, as soon as he appeared, was sent on the run for Emilie. When the man fled, David felt back exhaustedly against his pillows and waved Brighton off.

"I think you had better go now," he said. "Our conversation is finished."

Brighton understood, although he still wasn't sure why Willow had cursed him so. Perhaps it was because he was trying to interfere in the relationship between Adalind and Maddoc and, to that end, he could see her point. He *was* hateful. Perhaps their conversation was indeed over for the night, at least until the next time he could bring it up to David. He knew there would be a next time.

"Very well, my lord," he said, backing out of the tent. "Until the next time we meet, I pray your health returns."

He was nearly out of the tent when David called to him. "De Royans?"

Brighton paused in the open flap. "My lord?"

David's gaze, for as weary as he was, remained strong and intense. "There will be no next time on this subject," he said. "We are at an end."

Brighton dipped his head as if to understand, but he did not reply. The truth was that the subject was not at an end, not by any stretch of the imagination.

When he retired that evening, it was with his broadsword in his hand. He fully expected du Bois to descend on him and was rather surprised in the morning to discover that he was still alive.

***

"Stay away from him, Maddoc," David said threateningly. "I do not want blood spilled today, do you understand? I would have our trip home to Canterbury uneventful. I do not need to be worrying over you when I have more important things on my mind."

Maddoc wouldn't look at him, nor would he respond. On a cold and foggy morning following the evening's festivities, he had been ordered to break down their camp so they could return to Canterbury and he was, in theory, completing the job. He had issued orders to the men, and he and Gerid were overseeing the disassembly. However, there was more to it than that. So much more.

David, able to stand although he was hunched over and leaning heavily on a big stick the physic had given him, had not let Maddoc out of his sight since last night. Since the moment Brighton had left David's tent, there were dealings afoot. Because Willow hadn't kept her mouth shut on what she had heard between Brighton and David, David had been forced to tell

Maddoc that Brighton had made an offer for Adalind's hand. Maddoc hadn't reacted overly but David could see the smoldering fire in his eyes. That fire was meant to kill. God only knew, he was well aware of what the man was capable of. Walter de Burgh had found that out the hard way.

"Maddoc," David lowered his voice when he saw that the man was not responding to him. "Look at me. That is a command."

After a lengthy pause, Maddoc turned to look at him. When their gazes locked, David lifted his eyebrows.

"Do you understand what I am telling you?" he asked.

Maddoc nodded faintly. "I do."

David acknowledged his answer but he still didn't trust him. "Where is Adalind right now?"

"With her mother, grandmother, and sister. They are in the hall breaking their fast."

"Do you know where de Royans is?"

"He left this morning and rode east."

"You were stalking him?"

"Of course I was."

David's jaw ticked angrily. "Damnation, Maddoc, stop this posturing," he snapped. Then he sighed heavily, struggling to stay calm because it made his head hurt when he got truly angry. "De Royans is a suitor just like all the rest. You have dealt with four of them up until this point and de Royans is no different. Remain calm and stay away from him, and this too shall pass. I will deal with the man if the subject comes up again."

Maddoc was shaking his head even before David finished his sentence. "He is *not* like the rest," he said. "The man is cunning, strong, and tactical. More than that, he knows without a doubt that Adalind and I are betrothed yet he still went to you to try and convince you to break our betrothal. A man like this is not simply an annoyance; he is dangerous because he will do anything he can to win."

"You are threatened by him?"

"Worse - I understand him because I think the same way."

David watched Maddoc as the man spoke, noting how deeply Maddoc was struggling to maintain his self-control.

"So what do you propose?" David asked quietly. "Will you do to him what you did to Walter de Burgh? You killed a man because he was a threat to both you and Adalind. Is de Royans a threat as well?"

Maddoc averted his gaze. "Possibly," he said. "I will make all reasonable attempts to stay away from him, my lord, but if he does not stay away from me and from Adalind, I will challenge him. I will not tolerate his disrespectful or threatening behavior."

"The man has not threatened you, Maddoc," David said. "He has not brandished a weapon or made threats of any kind. Lad, you simply cannot go around killing every man who has an eye for Adalind. She will be your wife; men will look at her, and you will end up killing half of England. You will be the Great Murdering Husband of Adalind de Aston du Bois and all men will fear you as such. Would you truly shame the family in that manner?"

He said it rather humorously, trying to break Maddoc's stiff stance, and it was a struggle for Maddoc not to crack a grin. He cast David a sidelong glance.

"Then what would you suggest I do, my lord?" he asked. "What would *you* do?"

David shrugged. "I would marry her immediately," he said without hesitation. "That would solve nearly every issue. But I am not so sure you are ready for such a thing. I think perhaps you like fighting off would-be suitors and testing your strength against them. I think there is something about the flash of dark steel against warm flesh that excites your inner animal."

Maddoc did break down in a grin, then. "I am not so barbaric or so arrogant," he assured him. Then, he sobered. "But you are wrong about one thing; I am ready to marry Addie. I would do it today if I could."

David's blue eyes glimmered. "Perhaps not today," he said softly. "We must travel home first. But I will send a messenger on ahead for the Archbishop of Canterbury and tell the man we will have need of his services tomorrow. Will that suffice?"

Maddoc suddenly wasn't so stiff and angry anymore. He felt rather warm and excited, enough so that dark thoughts of Brighton de Royans faded.

"It will," he said. "Thank you, my lord. I am deeply appreciative."

David's smile faded. "Prove it," he said. "Make Adalind happy. That is all I ask, Maddoc. Think of her before you think of yourself in every situation and you can do no wrong. That is my advice to you."

Maddoc smiled. "I will take it to heart."

"See that you do," David said, pointing to the great hall of Shadoxhurst. "Now, go inside and collect the women you will soon be related to. You may inform Adalind of what is to take place tomorrow and let us see if she will stop hugging you long enough for you to mount your horse and ride home."

Chuckling, Maddoc made his way inside the keep. True to David's predication, it took some effort for Adalind to stop hugging him so he could settle her on her palfrey and mount his charger. Even then, they rode together the entire way back to Canterbury.

***

"He is waiting for you, Maddoc."

Astride his big charcoal gray charger as the gatehouse of Canterbury came into view, Maddoc was puzzled by Gerid's softly-uttered statement. The man had ridden on ahead to begin preparations for David's arrival but was now back with the party returning from Shadoxhurst. His expression suggested that all was not well in the world of Canterbury Castle.

"*Who* is waiting?" Maddoc asked.

Gerid eyed David, and Adalind, riding several feet behind Maddoc as the shades of sunset cast purple shadows across the land. The sun was nearly down now and the earth was growing cold.

"De Royans," he finally muttered. "The man evidently showed up a few hours ago and told the soldiers that he would wait for you."

Maddoc could feel his anger rise, like a tide, starting in his toes and working its way up his body. His brow furrowed.

"Is that so?" he asked, almost casually. "Then I would not want to disappoint him. Where is he?"

"In the bailey. In full armor. Maddoc, I do not think you understand; he is here to fight you."

Maddoc wasn't the least bit upset by the news. He didn't even have to ask why; he knew without question. He was already in full battle armor, as was usual when he rode escort, so there would be no preparation involved. He was ready, willing, and able to meet the fight head-on. In fact, he was looking forward to it. It saved him the trouble of having to hunt the man down.

"What is it?" David asked. He could see Gerid and Maddoc conferring quietly. "Gerid, what has happened?"

Gerid was reluctant to tell him. He started to open his mouth, looking to Maddoc for guidance on how he should phrase the news in front of the entire de Lohr family, but Maddoc seemed unconcerned with tactfully couching the information. He spoke before Gerid could.

"De Royans is here," he replied evenly. "It seems he has come to challenge me."

David was livid in an instant but before he could speak, Adalind cried out. "Nay!" she gasped, horrified. "Maddoc, you cannot do it!"

Maddoc turned around to look at her, seeing naked fear on her features. He smiled. "Not to worry," he assured her. "I have beaten him before and I shall do it again. I am sorry his appearance has upset our return home, however. I was hoping for a quiet evening before tomorrow's ceremony."

He winked at her as he said it but Adalind was in no mood for his attempts to soothe her. She was outraged and terrified that a man she had thought very highly of should do such a dishonorable thing. In fact, she was still having difficulty believing it.

When Willow had sobbingly told her of the conversation between Brighton and David, Adalind had run straight to David, who had explained the situation in a calmer fashion. In fact, Maddoc had been present because he, too, had heard Willow's weeping, so they both heard David's version of Brighton's visit.

Adalind had been furious and shocked at the news while Maddoc did more of what Maddoc usually did; a slow burn. He didn't show much emotion, mostly because he was internalizing his feelings and plotting Brighton's very painful demise. Knowing this, David had sent Adalind to bed but had refused to let Maddoc out of his sight. Now, Brighton had unexpectedly shown his face at Canterbury and there was nothing David could do to keep Maddoc away from the man. A storm was coming and there was no way to stop it.

Adalind knew it as well. She knew what Maddoc was capable of but she also knew the man was not immortal. He could be hurt, or worse, and that thought terrified her more than any other. To be so close to realizing her dream of marrying him was more than she could bear. She knew she would shrivel up and die if anything happened to him. If she could stop the confrontation, then she would. It wasn't the smartest decision, but she had to try. Digging her heels into her palfrey's sides, Adalind took off at a gallop for the gatehouse of Canterbury.

Startled, Maddoc took off after her but his horse was built more for strength and stamina than for speed, and the palfrey out-ran the charger by a wide margin. Once Adalind passed through the gatehouse, she was on the lookout for Brighton, coming across him in the torch-lit bailey off to the west of the keep. He was with all of his possessions, including his big cream-colored charger, and her gaze fell upon him in a corner of the shadowed yard. She ran straight at him.

"Brighton!" she screamed at him as she yanked her horse to a halt. Then she bailed off the animal, nearly falling when her skirts got tangled. "By all that is holy, what gives you the right to come here and challenge Maddoc? Have you gone mad?"

Brighton was quite calm. Hours of reflecting on his decision, waiting, had seen to that. He stepped away from his horse and possessions, coming into the flickers of torchlight. He was fully armed, for battle, a frightening and large knight that was clearly nothing to be trifled with. In the shadows of the coming night, his presence was eerie and unwelcome. The broadsword in his left hand gleamed wickedly.

"I am sorry, Addie," he said rather quietly. "I know this seems strange and sudden, and it more than likely is, but...."

"Why are you here?" she demanded, interrupting him. "Tell me why you are challenging Maddoc. *Tell me!*"

Brighton sighed as if saddened by the entire situation and took a step towards her. When she jumped back to keep distance between them, he came to a halt.

"Because I must," he said simply. "I am a better marriage prospect for you than he is. Perhaps you do not understand that, but you will in time."

"There will be no time!" she shrieked. "I want you to go away from here and never come back, do you hear me? I do not want you here and I certainly do not want to marry you."

By this time, Maddoc was thundering up behind her. Brighton kept his focus on the enormous knight as he replied to Adalind.

"You are young," Brighton said, backing away as Maddoc dismounted and began to approach. "Moments like this will fade from memory. I will do all that I can to ensure that your recollections of me, and of this moment, are only good ones. I will ensure you do not regret anything."

Adalind was frustrated and terrified to tears. She threw up her hands. "You speak in riddles," she said. "Brighton, you will listen to me – I do not want to marry you. I do not know whatever gave you the idea that I was interested in you because I am not. I love Maddoc and we are going to be married tomorrow. Do you hear me? Tomorrow I become Lady du Bois and this madness ends."

Brighton was still looking at Maddoc, who was by now marching quite purposefully toward him. Brighton began to move out and away from the wall of the keep, away from things that could allow Maddoc to trap him against. He needed room to move if he was to survive and emerge victorious, because his speed was perhaps the only advantage he had. Maddoc was big and powerful, and Brighton knew he could not use strength to overcome him. It would have to be cunning and speed. There was no other alternative.

Maddoc began to pick up the pace, charging at de Royans as he unsheathed his mighty broadsword. Then he was running at him, weapon wielded offensively, as Gerid suddenly appeared and pulled Adalind away from the battle that was sure to come. She screamed, startled and frightened, as Maddoc threw all of his weight into the first blow that sent Brighton reeling. The man flew back as if he had been hit by a battering ram, skidding onto his buttocks in the moist earth. But just as quickly he was on his feet again, rushing back at Maddoc with his sword leveled.

The epic battle had begun.

Today it is heaped at your feet, it has found its end in you
The love of all man's days both past and forever:
Universal joy, universal sorrow, universal life.

CHAPTER FOURTEEN

It was dawn in Kent. The mist that had formed in the pre-dawn hours was now hanging like a thick blanket across the land, shrouding the awakening world in a cold embrace.

David was standing in the entryway of Canterbury's mighty keep. His face was pinched from the cold as he leaned against the doorjamb, his eyes riveted to the scene below. He was wrapped in a heavy fur cloak, but it gave him little comfort. He had been standing there all night, watching and waiting.

The sounds of broadsword clashing had gone on throughout the night and now into the morning. Maddoc and Brighton had not eased their battle since the inception. It had been stronger at times, weaker at others, but there had been a constant fight since dusk of the previous evening. It had been brutal and bloody to watch, but now as the sun rose and a new day was dawning, it seemed to be gaining steam again.

David had sent the womenfolk inside when the battle started, including a hysterical Adalind. She wanted to stay and watch but David would not permit it. If Maddoc was to be killed, he didn't want her to witness it. He wasn't even sure if he wanted to witness it. Even now, he could see the combatants over to the curtain wall, moving like the walking dead with lethargy and strength and, at times, carelessness. David thought about calling an end to it but he knew it would do no good; they would simply start up again, at some point, so it was best to let them fight it out until a victor emerged. David seriously wondered who it would be.

Maddoc was showing remarkable stamina in the course of the battle. He had never let up, not even when he drove Brighton close to the curtain wall and, in the course of the fighting, was nicked in the shoulder by Brighton's blade when it ricocheted off the wall. The bouncing blade had caught Maddoc in the joint where the breastplate met the shoulder armor, and he had been cut although they did not know how badly. Blood was seeping but not pouring.

Brighton had fared slightly worse under Maddoc's strength and skill. Maddoc had made sure to go for his head at all times and, at some point a few hours in to the battle, managed to strike his helm so hard that it dented and torqued. This gave Brighton an inhibited field of vision as he fought because he could not pause to remove his helm. He had to keep fighting or be killed. But his diminished sight allowed Maddoc to cut him in the leg at one point, a deep gash to the back of his knee that had done some damage. Brighton was having trouble walking but he could not stop. His life depending on it.

So the morning began to dawn in shades of gray as David stood and watched the knights slugging it out over by the well. As he stood there, exhausted and grim, he felt a soft body beside him and a warm cup of wine appeared.

"So they are still fighting," Emilie handed her husband the mulled wine, which he took gratefully. "Will they ever tire?"

David sipped at the beverage. "Not until one of them is dead," he said. "I was standing here thinking that it was not so long ago that the ap Athoe brothers were battling it out in much the same fashion and Maddoc thought they were both idiots. He said they were an embarrassment to the knighthood and that he took personal offense at their behavior."

Emilie smiled. "That sounds like something he would say," she said softly, her gaze moving off towards the sounds of battle. "Now he understands what it is to fight for the woman he loves."

"He had no choice."

"He *does* love her."

David nodded faintly, acknowledging what they all knew, as he sipped at his wine again. "I am not surprised this battle has lasted this long," he said after a moment. "They are both very strong men."

Emilie could see them in the growing light, slicing at each other wearily. "Can you not stop them?" she begged softly. "Surely they will listen to you."

David nodded. "I can try," he said. "But they will only start up again once they have rested. This is a fight of passion and possession, Em. One cannot simply stop what has already started. They have to fight it out until...."

"Until one of them is killed," she finished for him. When he nodded reluctantly, she shook her head. "It could be Maddoc. What then? Do you have any idea how it will affect Adalind? Is she truly going to want to marry the man who killed the only man she has ever loved?"

"I will not allow her to marry de Royans," he said. "I have already denied the man. If he thinks he is fighting to win her, then he is wrong."

"Have you told him that?"

David shook his head, hard. "And risk injury?" he said as if she was daft. "Perhaps there is something you do not know, sweetheart; I do not move as quickly as I once did. Those men down there are big, young, and strong, and I am not about to get close enough to the point where they might run me down. Moreover, I might distract Maddoc if I did and give de Royans the opportunity to kill him. Nay, my lady, I am not going anywhere near that battle."

Emilie cocked an eyebrow. "Then stand here and yell at them, for Pity's sake. Let them hear you."

"Again, a distraction. Maddoc would hear me and perhaps de Royans would. I do not know. But I do know this; if Maddoc hears me, he will stop if I tell him to because I am his liege. It is de Royans I do not trust. I do not want to help the man kill Maddoc; therefore, it is best not to interfere."

Emilie sighed heavily even though she did not agree with him. She pulled her fur cloak more tightly around her slender body in the chill temperature. She glanced up to the sky, to the mist that was swirling overhead.

"Adalind has not slept," she said quietly. "Her bower window faces this side of the castle. She has been watching this all night."

David didn't like the sound of that. "Did you try to stop her?"

"Of course we did. She will not move. If it were you doing battle in the bailey, I would have to watch also. I could not bury my head in the sand and hope for the best."

David started to say something but was distracted when Brighton, being driven back by Maddoc, bumped into the well and was nearly pushed into it as Maddoc saw an opportunity. Brighton lost his balance momentarily but slugged Maddoc in the face with his right hand, shoving the man back, before regaining his balance and moving away from the well. David watched with a calculated eye.

"Maddoc is finally gaining the upper hand," he muttered with some satisfaction. "De Royans, as good as he is, is tiring. We should see an end to this soon."

Emilie watched the knights as the broadswords began to swing again. "Will Maddoc kill him?"

David nodded slowly, his eyes riveted to the battle. "He will have to." He watched a moment longer before turning to his wife. "Is Adalind still in her chamber watching all of this?"

Emilie nodded. "She was the last time I saw her."

David thought a moment. "Bring her down here," he finally said. "If she is going to watch this, let it be with me. That way, if something happens...."

Emilie understood. Kissing her husband's cold cheek, she disappeared inside, intent on collecting her granddaughter.

***

Adalind was not in her room.

Under the guise of going to the privy, she had slipped from the keep and even now stood against the southeast corner of the big, squat keep, watching Maddoc and Brighton battle in the distance. She had been watching the swordplay all night, knots in her belly as Maddoc fought for his life. This was supposed to be her wedding day, the happiest day of her life as she married the man she loved. She had prayed constantly since the contest started that it would not be the day she buried Maddoc. She would want to be buried right along with him.

Now, down on the floor of the bailey, she could see the happenings much better. Clad in a gray surcoat made from lamb's wool and a matching cloak lined with rabbit's fur, she blended in to the dark and misty dawn as she clung to the wall of the keep, waiting and watching just like everyone else. She could see her grandfather at the entrance to the keep, watching from his post where he had been all night, and she could also see the soldiers on the walls watching every movement. Even Gerid was up there. He had been watching all night, too.

Adalind had long since dried her tears over the situation. She had wept for several hours after the start of the battle, but those tears had faded in favor of a plan. She simply couldn't sit by as Maddoc fought for his life. It wasn't in her nature. All of this was her fault, anyway, so it was up to her to put an end to it.

Watching the fight from her chamber as Willow snored and her mother sewed, Adalind's bright mind began to formulate a scheme. By dawn, she most definitely had a plan, something that would stop the fight and make de Royans go away forever. She had to see it through.

In her hand, she held a small bejeweled dagger that her grandmother had given her long ago. She intended to use it on de Royans while Maddoc had him distracted. She wasn't sure how she was ever going to explain to Glennie how she had killed her brother, but she couldn't worry about that now. All she could think of was Maddoc and saving him from Brighton. She hoped she was brave enough, and strong enough, to do it. But for Maddoc, she was willing to do anything. Even kill.

As the day lightened around her, she was ready to enact that plan. The problem was that her grandfather stood between her and the combatants, and he would surely stop her before she could get to them. Therefore, she circled the keep and ended up on the west side, which was a little closer to the battle. More importantly, there was nothing between her and the knights so she had a clear field to operate in.

To her right, against the wall of the keep, stood Brighton's charger. Looking at the big cream-colored horse butt gave her an idea. As Maddoc knocked Brighton to his knees and nearly cut his head off with a weary swipe of the broadsword, Adalind picked up a rock, aimed at the horse's arse, and threw as hard as she could.

The charger squealed and, startled, took off at a dead run. A satchel came loose and crashed to the ground, spilling possessions. I was enough to distract both Brighton and Maddoc, who instinctively looked over when the horse brayed. It was the distraction Adalind had hoped for and she rushed out from her hiding place, straight at the knights. Brighton's back was to her but Maddoc was facing her, and when he saw her running toward them with a dagger flashing in her hand, he could hardly believe what he was seeing. In fact, it took him a long moment to process it. Then, he moved in her direction.

"Addie!" he boomed. "Get back! Get....!"

His words were cut off as Brighton used Maddoc's distraction to his advantage. Bringing up his broadsword, he took a blind stab at Maddoc and ended up goring the man in the torso underneath his right arm. It was in the seam where the breast and backplate joined, and he had, by sheer chance, penetrated it.

The heavy broadsword carved into Maddoc's big body but the man didn't go down. It slowed him down and he staggered sideways with the majority of Brighton's broadsword hanging out of his body. Brighton, however, was up and moving, rushing to Adalind and grabbing her before she realized what had happened. The dagger in her hand ended up in Brighton's grip, and he hauled her up against him with the lovely bejeweled dagger pointed at her neck.

Maddoc saw what had happened but his legs wouldn't move correctly. He tried to take a step in her direction but ended up collapsing on his knees. He couldn't breathe and his field of vision was fading. David was already flying off the stairs, moving far too fast for the injured old man, heading for Maddoc as Gerid and a host of soldiers also rushed in Maddoc's direction. In fact, the entire castle was in an uproar as Maddoc pitched forward onto his face.

Adalind screamed Maddoc's name as Brighton began dragging her across the bailey. She was crying loudly, the realization of Maddoc's injury driving home every horrible fear she had ever entertained. The fact that she had caused it with her foolish plan only made her scream louder. God help her, she knew she had killed him in her attempt to save him. She was shattered in so many ways, pieces of herself sparking into the cold gray dawn like shooting stars burning out in the night sky.

Every part of her was dying at the moment, her soul snuffed out as Maddoc lay on his face. In her grief, Adalind grabbed the dirk that Brighton was holding against her throat and forced his hand, driving it into her neck. The blood poured.

David roared with agony when he saw Adalind and the blood spilling down her chest. He was half-way to Maddoc but came to an unsteady halt as Brighton dragged Adalind to within a few feet of him.

"Nay!" David threw out his hands to Brighton. "Do not kill her; please, I beg you."

Brighton was somewhat horrified himself. "I did not do this to her, my lord, I assure you," he said. "She has done it to herself."

David was begging. "Please let me have her," he pleaded. "She needs a physic."

Brighton could feel her squirming in his arms and knew she had some strength left. Whatever injury she had given herself must not have been too terrible if she still had fight in her. He shook his head.

"I will find a physic for her," he assured him in an oddly calm voice. "Your physic must tend Maddoc. He is a good man and an excellent knight. Perhaps it is foolish to say so, but I am sorry for what I had to do. I had no choice."

David was pale with fury, with fear. It was a struggle to remain calm. "Damn you, de Royans," he hissed, trying not to look at Adalind as she gasped and wept. "I told you Adalind was not meant for you. You should have done the honorable thing and accepted my word. God damn you to hell; now you see what you have done."

Brighton's gaze flickered in Maddoc's direction. A host of soldiers hovered over him as Gerid rolled the man onto his back and checked him for signs of life. He refused to feel remorse.

"It is done," he said simply, hoarsely. "I cannot take it back. Now, give me my horse or I swear you will lose your granddaughter in front of your eyes."

"If you do, I promise you that you will not leave this place alive."

"Then give me my horse or she will bleed to death in front of you. Let me go with her or she dies."

"If she dies, you die."

"The longer we stand here and argue, the more her life slips away."

"Papa," Adalind sobbed. "Maddoc... I am so sorry. Please, Papa, *help him.*"

It was so pitifully spoken, the sorrowful pleas of a young woman about to lose what was most precious to her. David looked at Adalind and he couldn't stop the tears filling his eyes. It was as horrible as it could possibly be and he was sick with the realization.

"Oh... Addie," he murmured. "It is not your fault, sweetheart."

Adalind was weeping deeply. "Papa, help him," she cried. "I cannot live without him. I want to die, too."

David could feel her grief, a physical pain reaching out to squeeze his heart. He could hardly breathe with the force of it. As he turned to look over his shoulder at Maddoc, who was now being tended to by Gerid and several soldiers, screams from the keep caught his attention and he looked up to see Emilie and Christina in the doorway surveying the carnage.

Torn between Adalind and Maddoc, David was swept up with the vision of his grief-stricken wife and daughter. His first instinct was to bolt towards the keep, and he did. God help him, he went with his instinct because he knew he wasn't strong enough to fight Brighton for Adalind. He needed help, and his help was dying on the ground with a broadsword in his torso. He knew Brighton served Norfolk so he knew where the man would take her. When David showed up to claim his granddaughter, it would be with his army and his brother's army, and Norfolk would have no choice but to surrender. Then they would burn Arundel to the ground.

With David no longer blocking his path, Brighton hauled Adalind across the bailey, holding the dagger to her throat so no man would stop him. Soldiers followed him a close range but no one made a move to attack him, fearful that he would kill Adalind. She was bleeding all down her neck and chest, wounded in the battle for her hand. Behind them, her mother and grandmother screamed their anguish.

As the soldiers followed in an uncertain group, Brighton came across his charger over by the far end of the bailey and tossed Adalind up into the saddle. He vaulted on behind her and, reins in one hand and holding both Adalind and the dagger in the other, he made haste from Canterbury's chaotic keep.

We have played along side millions of lovers, shared in the same
Shy sweetness of meeting, the same distressful tears of farewell-

CHAPTER FIFTEEN

She wouldn't let the physic touch her.

Fortunately, the wound on Adalind's neck had stopped oozing but she wouldn't let anyone near her to tend it. Whenever they tried, she screamed and threw fists and feet until they backed away. She was like a caged animal, incoherent and mad, causing chaos and concern with her behavior.

His first thought after leaving Canterbury was to find a church so they could be married right away. He would have the priests send for a physic to attend to Adalind's wound, but that plan had not worked out as he had hoped. Adalind cowered in the corner of the sanctuary at the small parish church of St. Barnabas, absolutely out of her mind with grief and terror. Every time Brighton approached her, she screamed as if he was preparing to murder her.

The priests; three of them, had no idea what to do. There was a man in charge, Fr. Matthias, who was a sane and just man who had once been a knight. While his two subordinate priests spoke in hushed and fearful tones, he remained silent, watching the well-dressed but blood stained lady collapsed against the cold stone wall on the western edge of the sanctuary. A physic they had brought from the town sat on the floor several feet away from her, trying to coax her into allowing him to tend her wound, but she put her hands over her ears and blocked him out.

The big blond knight just stood and watched her. The man had hardly said five words to them in the hour or more that he and the lady had been there, and even then it was to demand a physic. Since that time, the man hadn't uttered another sound; he wouldn't answer any questions from the confused priests. He simply stood about a dozen feet away from the lady, watching her, his face etched with exhaustion and quite possibly anguish. It was difficult to know. One thing was certain, however; whatever was happening between them was horrible and tumultuous.

Fr. Matthias was observing the situation just as the knight was, only he was observing the entire scene. The knight seemed to only be focused on the lady, but Fr. Matthias envisioned the global view. Nothing escaped his scrutiny. Nearly two hours after the knight had brought the kicking and screaming lady through the door, Fr. Matthias had enough curiosity and concern.

At first, he hadn't wanted to involve himself in the situation. It was safer sometimes to stay out of these hectic situations and hope that they simply go away. But this one was not going way. He wanted to know what was going on and what all intentions were from both the lady and the knight. He suspected the knight would only tell him the arrogant and self-important versions that knights were so capable of, and thought the lady might be the only one to give him any semblance of the total truth. If he could only ease her fear.

Fr. Matthias broke away from his anxious companions and made his way towards the lady. The physic, a younger man with a bald head, sat on the ground several feet away in his attempt to communicate with her. Fr. Matthias moved past the priest but didn't get too close; he'd seen what happened if the lady felt threatened. He moved to the stone wall, so cold and moist, and leaned against it as he focused on her terrified and huddled form.

"My lady?" he said softly. "I am Father Matthias. My lady, I realize you are frightened but I do not know why. Will you please tell me what has happened?"

Adalind was in a haze of terror and grief. She heard the man speak but started to press her hands over her ears again until she heard him introduce himself as the priest. Then, her head came up from the protective embrace of her arms and her big green eyes were abnormally bright within her pale face. She wiped unsteadily at the mucus and tears smeared over her face.

"Please," she whispered. "Help me."

"What help do you need, my lady?"

Adalind couldn't even bring herself to look at Brighton but she knew he was standing nearby. She could feel it.

"The knight," she murmured. "He has killed my husband and has abducted me. Please… give me sanctuary. I beg of you."

Fr. Matthias frowned as he dared to move closer to the lady. He crouched down beside her, putting himself more on her level as he spoke calmly and softly.

"Who are you?"

Adalind swallowed. "The Lady Adalind de Lohr de Aston," she said. "My grandfather is the Earl of Canterbury. Please give me sanctuary and send word to my grandfather and tell him I am here. He must know."

The priest was rather shocked to hear the woman's name. He looked up at Brighton, still standing like a great stone sentinel several feet away.

"Is this true?" he asked. "She is Canterbury?"

"She is."

"Did you kill her husband and abduct her?"

Brighton sighed heavily. "I did not kill her husband," he said, trying not to sound as if he was defending himself. "He was her betrothed. I challenged him and I won. She is rightfully mine and I will marry her today."

Adalind began sobbing pitifully at the mention of Maddoc. "You murdered Maddoc, you contemptible bastard," she cried. "I will kill myself before I will marry you, do you hear me? I hate you, and I hope you die a horrible, painful death and then I hope you spend Eternity in Damnation's fiery pits. I hope you burn!"

She was off crying again and the priest hastened to reassure her. "My lady, please," he said, daring to put a hand on her head to soothe her. "Do not upset yourself so. I will help you, I swear it."

Brighton unsheathed a long, wicked-looking dirk that had been in the folds of his armor. "You will marry us now."

Fr. Matthias looked up from Adalind's lowered head, unimpressed by the weapon as it flickered in the weak light. "Are you to kill me, too, if I do not? There will be no hope for your soul then. "

"Marry us *now*."

"No."

"Do it or I will kill all of you and burn this place over your heads."

Fr. Matthias didn't doubt him for a moment. The knight had an edgy look about him. Moreover, Matthias was unarmed and in no position to enter into a physical altercation with the knight. At least not at the moment. He would have to be more clever than that to gain control over the situation.

"Perhaps some food and rest will make you both feel better," he said. "I have no desire to lose my church or die in the process, so let us make the lady a priority between us. The physic will tend her wound while you and I discuss your immortal soul and the fact that you are so close to losing it."

Adalind looked at the priest fearfully. "But... please... I must...."

Fr. Matthias patted her hand, cutting her off as he stood up. "Allow the physic to tend your wound, my lady," he said evenly. "I will speak with your suitor until you are satisfactorily rested and fed. Do not worry."

Adalind didn't want anyone touching her. In fact, she started to panic. Bolting to her feet, she ran away, darting around the sanctuary as the physic and Fr. Matthias attempted to calm her. Brighton kept his eyes on her as he backed up to be near the door so she couldn't slip past him. When Adalind dodged between a pair of pillars and realized her exit was blocked, she went even further into madness.

Off to her left were dozens of candles against a small statue of the Virgin Mary. Some were lit, some were not. She raced at the candles and began throwing then at Brighton, making contact with him more than she missed. Brighton found himself fending off a barrage of heavy tallow candles, at times being sprayed with hot wax across his mail. As Fr. Matthias pleaded for calm, Adalind hurled insults and declarations of her hatred for Brighton along with the candles. Her screaming lifted to the rafters.

When her supply of candles ran out, Adalind looked around for other things to throw, but the sanctuary with its cold dirt floor and beamed ceiling was scantily furnished. It was then that she noted that the sanctuary was lined with thin lancet windows and she realized that a couple of them were low enough to the ground that she could possibly escape from them.

Gathering her skirts, she raced across the sanctuary and threw herself at one of the windows, realizing too late that it was a tighter fit that she thought. Struggling through the window gave Brighton time to come up behind her and pull her, kicking and screaming, out of the window.

Adalind fought him for everything she was worth. Feet and fists were flying, smacking him as her body twisted violently, but Brighton held fast. She was surprisingly strong for a woman and twice he lost his grip as she twisted, but he managed to regain her again. At one point, she hit him in the nose and blood trickled, but he remained relatively calm. He never tried to hit her back or otherwise hurt her. He only attempted to restrain her. But when she started biting, he snaked his hand into her blond hair and held her head still so she couldn't snap at him. Then, he sought out the priest.

"You will marry us now," he commanded.

Fr. Matthias, standing a few feet away, shook his head. "I will not."

Brighton's ire began to rise. "Do it or you all die."

"You cannot kill us and hold her at the same time."

He had a point, although Brighton wouldn't admit it. Not now; he'd come this far and his entire mission was beginning to smack of pride more than passion. He could not, and would not, surrender. Being a clever man who achieved his means through any way possible, he was not at an end. He had a plan. Using the butt-end of the dirk he was carrying, he balled his fist around it and hit Adalind in the head fairly hard. She yelped and went limp but was not fully unconscious, so he hit her again and knocked her out completely. Lowering her carefully to the ground, he turned on the priests.

Fr. Matthias; startled but not surprised at what the knight had done, took off at a dead run. There were weapons in his chamber if he could only get to them. Being a former knight, he felt naked without some manner of weapons and kept them safely hidden. Brighton bolted after him and they raced through the sanctuary and into an alcove that had a small door used only by the priests. The door led to a courtyard outside and Fr. Matthias ran to another section of the complex, a low-ceilinged structure that housed the priests. But the door latch jammed as he tried to open it, allowing Brighton to catch up with him.

When Brighton grabbed him, Fr. Matthias balled a fist and slugged Brighton in the face. The knight stumbled back but still managed to grab the rather muscular priest, and the two of them went blow for blow across the cloisters. It was a dirty fight, and brutal, but Fr. Matthias held his own for several minutes before finally succumbing to Brighton's stronger fists. The priest hadn't been in a fight in years and was therefore not particularly prepared for this one. One last hard blow from Brighton eventually knocked him out completely.

With Fr. Matthias out of the way, Brighton staggered back into the sanctuary where Adalind was just starting to come around. Gathering her into his arms as she tried to slap him, he ordered one of the subordinate priests to perform the marriage mass but the brother wasn't fully ordained yet and could not complete the task. Frustrated, Brighton could see that his visit to St. Barnabas was at an end and carried Adalind out into the late afternoon, mounted his charger, and continued on his quest to find a priest who would marry them.

After his experience at St. Barnabas, he wasn't so sure he was going to find the task particularly simple. In fact, he was starting to doubt all of it.

Old love but in shapes that renew and renew forever

CHAPTER SIXTEEN

Two weeks later

David could hear the sentries shouting.

Sitting in his solar on a lazy afternoon, he could hear the excitement and he rose from his chair before the fire, shoving the dog aside as he made his way to the keep entry. He took the stairs slowly, as he was moving slow in general these days, listening to the shouts going on around him. By the time he hit the bottom of the stairs, he could see the guards scrambling at the gatehouse and the old iron portcullis straining against its chains as it was slowly lifted. Gerid, who had been at the gatehouse with the commotion going on, went to meet him.

"My lord," he greeted. "Your brother has been sighted."

David sighed with a huge amount of relief. "How far out is he?"

"Not far," Gerid turned to the gatehouse and pointed. "Perhaps a half mile or so. It looks as if he is bringing half of the Welsh Marches with him."

David nodded as Gerid excused himself and ran back towards the gatehouse. David followed, thinking of the past two weeks and the anguish that had affected his family. He was too close to the situation, far too shaken to be of any real use, so he did what he'd done all his life when he was in trouble; he sent for his brother. He thought perhaps Christopher could help, at least with the mental health of his family if not the physical health. Seeing Uncle Christopher would do them all a world of good because the past fortnight had been very bad, indeed.

So he made his way to the heavy, squat gatehouse just as his brother's army appeared on a small rise in the road leading towards the castle. He stood there and watched the army come closer, grow bigger, until he could make out the knights and the infantry, and standard bearers hanging the blue and gold banners of the Earl of Hereford and Worcester. It was a truly awesome sight of one of the finest fighting forces in England. As the army began to pass beneath the portcullis, David could only feel relief. In fact, he was nearly weak with it.

His relief grew when he spied his brother astride a big golden charger, heading in his direction. The horse was a young one, and hard to handle, but his brother was making a good show of it. For an elderly man, he was giving it all he had. David bit off a grin as the man came within range.

"What are you doing with a horse like that?" he demanded. "This animal will put you in your grave if you are not careful. What does your wife say about it?"

Christopher de Lohr, Earl of Hereford and Worcester, Baron Malvern and Leominster, First Guardian of the Welsh Marches, and Keeper of the Borders, flipped up his visor and gave his brother a scowl. But he couldn't hold out long so he ended up laughing.

"Dustin tells me that I am old and foolish," he told him. "But it was a gift. My son, Douglas, gave me this animal for my birthday a few months ago and I will be damned if I will let anyone else ride the beast. Already, my grandsons are begging to have the animal but I will not surrender him. At least, not yet."

David smiled at his brother, reaching out to grab the enormous gloved hand that was extended to him. It was a reassuring moment, one of comfort and faith, of a human touch that David had sorely missed. He and his brother were closer than most, having fought together and suffered innumerable tragedies and triumphs. Christopher was the steady rock and David was the fire. When they were apart, he missed him deeply.

"You should let them have it," he said, shaking the hand gratefully. "You are too old to be riding him. In fact, I do not believe I have seen you dressed for battle in years. You usually ride to the rear in a less combative role."

Christopher let go of his brother's hand and laboriously climbed off the charger. He was a very big man, at least a head taller than David, and older by three years. As he moved near the head of the horse, the animal turned on him and tried to bite him. He slugged the beast in the neck and handed him off to one of the weary foot soldiers as the army passed him by.

"Damnable horse," he muttered. "He has been trying to bite me nearly the entire journey. I almost lost a hand."

David shook his head. "Not a particularly illustrious way to receive an injury for a man of your stature."

Christopher conceded the point. "Definitely not," he said, getting a good look at his younger brother. Usually handsome, spry and healthy for a man of sixty-four years, he seemed to have aged terribly. "God, you look old. What in the hell is going on around here?"

David's smile faded. "Did you read my missive?"

"All of it. That is why I am here. But I want to hear exactly what is happening, not an ambiguously worded missive."

David gazed into the face, so very familiar, so very wise, and finally shrugged his shoulders.

"I do not even know where to begin," he said as they both turned for the keep, their pace slow. "It all started when Adalind returned from Winchester Castle a few weeks ago. Suitors followed her, fighting over her, making a nuisance of themselves. But you cannot blame them – Adalind has grown into the most beautiful woman you have ever seen."

Christopher was listening intently. "I do not doubt it," he said. "But what is this about Maddoc? How is he involved?"

David visibly sobered. "I betrothed him to Adalind," he said. "Do you remember how she used to follow him around when she was a young girl? She was like a puppy, following him everywhere."

"I seem to remember something about that."

"Her persistence must have paid off. When she returned from Winchester, it took Maddoc three days to declare his interest in her. She was thrilled, of course, and when Maddoc was not beating off suitors, he and Addie spent a great deal of time together and eventually fell in love."

Christopher lifted his eyebrows. "I am happy for them, of course. But that does not explain the contents of your missive or why I am here."

David's jaw began to tick. "A suitor, a knight by the name of de Royans who serves Norfolk, challenged Maddoc for Addie's hand," he said, feeling miserable even as he said it, as if he was living it all over again. "It was a brutal battle, like nothing you have ever witnessed before, and you and I have certainly seen our fair share of fights. It all happened so fast... Adalind tried to intervene and Maddoc was gored when he tried to protect her. At least, that's what I think happened. As I said, it happened so fast that before I knew it, Maddoc had a broadsword through his chest and de Royans abducted Adalind."

Christopher's bearded features were grim. "Is Maddoc dead?"

David shook his head. "Nay," he replied, "although God knows, he should be. The wound was bad. The physic said it punctured a lung and sliced other vital organs, but the wound did not kill him. However, he has been gravely ill from infection the past several days. He has a raging fever that is weakening him. The physic seems to think that if he continues along this path, he will not survive much longer."

They came to a halt in the middle of the bailey as the rest of Christopher's army lumbered through the gatehouse. Christopher pulled off his helm and peeled back his hauberk, revealing a full head of hair that once blond, had now turned mostly gray. With his neatly trimmed beard that he had kept since he had been a young man, he presented a strong and stately appearance. But at the moment, he looked despondent and worn. The news was sad, indeed.

"Did you send for Rhys?" he asked quietly.

David nodded. "The same day I sent for you," he said. "He should be here at any time. If Maddoc passes, I want his father to be with him."

Christopher thought of Maddoc du Bois, the young and strong and extremely skilled warrior he had knighted himself when Maddoc had only been seventeen years of age. His father, Rhys, had served Christopher and when Maddoc grew into manhood, Christopher had seen his father's strength and brilliance in the serious young knight. He was wise beyond his years and vastly trustworthy. Every good quality a knight should have, Maddoc possessed. To see such genius come to such a tragic end was sickening.

"God," he finally hissed. "I simply cannot believe any of this. Rhys will be beside himself with grief."

David nodded. "I know," he said quietly. "You should also know that I have sent for Forbes."

Christopher looked at him, surprised. "Gart?" he repeated. "Why?"

David sighed heavily. "Because I need help in recovering Adalind," he said. "Rhys will be useless, as will Maddoc if the man survives, and I am not entirely sure I can be rational about regaining my granddaughter. All I want to do is kill de Royans and punish Norfolk for having the audacity to command such a man. If I am out of control, it will be up to you to keep me sane, and if you are occupied with my madness, the rescue of Adalind will fall to someone who is not so emotionally attached to the situation. That is why I need Gart. I need his wisdom and sense of control. There is no one finer."

Gart Forbes, the man Adalind had seen in Winchester those weeks ago, was a former vassal of the de Lohr war machine, a knight that the foot soldiers used to call 'sach'. It was a loose Gaelic term for madness, which adequately described Gart when the man was in the heat of battle. He had been David's right hand those years ago, just as Rhys had been Christopher's. Both of these exceptional and powerful knights had eventually left the House of de Lohr, establishing their own houses and their own individual reputations for greatness.

Now, they were returning to assist the de Lohrs for one final and great mission; old men who would answer the call of duty one last time. It was both a pleasing and sobering thought, given the circumstances for the reunion. Still, Christopher rolled his eyes at his brother's statement. He couldn't help himself.

"You must be insane," he muttered. "Gart will roll over Norfolk like the hand of God and obliterate him completely. He will burn East Anglia to the roots and smite all to dust. Once he is finished with that, he will chop

Norfolk and anyone associated with him into little pieces and feed them to the dogs. The man is the devil."

David grinned wearily at the dramatic interpretation of Gart Forbes' attributes. "That may be, but if you had to pick one man to rescue one of your womenfolk, who would it be?"

Christopher wasn't hard pressed to acknowledge the point. He puffed out his cheeks and sighed heavily. "I suppose it would be Forbes."

"I thought so."

They were nearing the keep, lost in conversation, when a shout came from the gatehouse. David and Christopher turned to see a big knight astride a bulky brown warhorse approach. The horse was full of spirit and the knight rode him effortlessly. David's expression, so recently heavy with grief, washed with joy and recognition.

"Daniel," he breathed.

Christopher grinned. "I ran in to him on the road about an hour go, heading in our direction," he said. "I forgot to tell you that I found your prodigal son."

David was so glad to see Daniel that there were tears in his eyes. He smiled with true delight as Daniel brought his charger to a halt and dismounted.

Tall like his Uncle Christopher but with his father's chiseled features and deep blue eyes, Daniel Hampton de Lohr, Lord Thornden, looked like a Viking god. Blond, muscular, and something of a wandering spirit, he smiled broadly at his father as he removed helm. Then he opened his arms and sucked the man into a powerful embrace.

"Greetings, Father," he said, releasing his father so he could look the man in the eye. "Imagine my surprise when I ran into Uncle Christopher's army. He said that you called him to Canterbury."

David touched his son's cheek as if to reassure himself that he wasn't dreaming. It had been months since he'd last seen his boy.

"We were expecting you last week," he said. "What kept you?"

Daniel shrugged carelessly. "A lovely baron's daughter in Dorset," he said. "In fact, her father wishes to speak with you but do not listen to him. I did none of those things he has accused me of."

Daniel truly had a lively, devil-may-care personality. He was the life of any gathering; the wit of any party. He was loved and revered by his family and friends. As Christopher snorted at his nephew, David shook his head reproachfully.

"Another father I must pay off because of a compromised daughter?" he said, outrage in his tone. "I have raised you better than that, Daniel. What am I going to tell your mother – again?"

Daniel laughed, mostly because his uncle was laughing and it truly was funny to watch his father stew.

"Tell her I am a rake and a cad, and that no woman should ever trust me." He snorted when his father scowled, and put his arms around the man again, hugging him and kissing his head. "I jest with you, I promise. I simply like to see those veins on the side of your head throb."

David just shook his head again, somewhat disgusted, but mostly thrilled. He loved his son more than anything on earth, rascal that he was.

"So now you have," he said. "Satisfied?"

Daniel grinned. "Until the next time," he said. Then, his gaze moved over the keep he hadn't seen in a long time. "You did not answer my question – why is Uncle Christopher and his army here? What is happening?"

David's good humor left him. He was dreading telling Daniel given that he and Maddoc were very good friends. He had no idea how his son was going to take the news.

"Adalind returned home from fostering a couple of weeks ago," he said quietly. "I know you are aware of the history between Addie and Maddoc, so I know you will be surprised when I tell you that Maddoc has asked for Adalind's hand in marriage."

Daniel's face lit up and he crowed with laughter. "Oh, my giddy young man," he howled. "How on earth did this happen? She used to follow him around to the point of madness and now he... well, I simply cannot believe any of this, not until I have spoken to him myself. He has a lot of explaining to do, that foolish whelp. Where is he?"

Looking forward to harassing Maddoc about the turn of events with Adalind, Daniel started to push past his father so he could seek out his reckless friend. David grabbed him before he could get away.

"Daniel, listen to me," he said. "Adalind had other suitors. They showed up here in droves and Maddoc chased them all away except one. This knight, named de Royans, asked for Adalind's hand and when I denied him, he challenged Maddoc. I am afraid Maddoc was badly injured in the fight and the knight absconded with Adalind. Maddoc is inside the keep but he is very ill. The physic thinks he may die. Your uncle is here because we must go after Adalind and rescue her from the knight that took her."

As he neared the end of his sentence, he could see that Daniel's features had gone from happy and laughing to disbelief and grief. Daniel stared as his father, stunned, as the words sank deep.

"Maddoc is *dying*?" he repeated. Even as the words left his mouth, he shook his head. "That is impossible."

"I am afraid not."

"It is!"

"Nay, Daniel, it is not."

Daniel's grief grew as he realized his father was very serious. "But he is the best knight I have ever seen – the best knight *England* has ever seen. There is no way in which he could have been injured in a fight. He is too damn talented."

David could see that Daniel was growing agitated and hastened to calm him. "Aye, he is," he agreed. "What happened was purely by chance. It should never have happened but it did. Daniel, I realize Maddoc is your friend, but I need your level head now. If we are going to save Adalind, I need your wisdom and confidence. Can you do this for me?"

Daniel heard his father but his eyes were on the keep. He nodded, haphazardly. "Of course," he said, distracted. "Where is Maddoc? I must go to him."

David could see he would get nothing more out of his son until he took him to Maddoc, so with a weary nod of the head, he grasped Daniel by the arm and headed up the steps leading into Canterbury's keep.

It was cool and quiet in the big keep, the smaller hall straight ahead. Servants moved about in the darkened hall but for the most part it was empty. David led Daniel and Christopher up to the second floor where the bedchambers were located. There were four of them, all fairly large, and then three smaller chambers meant for servants.

It was eerily quiet on this level, as if it was forbidden to speak in anything over a whisper. There was a feeling of sadness; they could all sense it, a fog of sorrow that enveloped everything it touched. The corridor was dim as they made their way, the heavy oak doors closed to prying eyes except for one. That panel was half-cocked, weak light emitting from inside. David took them to that door and pushed it open wide.

The first thing Daniel noticed was that the bed took up nearly the entire room. An oilcloth hung over the small window that allowed for light and ventilation into the room, and it smelled heavily of cloves and mint, pungent scents in their own right but nearly staggering when combined. A very old man sat against the wall as he fussed with some items on the table next to him, looking up when he heard movement in the doorway. Three enormous warriors stood there, all of them appearing somewhat hesitant.

"My lord," the little man greeted David directly, stiffly standing. "There is no change to report on the knight. His fever rages still. He rests."

All three of the men in the doorway looked at the bed where Maddoc lay. He was stripped from the waist up, his muscular chest gleaming with sweat in the weak light and an enormous bandage wrapped around his midsection. Surprisingly, his eyes were open and when he saw Daniel, he tried to get up.

"Daniel," he said weakly. "You have come."

When they saw that Maddoc was trying to rise, they all hastened to the bed to hold the man down. Daniel was at his head, his big hands on Maddoc's broad shoulders.

"Easy, man, easy," he said, filled with grief over the sight of his friend and struggling to keep a smile on his face. "Stay where you are. You look as if you have seen better days, my friend."

Maddoc's bright blue eyes were unnaturally intense as he practically clung to Daniel. It was such a desperate hold, one not unnoticed by David or Christopher. Maddoc was hanging on to Daniel with a death grip.

"He took Adalind," he told Daniel, his voice terribly weak and unlike the Maddoc they all knew. "His name is Brighton de Royans. He is a vassal of Norfolk so he must have taken her to Arundel Castle. I know she is very frightened and she must fear that I am dead, but you must find her and tell her that I live and I will come for her when I can. Will you do this for me?"

Daniel patted the big hands that held on to his arms, cold fingers digging in to his flesh. He could see that Maddoc's mind was hazed with fever, for the man wasn't thinking clearly. It was obvious in the way he spoke, and his heart sank.

"Of course," he assured him strongly. "I will go today. But if I find her, wouldn't you rather have me bring her back?"

Maddoc blinked as if that thought hadn't occurred to him. He began to nod. "Aye," he agreed. "Please bring her back."

Daniel was having a difficult time with his composure. His mightiest and dearest friend was verging on delirium and death, and he could hardly stand the grief. So he nodded his head firmly, held Maddoc's face in his hands, and kissed the man loudly on the forehead. He was struggling so very hard not to weep.

"I will," he said hoarsely. "I swear I will bring Addie back to you. You must not die until I can bring her back, do you hear me? You must stay alive. Do you promise?"

Maddoc nodded weakly, his strength failing him as he sank back against the mattress. "I promise," he muttered, evidently relieved that something was going to be done about Adalind's abduction. "When you find Addie, please tell her that I am not dead. Please tell her... Danny, tell her that I love her. What I feel for her is timeless and unending. Will you do that for me?"

Daniel lost the struggle against the tears. They began to well in his eyes. "Do you truly love her?"

"I do. I regret deeply that I have not told her. I should have."

Daniel flicked a gloved finger at his eyes so the tears would not fall and make him look like an idiot. "Addie has been telling you that she loves you since she was five years of age," he said. "Now you are finally loving her in return? Great Gods, you are a slow and dim-witted man."

Maddoc's lips twitched with a smile. At least his humor wasn't gone completely. "I know," he whispered. "Please tell her."

"I will, but when I bring her back, you had better tell her yourself. She will want to hear it from you."

"I swear, I will." Maddoc turned his head slightly and noticed Christopher and David standing at the foot of his bed. He hadn't been aware of their presence until this moment, so focused he had been on Daniel. When he realized there were two earls standing next to his bed, he started to get up again. "My lords, I did not see you. I apologize I am unable to greet you properly."

Daniel pushed him down again as Christopher came around to stand next to his nephew. "You are forgiven," he said to Maddoc, his sky-blue eyes twinkling although his heart was breaking at the sight. "Your father will be here soon, Maddoc. He will be very glad to see you."

Rhys looked surprised. "My father?" he repeated. "Why is he coming?"

Christopher didn't want to put the reason in to words. He just couldn't bring himself to do it. "He is coming to help regain Adalind, of course," he said the first thing that came to mind. "Daniel cannot go alone."

In Maddoc's fever-ravaged mind, the reason made sense. "Is that why you are here?"

"It is."

Maddoc extended a hand and Christopher captured it, holding it strongly. "Then I thank you," he said faintly. "She means everything to me."

"We shall bring her back, Maddoc. Have no fear."

"I will not."

They could all see that he was growing exhausted from the conversation. David in particular was very concerned. He turned to the physic as Maddoc, completely worn out, closed his eyes.

"What are you giving him for the fever?" he demanded.

The physic wasn't intimidated; he'd been in his profession far too long to show response to demanding lords. He faced David calmly.

"Boiled bark from the white willow, my lord," he said. "I have also placed a poultice of mustard and moss against the wound, which has been drawing the poison out of his chest. But, most importantly, I have been forcing him to drink a rotten brew that has proven its worth many times over in healing the sick. I have great hopes that it will cure him."

By this time, Christopher was listening to the old man. "Rotten brew?" he repeated. "What madness is this?"

The old physic looked to Christopher. "I learned my trade on the sands of The Levant during Richard's crusade," he replied. "The savages had a brew they called 'Rotten Beer' that they made from bread that had gone bad. It is fermented until green hair covers it. Steeped in warm water, it is held warm for several days until it can reach full strength, and then it has a miraculous medicinal quality that cures anything. I have used it time and time again. I am using it on Sir Maddoc in the hopes it will ease the poison in his chest. If it does not work, I fear we will lose him."

David sighed heavily, looking over at Maddoc where Daniel was still sitting beside the man, holding his hand and stroking his head. Knight to knight, brother to brother. In the dim and pungent room, it made for a tragic scene. He felt sick and so very sad.

"Very well," he replied. "Do what you must. But keep him alive. He has much to live for."

The old man nodded and turned back to his table, which had an array of odd medicaments and vessels on it. As Christopher lingered at the old physic's table to inspect the odd and miraculous things upon it, David went back over to Maddoc's bedside. He put a hand on his son's shoulder.

"We should let him sleep now," he said quietly. "Come with me. Your mother will want to see you."

Daniel nodded reluctantly, gave Maddoc's hand one last squeeze, and stood up. Maddoc was already asleep so they quietly left the room, heading out into the dim corridor. Once in the hall, Daniel exploded.

"Who is this de Royans?" he demanded, smacking in open palm with his fist. "Who is this bastard who has done this to Maddoc? Does he truly serve Norfolk? I am leaving right now to find him and when I do, I will draw and quarter him and take great pleasure in every scream of pain he utters."

David put a calming hand on his son. "We will go after him, I assure you," he said. "That is why I sent for your uncle and for Maddoc's father and other allies. Trust me when I say that de Royans and Norfolk will suffer. This offense against Maddoc and Adalind will not go unpunished."

Daniel looked at his father, his uncle, and then started to charge down the corridor. "I am leaving now," he said resolutely. "I am going to find this whoreskin and destroy everything about him."

David grabbed his son, halting the man's progression. "Surely you are not forgetting about Adalind," he said. "De Royans has her. We must make sure she is safe before we punish him. We need your calm head, Daniel, not your rage."

Daniel's jaw ticked. "You realize that if he abducted her, he has probably already married her," he said, lowering his angry voice. "And if he has not married her, then he has, at the very least, compromised her."

David closed his eyes to the words had been afraid to voice. "If he abducted her with the purpose of marriage, then I am sure he has not harmed her in any way," Christopher said, seeing his brother's grief. "Why harm the woman he wants to marry? It would make no sense. David, did you get the impression that he was a violent and reckless man other than challenging Maddoc?"

David shook his head. "Nay," he said honestly. "In truth, he was very polite and well-spoken. I never received the impression that he was malevolent or mad. He simply wanted to marry Adalind and I denied him. He must have either been terribly insulted or unused to denial to go after Maddoc the way he did. He was determined."

Daniel had heard enough. "I am going to find him," he rumbled threateningly. "I am going to find him and find Adalind, and I am going to make him pay for what he has done. I sincerely hope the man is right with God because when I am finished with him, he will wish he had never heard the name of de Lohr. In fact, I...."

His rant was cut off by the sounds of heavy footfalls in the corridor. Daniel, David, and Christopher turned in the direction of the sounds to see the hulking figure of Rhys du Bois emerging from the darkened stairwell.

They were all startled by the sudden appearance of Maddoc's father. The man, so handsome in his youth with the black hair and brilliant blue eyes that Maddoc had inherited, looked old and gray and exhausted, as if he hadn't slept in a hundred years. There was grief and sorrow lining every inch of his face, so much so that the physical impact was unavoidable. They felt as if they had all been hit in the gut with it. Christopher broke away from David and Daniel.

"Rhys," he said, holding out a hand in greeting. "It has been a very long time, my friend."

Rhys took Christopher's hand, the brilliant blue eyes already filling with unshed tears. He could hardly speak. "My son," he said hoarsely. "Is he dead?"

David cut in, shaking his head. "Nay," he assured him. "The physic is doing all he can to heal him. Come and see him."

Christopher and David began pulling Rhys down the hall as Daniel stood by and watched. He was so consumed with rage and agony that he could hardly move. Two young men were with Rhys, emerging from the stairwell behind him, and Daniel recognized them as two of Rhys' sons.

Evan de Foix was another black-haired and blue-eyed son but Trevor de Foix resembled his mother to a fault with his reddish blond hair. De Foix was the name the family used in France where they lived, as relatives of the Duke of Navarre, and Daniel extended his hand to the brothers as they came near. They looked just as exhausted as their father.

"How is my brother?" Evan asked in a pleading whisper, gripping Daniel's hand.

Daniel wasn't sure how much more sorrow and grief he could take. Every man felt it, radiated it, until it sucked all other emotions out of the air.

"He lives," Daniel replied softly. He nodded his head in the direction they were taking Rhys. "Go with your father and you shall see for yourself."

Solemnly, Evan nodded his head and continued on after his father. Trevor, very young and quite tall at his age, nodded grimly as he passed by. Daniel watched them move down the corridor, crowding into the small room where Maddoc was. He could hear voices, mostly David and Rhys', until he began to hear sobbing.

Quietly, he moved back down the hallway and peered into the room where Rhys had Maddoc's limp body in his arms, sobbing low and mournfully. The father rocked his son gently, devastated over the turn of events. It was the worst thing Daniel had ever seen.

Turning on his heel, he came face to face with his mother and older sister. Startled at their appearance, and the fact that they had snuck up behind him, Daniel did the first thing that came to mind. He threw his arms around them both, hugging them tightly as they began to weep softly. He couldn't even speak; all he could do was hug. Words, at the moment, were unnecessary.

As he hugged his weeping mother, he kept thinking of the horrid things he would do to the de Royans bastard once he got his hands on him. For the man to cause so much grief to his family and friends was unforgivable.

He would make him pay with every last bone in his body.

You and I have floated here on the stream that brings from the fount.
At the heart of time, love of one for another.

CHAPTER SEVENTEEN

"Why in God's name did you bring her here?" came the plea. "You will bring the entire House of de Lohr down on us, and for what? To sate your lust with one of their own?"

Brighton stood in the solar of the Earl of Norfolk, Hugh d'Aubigney. Hugh was a younger man, of ill health, but with a good and steady mind. He was the fourth earl in a long line of powerful earls and perhaps one of the finest of the line. He was well-respected. But now, as Brighton stood before the good earl, he was coming to think that everything about this venture with Adalind de Aston was going to crush him. Everything he had worked for was now at risk. The good earl was not the bit supportive of what his senior knight had done, and he did not mince words.

"It was not to sate my lust, my lord, I assure you," Brighton replied steadily. "She is a marriageable prospect, as am I. Marriage is made in such ways."

"Wars are made in such ways," Hugh fired back. His head was aching and his stomach rolled, paining him greatly. He sank into the nearest chair as a dog tried to jump on his lap. "Brighton, we have more civilized ways of obtaining a bride these days. That is why there are contracts and negotiations. Do you have any idea what you have done with your barbaric abduction? You have put me in the sights of the House of de Lohr and they will crush me to get to you. Did you stop to think of this before you kidnapped their kin?"

Brighton stood his ground although it was an increasing struggle. He was beginning to grow hot, thinking it was perhaps from the snapping fire in the hearth next to him, so he moved away from the flame. He was still hot even after he moved, now with the added discomfort of doubt in his actions. He tried not to let uncertainty overwhelm him.

"I challenged her betrothed and I emerged the victor," he said. "I did not abduct her. She was the prize."

Hugh rolled his eyes as he helped the big, shaggy dog climb up onto his lap. The dog brought warmth, which he craved in his slender body. Dogs were often on his lap for that purpose.

"She is *not* a prize," he snapped softly. "That woman is a mess, Brighton. She screams and kicks and fights anyone that comes near her. That is not the behavior of a prize but the behavior of a captive."

Brighton sighed heavily, lowering his gaze to regroup. "She is unsteady, that is true," he replied. "But it is her exhaustion. We have been traveling for ten days. Given time...."

"Given time she will still feel the same way," Hugh cut him off strongly, pointing fingers. "Brighton, I want you to listen to me very carefully. You are a brilliant young knight and I have always been very proud to have you in my stable but, at the moment, I fear you have done something horribly foolish. The Earl of Canterbury's granddaughter must be returned home immediately."

"She is mine."

"She cannot stay."

Brighton didn't want to argue with the man but he wasn't going to return Adalind, either. He tried another tactic.

"It is my intention to marry the woman," he said. "We stopped at three parishes on our way from Canterbury but the lady would not... that is to say, circumstances did not permit us to be married. I was therefore hoping Fr. Trudo could perform the mass. Arundel has been my home for several years and I would like to be married here and raise my family here."

He made it sound soft and sentimental, but Hugh would have none of it. He shook his head. "Get that woman back to her family," he commanded. "If you refuse, then I will throw you in the vault and have someone else return her. Is that clear?"

Harsh orders that had Brighton backed into a corner. He had to question himself at that moment – was he willing to throw away a bright future and an impressive career over a woman who didn't want him? He didn't want to deliberately disobey the earl, but he was disinclined to follow a direct order. It would be career suicide if he refused. After a moment, he sighed again.

"My lord," he began carefully. "If I can obtain her agreement for this wedding, will you allow us to stay?"

Hugh looked at him as if he was daft. "The only way I will allow her to stay is if you can get written permission from her grandfather and his assurance that he will not attack Arundel," he said. "Given the circumstances, I am not entirely sure such a thing is possible."

"But you will consider it?"

"It is an impossible task."

"But you *will* consider it, my lord?"

Hugh met his gaze steadily. He had known Brighton de Royans for seven years and never in that time had he known the man to behave stupidly. There was a first time for everything, he supposed, but based upon the fleeting glimpse of Adalind de Aston, perhaps he did understand Brighton's infatuation with the woman just a little. She was exquisite. However, it didn't change the way of things.

"I will consider it if you can bring David de Lohr to my doorstep, in peace, to discuss it," he said. "But until that time, stay away from the lady. I am sending Isabelle to tend her and perhaps bring her some comfort after what you have done. After that, she will be returned."

Brighton didn't argue with him further, mostly because he was going to disobey him by keeping Adalind at Arundel until he could figure out a solution to everything. He knew Adalind was wild with hatred against him, but he hoped that time and his gentle persuasion would see that situation change. He would hope for it. Until then, however, he had to figure out how to hide a woman who was not exactly the shy and meek type.

He had to hide a banshee from discovery.

***

Arundel Castle was the biggest castle Adalind had ever seen, and she had seen quite a few castles in her short life. The enormous motte had a keep set deep within its crest and a gigantic curtain wall surrounded the castle using the motte as a center point, creating two baileys. On the north side of the castle were structures that housed apartments and stables, while the south side contained the biggest hall in all of southern England. Truly, the sheer size and pageantry of Arundel Castle was overwhelming to the senses.

Overwhelming for normal visitors, that is; to Adalind, it was her prison, a corner of hell that she had been relegated to with her jailor as Brighton de Royans. She wasn't impressed with it, or anything else for that matter. Anyone that approached her was screamed at. She had no sense of propriety or manners. She was distraught and overwhelmed; seventeen days after her violent extraction from Canterbury. She simply couldn't wrap her mind around anything other than her grief.

They had arrived at Arundel the day before. Brighton had put her in a room on the northern block and had assigned people to see to her comfort since she would take none from him. Their travel to Arundel had been nothing short of hellish because she fought, kicked, scratched, and bit every step of the way to the point where Brighton was forced to bind her as they traveled. There was no other way to accomplish it because she tried to run every chance she was given and when she wasn't running, she was trying to hurt him.

Moreover, he'd stopped at three churches after he had left St. Barnabas in the attempt to marry Adalind but she fought him so much on it, literally, that he had given up by the fourth attempt. He didn't want to marry a woman he would have to restrain during the mass and it was quite clear that Adalind wasn't going to make it easy for him.

In her filthy surcoat that she had been wearing for almost two weeks, Adalind sat huddled in a corner of the decently appointed chamber she had been consigned to. Her blood had stained the neckline of the garment, drying long ago into dark brown stains, and the wound from whence the blood flow sprang was now a large scab near her right collarbone. It was healing nicely but would leave a scar.

Still, she didn't care. There wasn't much she cared about at the moment other than another scheme to escape Brighton. It had been hours since their arrival to Arundel and even though there was a bed in the small, neat chamber, she hadn't used it. When someone came in to stoke the fire, she had screamed at them and threw whatever she could get her hands on. Now no one wanted to come into her room, which was how she wanted it. She wanted to be left alone with her grief.

Her last vision of Maddoc was of the man face-down in the bailey of Canterbury. She could still see the moment Brighton swung on him and plowed the broadsword into his torso. She was haunted by the expression on Maddoc's face, surprised by the fact that Brighton had actually gored him. All of these things assaulted her senses until she couldn't think straight and the guilt of her actions was the most damaging thing of all.

She had caused Maddoc's death. At first, she wanted to die, too. She was eager for it. But after days of travel and reflecting on her actions, she came to realize that killing herself would only condemn her soul to Purgatory where she would never see Maddoc again. If she wanted to see him in the afterlife, then she would have to live out her worthless and meaningless life until such time as death naturally took her. She could only hope it was soon.

The only place that seemed like a safe haven to her now, a place that was closer to Maddoc's soul than any other, was a convent. It was a place closer to God and, subsequently, closer to heaven than anywhere else she could think of. Once, she had wanted to join the cloister because she would not marry the man she loved. Now, she wanted to join for the same reason. But in order to commit herself, she would have to escape Arundel and Brighton, and she knew that would not be a simple thing.

Oh, God, she moaned inwardly, laying her head on the bended knees that were clutched against her chest, *please forgive me for what I did to Maddoc. Please embrace him within your bosom, O Lord, until such time as we can be reunited again. My love for the man is unending and timeless, and it is stronger than the cold fingers of Death. We will be together again, someday.* She had prayed that prayer many times over the several days, usually accompanied by sobs. Today was no different. But as she prayed the prayer, the only thing that brought her any measure of comfort, there was a soft knock on the door.

Adalind's head popped up, her eyes narrowing. She looked around the room, quickly, noting that there was nothing left for her to throw unless she wanted to toss tables and chairs. She had exhausted her ammunition supply within the first hour of her arrival. Gearing up for another fight, she balled her bruised hands and didn't say a word as the knock came again. After a lengthy pause, the door slowly creaked open.

A small woman with a tightly wimpled head and big brown eyes peered into the dim room. She had evidently been warned about Adalind because the only thing visible was her head. She wasn't about to step into the room. After a moment, she spied Adalind huddled up in the corner against the wall, rolled up into a protective ball. The woman smiled timidly.

"Lady Adalind?" she said in a very soft and sweet voice. "I am the Lady Isabelle, Countess of Norfolk. I promise I have not come to hurt you in any way. I have simply come to make sure you are taken care of. May I please enter?"

Adalind gazed at the woman a moment longer before turning away. She didn't want to look at her and she didn't want to talk to her. But she stayed huddled up in her protective ball and that was evidently good enough for Lady Isabelle. As long as the Lady Adalind wasn't charging, she would be brave and enter the room.

There were a pair of female servants behind Lady Isabelle and when Adalind caught sight of them out of the corner of her eye, she rolled to her knees, preparing for some manner of a physical confrontation because it appeared to her as if Lady Isabelle was bringing reinforcements. When Lady Isabelle saw Adalind's reaction, she held out a swift hand to the women behind her, ordering them to stop in their tracks. They did.

"My lady," Isabelle said calmly, soothingly. "I assure you, we will not harm you. We have brought food and clothing and warm water for you to bathe in. I promise I only wish to help you and I swear no one will hurt you. Will you please allow us into your chamber?"

Adalind wasn't ready for any human contact. She growled as she spoke. "Get *out!*" she snarled. "You are not welcome here. Get out and leave me alone!"

The servants cowered but Lady Isabelle remained strong, at least for the moment. "My lady, I understand you have been through some very trying times," she said. "I do not wish to aggravate or harass you – I swear I only want to help. Will you please let me?"

"Nay!" Adalind barked. "Get out before I throw you out!"

Isabelle studied the woman, looking like a wild animal in her torn and stained clothing, her long blond hair dirty and askew. But she also noted her face and she could see that the Lady Adalind was a truly beautiful woman underneath the dirt and snarling. She could also see just how shattered the woman was. She began to feel a tremendous amount of pity for her.

"My lady," Isabelle tried again. "My husband has ordered Sir Brighton to return you to Canterbury. You cannot go home in rags and dirt. Will you please allow me to clean you up so you can be returned home looking as a daughter of de Lohr should?"

That gently uttered statement seemed to suck all of the fight out of Adalind. She stared at Isabelle, her features pale with shock. For the first time in weeks, the wild and frightened animal subsided.

"Home?" she repeated. "I... I am going home?"

Isabelle smiled timidly. "Aye," she said. "May I help you prepare?"

Adalind was truly astonished. She stood up, unsteadily, her eyes wide on Isabelle. "Where... where is Brighton?"

"He is with my husband."

"Will he punish him?"

"I do not know, my lady. That is for my husband to decide."

"I will not see him again?"

"I do not know, my lady, but if I have any say in the matter, he will be kept from you."

"When can I return home?"

"I am not for certain, but it will be soon. Will you let me help you now?"

Adalind stood there a moment, dazed as she reflected upon Lady Isabelle's words, before finally nodding her agreement. The lure of getting away from Brighton, for the moment, blurred all else in her mind. Her nod was brief but enough to send Isabelle into action. Soon, the woman was barking orders like a commander as the small army of servants she brought with her swung into action.

Adalind ended up in the corner again, watching the activity with anxiety. Isabelle went to her and spoke softly enough, sweetly enough, so that Adalind calmed somewhat and Isabelle was able to put her arm around her to comfort her. She stood there and held her, explaining the actions of the servants as if she was explaining the situation to a small and frightened child.

Adalind let the woman comfort her. In truth, she needed it. The warmth of human contact was not to be underestimated and it was the first time in three weeks that she felt safe. She was exhausted, emotional, and hungry, and Isabelle must have sensed her immediate needs because she directed two servants bearing trays to set them down on the table near the small lancet window.

There was a pitcher of wine, bread, cheese, fruit, and a big trencher that contained an entire roast fowl and a steaming bowl of boiled carrots. As Isabelle continued to direct the servants in the filling of a great copper tub and the building of a fire in the dark and sooty hearth, Adalind nearly collapsed into one of the chairs and began tearing at the food.

As she stuffed food into her mouth, she began to notice that some of the servants were passing through a small and hidden doorway that was built in next to the hearth. It was a servant's passage, not unusual in fine houses that usually led to a kitchen or other service part of the structure. She hadn't noticed the door before because it blended seamlessly into the wall, but she was coming to think that perhaps she could use it to escape. The main door into the room was bolted and locked, but it was quite possible this one was not. She tried not to pay too much attention to it, fearful that Isabelle or someone else might catch on that she had noticed it.

When can I return home? She had asked. Isabelle had not provided a satisfactory answer and Adalind had no intention of remaining at Arundel any longer. She had to get out, to find a nunnery somewhere, somehow, that would accept her pledge. There was no use in returning to Canterbury because there was nothing left for her there. She knew they had already buried Maddoc, as it had been weeks since his death, and the thought that she had been unable to attend his funeral brought instant tears. Her chewing slowed as tears coursed down her cheeks, and Isabelle happened to notice.

"Oh, my lady," Isabelle sighed, going to Adalind and putting her hands on her shoulders to comfort her. Then she looked up at the servants milling about in the room. "Everyone get out! Get out now!"

The servants made all haste for the door, including those bearing hot water for the tub, but Isabelle yelled at those men to deposit their load before leaving. Water was dumped and people scattered, eventually leaving Isabelle alone with Adalind and a lone remaining serving woman who was cleaning up the splashed water on the floor. When the door finally shut, the room was suddenly still and quiet. Isabelle turned to Adalind.

"Now, my lady," she said kindly. "Let us strip you of your soiled clothing and wash the dirt from your skin. You will feel better when you are clean again."

Adalind's tears for Maddoc had faded and her focus had returned to the servant's door. She wasn't thinking about anything else; food, bath, or rest. All she could think of was slipping from that door and losing herself in the maze of Arundel Castle, finding a way to escape the towering walls that were boxing her in.

Weeks of travel, of chaos, had shaken her usually steady mind. Grief had further shattered it. She was thinking the thoughts of a desperate person as if she couldn't comprehend anything else. She wanted out. But in order to accomplish that, she had to rid herself of Lady Isabelle and the servant woman. She had to be clever. Sensing the woman was already very sympathetic towards her situation, she knew she had to exploit that. Not usually sly or conniving, Adalind dug down deep to find the necessary trait.

"I... I am not feeling very well," she lied. "I realize you have gone to some trouble to bring a bath, but I cannot... I simply want to lie down. I do not wish to bathe now."

Isabelle wasn't entirely unsympathetic. "I understand you are pushed beyond your limit," she said. "I promise we will make quick work of your bath and you will feel much better when we are finished."

Adalind shook her head. "Nay," she insisted weakly. "Please let me rest for a time and then I will submit to your attention. I simply do not feel strong enough now."

Isabelle was indecisive but she didn't want to push her. It was the first time since Adalind had arrived at Arundel that she wasn't screaming or throwing things, so she didn't want to pressure the woman back into her animalistic behavior. Therefore, she graciously backed down.

"As you say, my lady," she said. "We will return before the evening meal and perhaps you will feel better then."

Adalind kept her gaze averted, her dirty hair hanging over her face. "Perhaps."

"I shall leave the food. Perhaps you should eat a little more and regain your strength."

"I will try. Please leave me alone."

Isabelle was reluctant to leave her but forced a smile, accepting her guest's wishes courteously. There was something so desperate and sorrowful about Lady Adalind, something that compelled her to want to remain with her. Something wasn't right with the woman, but she honestly didn't know what. All she knew was what her husband had told her. She wished she could engage the lady in a calm conversation but now was not the time. Perhaps later, after the lady rested, would be more appropriate.

Adalind sat in the chair, staring at the floor with her hair hanging over her face, as Isabelle and the serving woman silently quit the room. When the door shut softly, Adalind's head shot up, her gaze on the closed door. She could hear voices in the corridor outside, Lady Isabelle's mingled with a man's voice. She didn't recognize it and assumed it was a guard of some kind. When Lady Isabelle's voice disappeared, Adalind bolted up from the chair.

With great silence, she skittered across the cold wood floor to the servant's door. The panel was flush against the wall and the seams were nearly invisible, so it took Adalind a couple of pushes against the wall before the panel finally shifted. Another push and it swung open. Thrilled, Adalind peered down a set of narrow and dark stairs that lead down into blackness. She couldn't even see the bottom. But that didn't matter to her and with tremendous care, she slipped inside the door and cautiously descended the stairs.

Adalind's heart was racing as she came to the bottom of the dim steps, terrified every second that she was going to come across a servant or a soldier. The stairs dumped out into a low-ceilinged corridor with an arched roof and Adalind paused at the base of the steps, hearing voices off to her right and deciding that she would therefore go left.

As she slipped down the passageway, Adalind could see that she was in the storage area below the living level of the keep and there were several rooms that were stacked with items she couldn't stop to explore. All she knew was that she was feeling freedom in her veins, escape from Brighton and the hell he had put her through the past seventeen days, and an overwhelming need to break away. She had to get out or die trying.

At the end of the corridor was a small kitchen with a blazing fire in a brick reinforced hearth and two women moving about their duties. There was also a small, heavily fortified door that was cracked open. Smoke from the malfunctioning fireplace seeped out into the yard beyond. Adalind burst into the room and, seeing the startled women staring back at her, rushed out through the half-opened kitchen door like a runaway horse. The lure of the yard beyond was too great and she couldn't control herself.

The kitchen yard outside was boxed in but not too terribly. Even though it was the spring season, it was rather cold outside, and wet, as Adalind rushed into the center of the yard. Almost immediately, she spied a small gate that, once she charged through it, opened up into another yard, larger, with a fish pond and a big well. Adalind had visited enough castles during the course of her fostering and traveling with the entourage from Winchester that she knew most of the larger castles had postern gates, usually near the kitchens, for easy access to the yards and ponds. These postern gates were usually very small and extremely fortified in case of a siege. As Adalind ran a rather desperate circle around the yard, she spied a small iron gate set within the wall.

Making a mad dash for the gate, she saw that it was bolted well from the inside with a huge iron bolt. She grunted and groaned as she worked the bolt, trying to loosen it, and eventually the rod shifted enough so that she was able to slide it free. It took two good yanks to pull the gate open enough so that she could slip through because the mud and muck beneath it prevented easy movement.

From that point, it was a clear shot down the slopes of Arundel and into the woods that clustered around the fortress on the north east side. Spring rains had left everything extremely wet and muddy, but Adalind didn't care. All she could taste or feel was freedom. Once into the dense woods with their shielding trees and canopies of branches, she oriented herself to the direction she wanted to go via the main road that led to Arundel, knowing that road approached from almost due east. She had heard Brighton say so at some point. She also knew that Canterbury was almost due east.

Sticking to the fields and bramble, she made her desperate escape.

You become an image of what is remembered forever

CHAPTER EIGHTEEN

"Unfortunately, Daniel has gone without us," David said, looking particularly pale and drawn. "Seeing Maddoc on his deathbed was too much for the man to take. He has gone to seek vengeance against de Royans and against Norfolk."

The solar of Canterbury was a crowded place. Dogs milled around, looking for scraps, as a host of powerful men filled the small room. It was, in truth, a legendary assembly of de Lohr and their allies, something that had not been witnessed for a very long time and perhaps would never be seen again. Men of power, breeding, and skill lined the walls as David spoke the sorrowful words.

"Then he is going to get himself killed." The reply came from Gart Forbes who, having arrived only hours earlier, now found himself in the middle of a deepening crisis.

Very tall, very broad, and with chiseled features and a great bald head, as Lord Gallox, a vassal of Baron Buckland who also happened to be his step-son, Gart commanded an exceptionally powerful fighting force because simply put, Gart was a warrior's warrior. He had once been the best fighting man in the realm and still managed to maintain something of a very powerful reputation with an army of men sworn to him that had been compared to the precision and strength of ancient Roman troops. More than Gart's intelligence or tactics, it was his sheer fighting ability that was greatly respected, even at his age.

David glanced over at the big man in well-used mail standing near the hearth. "Daniel is quick to temper," he admitted, rolling his eyes at his brother when he caught the man smirking. "I realize he gets that particular attribute from me, but he also has the ability to see a situation from all sides once he has cooled. I would hope, at some point, he will realize he cannot take on the whole of Norfolk alone and return to us. But in the meanwhile, we must prepare to lay siege to Arundel Castle if, in fact, Adalind is there and they do not release her upon demand."

The room fell silent for the most part, each man to his own thoughts, not wanting to voice the obvious. There was one thing they were all thinking but reluctant to mention it. It was too sad to comprehend. Still, it needed to be addressed.

"David," Rhys finally broke the stale silence. "If de Royans has married her, there is nothing we can do about it. Surely we can lay siege to Arundel in vengeance for what de Royans did to Maddoc, but if Adalind is married to the knight, even though it is a forced marriage, the fact remains that she belongs to him and we cannot take her back."

David looked at the man seated on the other side of his enormous and well-used desk. "Then I will charge him with thievery and I will charge Norfolk with harboring a criminal," he hissed. "De Royans will not keep Adalind even if they are legally married, I assure you. I will take my grievance straight to Henry and let the king hear my evidence. De Royans stole my granddaughter and he will pay."

"And he gravely injured my son," Rhys shot back quietly. "No one wants to see the man pay more than I do but the matter of Adalind is separate from the matter of Maddoc. If she is de Royans wife, we cannot break that bond with all of the sieges and all of the weapons in the world."

"Then I will kill him," Evan de Foix, standing in the shadows behind his father, piped up. "He has virtually killed my brother so I will kill him. It is an honorable reckoning and once he is dead, we can claim the lady."

Rhys held up a hand to silence his rather rash son. "I do not need two dead sons on my hands, Evan."

"But you sit by and discuss details that are not insurmountable, Father," the young man insisted. "If de Royans is dead, Adalind is no longer his wife."

Rhys turned to look at his son. He had an identical twin brother just like him, left home to protect Bellay Castle in their absence. Both young men were quick to temper and rather reckless, something Rhys, with his infinite patience, had been trying to work out of them. He was still working on it.

"You will kindly let the earl decide what is to be done," he said, lifting his dark brows for emphasis. "Be still, now."

Upset but obedient, Evan sank back into the shadows with his brother and Gart Forbes' son, Brydon, who was a well-established knight in his own right. Brydon had ridden to Canterbury with his father at the head of a nine hundred man army, silent and big like his father, watching and waiting from the shadows for actions to be planned and commands to be given. Rhys eyed the sons of the great knights in the room for a long moment before returning his attention to David.

"This is a critical and evil time, David," he said quietly. "You know I respect your opinions and your decisions, but I would be remiss if I did not point out that your emotions could cause you to make a rash decision. I cannot reach a logical conclusion because my son is involved, and neither can Chris because of you and Adalind. I would suggest we ask Gart to lead us on this matter since he is the only one without a child involved."

David looked at Christopher for the man's reaction. It was as David had originally told his brother, in much the same scenario – everyone had an emotional stake in this endeavor except for Forbes. Rhys saw that, too. Christopher wasn't one to relinquish control of a battle march but he had to admit that, at this juncture, it was the wise thing to do. He looked at Gart.

"It would seem you are the most level headed and responsible out of all of us at this time," he said, rather dryly. "You have heard the facts. You know the situation. What would you suggest?"

Gart's gaze was steady. He had deep set eyes that were intense and mysterious, as if they hid a thousand secrets and a thousand emotions. With his gaze still lingering on Christopher, he spoke.

"Brydon?" he asked. "What would you do, lad?"

It was an invitation for his son to do what he did best; Brydon was a master of tactics and planning, and Gart relied heavily on the man. When all else was crumbling, Brydon held strong and steady, observing all, seeing all. The young knight heard his name, the softly uttered question, and stepped forward.

"It must be assumed that de Royans has married the lady already," he said, his mind working quickly. "If I abducted a lady for the purpose of marrying her, I would not wait. Therefore, we must assume that Lady Adalind is now Lady de Royans. That being said, Lord du Bois is correct; we cannot simply wrest her away from her husband because the Church would side with him. Man cannot break what God has brought together."

As the men in the solar shifted somewhat uncomfortably, knowing he spoke the truth, Brydon continued.

"It would seem to me that we should isolate the true reason behind our might force," he said, his voice quiet but calculating. "Are we gathering in anger to blindly raze Arundel out of sheer fury and vengeance, or are we gathering to accomplish a clear purpose? We must define that purpose, my lords. Is it to regain the Lady Adalind, or is it to avenge Maddoc?"

"Both," Evan spat. "My brother deserves justice."

Brydon nodded in agreement before Rhys could quiet his son. "And he shall get it, but we must be smart with our actions," he said. "It is my sense that we should march on Arundel and show him our strength. D'Aubigney will know that we mean business when he sees a two thousand man army on his doorstep. But before we let a single arrow fly, we ask what has become of the Lady Adalind. If she is married, then we must call out de Royans to face our challenge, one on one. I will volunteer to face him but I am sure there are others that would take precedence over me. If de Royans refuses, not only is he a coward, but he is a thief, and at that point we will make demands to d'Aubigney to turn him over to us to face justice. Only if he refuses do we lay siege as a last resort. Is everything I have said so far making sense?"

While Gart grinned with pride, the others in the room nodded stiffly. No one liked what they were hearing but it was composed and reasonable. Brydon had a calming air about him that Gart did not have, making him ideal to deliver serious or bad news.

David nodded to Brydon's question, leaning against the table with his chin in his hand. "You make complete sense," he said, sounding rather depressed, "and you are correct - we must define our purpose. I will agree to your plan on how to handle this situation because it takes vengeance out of the mix and replaces it with justice. That is all I want for Maddoc and Adalind, truly – justice."

Brydon glanced around the room, reading the various expressions, until he came to his father. Gart winked at his son, so very proud of the man. Brydon smiled faintly in return.

"If we are all in agreement, I will have the sergeants begin assembling the troops," Brydon said, winding down his speech because there was action to take. The time for talk was over. "It is at least one hundred miles to Arundel which means it will take us at least six days to reach it. The sooner we start, the sooner we can resolve the situation."

David nodded at him and he quit the room swiftly, followed by Evan and Trevor. Christopher, David, Rhys, and Gart could hear the young men as they began to bark orders, their strong and steady voices wafting through the solar's lancet windows. They were young men who had been well trained, bred from fine stock, now becoming the strongest generation as their fathers grew old and prepared to pass on their responsibilities. It was a rather pivotal moment as the men in the solar, the great knights of old, realized this might quite possibly be the last action they ever saw together. The feelings were bittersweet.

"As I listen to Brydon, I can only think that I have accomplished what I set out to do in life," Gart murmured, glancing up at the three faces so familiar to him. "His mother and I have raised him correctly. He is a fine man with a fine heart. Even if I had conquered the entire world and all within it, at this moment, Brydon would still be my greatest accomplishment. I am content."

David nodded, a faint glimmer in his eye. "I feel the same," he said softly. "When I see Daniel, I feel as if I have truly accomplished something great in life."

Against the wall, Christopher snorted softly. "Even when he teases you until your veins bulge?"

"Especially then."

Christopher's gaze was warm upon his brother. "We have done well, you and I," he said. "We have six sons between us and the name of de Lohr will live on. Already, it is strong and will only grow stronger. We have given our sons that legacy, the best part of both of us."

"The best part of me is lying in a bed upstairs," Rhys' softly uttered statement filled the air. He had been staring at his hands but when he looked up, he saw three sad expressions gazing at him. It was difficult not to give in to their sympathy. "All moments in my life have led up to this one. I agree with Brydon; we will have a plan when we march upon Arundel, but make no mistake – the only man entitled to seek a reckoning for Maddoc is me. It is my right."

"You are too old," David sighed. "Rhys, you will be facing a man twenty or thirty years younger than you are. As great as you are, and you are the greatest, you cannot compete with youth and speed."

"Perhaps," Rhys whispered. "But it is my right and I will not allow anyone to take it from me."

Christopher and David passed concerned glances, finally looking at Gart, who was stone faced as he looked at Rhys' lowered head. When Gart felt their stares, he looked up at them both. The stone-faced expression morphed into one of resignation.

"It is his right," he finally muttered. "If we were speaking of Daniel or Brydon or any one of Chris' sons, we would feel the same way. For my son, I would seek justice a thousand times over no matter what the risk, and if I die, I die in the quest for my son's justice. There is no wrong in that."

There was nothing more any of them could say to that. They all knew the stakes and they all knew the plan. As their sons organized the armies down in the bailey of Canterbury, David wearily rose from his seat and extended a hand to Rhys, who took it and laboriously stood. They were old, that was true, but they were still knights, and they would do what knights do best.

They would fight for honor, justice, and the bonds of family and allies. One last time, they would fight.

***

He could hear the shouting from the bailey. In fact, he had been dreaming about something, something military or violent, and those shouts were a part of that dream. It took him some time to realize that he was awake, listening to the voices of soldiers and commanders down in the ward.

Maddoc stared at the ceiling for the longest time. He didn't even know how long. It seemed like a lifetime. Then, it started to occur to him that he was very thirsty and his eyeballs no longer felt hot. The fever that had ravaged his body had made everything hot, even his eyeballs. It was odd not to be excruciatingly hot all over, but rather comfortable. Odd, indeed.

Maddoc turned his head slightly, noting the old physic sleeping in his chair up against the wall. A soft breeze blew the oilcloth covering the lancet window and he could see that it was daylight outside. He had no idea what time it was, or even what day it was, but it was indeed daytime. He could smell the dung and dust from the bailey blowing in through the window. It was a very comforting smell.

Slowly, he lifted a hand, which was more of a chore than he could have ever imagined. He was extremely weak and lifting one big arm was like trying to lift so much dead weight. He had no idea his arm weighed so much. But he brought a hand to his forehead, feeling that his temperature was cool and normal. He was surprised. More than that, he was breathing easy and the agonizing pain that had gripped his torso for the past few weeks was less than agonizing. He twisted a little, just to see how he felt, and the pain was still there but not nearly what it was. In his opinion, it was manageable.

The physic was snoring softly. Without moving his head or body too much, Maddoc looked around and noticed a small table at his bedside with a bowl on it and other implements. There was even a wet rag. Picking up the bowl, because it was the only thing he could really get his hands on, Maddoc threw it at the physic and hit the man in the shoulder.

The physic woke up with a violent start, jumping sideways and toppling out of his chair. On his bum against the wall, he rubbed the back of his head where he had smacked it as he fell. His astonished gaze was on Maddoc.

"Did you throw that?" he asked.

Maddoc shifted in the bed, realizing his back and bum were extremely sore from having lain motionless for so long. His body felt like it weighed a thousand pounds, stiff and sore and aching.

"I did," he replied softly. "I am thirsty and I believe I could eat something."

The physic struggled to his feet and made his way over to Maddoc. His surprise was obvious. He peered into Maddoc's eyes, felt his pulse, and put his ear against the man's chest. After several moments of listening to the inner workings of Maddoc's torso, he lifted his head.

"Your fever is gone," he stated the obvious. "How do you feel?"

Maddoc sighed faintly. "Exhausted," he said. "Hungry. Thirsty. And my head hurts a great deal."

The physic peered under his eyelids and in his mouth. Then, he shook his head in wonder. "A small price, considering," he said. "I thought for certain you were dead to us. I see that I was thankfully wrong."

Maddoc didn't have much to say to that, so he drew in a deep breath and closed his eyes. It was difficult to keep them open. There was some pain when he breathed but not much. More than that, he didn't feel winded or faint. Other than being extremely weary, he truthfully didn't feel all that bad, considering.

The physic, still shaking his head with wonder, went to the door and called for a servant. When an older, toothless woman appeared, he instructed the woman to bring bread and broth. The woman went on the run as the old physic returned to Maddoc's bedside and began unwrapping the bandages around his torso.

Maddoc dozed as the physic removed the moss and mustard poultice, noting that the wound was developing a hard scab. No more oozing, which was a good sign. He replaced the wrappings with boiled linen, clean and tight around Maddoc's chest, something he had learned during his years in The Levant where the old Arab physics who had bred and practiced their methods on the hot sands of the east had taught him that only boiled things should touch a wound. It was knowledge that had served him well, as Maddoc was showing evidence.

By the time the physic was finishing with the wrapping, the servant returned with strained beef broth and big hunks of hard crusted bread. As the physic broke up the bread, softened it in the broth, and fed it to Maddoc, more shouting and commotion could be heard from the bailey. It was enough to rouse Maddoc's curiosity.

"What is happening?" he asked the physic.

The old man spooned the softened bread into Maddoc's mouth. "I do not know," he said. "There are many soldiers in the bailey. Perhaps they are going to war."

Maddoc's brow furrowed as he swallowed the mushy but tasty bread. "War?" he repeated. "With whom? Where is Lord David?"

"With your father, I would imagine. In fact, I...."

"My *father*?" Maddoc repeated, startled. "My father is here?"

The physic nodded, putting a hand on Maddoc's big shoulder to steady him. "He came yesterday," he said. "Do you not remember?"

Maddoc was distressed, struggling through the mental cobwebs to put his last memories into perspective. After a moment of concentrated effort, he shook his head.

"I do not recall anything much," he admitted. "In fact, the last I remember, I was in the bailey with... oh, dear God... Adalind... where is Adalind?"

The physic could see that his patient was genuinely upset. Illness had a way of erasing memory; he knew that. He patted the man on the shoulder in a weak attempt to comfort him.

"Your father and other knights have come," the old man said patiently. "I have spent nearly all of my time with you so I am uneducated as to the exact details, but I was told by a servant that your father and Lord David are going after the lady. She is at Norfolk."

Maddoc was now struggling to sit up. "Addie," he muttered. "Sweet Jesus... it was de Royans, wasn't it? He took her. He fought me for her and... God, why can I not remember what happened after he gored me? My mind is like mud."

The physic wasn't strong enough to keep Maddoc in his bed; even though the young knight had spent the past three weeks ill and with fever, he was still a very big and very strong man even in his weakened state. The physic tried to hold him down as he hollered for a servant. Maddoc had one leg over the side of the bed and was struggling to push himself up when the servant appeared and the old physic sent the woman on the run for David.

Maddoc heard the command but it did not concern him. All he cared about was regaining his armor and riding for Adalind. His head was swimming and his body trembling with weakness, pain, and exertion, but he had to get up. He had to find Adalind and save her from de Royans because in his mind, it was the very last thing he remembered and the urgency was still very strong. As he struggled to his feet, he pushed the old physic out of the way. The old man fell to the floor and Maddoc lost his balance, toppling over and collapsing against the wall.

But he wasn't down for long. Maddoc rolled on to his knees as the physic picked himself up and went to help him stand. But the physic tried to direct him back to the bed while Maddoc wanted to head out of the door. It was quite a battle until the sounds of running boots filled the corridor outside and the door panel flew open.

"Maddoc!" Rhys exclaimed. He was so started that he actually stumbled back into the door jamb. "God's Blood, we thought you were... the servant said to come quickly and we thought...."

Maddoc reached out a big hand and his father caught it, steadying him. Although Rhys was a very large man, and very strong, Maddoc was taller and heavier than his father. Supporting nearly all of Maddoc's dead weight against him, Rhys practically carried his son back to the bed and sat him down as David and Christopher, having followed Rhys on his panicked flight into the keep, moved in to assist. Between the three of them, they managed to get Maddoc back to the bed, but he wouldn't lie down. He kept trying to get back to his feet.

"I have to get dressed," Maddoc told them. "I have to find Addie."

Rhys was thrilled to death that Maddoc was evidently recovered, so much so that he sat down next to him and threw his arms around him.

"Praise to God," he whispered, hugging his son tightly. "I thought we had lost you."

Maddoc realized they weren't going to let him get up. It was three against one and he wasn't strong enough to fight them all off. Thwarted for the moment, he paused long enough to appreciate his father's show of affection. It was obvious that Rhys was very emotional as he embraced his eldest child.

"You have not lost me," Maddoc assured the man, his gaze moving to David and Christopher standing in front of him. "What has happened? Will someone please tell me where Adalind is? I was told she was at Norfolk."

David was so relieved to see Maddoc up and about that he could hardly verbalize it. He thought for sure that the harried servant had come with news of the knight's demise and was more than surprised to see that the case was exactly the opposite. He bent over Maddoc and put a hand to his forehead.

"No more fever?" he asked.

"No more fever, my lord," the physic answered, standing behind them. "He awoke a short time ago clear of fever or infection and asked for food. I can find no trace of illness in him. It would seem that Sir Maddoc is something of a miracle."

David took his hand off of Maddoc's head, his blue eyes glimmering with warmth as he gazed down at the knight. "Thanks be to God for his holy and just miracles," he murmured. "I did not truly believe we would see this moment."

Maddoc knew he had been ill but the severity of it was finally beginning to sink in because they were all looking at him as if he was a ghost. He looked at his father, still hugging him, and patted the man's arms in a comforting gesture as if Rhys was the one that needed soothing.

"It could not have been that bad," Maddoc muttered, somewhat embarrassed.

David rolled his eyes. "Do you not remember any of this, Maddoc?" he asked. "De Royans gored you and badly injured you. Fever set in and we thought we were going to lose you. Truly, I did not think we would see you alive and well ever again."

Maddoc was ashamed he had been so much trouble. "I remember fighting de Royans," he admitted. "I remember seeing Adalind... she had a dagger in her hand and she was running toward us. I think she was trying to help me. I tried to stop her but de Royans cut me. After that... I do not recall much at all."

Rhys let go of his son, listening to the man's recollection of past events. "She is a brave woman if she was indeed trying to help you," he muttered. "Foolish but brave. She reminds me of my wife in that respect. Elizabeau has been known to show astounding bravery."

While Maddoc gave his father a weak grin, David explained what the man had wanted to know.

"After de Royans gored you, he grabbed Adalind and fled Canterbury," he said. "We assume he took her back to Arundel Castle but we do not know for certain. I have called upon my brother, your father, and Gart Forbes to help us reclaim her and to seek justice for what de Royans did to you."

Maddoc gazed up at him, digesting what he was told. He was coming to understand the sequence of events. But one thing was unclear to him.

"How long have I been ill?" he asked.

"Almost three weeks."

Maddoc's eyes widened. "Three *weeks*?" he repeated, shocked. "De Royans took Addie three weeks ago and you are only now going to reclaim her?"

There was accusation in his voice as Maddoc grew agitated. David and Rhys hastened to calm him.

"Maddoc, there was much involved," David tried to explain. "I am still recovering from the beating I took at Victoria du Bose's mêlée. I knew I could not go after Adalind alone so I sent for help from my brother and your father and Gart. They have only just arrived and now we intend to mount our massive army and ride for Arundel. Believe me that the delay was not by choice but necessity. To go after de Royans myself, or to send Gerid or one of the other knights after him, would have been a foolish venture."

Maddoc was still staring at David in distress and outrage. "So you let him take her with no recourse? Just like that?"

"I had no choice. He had a dagger to her throat and threatened to kill her multiple times. I truly had no choice, Maddoc, believe me."

Maddoc was shaking with anguish, with nausea, at the thought of Adalind with de Royans. His mind was becoming clearer, however; he knew what had more than likely already happened during the time he had been ill. The realization brought tears to his eyes.

"He would have married her as soon as he could," he muttered, closing his eyes against the mere idea. "She is already Lady de Royans."

"We do not know that for certain," David said softly.

Maddoc would not be eased. He collapsed forward and put his face in his hands. "Oh, Addie," he whispered tightly. "I am so sorry, sweetheart... so very sorry I could not prevent this. God forgive me for failing you."

Rhys put his arm around Maddoc's slumped shoulders. "You did not fail her, lad," he assured him quietly. "Maddoc, even if de Royans has married her, David plans to charge him with thievery and quite possibly the marriage could be annulled on those grounds. There is hope, son. There is hope."

Maddoc wallowed in sorrow for a few seconds longer before wiping his face and lifting his head. The emotion in his expression was naked, his pain raw, but his jaw was set resolutely. He was weak with injury and his body wasn't nearly healthy enough to go after Adalind, but there was no question in his mind that he was bound by love and honor to find de Royans and beat him down until one or both of them was dead. He had to punish the man and regain Adalind or, at the very least, free her from him forever. Even if he perished, Adalind had to be freed.

He knew what he needed to do.

"I am riding for Arundel," he muttered, emotional. "I will challenge de Royans and I will kill him. Then I will bring Addie home and marry her as I should have done those weeks ago."

David put a hand on his shoulder. "You are still a very sick man," he said, trying to be gentle with him. "I know it is asking you to trust others where Adalind is concerned, but I am asking you to please trust us. Trust *me*. Adalind is my flesh and blood, and I swear I will not fail you. I will get her back for you."

It was a kind way of trying to keep Maddoc out of the battle, but they all knew it was of no use. Maddoc gazed at David, his liege, a man he'd known since childhood and a man he respected greatly. He trusted him. He believed in him. But he could not let the man fight his battles for him. After a moment, he simply shook his head.

"I understand your point, my lord," he said quietly. "But I must do this. For Adalind, as well as for me, I must do this. De Royans aggression was against me and I cannot let the man win. The cost is too high. I must regain what is mine and reclaim my honor as a knight, something that de Royans tried to take away from me. You will understand when I say that I must do this myself."

David knew that. He sighed heavily, looking at Rhys, whose gaze was fixed on his son. There was such sorrow in the air, such anguish, because more than anything, the old knights understood Maddoc's point of view. The man had been raised to understand honor and loyalty, love and commitment, so his stance in the matter was not a surprising one. It was expected.

"I understand," David finally said, dropping his hand from Maddoc's shoulder. "We will be prepared to leave when you are up to the task. For now, I will have...."

Maddoc cut him off. "I will be ready in an hour."

Rhys cut in. "Maddoc, you are still recovering from a near-death experience," he said. "At least eat and get a good night's rest. We will leave at dawn. Whatever has become of Lady Adalind, delaying until morning will not change her fate. A few hours will not make a difference to her but it will do *you* a world of good."

Maddoc looked at his father through his haze of determination and reluctantly agreed. A few hours would not change the situation with Adalind, wherever she was. He could feel himself getting apprehensive and edgy over the thought of a delay but he fought it. He hated to admit that he still felt very weak, so perhaps a good meal and some sleep would help him in regaining some of his strength.

He was going to need all of it for what he was about to face.

As I stare on and on into the past, in the end you emerge,
Clad in the light of a pole-star piercing the darkness of time:

CHAPTER NINETEEN

Brighton was furious. Really and truly furious. He was angry with d'Aubigney and his wife for allowing Adalind to escape. The blame just couldn't be placed anywhere else; Lady Isabelle had allowed Adalind to somehow slip away, through a servant's passage, he was told. A couple of cooks had seen her as she had made her escape but they had no idea who she was and made no effort to stop her. Those cooks had been punished but Adalind was gone nonetheless.

Her disappearance had occurred well before sup. No one even realized she had left until the evening meal, when the sun had gone down, and Lady Isabelle had gone to check on her. The room had been empty and the Lady Adalind, vanished. It had been at least five hours since the last anyone had seen of Adalind so there was no telling where she was or how long she had been missing. Even so, the castle was locked down and every inch of it searched for the lady. Not surprisingly, she was not to be found.

Now it was dark, with a fat half-moon illuminating the night sky, and Brighton was preparing to depart Arundel in his search for Adalind. In the knight's quarters in an outbuilding attached to the castle's curtain wall, he finished securing his armor and weapons. Gloves were strapped and secured. Every movement was sharp and edgy, indicative of his anger. As he plopped his helm on his head and gathered his traveling satchel, he determined that the moment he found Adalind, he would hunt down a priest and force the man to marry them. He was no longer to be sensitive to Adalind's nonsense. He was finished feeling pity for her. Her escape had erased any measure of compassion he had ever felt for her.

Departing Arundel without so much as a word of farewell or warning from d'Aubigney, Brighton set off into the night. True, it wasn't particularly wise to travel at night, much less travel alone, but he had no fear as he took the road east. He suspected Adalind would be heading in the same direction in her haste to return to Canterbury. He was fairly certain that she was on foot, which meant he would overcome her fairly quickly if she stayed true to the road.

Of course, there were many towns between Arundel and Canterbury, and it would take weeks for her to reach Canterbury on foot, so he would be vigilant. He was certain he could find her. But his true hope was to find her before something terrible happened to her. More than her escape, more than d'Aubigney's negligence, he was genuinely angry over the lady's determination to put herself in such danger. He planned to tell her so when he found her. And then he would marry her and, as her husband, perhaps take a switch to her lovely backside to drive home his point.

Shortly after midnight, the clouds rolled in and a heavy rain fell.

***

Three days out of Canterbury, Daniel found himself heading south in a blinding rain storm. It was so bad that the air itself was gray, nearly obliterating any glimpse of landscape around him. He could have been passing through hell's half acre for all he knew because he couldn't see a thing with all of the mist and inclement weather. It was enough to tip his already-foul mood into overload.

Two long days of travel had given him a good deal of time to think. An inherently lonely man in spite of his enormous family and close friends, he rather preferred his own company to the company of others and preferred to travel alone, so his current situation was nothing new. He liked it that way. But it did give him time to reflect on life in general, on his father and his niece, and on Maddoc. More than once over the past few days thoughts of Maddoc, and their adventures together, had brought a smile to his lips.

Daniel and Maddoc were born ten months apart, so they were essentially the same age. When Maddoc had fostered at Lioncross Abbey Castle on the Welsh Marches, Daniel had as well. They had met under Christopher de Lohr's roof and had been strong friends ever since. Maddoc had been a big child, rather silent and intense, while Daniel had been loud and brash. It had been Daniel who would coerce Maddoc into his schemes, such as stealing cheese or lifting the coin purse off a sleeping knight, but it was Maddoc who would take the punishment when they were caught. The earl's son was rather untouchable, especially since his uncle was also an earl, but the grandson of the Duke of Navarre was fair game.

In spite of the times Maddoc had taken the punishment for Daniel, their friendship was unbreakable. In their first battle together, squiring for other knights, Maddoc had saved Daniel's life when a rogue soldier had tried to kill him and Maddoc ended up spearing the man. Daniel had reciprocated the next year in much the same situation.

Daniel laughed when he thought of the time when he and Maddoc, newly knighted and off to travel for a few months, had stopped at an inn in Cumbria where a busty and lusty serving wench had set her sights on Maddoc. Being young, rather virginal, and also rather hot-blooded at that point in his life, Maddoc had fallen for the woman's charms and ended up in bed with her. At least, that was the plan. But before that rendezvous could take place, Daniel had swapped out the young wench for one three times the woman's age. Maddoc had retired for the night to what he thought would be a hot bit of flesh and instead ended up in bed with a shriveled old corpse. Daniel could still hear the man screaming. It had been hysterical fun.

More adventures followed the pair as they grew older, but Maddoc's focus was on his career while Daniel's remained on travel and adventure. Maddoc settled in at Canterbury and the pair went on with their lives as they chose them, but they had always remained very close. As Daniel plodded along through the pouring rain, he alternately laughed at the memories and raged at the current situation. All he knew was that Brighton de Royans was going to suffer a painful and lingering death. He hated a man he had never even met. He was going to kill him with his bare hands.

As the day began to wane and the thunder rolled, Daniel was seriously thinking about seeking shelter. In spite of the weather, he had managed to travel between twenty and twenty-five miles a day, mostly because he traveled so much and new how to get the most mileage out of the day no matter what the conditions. He was seasoned, and he was hearty. As he directed his steed off of the pitted road and up onto an embankment of smooth, wet green grass to make the path easier for the horse, he noticed that he was coming upon a town. Coming down off the embankment and back onto the road where it leveled out near the edge of town, he decided this would be the place he sought shelter for the evening.

Wet homes and businesses passed him by as he plodded along the road. He kept an eye out for an inn and came across one near the center of the town. There was actually a square of some kind with a big trough in the middle of it which he realized was a well as he drew close. It was the town meeting place, usually full of vendors and buyers, now empty as the rain pounded. As he approached the inn, he noticed a church off to his left, a gray-stoned building blending in with the gray rain and mist. It appeared cold, as churches often did, and crowded, oddly enough. He could see people standing just inside the entry, perhaps seeking shelter from the rain just as he was.

Finding some shelter for his horse behind the inn in a rather crowded stable, he paid the boy tending the horses a pence to see to his stallion and proceeded to make his way towards the rear of the inn. He sloshed through the mud, knowing he was going to have to pay someone to clean the rust off his mail that night. The stuff would seize up if he didn't have it cleaned off and he wouldn't be able to wear it.

Opening up the inn door, he was hit in the face with heat and the stench of smoke and too many dirty bodies. The place was absolutely packed and he took a couple of steps in, scoping out the landscape, before realizing there was no use in going any further. Every single corner was jammed with people. Frustrated, he quit the inn and left the back door hanging open as he made his way back to the stables.

He was half way across the swampy yard when it occurred to him that there was a church across the road. At least it would be dry shelter and perhaps he could impose upon a priest to direct him to a family willing to provide him with a meal for a few coins. Wiping the water out of his eyes, he shifted direction and headed in the direction of the church.

The weather was worse now, if such a thing was possible. He'd never seen such rain. Making his way quickly across the square, he headed for the enormous church that was now looming ahead through the gray. He had his satchel and broadsword under his left arm, trying to keep both of them dry as he made his way through a rock-filled lake that was really the walkway leading up to the church. At this point, all he could think of was getting dry until the sounds of screams filled the air.

At first, he didn't pay much attention. He wasn't about to involve himself in someone else's affairs but he did keep an eye out just so he wouldn't inadvertently get caught up in something. There was always someone looking to challenge a well-armed knight, wanting to make a name for himself, so his plan was to stay clear of whatever was going on and stick to the shadows. Then he'd find that priest who would direct him to a family in need of coin in exchange for a dry spot and hot food.

At least, that was his hope until he spied the commotion that was causing the screaming. He could see it, clear as day, as he entered the church. There was a pair over near a small alcove, a man and a woman in mortal combat. It took him a moment to process what he was seeing and when realization finally dawned, his satchel hit the floor as did the heavy leather sheath for his broadsword. The weapon was unleashed and so was Daniel.

Before he could draw two true and steady breaths, Daniel charged across the sanctuary floor with his broadsword held high and murder in his heart.

He was out for blood.

Whenever I hear old chronicles of love, it's age-old pain,
It's ancient tale of being apart or together.

CHAPTER TWENTY

The storm was legendary. In fact, Adalind had never seen such rain. It was as if God himself was angry, casting down big lightning bolts with his eyes and creating thunder with his loud booming voice. She tried not to think that the weather was the result of God being angry with her, personally, for all of the sins she had committed over the past five days. She hoped he was an understanding God. If he wasn't, then she hoped one of those lightning bolts wasn't aimed at her head.

It all started after her escape from Arundel. Adalind never knew she had a mind like a criminal but she evidently did because the first thing she did was steal some clothes that had been hung out to dry. As she had crossed through the town, a mad-like dash to get away from the castle, she ran through a cluster of poorly constructed homes where washed clothing had been hung out to dry on a sapling tree.

As she ran, she almost passed it by but the thought that Brighton, or anyone else for that matter, would be able to spot her in her fine clothing had her stealing what she could off the tree and dashing into the woods with it.

A quick inventory in the undergrowth showed that she had stolen a coarse linen shift, a type of surcoat, dyed red, that was more of a girdle with a skirt attached, another large red tunic that was more like a cloak than an actual tunic, and a pair of hose that were surprisingly soft. Very quickly, she had pulled off her fine clothing, all except her shift and corset, and pulled on the girdled skirt, hose, and cloak-like tunic. The material was rough, and the dye job was uneven, but the clothes were surprisingly clean and comfortable. They also blended in and made her look like a peasant. Please with her acquisition, she buried her fine clothing under a pile of moldering leaves and continued her flight.

As the evening fell on the first evening, she was afraid to travel in the dark so she sought shelter in a barn with a pair of cows for company. The barn was part of a small farm, for she could see the farmhouse in the distance, and she hid in the loft that was filled with dry and crunchy grass.

As the sun set completely, the farmer brought his big shaggy horse into the barn and fed and watered all of the animals as Adalind hid in the loft and prayed he would not find her. He left, eventually, and went to the house, leaving Adalind with the animals and building up a powerful hunger.

So she had crept out of the loft and scooted over to the house, staying to the shadows as the man and woman came outside and moved in and out of a cellar of sorts that was made out of stone. The old man would roll the stone door away and the woman would gather food items and take them back into the house.

It gave Adalind an idea and before the night was over, she had managed to steal quite a bit of food from the stone cellar and the farmer's shaggy horse. She left in the middle of the night, fearful she would be caught if she tried to leave before dawn because farmers were always up before the sun. Therefore, by the light of the half-moon, Adalind and her stolen horse traveled north.

On the run, she began to think like the hunted. It was easier than she thought. She knew Brighton would have discovered her absence and she was positive he was trailing her so she had to be smarter than he was. She had to find a convent, a church, anywhere that would provide her sanctuary. It was her only hope because she had to assume she could not outrun Brighton over the long run. He would catch her and marry her and she would live in hell for the rest of her life. She couldn't allow that to happen.

Therefore, thinking like an outlaw became easier. She stole food when she could, hid in the shadows, and traveled in the trees that paralleled the road so she could stay away from those that traveled in the open.

On the eve of the third day, she came across a small encampment and watched from the bushes, like a thief waiting to pounce, only to discover that the man she thought was sleeping by the fire was actually dead, so she stole his horse and most of his possessions. Coinage, food, weapons... it all became hers, and she rode off on a fine Belgian warmblood, feeling bad she had stolen everything but concerned only with her survival.

With the money and her stolen wardrobe, she was able to pay for food for the next couple of nights and she even slept on a bed on the fourth evening. Being paranoid that Brighton would happen upon her at any moment, she stayed in a small inn with terrible food and a horrible stench. Surely Brighton would never stay in such a place and surely he would never look for her in such a place. It was the best night's sleep she'd had in almost a month, safe in the arms of that smelly hostel.

The fifth day had dawned stormy and windy, and she had traveled a short way before deciding to seek shelter from the elements. She entered into a larger village with a town center and a big well, riding comfortably because she was covered up with the dead man's enormous cloak.

Almost immediately, she spied the bell tower of a church and she made her way towards it. As she drew closer, she could see that it was a fairly large church with a cloister attached and she began to pray she found a safe haven that would protect her from Brighton. She could only imagine where the man was, nearby, on her tail, at any moment ready to capture her, so she was thrilled to have finally found safety. She was sure of it.

There was a livery behind a small inn across the street from the church and she paid the boy handsomely to feed and water the fat Belgian warmblood that had thusfar been a smooth and steady ride. He was a good horse. She left the stable as the boy was drying the horse off, lugging the big satchel with all of the possessions she had stolen. Other than the saddle, she wasn't going to leave anything behind in the stable where it could be filched. Covering her head with the hood of the enormous cloak, she made her way through the mud and rain to the church across the square.

It was fairly crowded inside and the soot given off by the tallow candles gave the air a greasy smell. It was stuffy, but it was dry and relatively warm, and Adalind peeled off the hood of the cloak as she wandered into the cavernous sanctuary. She was looking for a priest, someone she could speak with about her quest for sanctuary and eventual commitment to a nunnery. There were plenty of peasants and travelers in the church, huddling in quiet groups, but it took her several minutes before she came across an acolyte who directed her to an alcove near the door where the priest was.

Retracing her steps towards the front of the church where an arched doorway evidently led into the priestly alcove, she was about to enter the room when she heard a familiar voice. Not a friendly or comforting voice, but one from her nightmares. It took her a moment to digest what she had heard and come to a confused stop. Confusion turned to fear. Startled, she threw herself against the wall next to the door and, with a deep breath for courage, peered around the corner.

Brighton was standing with the priest several feet away. He was in conversation with the man in stained brown robes, his back partially to the entry, but it was all Adalind needed to see. Panic filled her as she scampered away, trying not to make too much noise, struggling to camouflage herself in the groups of people that were huddled in the sanctuary seeking shelter from the elements. It was a harried flight, one that attracted some attention, as she made it to the other side of the church where shadows concealed the corners.

Dear God, he is here! She thought frantically, throwing herself behind a big stone pillar that was part of the roof support. Her breathing was coming so fast and furiously that she ended up breaking down into terrified tears, covering her mouth so she wouldn't make any sounds. Still, the shock was too great and she allowed herself a few seconds of hot, frightened tears. She knew he would come after her and was unhappy to realize she'd been correct. Of all the towns between Canterbury and Arundel, they both happened to stop in the same one. The irony was unfathomable.

So she struggled for calm, wiping her tears, staying behind the pillar because she thought it would be better to stay where she was and not try to leave. He might see her and she was fairly certain she couldn't out run him on the fat Belgian stallion. Therefore, the most logical thing was to wait him out until he left and not try to run.

... please, Brighton, go!

As she sat behind the pillar, shielded, she began to calm. There were quite a few people in the sanctuary, enough to distract the knight, and she quickly pulled the hood up over her head to shield her features. In fact, she drew up her legs and buried her face in the top of her knees, praying furiously for both control and protection. Surely God would listen to her pleas.

Please, God, send Brighton far away so I shall never see him again. And please... if Maddoc is with you, perhaps you can send him to protect me. I need a guardian angel, God... please send him to me.

Adalind must have prayed the same prayer a dozen times. Over and over, she asked for Brighton to be sent away and for a guardian angel to protect her. Outside, the storm raged and time passed, and Adalind remained pressed up against the stone pillar, listening to the weather howl and wondering where Brighton was. She didn't dare move, peering around the pillar and risk being spotted. She couldn't hear any voices, not from anyone, because the rain and thunder were so loud. On into the afternoon, she sat... and she waited.

It was a long and apprehensive wait. Adalind kept her face down and her hood over her head, listening to the rain, praying for protection and desertion – protection from God, Brighton's desertion. She also found her thoughts wandering to Maddoc, wondering what it would have been like had Brighton de Royans never made an appearance and she had married Maddoc as she had always planned.

They would have remained living at Canterbury, a newlywed couple just starting out in life. She thought on the children they might have had, all sons she was sure, who would have all looked just like Maddoc with his blue eyes and black hair. Perhaps they would have even had his smile, with the big dimples in each cheek, and his chin with the defined cleft in it. There was so much about him that was distinctive and wonderful, now dead and buried. It was a struggle to remember the wonderful things about him and not the last time she saw him. Maddoc, her beautiful angel, now gone forever.

The afternoon continued on and, at some point, she fell asleep with her knees drawn up and her head covered. She was weary, and hungry, and dozed periodically, waking herself up in a panic when thoughts of Brighton would come about. Then she would pray for that guardian angel again, pleading with God to send someone to protect her. As the afternoon began to wane, she dared to lift her head to look around and see what was going on around her.

For the most part, people seemed to be sitting on the ground, or praying, or milling in small groups. Adalind could see that everything was still and relatively quiet, and she began to feel somewhat brave. Cautiously, she moved, very slowly, to peer around the pillar into the main body of the church.

Several seconds of frantic searching did not reveal Brighton. In fact, there were hardly any people in the chapel at all, as if everyone had finally meandered home to hearth and a good meal. A few people continued to mill around by the entry, coming in and out, but the crowds seemed to have vanished. Fortified with confidence, Adalind moved out of her hiding place and began to move back across the sanctuary in her hunt for the priest.

All the while, however, her gaze moved over the cavernous hall, making sure Brighton was nowhere to be found. Making sure he was gone. Maybe she wouldn't need that guardian angel, after all. As she made the turn into the alcove where she had seen Brighton and the priest speaking, she ran headlong into an armored body.

It was an unexpected and terrifying encounter, one that sent Adalind from calm to hysterical in split second. Brighton grasped Adalind as a reflex to steady her when she bumped into him, realizing before it was almost too late whom he held in his grasp. The moment they laid eyes on each other, Adalind let out a horrific scream and yanked her arm from his grasp. The battle was on.

Brighton didn't even say a word; he didn't have to. He had his hands full trying to grab Adalind as she screamed and fought and kicked. The entire sanctuary was in an uproar as the lady did battle against the big knight, throwing her fists, and everything else, at him in an attempt to get away. A bank of candles ended up on the ground as the lady tried to pick it up and hit him with it, but it was too heavy. It rolled to the ground as he managed to get a hold of her wrist. Adalind grabbed a candle and smashed it, flame-side, into Brighton's face. Hot wax burned his skin.

But Brighton was tough. He didn't utter a sound as the wax burned him. He had Adalind by one wrist and was going for the other, but Adalind wasn't going to go down without a fight. He was going to have to kill her first. She twisted and screamed, and ended up throwing herself down on the ground in an attempt to break his hold. Then she put her feet up and tried to kick him in the groin. Brighton had to move quickly or risk serious injury.

"Adalind," he said firmly. "Stop fighting me... you are going to injure yourself."

Adalind was incoherent with fright. "Let me go!" she hollered. "Let me go!"

"I am not," he said, his voice low with resignation and hazard. "Please stop fighting before we both get hurt."

That only seemed to feed Adalind's frenzy. She yanked and pulled, swung fists and feet. Even though Brighton was armored, he was still on the receiving end of some seriously strong blows. Panic fed Adalind's strength and she recklessly battled. She was attempting to kick him in the groin again when Brighton suddenly let go of her. Adalind tumbled to the ground, clawing at the dirt in an effort to crawl away, when a shadow suddenly passed over her and she heard the distinct sounds of broadsword against broadsword.

It took Adalind little time to figure out there was a fight going on over her head. Startled and frightened, she scrambled to get out of the way, trying to cover her head with her arms, as she was accidently kicked by a massive boot. It smacked her in the hip as she crawled on all fours nearly halfway across the sanctuary before she allowed herself to turn around and see what was going on.

Someone had intervened on her behalf. She could hardly believe it but was thankful with all of her heart. *Perhaps the guardian angel I prayed for?* Perhaps God had listened to her, after all.

She could see a very big knight going up against Brighton as the man fought for his life. The knight was fully and heavily armored so she couldn't see his face, but he was a man with power and skill. Brighton had been caught off guard and was struggling to defend himself, as he'd barely had time to unsheathe his broadsword and had an awkward grip on it.

In fact, as Adalind watched, the unknown knight managed to knock Brighton's sword from his grasp and send it sailing off into the shadows. At the same time, he kicked Brighton in the side of his left knee and caused the man to collapse onto his knees. As the thunder rolled and the rain pounded, the unknown knight pointed the tip of his broadsword at Brighton's eye.

Brighton knew he was defeated but he would not give up. He took a swipe at the broadsword and tried to roll onto the ground in an attempt to take out the legs of the unknown knight, but he was rewarded when the knight kicked him in the neck. It was a hard kick, right in the throat, and as Brighton lay there and gasped for air, the unknown knight flipped up his visor.

It was Daniel.

"Uncle Daniel!" Adalind screamed.

Daniel glanced up at his niece, holding out a hand to her to prevent her from coming closer because she was struggling to her feet, trying to run to him. When he held out his hand, she stopped. His focus returned to Brighton, laboring to breathe. All he could feel at the moment was pure, unadulterated anger and hatred as he gazed down at the man. Infuriated, he kicked him again in the neck, and then in the head. Half-conscious, Brighton struggled to stay alert.

"Before I kill you, I want you to know who I am and why I am going to end your miserable life," Daniel rumbled. "My name is Daniel de Lohr. Lady Adalind is my niece and Maddoc du Bois, the man you stole her from, is my closest friend. You are wholly unworthy to have faced Maddoc in a challenge and wholly unworthy to have made an attempt on his life, so listen to me now; your death is in vengeance for Maddoc's death. It is a small price to pay and will not nearly settle the debt, so know this – I will ride to your family and slay every one of them. I will burn your home, steal your possessions, and slay everyone who ever knew you. I will wipe your name from this earth and take pleasure in it. Perhaps then will I consider justice served for Maddoc and Adalind. Perhaps then will your debt be settled with me. Look at me now."

Brighton could barely open his eyes but he tried. His hands were around his neck, trying to protect himself should Daniel try to kick him again. Daniel bent over, looking Brighton in the eye.

"Do you understand me?" Daniel hissed. "You worthless son of a whore, do you understand why you are seconds from death?"

Brighton tried to inhale deeply but it was difficult. He eventually closed his eyes because it was just too difficult to keep them open.

"Maddoc... was a good knight," he whispered. "I regret his death but as knights, death is our shadow. It is always there. I fought Maddoc for Adalind because I wanted her. There is no dishonor in a challenge."

Daniel could see that the man was calmly accepting his fate. It both infuriated him and inspired some measure of respect. He couldn't really decide which reaction was stronger. With a heavy sigh, he stood up and dared to glance over his shoulder at Adalind. She was standing up, looking disheveled, and watching him with enormous eyes.

"Are you well, Addie?" he asked softly.

Adalind nodded vigorously. But as she did, Brighton kicked out his legs and caught Daniel around the ankles, toppling the man over. His broadsword went flying as he landed in a heap of mail and armor. Adalind shrieked and jumped back as Brighton rolled onto his knees and went after Daniel with a vengeance. Brighton had his hands wrapped around Daniel's neck, choking the life from him, and Adalind's panicked gaze found Daniel's broadsword a few feet from the tussling knights.

She rushed over and picked up the weapon, quickly realizing it was very heavy. Struggling to hold it aloft, she could see that Brighton was focused on killing Daniel. He wasn't looking at her. Getting a good grip on the sword, she did what she had to do in order to save her uncle's life. Perhaps there was more to it; weeks of horror, of fear, and of grief over Maddoc's fate. The man had caused her so much pain she would never be rid of it all. All of that anger and grief built up to the point where she ran at Brighton and rammed the broadsword squarely into his back.

Brighton groaned and fell forward onto Daniel. Shrieking at what she had done, Adalind took hold of Daniel's arm and yanked, trying to move him out from underneath Brighton, but Daniel's substantial weight prevented her from rendering much aid. Daniel managed to remove himself from Brighton under his own power, shoving the man off of him and struggling to his feet. He eyed the knight, now collapsed on the dirt floor of the sanctuary with a broadsword in his back, as he rubbed his neck. Then, he turned to Adalind.

She was sobbing with fear, with relief. Daniel could see the emotions rippling across her features. He staggered over to her, wrapping his arms around her and hugging her tightly.

"All is well, Addie," he assured her hoarsely. "All is well, I promise. Let us go home now. I will take you home."

Adalind forgot all about joining the convent at that very moment, never to consider it again. To be back in the arms of her family was of more comfort to her than God ever could be. She needed and wanted to go home, to face whatever she had to face within the bosom of her loving family. She had been foolish to think she could ever leave them.

"Thank you, Uncle Daniel," she sobbed. "I... I prayed to God to send me a guardian angel and then you appeared. "

He gave her a final squeeze before letting her go. "That is because God told me to come and find you," he said, half-teasing her as he wiped tears from her face. "He told me to come right to this place, at this very minute, and I did."

Uncle Daniel liked to jest; Adalind knew that. She smiled weakly. "I never considered you an angel. Papa always said you had the devil in you."

Daniel laughed softly, displaying big white teeth. "Perhaps you will tell Papa otherwise now. Perhaps he will think better of his wayward son."

"Perhaps," she murmured, looking up at him with her watery green eyes. "Have you been to Canterbury? Did they tell you of Maddoc's death?"

Daniel sobered. "He was not dead when I saw him," he said, watching the surprise and astonishment register on her face. "He was very ill with fever, however. His wound was great. He asked me to come and find you and tell you that he would come for you when he was feeling better."

Adalind's mouth popped open. "He is *alive?*"

Daniel nodded, forcing a smile to be encouraging to her but he did not feel such things in his heart. He felt sorrow and grief. "He was when I saw him," he said quietly. "That was only a few days ago. We should hurry back to Canterbury right away so that he will not worry any longer."

Adalind was beyond tears. She was so astonished that Maddoc was alive that she could think of nothing else. It filled her mind, consumed her body, leaving an imprint of hope and joy like she had never before experienced. She ran to collect the stolen satchel she had dropped in her fight with Brighton and began heading for the entry door. She had to get home.

"Uncle Daniel, come *now*," she commanded. "I must return to Maddoc."

Daniel could see how eager she was and he could only pray that Maddoc had not passed away in the few days he had been gone from Canterbury. He didn't want to kill her joy but he didn't want to promise her all would be well, either.

"I know," he said, taking a few steps in her direction. "Addie, he told me to tell you something."

She paused by the entry, the great Norman arch that allowed God's faithful to enter his holy domain. "What did he tell you?" she cocked her head.

"That he loves you and he is sorry he has not told you before."

He saw the pallor of Adalind's face change; it went from rather pale to something that could only be described as glowing. A smile spread over her lips, one of joy and peace and comfort. It was an expression Daniel had never seen before, from anyone, and knew he never would again. It was an expression of abundant and true love.

"I know he does," she said after a moment. "He did not have to tell me. I already know he does."

Daniel was, in truth, rather surprised to see how much his niece had changed since the last time he had seen her. She had always been beautiful, that is true, but there was something different about her now, something mature and settled. Perhaps Maddoc had done this for her; perhaps not. Perhaps it was something she did on her own. All he knew was that he felt an overwhelming desire to return her to Canterbury. She had such love for Maddoc and always had. Now that he returned that love, it was unnatural for them to be separated.

Daniel smiled at the wisdom of her reply, not those of an insecure or flighty woman, but one who knew she was truly and wholly loved.

"He wanted me to tell you anyway," he said after a moment. His attention turned to Brighton, still on the floor of the church, and he moved in his direction. "Let me retrieve my sword and we shall leave."

Brighton was stirring as Daniel reached him and he bent over, swiftly pulling the sword from the man's back and listening to him groan. His wound was mid-back, above his kidneys but below his shoulder blade on the right side of his torso. From what Daniel could see, the broadsword had penetrated several inches into the man's body. It was deep. With his boot, he rolled Brighton over on to his back.

The man was conscious, gazing up at him with half-lidded eyes. His breathing was unsteady.

"If you are going to finish the job," Brighton whispered, "all I ask is that you be merciful."

Daniel gazed down at him seriously. His jaw began to tick. "Why?" he asked. "In return for the mercy you showed Maddoc when you gored him? For the mercy you showed Adalind when you ripped her from her family and stole her away? For all of that, I will make sure you suffer. I will cut you and bleed you and take great comfort in your anguish."

Brighton simply closed his eyes. He would not plead for his life and there was no use arguing with a man bent on vengeance. As Daniel took a good grip on his sword and lifted it with the intention of cutting deep in to Brighton's body, he heard a soft voice behind him.

"Nay, Uncle Daniel," Adalind came up beside him, gazing impassively down at Brighton. "Do not kill him."

Daniel paused in mid-stroke, turning to look at her. "Why not?" he asked, confused. "Why should I not gut him and take joy in every stroke for what he did to you and did to Maddoc?"

Adalind continued to gaze at Brighton. For the first time in a month, she thought not on her currently relationship with the man, but back to the knight before the challenge, the abduction, the humorous and intelligent knight she had come to know through Glennie. She had always liked Brighton a great deal until the change. She knew that Glennie loved her brother terribly. She could only imagine Glennie's pain when she learned of Brighton's death. She began to feel confusion and remorse. With a heavy sigh, she crouched down next to Brighton's head.

"For every pain and horror you have caused me, I should let Uncle Daniel seek vengeance," she murmured. "I cannot say that I have not thought of killing you myself over the past several weeks, because I have. And I can say with certainty that I will always hold great resentment and hatred for you against all that you have caused. It is not unlike the pain and suffering I endured during those years at Winchester Castle when your sister was the only friend I had. But she saved me then as she will save you now. For her, I will spare your life because she was my salvation during those hellish years and because of her, I found the strength to be strong day after day. I know your death would cause her great sorrow and I would never knowingly hurt her, not after everything she did for me. At this moment, I simply want to be free of you and never, ever think of you again. Do you understand me?"

Brighton's eyes opened and he looked at her, a flash of great longing crossing his features. But it just as quickly vanished, futile as it was.

"I understand," he muttered.

"You will never again show your face at Canterbury?"

He closed his eyes and looked away. "Never."

"Swear it."

"I swear."

Adalind stood up, looking down on him and wondering if she was making the right decision. She hoped so.

"The moment I leave this church, you will cease to exist to me, Brighton de Royans," she murmured. "God forgive you for what you have done to me and to Maddoc, for I certainly will not."

With that, she turned away from him and marched from the sanctuary. Daniel's gaze lingered on the fallen knight before finally sheathing his sword and following Adalind's trail.

The thunder rolled and the rain fell as the priests moved in to aid the wounded warrior.

My spellbound heart has made and remade the necklace of songs,
That you take as a gift, wear round your neck in your many forms,
In life after life, in age after age, forever.

CHAPTER TWENTY-ONE

Maddoc was having a hard time riding comfortably astride his big gray warhorse, mostly because his left side was paining him greatly and in order to ease the pain, he had to shift his balance, which put strain on the other parts of his body. His entire body was one giant mass of soreness.

But he was thankful for the pain, thankful he was able to ride, to remain upright for extended periods of time, and thankful he was alive. There was so much to be thankful for as he saw it, but the one thing he was singularly focused on was Adalind. He was thankful he was able to ride to claim her. However, the worst part was the not knowing; not knowing where she was, how she was, or what had becoming of her. It was tearing him apart but he tried not to show it. He tried to stay focused and strong, riding with legendary knights all around him. When he pulled his head out of the clouds and looked around, it was perhaps the most impressive force he had ever seen.

Christopher and David rode up at the head of the column, keeping each other company like in days of old when they would ride for Richard the Lion Heart, batting his evil brother John from one moment to the next. The battles those two had fought had gone beyond the world of legend into the realm of myth nowadays. Behind them rode Gart and his son Brydon; riding more to the flanks of David and Christopher and so heavily armed that Maddoc was certain their weapons and armor weighed more than the horse.

To the rear of the column rode Gerid, Evan, and Trevor, covering the retreat of the army, while Maddoc and his father rode well behind Gart and Brydon. Because of Maddoc's vulnerability and injury, the only way Rhys and David would allow him to ride was if he was in a somewhat protected position. Maddoc had pitched a bit of a fit but had finally agreed. He knew he was a still a sick man when he put on all of his armor and felt as if he was walking around with a thousand pounds of steel on. It was almost too weighty to bear. But he kept his mouth shut, not wanting to worry his father, until he mounted his horse and almost fell off. That brought his father down on him and it was another hour before he could convince everyone he was well enough to travel. Rhys agreed under one condition – that the old physic ride with them. Maddoc reluctantly acquiesced.

So the old physic rode in a wagon to the rear, there for Maddoc and Maddoc alone. When Rhys asked the physic his name, the old man simply shook his head and told him his name was Man. So Man rode in the wagon, clutching his large satchel with the medicaments in it, appearing comfortable with all of the knights around him. Having learned his craft, as he had told David, on the sands of The Levant, he was comfortable with armored men and their weapons, and at his age nothing much bothered him.

The pace on the first day was rather slow to accommodate Maddoc but when he realized it would take them weeks to arrive at Arundel, Maddoc ordered the pace increased on the second day and they managed to make excellent time. The result with Maddoc, however, was excruciating pain in his back and blood in his urine, but he kept it to himself, fearful that David would send him back to Canterbury. On the morning of the third day, he woke up barely able to move but, again, put on a brave face for the sake of his father and the other knights. His brother, Evan, was already watching him like a hawk so he didn't want to give the man fuel for his apprehension. He pretended that everything was fine no matter how badly he felt.

The rain, which had fallen intermittently since they had left Canterbury, began falling in sheets on the morning of the third day. Everyone and everything was soaked to the skin as the army tried to light a few cooking fires for the morning meal but were unable to do so. Everything was soaking. The knights, covered in wet and slop, mounted their equally wet and sloppy steeds and resumed their positions about the column.

This day, however, Gart and his son were at Point, leading the army down a particularly shrouded stretch of road as the rain fell and the thunder rolled. Twice, Gart thought he saw a threat and sent the younger knights out to check it out. Maddoc and Rhys began to suspect Gart was just doing it to give the younger, and edgier, men something to do, because they would always return empty-handed and disappointed. But they certainly seemed to love the initial rush of excitement when Gart sent them on a run. The thought of apprehending bandits or other outlaws was a great lure.

Nearing noon, the weather was so bad that David was considering calling a halt so that they could find some shelter for a few hours simply to dry off. Maddoc did not take kindly to that suggestion so the army continued on a little longer, struggling through the driving rain and epic mud. At one point, the wagon carrying provisions and the old physic got stuck in a massive rut, bringing a swarm of knights down around it as they tried to free it.

Gart, Brydon, Evan, Gerid, and Maddoc leapt off their war horses and threw their considerable strength into shoving the extremely heavy wagon from the rut, rain pouring in their faces as they tried to move it. Maddoc strained himself after the second huge push and was forced to back off as Trevor and Rhys took his place, along with a host of men at arms, and the wagon finally rolled out of the run and continued along the road. The knights re-mounted and returned to their posts.

By early afternoon, even Maddoc was forced to agree that the army needed to take shelter from the storm. The wind was whipping up and lightning bolted across the sky, creating more havoc. As the younger knights bolted off the road in search of a sheltering area they could camp in, Maddoc wandered to the head of the army, his gaze on the road heading southwest.

Emotions he had been fighting off for days began to swamp him again, feelings of failure and guilt. He seriously wondered if Adalind would look at him differently after this event, questioning his ability as a knight and as a man. In her eyes, he had been perfect up until that moment. He wondered if that would still be the case after all was said and done.

Behind him, he could hear orders being shouted at the army to disburse in the trees and begin setting up camp. Men and horses began to move, but Maddoc remained in the middle of the road as the rain pounded, his bright blue gaze fixed on the horizon as he lost himself in thought. But as he stared at the road, he began to see a rider appear through the mist and rain.

It was a lone rider, well camouflaged by the weather. Maddoc's eyes narrowed as he tried to make out details. Whoever it was seemed be riding fairly swiftly for such bad weather. His attention was fixed on the incoming object when he heard a voice beside him.

"A rider," Rhys muttered.

Maddoc nodded faintly. "Riding like a madman in this weather," he said. "He is covering a lot of ground very quickly."

Rhys flipped up his visor and wiped the water from his eyes. "Can you make out any standards or colors?"

Maddoc shook his head. "Not in this rain," he said. "All I can see is a rider and a horse. Beyond that, 'tis difficult to...."

He suddenly trailed off, straining to see. Rhys didn't think much of it, watching the rider approach, until Maddoc suddenly hissed.

"Daniel," he breathed. "My God, it is Daniel."

Like a shot, Maddoc was off, tearing down the road with mud flying behind him. Startled, Rhys took off after him. Seeing Maddoc and Rhys galloping madly down the road towards a lone rider, David and Chris strained to see what had their interest until both of them, at the same time, looked at each other in shock.

"Daniel!" they said in unison.

For elderly men, they managed to vault onto their horses with a good deal of agility, following the trail of Rhys and Maddoc. The other knights caught sight of what was going on but Gart held them back, unsure what was happening and unwilling to separate the rest of the knights from the army. But he did remove his enormous broadsword, a wicked looking thing with a nasty serrated edge. He was ready for a fight. When the younger knights saw what Gart had done, they whipped out their broadswords and began posturing like barbarians. Gart caught sight of all of the raging going on behind him and fought off a smirk. Oh, but it was good to be young and strong, and so very foolish....

Maddoc was the first one to reach Daniel down the long stretch of road. It seemed like he had been riding for miles when, in fact, it had been a relatively short distance. Daniel loomed closer and closer on his wet and irritated steed, coming at breakneck speed, and when he tried to pull the animal to a halt, the horse ended up sliding in the mud. Maddoc had to act fast so he would not be hit by the sliding horse, driving his charger off the road and onto the wet and green embankment.

There was panic in his thoughts and in his movements. By the time Maddoc turned around, he realized that there were two people on Daniel's horse. The second person, much smaller than Daniel, had been concealed behind him. As he brought his horse around and headed for Daniel, the small figure on the back lifted its head and the face came into view. The hood partially came away, revealing tuffs of blond hair. It was a very familiar face that had Maddoc gasping at the sight.

"Adalind!"

Maddoc couldn't believe what he was seeing, his astonishment overwhelming him. His breath caught in his throat and as he tried to dismount his horse, his foot caught in the stirrup in his haste and he ended up falling to the ground. The visor flipped up, bright blue eyes focusing on a sight he wasn't sincerely sure he would ever see again.

By this time, Rhys and David and Christopher were upon them and Adalind began weeping when she realized she was looking at Maddoc. She hadn't been aware of anything until the knight swung around, fell off his horse, and lifted his visor. She knew those eyes; dear God, she knew them! Leaping off the back of Daniel's charger, she slipped in the mud and scrambled to her feet as she struggled to reach Maddoc. The mud was so slick, preventing her from moving quickly, and Maddoc was having an equally difficult time regaining his footing. It was agonizing, trying to come together while the elements worked against them.

Muddy, wet, and sobbing, Adalind crawled up onto the embankment, half on her feet, half on her hands and knees. Maddoc had rolled to his knees, trying to get up, but Adalind was faster, and healthier, and she threw herself into Maddoc's arms, knocking the man off balance. He felt onto his back with Adalind clutched against him, holding her so tightly that he heard her back crack.

On the ground, in the mud, with the rain pouring down on them, Maddoc and Adalind finally found each other.

"Maddoc!" Adalind wept, her hands on his face through the raised visor as if to convince herself she wasn't seeing a phantom. "You are alive! Oh, God, I thought you were dead!"

Maddoc was trying to hold her and remove his helm at the same time, but the latches were rusting and he ended up ripping the helm off his head. The helm went sailing and his hands were in Adalind's hair, holding her fast as he kissed her furiously. She tasted like Joy.

"I am not dead," he whispered in between gleeful and furious kisses. "I am well and whole. And you? Are you well? Did he hurt you?"

Adalind shook her head, her hair wet, slapping the both of them. "I am unharmed. I swear that he did not harm me."

The furious kisses slowed and they paused a moment, drinking in the sight of each other. For a brief, warm and glorious moment, they just stared at each other. Realization settled. They were together again. Maddoc had tears in his eyes, mingling with the rain, running down his face.

"Addie, I love you," he said hoarsely. "I should have told you before and I beg your forgiveness that I did not. I love you with all that I am. Please know this."

"I do," she whispered, feeling glorious and ecstatic at his declaration. "Oh, Maddoc, of course I do. I love you also, with all of my heart and soul. From the beginning of time until the end of it, I will love you and only you."

He kissed her, hard, his lips trembling with emotion. Everything about him was quivering with delight and fear and relief. "Now," he began softly. "Tell me what has happened. Are you Lady de Royans?"

She shook her head before he even finished his question. "Nay," she murmured, her fingers on his lips. "He tried, but I would not let him. I fought him every second of the day, every waking moment. The man never had a moment's peace because I would not allow it. He tried to force priests to marry us, three times he tried, but each time I would not let him. I think he finally gave up."

The understanding that she was unmarried, and untouched, drove him to new tears. He threw her into a fierce hug, his face buried in the side of her head, listening to her soft weeping and shedding grateful tears of his own. He could hardly believe it; although he'd hoped for the best, he never truly believed the situation would work out in their favor. He was shocked and thankful to realize it had.

"My sweet, sweet girl," he murmured. "I am so sorry for everything that happened. If I could only take away the sadness and fear, I would gladly do so a thousand times over. Please forgive me, Addie."

She pulled back to look at him, curiosity mixed in with the joy in her expression. "For what?"

He sighed faintly, drinking in the sight of her face, studying her, wondering if all would ever be the same again between them.

"For failing you," he whispered. "For letting de Royans get his hands on you. I am so sorry, sweetheart. "

She was genuinely puzzled. "It was not your fault," she insisted. "It was my fault. I should not have tried to interfere. Maddoc, 'tis I who should be asking for your forgiveness. Had I not tried to interfere, none of this would have happened."

"Interfere?"

She nodded, sickened by her confession. "I tried to help," she said, haltingly. "I had a dagger and I was going to stab de Royans with it so you would be able to best him. I was only trying to help, Maddoc. I swear I was."

He thought back to that moment in time, nearly the only thing he remembered over the past several weeks. After a moment, he nodded in understanding. "I saw you with the dirk," he said softly. "I thought you might be trying to help me but I was terrified you were going to be struck."

"That was when Brighton gored you."

Her eyes were filling with tears again and he pulled her back into his embrace, comforting her as the situation began to clear. Now, he understood for certain what had happened and it had been as he suspected. No one was to blame. But he still felt guilty for the outcome and perhaps always would.

As he comforted Adalind, he began to notice that they were surrounded by several knights, including David. Maddoc locked gazes with David and a smile came to his lips.

"Addie," he murmured, kissing the side of her head. "I think your grandfather wants a hug, too."

Adalind nodded, but she didn't let go. "I am not finished holding you yet. He will have to wait."

Maddoc grinned, hugging her tightly for a few moments longer before patting her on the back. "Let us get up and out of this mud," he told her. "You are soaking wet and I would remove you from this rain."

Adalind nodded but she wasn't so inclined to let go of him until David and Christopher reached down and gently pulled her up. As she hugged David, Christopher and Rhys stepped in to pull Maddoc to his feet. As soon as Maddoc regained his balance, he caught sight of Daniel standing next to Rhys, grinning like a fool. He ran at Daniel and threw the man in a hug.

"You found her," he muttered, giving Daniel a squeeze before releasing him. "How in God's good name did you find her?"

Daniel was still grinning. "It was purely by chance, I assure you," he said, looking Maddoc up and down. "And you, my friend... last time I saw you, it appeared you were on your death bed."

Maddoc shook his head. "I am told I was very ill but I do not remember any of it," he said. "I do not even remember your visit. I was told you went after de Royans to avenge me and to regain Adalind. My thanks is not nearly enough at this moment, Daniel. I cannot put into words how very grateful I am."

Daniel slapped him on the shoulder. "You would have done the same for me," he said. "I consider it an honor to have avenged you."

The warm look in Maddoc's eye faded. "Tell me everything," he said, his voice low. "Where is de Royans?"

Adalind chose that moment to press herself up against Maddoc again, wrapping her arms around his armored body. Maddoc put his arm around her, kissing the top of her head, as Daniel eyed them both.

"That is a story I will gladly tell you when I am warm and dry and fed," he said to Maddoc. "Adalind and I have been traveling in brutal conditions."

Maddoc could see that he'd get nothing more out of Daniel with Adalind around, which concerned him. He wondered why. Perhaps it was a bad tale, indeed. He hugged Adalind to him and kissed the top of her head again.

"Then we shall do what we can to dry you both out," he said. "We are setting up camp about a quarter of a mile up the road. Let us dry off and partake of a good meal. I feel like celebrating."

With that, the group moved back to the road, collecting horses before heading back to the clearing where the army was setting up their encampment. Maddoc collected Adalind, and his horse, walking beside Daniel as they made their way back to the armies that had been collected to find Lady Adalind and bring her back safely.

The moment they got back to camp, the rain tapered off and the clouds parted, revealing a glorious sunset on the western horizon.

***

"He was injured badly enough that I believe he could not have left the church under his own power," Daniel said. "It is my assumption that the priests are taking care of him until he is well enough to travel. And with that, you now know how I came across Adalind and what transpired with de Royans."

It was a cold and wet night after the vicious rain, but the clouds had moved away to reveal a diamond-night sky and a nearly full moon. It was bright and glorious as several fires burned steadily into the night. Some of the men had managed to find wood in the undergrowth that wasn't saturated, and the warm fires burned brightly.

Daniel was sitting before one of those fires with Maddoc, Adalind, David, Christopher, Rhys, Gart, Brydon and both of Maddoc's brothers. They were crowded around the biggest fire, drinking tart wine and eating the succulent venison that Gart had managed to take down when the rains cleared and the animals had emerged to feed. Gart and Rhys had butchered the animal into several pieces so it would cook faster, which it did, and the air was filled with the smell of roasting meat and the sounds of happy men.

Adalind had stuffed herself ill on meat and now sat in a miserable and weary heap against Maddoc, who hadn't let her out of his sight, or more than a foot away from him, since their reunion that afternoon. Now, they sat discussing the crux of the issue, between Adalind's story and Daniel's, up until the point where Daniel had left Brighton injured on the floor of the church. Maddoc knew everything now. He was sickened by Adalind's tales of fending for herself and stealing but he was hugely grateful for the happenstance that brought Daniel and Adalind together. It could have been so much worse. While Daniel stuffed his face, Maddoc stewed.

"Then you did not kill him," Maddoc clarified.

Daniel shook his head. "I did not," he replied, eyeing Adalind because of her hand in his reasons for not killing de Royans. He took the chivalrous route and took the blame. "I had an uncharacteristic flash of mercy. Besides, I thought it more important to remove Adalind. She was a hysterical mess."

Maddoc cocked an eyebrow, looking at Adalind as she sat with her head against his chest, struggling to keep her eyes open. He turned back to Daniel.

"Then it stands to reason he is still at the church," he said softly.

Daniel nodded. "As I said, the man could not travel. It will take some time for him to recover enough to ride."

Maddoc didn't say anything. He gazed at the fire with Adalind dozing against him. He shifted so she would be more comfortable, his arm around her protectively. He seemed distant and pensive, not realizing that most of the older knights were watching him. Being wiser, and with many years of experience in such things, there was not one among them who did not suspect what Maddoc was thinking. David was brave enough to voice it.

"What are you thinking, Maddoc?" David asked softly.

Maddoc paused before replying. "I am thinking that de Royans is still a threat so long as he lives," he murmured. "I will be looking over my shoulder for the rest of my life."

"That is not true," Adalind yawned. "He promised he would never return."

"And you believe him?"

She shrugged and yawned again. "He is a knight," she said simply. "I believe his word just as I believe yours. Maddoc, you must remember that I knew Brighton before all of this. He was an honorable man then. Perhaps he has regained his senses."

"Honorable men do not challenge other men for their wives," Maddoc countered quietly. Then he looked at Daniel. "Where is this church where you left him?"

Daniel was chewing on a big piece of meat. "A day and half ride that way," he pointed to the road leading south. "Maresfield, I believe, is the name of the village. It has a big church in the center of town."

Maddoc was watching Daniel eat. "You should have killed him."

Daniel slowed his chewing; he knew this moment was coming and he prepared himself. "Maddoc, I am sure the man will return to Norfolk," he said. "I beat him soundly and he was badly injured with a wound to his back. He knows what will happen to him if he shows his face at Canterbury again."

"Why did you not kill him?" Maddoc would not let up.

Tension was rising around the campfire. Adalind, half-asleep, could sense it and she lifted her head, speaking before Daniel could.

"Because I asked him not to," she said.

Maddoc looked at her, rather incredulously. "Why would you ask such a thing?"

Adalind could see he was bent on honor, on justice, and her emotions began to rise. She pushed herself off of him, wrapping her stolen cloak more tightly around her as she thought on her answer.

"Because...," she said, searching for the right words. "I am not even sure I can explain it. Brighton put me through hell for weeks. It... it was as if I had become no better than an animal, fighting him day and night, trying to hurt him so I could escape, screaming and hitting every time he would come near me. I told you that he took me to Arundel."

"You did."

She continued. "When he took me there, I found a way to escape. I had to; I could think of nothing else. I spent days on the road running from him, hiding out like a common thief, terrified every minute of every day. Even so, he still managed to find me. Daniel found me, too, and he and Brighton had a horrible fight." Her voice softened. "But as Brighton lay on the ground, injured... it was so strange. It was as if the animal in me went away and I felt like myself again. I felt safe because I knew Brighton could no longer hurt me. And I thought of Glennie, his sister, who had been so kind to me all of those years at Winchester and I knew how badly his death would hurt her. I did not want her to go through that. I had suffered so much pain, Maddoc, but with Brighton... I suppose Glennie saved his life. I asked Daniel not to kill him because of Glennie. Perhaps it is an odd sense of mercy, but I felt it nonetheless. I simply wanted to be away from the man. I was tired of fighting and bloodshed. I wanted to be done with it and if Daniel killed Brighton, his blood would be on my hands and I would never be done with it. I could never forget."

She trailed off, unable to explain it better than she had, and Maddoc reached out and stroked the back of her blond head.

"I cannot say I understand your reasoning, but I respect it," he said. "Surely you must know that I cannot let the man live. I cannot have that threat against you, against me, for the rest of our lives."

She nodded sadly, staring down at her hands. "I know," she sighed. "I suppose in hindsight, it was foolish to spare his life. I suppose... I suppose I felt that there had been too much pain and suffering all around. It had to stop somewhere. I stopped it with him."

Maddoc continued to stroke her hair. "I must find him. And I must kill him."

"Maddoc," Rhys spoke up from across the fire. "I would never question your knightly honor because I understand it all too well, but you are still a sick man. You are still recovering from a very bad wound. Perhaps you should wait to confront Brighton. You have Adalind back and that is the most important thing, is it not?"

Maddoc glanced over at his father. "You are speaking like a man who does not want to lose a son," he said. "If this had happened to your wife, how would you feel?"

Rhys met his gaze steadily. "It *did* happen to me," he said quietly. "When you were about three years of age, Elizabeau was abducted by forces loyal to King John. I spent months searching for her. Ask David and Chris, for they were there. They saw what happened to me; during the course of the experience I transformed into something I never believed myself capable of. I became a hunter, obsessed with finding the woman I loved. I found her, but not without great personal sacrifice. You already know the story."

Maddoc nodded seriously. "I know the story," he confirmed softly. "Forgive me, Father. I did not mean to patronize you. You of all people understand my conviction. It is more than justice – it is essential for my survival and the survival of Adalind. I *have* to do this."

Rhys nodded. He indeed understood. Then he hung his head. He couldn't stand the thought of losing him.

"I know," he murmured, glancing up at David, at Christopher, and at Gart. The old knights had that same look of resignation that he did. "We all know. We will leave on the morrow for Maresfield."

Maddoc shook his head. "There is no need to move the entire army," Maddoc replied. "I will go alone. You will return to Canterbury."

Adalind was the one to leap up first. "I am going with you," she demanded. "I will not let you go alone."

Maddoc could see she was gearing up for a battle and hastened to soothe her. But before he could speak, others began chiming in.

"I am going also," Rhys said flatly.

"As am I," David conceded.

Maddoc turned to the men to dispute them but was interrupted when Christopher suddenly stood up and stretched his big body.

"We had all better try to get some rest if we are heading to Maresfield in the morning," he said, looking at Brydon. "You will take the army back to Canterbury with Gerid, Edward, and Trevor. Your father and the rest of us are going with Maddoc. Settle the army in once you reach Canterbury but do not let any of them wander, for we shall not be long."

The men started to move, leaving Maddoc sitting there, wondering how he had lost control of this venture. A solitary undertaking was now turning in to a group effort. David pulled Adalind to her feet but Maddoc stopped him from going any further.

"Where are you taking her?" he asked.

"To bed," David lifted his eyebrows. "With me. You did not believe for one minute that I would leave her with you, did you?"

Maddoc would not be deterred. He stood up as well and tried not to make is sound like he was trying to coerce David into giving permission for something unseemly.

"I have been without her for a month," he said, his voice low. "It is my intention to never let her out of my sight again. That being the case, I suggest you send someone to find a priest who will come here and marry us before the night is through so that when she sleeps in the same bed as I do, you will not want to cut my head off for it."

David lifted a wry eyebrow. "Your head is not what I would cut off."

Maddoc fought off a grin. "I believe we passed a small church about five miles back. Send Edward and Trevor to retrieve the priest. Adalind and I will wait here."

By this time, Adalind was smiling up at Maddoc. "Please, Papa?" she begged softly. "Will you please do this?"

David could see he hadn't much choice. Moreover, if Maddoc and Adalind were truly married, then it would lessen de Royan's threat, at least in their own minds. She would be safer. And they deserved to be together after all they had been through. Gazing into Adalind's hopeful face, David knew he couldn't deny her.

"What am I going to tell your mother and grandmother?" he wanted to know. "They will be hurt to know you married Maddoc without all of the preparation and ceremony they wanted to give you."

Adalind squeezed his hand. "They can still plan a grand celebration," she said. "We can be married twice. *Please*, Papa?"

David's gaze lingered on her a moment before kissing her on the forehead and wandering off into the darkness, calling out to Edward and Trevor, who were more than happy to rush off into the night for a daring adventure. As the knights got mounted, Maddoc and Adalind stood together by the fire, arms around each other, thinking that this night would finally bring the culmination of their dreams. After weeks of horror, the realization was euphoric.

Rhys was still sitting by the fire. He hadn't left when the others had. He was watching his son and de Lohr's granddaughter, seeing the love and affection between them, appreciating it because it was something he had with his own wife. He knew what it was like to love someone so desperately that you would risk everything for them. A long time ago, he had done just that.

He stood up, grunting when his weary bones pained him. Maddoc glanced over at his father, not realizing the man had still been present. He'd been so focused on Adalind that he hadn't noticed. Adalind glanced over as well, smiling at the older man who looked a good deal like Maddoc. They had been properly introduced earlier in the evening, an introduction that had been brief as all of the knights had moved in to help settled the camp. Now, with just the three of them, she had a bit more time to focus on her future father-in-law. She smiled up at him.

"It is truly uncanny how much you and Maddoc look alike," she said. "I am so glad to have finally met you. Maddoc has always spoken so highly of you, as has my grandfather. He told me you used to carry two broadswords that you kept sheathed on your back. Do you still carry them?"

Rhys grinned. "I do," he replied. "Although I have not used dual blades in years, I still carry them with me just in case I meet a challenge where a single blade will not do."

"Have you come across such a thing recently?"

"Nay, but you never can tell."

They shared a small laugh and when they sobered, Rhys's expression turned serious. "I would like to congratulate you both on your impending marriage," he said to them. "Maddoc, I will have a lot of explaining to do to your mother about the swiftness of this marriage."

Maddoc grinned. "Tell her it was necessary," he said, then thought on that answer and laughed softly. "Well... not *necessary*, but important. Aye, that is a better word – important."

Rhys grinned. "Important, indeed," he agreed, looking between the pair. "My wife and I were married hastily also, and it was important. I think she will understand."

"I am looking forward to meeting Elizabeau," Adalind put her hand on Rhys' arm, sincerity in her expression. "Maddoc has told me of her over the years. I am anxious to know her."

"And you shall," Rhys said with a twinkle in his eye. Then, he looked at his son and his good humor seemed to fade. "This is a momentous moment, Maddoc. I suppose if I could give you any advice it would be to be faithful, be patient, and love her more than anything else in the world. Beyond that, you will have to find your own way in this marriage."

Maddoc smiled faintly. "It is something I am looking forward to," he said, the emotion of the moment not lost on him. There was something else not lost on him and he reached out, taking his father's hand. "I am so glad you are here, Da. Thank you... well, for everything. You are my rock and I shall never forget that."

Rhys touched his boy on the cheek, winked at Adalind, and left them alone by the fire. As a father, his job was finished and as he walked away from the glowing flames, he found himself thanking God that he was experiencing this moment. Up until a few days ago, he didn't think he would ever see this moment with Maddoc. He cherished it.

And he further prayed that after Maddoc found Brighton, he would not be left comforting the widow.

I seem to have loved you in numberless forms, numberless times...
In life after life, in age after age, forever.

CHAPTER TWENTY-TWO

The anxiety was building.

The rains had cleared out, leaving the days for traveling bright and sunny if not cool. As the six knights from Canterbury and one small lady made their way into the town of Maresfield, the town looked completely different than it had only days earlier. People were out, the sun was out, and everyone was going about their business. But at the appearance of so many knights into the town center where a plethora of clothes washing was going on, people became understandably nervous. That many knights, in one place, was never a good thing. Trouble was coming.

Adalind rode with Maddoc. As they approached the church, Daniel spurred his charger on ahead, as did Gart. They dismounted their steeds as the rest of the group approached, heading into the church to scout it out for Brighton. Several seconds after they entered, worshippers came shooting out of the front door, scattering in the street. Maddoc, David, Rhys, and Christopher came to a halt in front of the church, watching people run out of it as if the devil had just made an appearance inside.

The knights dismounted, feeling the fear from the villagers. It was like a fog, covering them all, spreading out from the church with invisible fingers. Maddoc climbed off his horse and held up his arms for Adalind, who slid down into them. He lowered her to the ground and took her hand, his gaze moving over the large church that was more like a cathedral. He had his own apprehension to deal with, that was true, but only in the sense that he was eager to confront Brighton and settle this matter once and for all. He could feel his father behind him and sense the man's disquiet, but he would not acknowledge it. He knew his father was worried. They were all worried. There was no use in speaking of it, mostly because he didn't want to upset Adalind.

His new wife had put on a very brave face for the past day and a half. He hadn't consummated their marriage on the night they were joined, mostly because it had been so late by the time the priest was finished that Adalind was exhausted. She fell asleep before he could make a move on her. Last night, whilst traveling, there simply hadn't been any privacy for the act with his father and four other knights around, so he and Adalind had simply gone to bed and slept in each other's arms.

Now, this morning, they found themselves in Maresfield, preparing for something that would either end him or free him. He hoped it was the latter. He was more determined than ever to rid them of Brighton once and for all. The face-off was coming and he welcomed it.

At the entry to the church, he paused and turned to Adalind.

"I will go in alone," he said softly. "I want you to stay with my father. I promise this will be over shortly."

Adalind had held her fear admirably until this moment. It was as if she realized he was utterly serious and really intended to go through with it. Perhaps until this moment, she'd held out hope he would back off and turn away. It had been a foolish hope, really; Maddoc never gave up and he never backed down. It was here, and now, and it was real. When Maddoc tried to turn Adalind over to Rhys, she clung to Maddoc's hand and refused to let go.

"Maddoc," she begged softly, "please... I know you must do this and I understand your reasoning, but I wish you would not. I would much rather have you healthy and whole, looking over your shoulder for Brighton for the rest of your life than a victim of his sword."

He smiled and kissed her. "I would not worry so," he said. "If what you and Daniel have told me is still true, Brighton is as injured as I am. That will make the odds in my favor because I am a better knight than he is."

He was trying to make light of the situation but she would have none of it. "Please," she whispered. "I am so frightened for you."

He kissed her again, stroking her cheek with his gloved hand. *His wife.* He still couldn't believe it as he looked at her. It didn't feel like they were married but he intended to remedy that tonight, sleep and travel be damned. When he should have been thinking about the coming battle, his mind turned to sex. It wasn't entirely unexpected, given he was a bridegroom, but most misplaced. Shaking himself of lustful thoughts, he focused on the task at hand.

"I know you are," he murmured. "But comfort yourself with your faith in my abilities. You *do* have faith in me, do you not?"

She was pouting, brow furrowed and lips puckered. "Of course I do."

He held her chin between his thumb and fingers, kissing her on the lips. "Thank you," he murmured, kissing her again. "I love you, sweetheart. Always remember that."

Her pouting was turning to something more, something uneasy and dark. "As I love you," she told him. "Why do you make it sound as if it will be the last time you ever tell me such a thing? If...."

Daniel and Gart emerged from the church, crowding Maddoc and cutting her off. "He is still here," Daniel announced. "I must say that I am rather insulted he was not happy to see me."

Adalind rolled her eyes miserably at her uncle's sense of humor but Maddoc found it amusing. "Where is he?" he asked.

"The priests moved him into the cloister," Daniel pointed into the darkened church. "He is to the rear of the cathedral in a long building that serves as their sleeping chamber."

"Is he bedridden?"

Daniel eyed Gart as he spoke, as if the two of them shared a secret. "Nay," he replied, scratching his neck. "At least, he was not when we came upon him, but he tried to attack Forbes and was summarily beat back. He knows you are coming for him, Maddoc. The man is unafraid of you or whoever you bring with you as support."

Maddoc cocked an eyebrow as he tightened up his gauntlets. "Is he moving well?"

"Well enough. He was getting out of bed when we left him."

"Excellent," Maddoc said with quiet sincerity. "Then this shall be a fair fight."

Without another word, he walked into the church. Adalind watched him take about ten steps before she tried to follow. Rhys held her back but she didn't take kindly to it so David stepped in and put his arms around her, trying to soothe the very frightened young woman.

"He shall not be long," he told her confidently. "He will easily dispatch Brighton and then we shall be on our way home."

Adalind was still trying to pull away from him, straining to catch a glimpse of Maddoc in the darkened church. He had faded from her view and she was becoming panicky. He was out of her sight and her imagination began to run wild. She told him that she understood his reasons for confronting Brighton but the truth was that even though she understood, she still did not want him to fight. She was rife with anxiety.

"We should go with him," she insisted. "He will need our support."

"We can only distract him," Christopher told his grandniece. "You in particular will distract him, sweetheart, and distraction in this profession is deadly."

They all seemed rather calm about it, which infuriated her. Adalind turned to the great knights surrounding her, legendary men who had shaped the future of England, frustration and desperation in her expression.

"How can you be so casual about this?" she demanded. "Maddoc is going to challenge Brighton, a man he has already fought twice. Brighton is more than capable of meeting Maddoc's challenge and I, for one, am appalled at how... how *calm* you all are about this. Do you not care for Maddoc more than that? Do you not wish to help him?"

While Christopher and Gart fought off something that looked suspiciously like a knowing grin, David addressed his granddaughter.

"Addie, you have been raised with knights," he said. "You spent years at Winchester around knights and fighting men. You understand their code of honor. You also know that this is something Maddoc has to face alone because if we all go in there to provide support, it will make him look and feel weak, as if he cannot do this alone. Is that what you want to do? Undermine his confidence?"

She sighed heavily. "Of course not," she said. "I know he is very capable. But... but can you not help him?"

"How?"

She threw up her hands. "Dispatch Brighton for him!"

"And rob him of the privilege?" David shook his head. "This is Maddoc's fight, Addie. You must let him fight it alone."

He made perfect sense but she was exasperated and furious about it. With a grunt of frustration, she turned away and took the steps up to the church entry but stopped short of actually going in. She stood there, ears straining to catch wind of what was transpiring. She couldn't hear a thing, not yet. Edgy, she turned to the five heavily armored men standing at the bottom of the steps.

"What happens if he needs help?" she demanded. "What happens if Brighton gains the upper hand and it is clear he will win? What then? Will you all still stand around and recite the code of knightly honor as my husband is killed?"

Out of all of the knights, only Rhys shook his head. "Should it come to that, I will not allow Maddoc to be killed," he said quietly. "I will step in if such a thing were to happen."

"Thank you," Adalind said sincerely, gathering her skirts and racing down the steps until she stood in front of Rhys. "Thank you for your show of support. I knew you would."

Rhys lifted his eyebrows. "He is my son," he said simply. "I nearly lost him once. If I can at all prevent it, it will not happen again. I do not intend to outlive Maddoc."

Adalind decided she liked Rhys very much at that moment, the one man who was willing to step in and help Maddoc should he need it. She wrapped a hand around his elbow, smiling at him. Before she could speak, however, the distant sounds of broadswords could be heard and her stomach lurched. Smile vanished, she turned in the direction of the sounds just as they all did. The sounds of metal against metal were ominous and evil. It seemed as if the entire town had come to halt when the sounds began, everyone hearing the combat upon the wind. But no one heard it more strongly than Adalind.

"Dear God," she breathed. "Please protect him."

The prayer was not unexpected. David, however, said what they were all thinking.

"And so," he murmured, "it begins."

***

The dormitory-like building to the rear of the chapel was large indeed. It was a single story structure made from the same dark stone as the church. As Maddoc approached, he unsheathed his broadsword just in case Brighton was waiting for him on the other side of the heavy oak and iron door. Cautiously, Maddoc pushed it open.

He paused a nominal amount of time, allowing his eyes to grow accustomed to the dim interior, before entering. When he did enter, his sword led the way.

The dormitory was like a great hall, cavernous and sparingly furnished, smelling of smoke and dust. It had a very strong smell. There were a few beds lined up neatly against the walls and as Maddoc stepped deeper into the room, he could see movement on the far end of the room. He came to a halt, facing Brighton, who was standing on the opposite side of the dormitory.

They were far enough away from each other that it was difficult to make out details, but Maddoc could see that Brighton had on his mail but little else. No plate armor and his head was bare. But his broadsword gleamed in the weak light. Maddoc could see the weapon clearly.

"Surely you knew that if I had breath in my body, I would seek vengeance against what you did to me and to Adalind," Maddoc said, his voice echoing off the bare walls. "You must have been expecting this moment."

He could hear Brighton sigh on the opposite side of the room. "I was," he admitted. "I assumed Daniel left me alive so that you could have the privilege of exacting revenge."

"He left you alive because Adalind asked him to," Maddoc replied. "She was given to whims of mercy because of your sister. Know that I have no such whims."

"I did not think you did."

Maddoc began to walk towards him, slowly and deliberately, his enormous boots crashing against the stone floor like great weighty anchors.

"It did not have to come to this," he said after a moment. "Had you simply left Adalind alone, none of this would have happened. See what your lust has brought you?"

Brighton saw him coming but he did not back off. In fact, he began to walk towards him as well. "It has brought me heartache," he said, moving gingerly because his back still pained him greatly. The physic thought there was some organ damage. "I thought Adalind would forget about you. I thought that I could overwhelm her with my charms and soon you would be just a sad memory, but I was wrong. Whatever bond you and Adalind have is stronger than anything I have ever seen. It was a mistake to take her, I see that now. But there is nothing I can do except face that mistake."

Maddoc came to within ten feet of him and came to a halt. He noticed a big welt on his right cheek, fresh. He pointed towards it with his sword.

"What happened to your face?" he asked.

Brighton wriggled his eyebrows. "A big bald knight with fists the size of a hamhock punched me when I tried to shove him away," he said. "I do not like being crowded by armed men when I am on my back."

Maddoc fought off a grin. "That big bald knight is Gart Forbes," he said. "He is quite frightening. I am not entirely sure I would not run from a challenge by that man."

"Nor I."

It was an unexpected moment of levity and Maddoc struggled not to smile. He took a deep breath, sighing heavily as he faced off against Brighton.

"How badly are you injured?" he asked.

"Badly enough," Brighton replied. "And you?"

"I have been better."

"What do we do, then?"

"I must kill you. You know that."

"I am coming to."

"Let us get this over with."

Brighton lifted his eyebrow. "I am not entirely sure I am overly eager to die," he said. "Did Adalind come with you?"

"She did."

"You will tell her something for me."

Maddoc lifted his broadsword. "Be careful what you say about my wife."

Brighton stared at him. Then, he cracked a smile. "So you married her?"

"Of course I did."

Brighton nodded his head. Then, he shrugged. "Tell your wife I am sorry for what I did," he said after a moment. "I thought I could steal her from you. I was wrong."

"You *were* wrong, about a lot of things. But that ends now."

"We shall see."

Maddoc simply nodded. Then, he lunged forward and would have cleaved Brighton in half had the man been any slower at defending himself. In the blink of an eye, the epic battle had begun.

***

The battle hadn't been like anything any of them had ever seen - Rhys, David, Christopher, Gart, or Daniel. It was rather astonishing. It was like watching the battle of the titans, for each man was determined to take victory in any way possible. From the moment they heard the onset of the battle, it was truly something to behold.

It started in the dormitory as any other fight. Maddoc and Brighton were boxed in to the structure where it was assumed the fight would stay. But that ended when Maddoc, in the course of grappling with Brighton, literally threw the man through the entry door and the thing splintered. Tangled up in the shards of wood, Brighton had to fight off an intense offensive by Maddoc before he was able to free himself by kicking Maddoc in the knee. Maddoc stumbled back, allowing Brighton to break free, and then the fight was on again.

Into the cloister they battled, thrusting the heavy broadswords at one another, trying to take each other's head off. Supporting posts for the arbor got in the way and at one point, Brighton's sword became wedged into the wood. Maddoc got close enough to slug him in the jaw and make a grab for his sword as he recovered, but Brighton bounced back and kicked Maddoc in the torso, sending him staggering off balance. It was enough time for Brighton to free his sword and the battle continued.

The entry from the cloister into the church had been opened by frightened priests watching the fight. As Maddoc and Brighton drew near, the priests scattered and the knights entered the church, swords swinging. Adalind and the others were still standing at the entry to the church, startled when Brighton came flying into the structure from the cloister entrance, stumbling, and rolling several times until he was able to halt his momentum. Maddoc burst in after him, chopping at him with his heavy broadsword and catching Brighton in the shoulder. Even though the man had mail, the razor-sharp broadsword managed to cut him and the first blood was spilled.

A massive battle ensued inside the church. Daniel, Rhys and Gart went inside to watch, but David and Christopher kept Adalind outside. They didn't want her distracting Maddoc so they kept her clear of the church, walking her over to the now-empty trough in the middle of the town center in an attempt to keep her calm and out of the way. But from inside the church, they could hear sounds of a serious fight that went on for quite some time until Maddoc suddenly spilled out from the church and tumbled down the stairs.

Adalind opened her mouth to shriek but slapped a hand over her gaping lips so Maddoc would not look in her direction. She understood well that distraction was deadly so she did her best not to make a sound, even as Brighton came flying out of the church and attacked Maddoc. Maddoc, seeing the man descend on him, lifted his sword to prevent his head from being cut off, but he immediately retaliated and caught Brighton in an awkward position. With a clumsy hold on his broadsword, Brighton's weapon went flying.

Swordless, Brighton found himself at a distinct advantage so he threw two massive punches at Maddoc's armored head, as Maddoc had once done to him, and twisted the helm so Maddoc's field of vision was reduced. Maddoc's response was to bring up a booted foot and kick Brighton on the side of the head, dazing the man enough so that he lost his balance and fell over. Leaving his weapon in the dirt, Maddoc pounced on Brighton and the sword fight became a fist fight.

With the closer quarters fighting, the blood began to fly. Both men landed heavy blows to the facial area and soon, both of them were bleeding from noses and mouths. It was extraordinarily brutal as they staggered to their feet and continued the battle. Grappling, throwing punches, kicking and shoving, they battled their way across the town center and ended up collapsing one of the vendor's stalls on the opposite side of the square when Maddoc literally picked Brighton up and threw him into the wall.

From there, they tussled to the next vendor's stall and collapsed that one, too. Brighton became tangled up in a measure of fabric and Maddoc took advantage of it; collecting the heaviest thing he could find, which happened to be an enormous iron pot, he brained Brighton over the head with it and the man went limp.

As Adalind and the others watched with concern, fascination, and some horror, Maddoc grabbed the dazed Brighton by the arms and began dragging him over to the well. David pulled Adalind well back out of the way as Maddoc lifted Brighton up and shoved his head into the water of the trough. It was a deep trough, with a lot of water in it, and Maddoc held the man's head under as Brighton, becoming conscious, began to fight for his life.

Adalind's hand was still at her mouth as she watched Maddoc hold Brighton's head under water. The battle, so brutal and crushing, was coming to an end; they could all see it. Sickened, Adalind turned her head, unable to watch as Maddoc struggled to hold Brighton's head under water. She was thrilled the battle was coming to a close, thrilled Maddoc was winning, but sickened at the fact that she was watching a man die. She'd never seen a man die before. The realization was as eye-opening as it was sobering.

"For everything you have done to Adalind," Maddoc grunted as he held Brighton's head under, "let this be the last time you traumatize the woman. Do you hear me, you bastard? You tried to kill me and now, I will return the favor. But I shall not fail."

Brighton was struggling and kicking for all he was worth, but he was in a bad position the way Maddoc was holding him. There was nothing for him to grab on to, nothing for him to hold. His vision began to dim and his struggles lessened, but he lasted longer than he should have. It was another full minute before his struggles stopped entirely and his body went limp. Even then, Maddoc continued to hold his head underwater as if fearful the man would rise up and the battle would continue. He needed it to be over.

It was.

Adalind was still facing away from them, hand over her mouth, when David finally let go of her and made his way timidly towards Maddoc. Rhys and Christopher did, too, going to the young knight who still had his enemy's head shoved in the water even though the man was clearly dead. When they attempted to force Maddoc to let Brighton go, he refused. He stayed where he was, partially covering Brighton's body with his own, using his weight to pin the man down, as he held his head under the water.

"Maddoc," Rhys had his hands on Maddoc's wrists in an attempt to force him to release Brighton. "It is over, lad. Let him go."

Maddoc closed his eyes tightly and shook his head. "Not yet," he grunted. "It is not over yet."

Rhys and David exchanged concerned glances as David gave it a try. "Maddoc," he had his hands on the man's shoulders. "Let him go, now. He is dead."

Maddoc refused to release him. He was still in the heat of battle, still fighting for his life, and not at all convinced yet that it was finished. As his father, David, and even Christopher tried to force him to release the body, Adalind came up on the opposite side of the trough.

Her gaze was adoring yet sad, powerful yet soft. She stared at Maddoc, seeing such fear and pain in his expression. As strong as he was, she could see his vulnerability at that moment and it touched her like nothing else.

He had been afraid, too; afraid that he would lose the fight and everything he had dreamt and hoped for would never come to pass. The man, the perfect knight, was human, too. She had never seen that side of him before.

"Maddoc?" she said, her voice breaking. "Maddoc, please let him go. I want to go home now."

Her soft, teary voice caused Maddoc to lift his head and look at her. She was standing on the other side of the trough, looking down at him with tears on her face. When their eyes met, she reached across the water and peeled his fingers off of Brighton's neck.

"Please, Maddoc," she whispered. "It is over. I want to go home."

Grown men could not accomplish what one small lady could. Maddoc let her remove his hands and he allowed her to pull him away from the trough as Christopher and Rhys pulled Brighton out of the water. Maddoc tried to turn around, to look at the body of his opponent, but Adalind wouldn't let him. She put her arms around him and walked him away from the scene, directing them towards their horses.

When Maddoc tried once more to turn around and survey the scene, Adalind put her hands on his face and held him staunchly.

"Nay, Maddoc," she whispered firmly. "Brighton is dead. The battle is over. Now it is our time to live and love and enjoy. No more Brighton; no more anything. You did what you set out to do; you defeated him. Now let us speak no more about him, not ever. He no longer exists to us so we can get on with our lives."

Maddoc was starting to collect his wits, his composure, as he listened to her speak. He put his arms around her and hugged her tightly, so very weary and battered. But he had Adalind and that was all that mattered.

"Whatever you wish, Addie," he murmured, kissing her head, getting his blood on her hair. "We shall go home."

Adalind pulled back to look at him, wiping the blood from his nose and mouth with a corner of her cloak. He looked shaken while she felt strong; so very strong. She would remember the moment forever. It was the beginning of the rest of her life with him.

"I have waited for this moment for ages past," she whispered. "In so many forms and in so many lives, I have waited for this. I have been yours since the day I took my first breath and shall remain yours until the end of time. Take me back to Canterbury and let us begin anew, as husband and wife. I cannot tell you how thrilled I am for this moment, Maddoc. Finally, to have you as my own."

He was warmed and comforted by her words. The energy of battle was fading and he was starting to feel normal again, empowered, knowing there was so much more to life than he could possible imagine. The little girl who had annoyed him to tears and declared her love for him endlessly had grown up and become his all for living. He couldn't remember when he hadn't loved Adalind. She completed him.

"As I have you for my own," he murmured, kissing the tip of her nose. Then he tweaked it playfully. "When I entered the bailey those weeks ago to find the ap Athoe brothers fighting over you, I could have never known that, in the end, I would have been fighting over you as well. I suppose they were not idiots, after all, because they were right."

Adalind grinned. "About what?"

"You," he whispered, his smile fading and his bright eyes intense. "You are worth it."

As Adalind and Maddoc lost themselves in a kiss of pure love, pure joy, the sun came out from the clouds and the promise of a bright and beautiful day dawned clear and blue.

EPILOGUE

Four years later

His face was buried in her neck, smelling the sweet musky scent that had the ability to arouse him like nothing else. He could feel her soft breasts against his bare chest, feeling the sensual movement every time he thrust into her. Her legs were wrapped around his hips but he unwrapped them, holding them behind the knees, giving him more freedom of movement as he continued to pound into her sweet and yielding body. At some point, he shifted so his weight wasn't bearing down on her and bearing down on the babe in her belly. He shifted so they were on their sides, facing each other, as he slowed his thrusts.

Adalind had her hands on his lower back, stroking it, stroking his smooth buttocks as he made love to her. She loved it when he slowed his pace, withdrawing completely only to plunge into her again, slowly, driving himself to the very hilt and then repeating the process. Her hands drifted between their bodies, putting her fingers on his phallus as he joined his body with hers. Nothing seemed to drive Maddoc crazier than her fingers on his manhood and he groaned as she fingered him, gently fondling his testicles.

Shifting again, Maddoc captured a warm nipple in his mouth, suckling gently and tasting her milk. She was still breastfeeding their younger son but he couldn't help himself from sampling the sweet milk from her breasts. She had such beautiful breasts. He suckled strongly on the left one, tasting her, licking her flesh with her milk upon his tongue and then licking her again just to lick it off of her. One big hand came up to fondle her breast, kneading it, suckling until there was no more milk in the left one. When he moved to her right breast, she stopped him.

"No more," she whispered into his dark head. "What are you going to tell Macsen when there is none left for his morning meal?"

Maddoc growled, returning his attentions to the left breast and suckling even though there was nothing left.

"I will tell him that his father is greedy," he murmured against her flesh. "If he was any older, I would fight him for the privilege of claiming it all for myself."

Adalind giggled softly but her giggles turned to groans when his thrusting gained pace and she could feel herself building to a climax. It was before dawn, the best time to make love before their day began and their two little boys awoke and demanded attention. This was their time, warm and cozy under the covers, sometimes making love two or three times before the sun rose.

Maddoc could feel Adalind's tremors beginning and he thrust hard, grinding his hips against hers, and feeling her powerful release. As she panted beneath him, he erupted deep within her, loving the hot, wet feel of his seed in her body. He held her buttocks in his hands, holding her firmly against him as the last of his convulsions died. With a heavy sigh, he opened his eyes to say something to her but caught sight of a big blue pair of eyes staring back at him from beside the bed. Startled, Maddoc discreetly shifted so that Adalind's naked chest was covered from view.

"Good morn, Steffen," Maddoc greeted his eldest son calmly. "You are up earlier than usual."

Steffen de Aston du Bois had his father's bright blue eyes, dark hair, and big build. He also had his demeanor; rather calm and easy-going, except when he woke up in the morning. He and his younger brother by thirteen months, Macsen, were known to be unhappy terrors in the morning and Adalind often had her hands full with the both of them. At nearly three years old and nearly two years old, they were a joyful handful, and very smart. They were learning to unlatch doors and sneak up on unsuspecting parents.

"Dada," Steffen rubbed his eyes and yawned. "I am hungry. I want mush."

Adalind, buried under Maddoc's body, carefully pulled herself out from underneath him and fumbled around under the coverlet for the shift Maddoc had pulled from her body in the heat of passion.

"I am coming, Steffen," she assured her little boy as she found the shift and pulled it over her head. "Where is your brother?"

Steffen didn't say anything but he pointed under the bed. Maddoc looked over the side of the bed; hanging upside down and peering under the big rope and oak-framed bed to find another pair of bright blue eyes gazing back at him from the darkness.

"Macsen?" he held out his hand to the child. "Come out of there, lad."

Macsen de Lohr du Bois, the same size as his older brother even though he was more than a year younger, took his father's hand and let the man pull him out. As Adalind climbed out of bed and went in search of her robe, Maddoc reached out an enormous arm and pulled Steffen into bed with him. When Adalind found her heavy robe, put it on, and began hunting for her slippers, she happened to glance at the bed and saw that Maddoc was laying there with two dozing toddlers. Hands on her hips, she went over to the bed.

"What is this?" she asked, pointing to the bed. "What did you do to them?"

Maddoc grinned at his wife. "It was evidently a ploy to get you out of bed so they could steal your place."

Adalind rolled her eyes but she was grinning. "I would believe that," she said, turning away as she continued to hunt for her shoes. "They have been plotting since the moment of birth to deprive me of sleep. They have succeeded, too, for the most part."

Maddoc grinned, snuggling with his boys as his wife pulled on her doeskin slippers. "Perhaps the next child will be different," he said softly. "Perhaps that one will be more considerate and obedient."

Adalind rubbed her gently swollen belly; nearly seven months into the pregnancy, she was still round and rosy, not huge and ungainly that would come in the end months. Maddoc thought it was the most beautiful time of her life.

"This child shall be a girl," she said flatly. "She shall be sweet and obedient, unlike these boys you allow to rule the house and hold."

Maddoc struggled not to laugh. "I do not allow them anything," he said. "Blame your grandfather if you must. He pouts like a spoiled lad every time we discipline them."

Adalind threw up her hands. "Papa is an old man," she said. "All he ever wanted was boys in the family but instead, he got eight women. Of course he pouts when we discipline the boys. He is afraid we are killing their de Lohr spirit."

"They are du Bois offspring."

"They are descended from the House of de Lohr."

They'd had this argument many a time. Maddoc put his big hand over Steffen's head, muting his ears, when the boy stirred at the sound of his mother's raised voice.

"They do not look like a de Lohr," he whispered, taunting her. "They look like me."

"And this child shall look like me," Adalind said firmly. She waved a hand at the bed. "Get them up, Maddoc. 'Tis time to rise and break their fast and get on with the day."

Maddoc kissed each boy and tossed back the covers, climbing out of bed stark naked as he went in search of his clothing. The room was warm from the banked fire and rich furnishing so he felt no chill as he found his breeches and pulled them on. Meanwhile, Adalind went to the bed and pulled two sleepy boys from the covers. They clung to her, yawning, as Macsen started to whine. When Maddoc turned around and saw her carrying two toddlers with her petite size and pregnant belly, he immediately went to her and took the boys from her.

221

"Go downstairs," he told her. "I will finish dressing and bring them down."

She waved him off. "Willow is already down in the hall, preparing their meal," she said. "I do not have to lift a finger with my sister and mother around."

He smiled faintly. "I am surprised Willow is up and moving considering how late she stayed up last night."

Adalind fought off a grin. "The arrival of your brother was cause for celebration. "

"Celebration, indeed. I was hardly able to speak with him with Willow hanging all over him."

"Willow is in love with Trevor," she told him what he already knew. "She wants to marry him."

He grunted. "He is too young."

"He is twenty years and three. That is *not* too young."

Maddoc wasn't sure what to say, mostly because anything he said about his brother's age or reluctance to marry sounded like an insult towards her sister. But mention of her sister and Trevor's arrival reminded him of something else; a missive had come for Adalind yesterday via messenger, something that was delivered to David who in turn gave it to Adalind. She hadn't mentioned it to Maddoc but David had. He didn't know what was in it, but the rider had been from Yorkshire. Maddoc wondered who could be sending his wife a missive all the way from Yorkshire although he had a good idea.

"Perhaps not," he finally said. "He did bring a missive from my father, however. It would seem that my brother Evan is betrothed to a local heiress in Navarre. Perhaps we will have a wedding to attend next year, after all."

Adalind lifted her eyebrows, surprised and pleased. "That is excellent news," she said. "I hope he does not get married before the baby is old enough to travel. I have never been to Navarre, and I should like your mother and father to see their grandchildren."

"I will make sure Evan understands his life revolves around your schedule before making his wedding plans," he said, winking at her. In his arms, Steffen wanted to be set down so Maddoc lowered the boy to the ground. "Speaking of missives, your grandfather said you received one yesterday. You have not made mention of it."

Adalind's warm expression vanished. She lowered her gaze, grasping Steffen by the hand when the little boy toddled close. After a moment, she sighed.

"That is because I was not sure what to say about it," she said quietly. "I was going to tell you, of course, but the subject... well, it is a sensitive one."

"Who was it from?"

"Glennie," she said. "It would seem that she is getting married and has invited us to attend."

Maddoc sobered as he made his way over to the bed, sitting on the edge with a dozing Macsen cradled against his shoulder.

"She must not know what happened with Brighton," he said softly. "Otherwise, I am sure she would not have invited us."

Adalind nodded sadly. "Brighton was buried in Maresfield," she said. "The priests knew who we were but they did not know where Brighton hailed from. No one ever told them. And Norfolk... he knew that Brighton came after me when I escaped from Arundel. So if Brighton never returned to Arundel, surely d'Aubigney could figure out what happened. Surely he must have suspected Canterbury was involved in Brighton's disappearance, and if Brighton's family came looking for him, would Norfolk not tell them what he knew?"

Maddoc sighed faintly, stroking her blond head. "I have gone months or even years without any contact with my family," he murmured, kissing her temple because she looked so upset. "Daniel is even worse; we have gone years without seeing him at all. It has only been four years since everything happened with Brighton so it is quite possible the de Royans do not even know he is missing and presumed dead."

Adalind looked at him. "But if Glennie is getting married, surely they have sent word to Norfolk for Brighton, and surely d'Aubigney will send word that Brighton has not been at Arundel for four years. If she does not know of her brother's disappearance, then she will soon."

"What do you want to do, then? Do you want to tell her the truth?"

Adalind shook her head, picking Steffen up when the boy whined and setting him on the bed between them.

"I do not want to tell her," she murmured. "But she was so good to me for so long, Maddoc. She was my only friend during those dark years at Winchester. But she knows nothing about what happened with her brother and I do not see the good in telling her such things. Let her remember her brother as she wishes to, without my stories of abduction and battles. I would not burden her so with such things."

"She would think different of you, I suppose."

"It is not me I worry about. It is you."

"Why?"

She turned to look at him, a hint of a smile on her lips. "Because you are the most wonderful husband in all the world," she said softly. "You are the man I love; the man I have always loved, and we have the most wonderful life together imaginable. You are strong and true and loyal, and you did what you had to do. I will not have anyone hate you for doing your duty.

Not even Glennie. Let her remember her brother as she chooses, for I will remember you only as my hero."

He smiled faintly, leaning forward to kiss her on the lips and laughing softly when Steffen didn't take kindly to it. The child was rather possessive of his mother and tended to get upset when his father showed affection towards her.

"What will you tell your friend, then?" he asked. "She will be expecting an answer."

Adalind sighed thoughtfully, hugging Steffen when the boy stood up and put his arms around her neck.

"I will thank her for the invitation but tell her I cannot travel because of the impending child," she said. "We will leave it at that."

"Are you sure?"

"I am. But since I am being denied Glennie's wedding, you had better tell your brother to offer for my sister's hand. I have a yearning to attend a wedding this year and since I cannot travel, the wedding will have to be here."

Maddoc just shook his head, grinning, as he stood up from the bed. "I will not involve myself in that affair."

Adalind stood up and helped Steffen off the bed, following Maddoc to the door. "Aye, you will," she insisted. "You will do this for me."

"I will not."

"I wish it."

They argued all the way downstairs into the great hall. They argued off and on for the next three months until one cold evening, Adalind began feeling the pangs of labor and by morning had delivered a healthy daughter. Maddoc was so thrilled at the birth of Cathlina Elizabeau du Bois that on the day of her christening, he cornered his brother and nearly strong-armed the man into offering for Willow's hand. It wasn't much of a feat, considering Trevor hadn't returned home to France in over four months because of Willow, so much to Adalind's glee, Willow and Trevor were married the following summer.

For the de Lohr and du Bois legacy, life went on. David and Emilie watched as their grandchildren married and had children of their own. Willow and Trevor had a son in the year following their marriage and two years after Cathlina was born, Adalind gave birth to another girl, Rhoslyn.

In the coming years, David grew too old to move effectively and would spend most of his time sitting by the hearth, warming his old bones and reliving his glory days. Maddoc would sit with him and listen to tales of valor, many of them involving Maddoc himself, but told with David's spin to the point where even Maddoc came to believe he was greater than life. Steffen and Macsen would hear the same tales, retelling them over and over to their children, who passed the family legends down.

Centuries and generations continued to pass the tales down until they turned into lore. On a porch in the state of Indiana, in a place called America that neither David nor Maddoc, nor Christopher nor Rhys, could have ever imagined; an impressionable young girl listened to her grandfather tell stories of their ancestors. Stories that had been passed down for so long that no one really knew where they came from. They were part of the fabric of the family; stories that the impressionable young girl listened to with great interest and took to heart. But she did more than any of her ancestors did - Kathryn wrote them down.

Under her hand, Christopher, Maddoc, Rhys, David, Daniel, William, Paris; even Brighton, and all the rest of the heroes came alive again for future generations.

Tales of unending love.

'Unending Love' by Rabindranath Tagore

I seem to have loved you in numberless forms, numberless times...
In life after life, in age after age, forever.
My spellbound heart has made and remade the necklace of songs,
That you take as a gift, wear round your neck in your many forms,
In life after life, in age after age, forever.

Whenever I hear old chronicles of love, it's age-old pain,
It's ancient tale of being apart or together.
As I stare on and on into the past, in the end you emerge,
Clad in the light of a pole-star piercing the darkness of time:
You become an image of what is remembered forever.

You and I have floated here on the stream that brings from the fount.
At the heart of time, love of one for another.
We have played along side millions of lovers, shared in the same
Shy sweetness of meeting, the same distressful tears of farewell-
Old love but in shapes that renew and renew forever.

Today it is heaped at your feet, it has found its end in you
The love of all man's days both past and forever:

Universal joy, universal sorrow, universal life.
The memories of all loves merging with this one love of ours –
And the songs of every poet past and forever

Made in the USA
San Bernardino, CA
12 August 2017